PASTWATCH

THE REDEMPTION OF CHRISTOPHER COLUMBUS

TOR BOOKS BY ORSON SCOTT CARD

The Folk of the Fringe
Future on Fire (editor)
Lovelock (with Kathryn Kidd)
Saints
Songmaster
The Worthing Saga
Wyrms

THE TALES OF ALVIN MAKER

Seventh Son
Red Prophet
Prentice Alvin

ENDER

Ender's Game
Speaker for the Dead
Xenocide

HOMECOMING

The Memory of Earth
The Call of Earth
The Ships of Earth
Earthfall
Earthborn

SHORT FICTION

Maps in a Mirror: The Short Fiction of Orson Scott Card (hardcover)
Maps in a Mirror, Volume 1: The Changed Man (paperback)
Maps in a Mirror, Volume 2: Flux (paperback)
Maps in a Mirror, Volume 3: Cruel Miracles (paperback)
Maps in a Mirror, Volume 4: Monkey Sonatas (paperback)

PASTWATCH

THE REDEMPTION OF CHRISTOPHER COLUMBUS

ORSON SCOTT CARD

TOR®

A TOM DOHERTY ASSOCIATES BOOK
New York

PASTWATCH: THE REDEMPTION OF CHRISTOPHER COLUMBUS

This novel includes a summary of the novella "Atlantis," copyright © 1992, published in *Grails: Quests, Visitations and Occurrences*, ed. by Richard Gilliam, Martin H. Greenberg and Edward E. Kramer.

This book is printed on acid-free paper.

A Tor Book
Published by Tom Doherty Associates, Inc.
175 Fifth Avenue
New York, N.Y. 10010

Tor Books on the World-Wide Web:
http://www.tor.com.

Tor® is a registered trademark of Tom Doherty Associates, Inc.

Design by Patrice Federo

Library of Congress Cataloging-in-Publication Data

Card, Orson Scott.
    Pastwatch : the redemption of Christopher Columbus / by Orson Scott Card.
        p. cm.
    "A Tom Doherty Associates book."
    ISBN 0-312-85058-1
    1. Columbus, Christopher—Fiction. 2. America—Discovery and exploration—
Spanish—Fiction. 3. Time travel—Fiction. I. Title.
PS3553.A655P37   1996
813'.54—dc20
                                                                    95-44927
                                                                    CIP

First Edition: February 1996

Printed in the United States of America

0 9 8 7 6 5 4 3 2 1

For Tom Doherty,

The publisher from the planet Krypton:

His heart is gold,

His word is steel,

And he knows the territory.

Acknowledgments

My heartfelt thanks to:

Clark & Kathy Kidd, for good company, a "virtual" hermitage, and
Kathy's careful first response to many chapters;

Henrique Flory, voyager, for help and inspiration;

The citizens of Hatrack River on America Online, for pointing out
dilemmas that I didn't know I had;

Richard Gilliam, for patiently waiting for the Atlantis story in its
extended form;

Don Grant, for many beautiful books and for his patience waiting
for a novel whose creation defied the calendar;

Michael Lewis, for the Red Sea;

Dave Dollahite, for the Maya;

A complaint to Sid Meier, for the game *Civilization*, which seriously
interfered with my ability to concentrate on productive labor
(but I recommend it to those who want to have the experience
of altering history for themselves);

To my assistants, Kathleen Bellamy and Scott Allen, for countless
helps, small and large;

As always, to Kristine for making life possible, and to Geoff, Em,
Charlie Ben, and Zina for giving it meaning.

Contents

PASTWATCH

The Redemption of Christopher Columbus

Pastwatch

 Some people called it "the time of undoing"; some, wishing to be more positive, spoke of it as "the replanting" or "the restoring" or even "the resurrection" of the Earth. All these names were accurate. Something had been done, and now it was being undone. Much had died or been broken or killed, and now it was coming back to life.

This was the work of the world in those days: Nutrients were put back in the soil of the great rain forests of the world, so the trees could grow tall again. Grazing was banished from the edges of the great deserts of Africa and Asia, and grass was planted so that steppe and then savanna could slowly reconquer territory they had lost to the stone and sand. Though the weather stations high in orbit could not change the climate, they tweaked the winds often enough that no spot on Earth would suffer drought or flood, or lack for sunlight. In great preserves the surviving animals learned how to live again in the wild. All the nations of the world had an equal claim on food, and no one feared hunger anymore. Good teachers came to every child, and every man and woman had a decent chance to become whatever his or her talents and passions and desires led them to become.

It should have been a happy time, with humanity pressing forward into a future in which the world would be healed, in which a comfortable life could be lived without the shame of knowing that it came at someone else's expense. And for many—perhaps most—it was. But many others could not turn their faces from the shadows of the past. Too many creatures were missing, never to be restored. Too many people, too many nations now lay buried in the soil of the past. Once the world had teemed with seven billion human lives. Now a tenth that number tended the gardens of Earth. The survivors could not easily forget the century of war and plague, of drought and flood and famine, of desperate fury leading to despair. Every step of every living man and woman trod on someone's grave, or so it seemed.

So it was not only forests and grasslands that were brought back to life. People also sought to bring back the lost memories, the stories, the intertwining paths that men and women had followed that led them to their times of glory and their times of shame. They built machines that let them see into the past, at first the great sweeping changes across the centuries, and then, as the machinery was refined, the faces and the voices of the dead.

They knew, of course, that they could not record it all. There were not enough alive to witness all the actions of the dead. But by sampling here and there, by following this question to its answer, that nation to its end, the men and women of Pastwatch could tell stories to their fellow citizens, true fables that explained why nations rose and fell; why men and women envied, raged, and loved; why children laughed in sunlight and trembled in the dark of night.

Pastwatch remembered so many forgotten stories, replicated so many lost or broken works of art, recovered so many customs, fashions, jokes, and games, so many religions and philosophies, that sometimes it seemed that there was no need to think up anything again. All of history was available, it seemed, and yet Pastwatch had barely scratched the surface of the past, and most watchers looked forward to a limitless future of rummaging through time.

1

The Governor

There was only one time when Columbus despaired of making his voyage. It was the night of August 23ʳᵈ, in the port of Las Palmas on Grand Canary Island.

After so many years of struggle, his three caravels had finally set sail from Palos, only to run into trouble almost at once. After so many priests and gentlemen in the courts of Spain and Portugal had smiled at him and then tried to destroy him behind his back, Columbus found it hard to believe that it wasn't sabotage when the rudder of the *Pinta* came loose and nearly broke. After all, Quintero, the owner of the *Pinta,* was so nervous about having his little ship go out on such a voyage that he had signed on as a common seaman, just to keep an eye on his property. And Pinzón told him privately that he had seen a group of men gathered at the stern of the *Pinta* just as they were setting sail. Pinzón fixed the rudder himself, at sea, but the next day it broke again. Pinzón was furious, but he vowed to Columbus that the *Pinta* would meet him at Las Palmas within days.

So confident was Columbus of Pinzón's ability and commitment to the voyage that he gave no more thought to the *Pinta*. He sailed with the *Santa Maria* and the *Niña* to the island of Gomera, where

Beatrice de Bobadilla was governor. It was a meeting he had long
looked forward to, a chance to celebrate his triumph over the court
of Spain with one who had made it plain she longed for his success.
But Lady Beatrice was not at home. And as he waited, day after
day, he had to endure two intolerable things.

The first consisted of having to listen politely to the petty gentlemen of Beatrice's little court, who kept telling him the most appalling lies about how on certain bright days, from the island of
Ferro, westernmost of the Canaries, one could see a faint image of
a blue island on the western horizon—as if plenty of ships had not
already sailed *that* far west! But Columbus had grown skilled at
smiling and nodding at the most outrageous stupidity. One did not
survive at court without *that* particular skill, and Columbus had
weathered not only the wandering courts of Ferdinand and Isabella,
but also the more settled and deeply arrogant court of John of Portugal. And after waiting decades to win the ships and men and
supplies and, above all, the *permission* to make this voyage, he
could endure a few more days of conversation with stupid gentlemen. Though he sometimes had to grind his teeth not to point out
how utterly useless they must be in the eyes of God and everyone
else, if they could find nothing better to do with their lives than
wait about in the court of the governor of Gomera when she was
not even at home. No doubt they amused Beatrice—she had shown
a keen appreciation of the worthlessness of most men of the
knightly class when she conversed with Columbus at the royal court
at Santa Fé. No doubt she skewered them constantly with ironic
barbs which they did not realize were ironic.

More intolerable by far was the silence from Las Palmas. He
had left men there with instructions to tell him as soon as Pinzón
managed to bring the *Pinta* into port. But no word came, day after
day, as the stupidity of the courtiers became more insufferable,
until finally he refused to tolerate either of the intolerables a moment longer. Bidding a grateful adiós to the gentlemen of Gomera,
he set sail for Las Palmas himself, only to find when he arrived on
the 23rd of August that the *Pinta* was still not there.

The worst possibilities immediately came to mind. The saboteurs were so grimly determined not to complete the voyage that
there had been a mutiny, or they had somehow persuaded Pinzón

to turn around and sail for Spain. Or they were adrift in the currents of the Atlantic, getting swept to some unnameable destination. Or pirates had taken them—or the Portuguese, who might have thought they were part of some foolish Spanish effort to poach on their private preserve along the coasts of Africa. Or Pinzón, who clearly thought himself better suited to lead the expedition than Columbus himself—though he would never have been able to win royal sponsorship for such an expedition, having neither the education, the manners, nor the patience that it had required—might have had the foolish notion of sailing on ahead, reaching the Indies before Columbus.

All of these were possible, and from one moment to the next each seemed likely. Columbus withdrew from human company that night and threw himself to his knees—not for the first time, but never before with such *anger* at the Almighty. "I have done all you set for me to do," he said, "I have pushed and pleaded, and never once have you given me the slightest encouragement, even in the darkest times. Yet my trust never failed, and at last I got the expedition on the exact terms that were required. We set sail. My plan was good. The season was right. The crew is skilled even if they think themselves better sailors than their commander. All I needed now, *all* that I needed, after everything I've endured till now, was for *something to go right.*"

Was this too bold a thing for him to say to the Lord? Probably. But Columbus had spoken boldly to powerful men before, and so the words spilled easily from his heart to flow from his tongue. God could strike him down for it if he wanted—Columbus had put himself in God's hands years before, and he was weary.

"Was that too much for you, most gracious Lord? Did you have to take away my third ship? My best sailor? Did you even have to deprive me of the kindness of Lady Beatrice? It is obvious that I have not found favor in your eyes, O Lord, and therefore I urge you to find somebody else. Strike me dead if you want, it could hardly be worse than killing me by inches, which seems to be your plan at this moment. I'll tell you what. I will stay in your service for one more day. Send me the *Pinta* or show me what *else* you want me to do, but I swear by your most holy and terrible name, I will not sail on such a voyage with fewer than three ships, well equipped and fully crewed. I've become an old man in your service, and as of tomorrow night, I intend to resign and live on whatever pension you see fit to provide me with.'' Then he crossed himself. ''In the name of the Father, the Son, and the Holy Ghost. Amen.''

Having finished this most impious and offensive prayer, Columbus could not sleep until at last, no less angry than before, he flung himself out of bed and knelt again.

''Nevertheless thy will not mine be done!'' he said furiously. Then he climbed back into bed and promptly fell asleep.

The next morning the *Pinta* limped into port. Columbus took it as the final confirmation that God really was still interested in the success of this voyage. Very well, thought Columbus. You didn't strike me dead for my disrespect, Lord; instead you sent me the *Pinta*. Therefore I will prove to you that I am still your loyal servant.

He did it by working half the citizens of Las Palmas, or so it seemed, into a frenzy. The port had plenty of carpenters and caulkers, smiths and cordwainers and sailmakers, and it seemed that all of them were pressed into service on the *Pinta*. Pinzón was full of defiant apologies—they had been adrift for nearly two weeks before he was finally able, by *brilliant* seamanship, to bring the *Pinta* into exactly the port he had promised. Columbus was still suspicious, but didn't show it. Whatever the truth was, Pinzón was here *now*, and so was the *Pinta*, complete with a rather sullen Quintero. That was good enough for Columbus.

And as long as he had the attention of the shipworkers of Las Palmas, he finally bullied Juan Niño, the owner of the *Niña*, into changing from his triangular sails to the same square rigging as the other caravels, so they'd all be catching the same winds and, God willing, sailing together to the court of the great Khan of China.

It took only a week to have all three ships in better shape than they had been in upon leaving Palos, and *this* time there were no unfortunate failures of vital equipment. If there had been saboteurs before, they were no doubt sobered by the fact that both Columbus and Pinzón seemed determined to sail on at all costs—not to mention the fact that now if the expedition failed, they might end up stranded on the Canary Islands, with little prospect of returning anytime soon to Palos.

And so gracious was God in answering Columbus's impudent

prayer that when at last he sailed into Gomera for the final resupply of his ships, the banner of the governor was flying above the battlements of the castle of San Sebastián.

Any fears he might have had that Beatrice de Bobadilla no longer held him in high esteem were removed at once. When he was announced, she immediately dismissed all the other gentlemen who had so condescended to Columbus the week before. "Cristóbal, my brother, my friend!" she cried. When he had kissed her hand she led him from the court to a garden, where they sat in the shade of a tree and he told her of all that had transpired since they last met at Santa Fé.

She listened, rapt, asking intelligent questions and laughing at his tales of the hideous interference the king had visited upon Columbus almost as soon as he had signed the capitulations. "Instead of paying for three caravels, he dredged up some ancient offense that the city of Palos had committed—smuggling, no doubt—"

"The primary industry of Palos for many years, I'm told," said Beatrice.

"And as their punishment, he required them to pay a fine of exactly two caravels."

"I'm surprised he didn't make them pay for all three," said Beatrice. "He's a hard loaf, dear old Ferdinand. But he did pay for a war without going bankrupt. And he *has* just expelled the Jews, so it isn't as if he has anybody to borrow from."

"The irony is that seven years ago, the Duke of Sidonia would have *bought* me three caravels from Palos out of his own treasury, if the crown had not refused him permission."

"Dear old Enrique—he's always had far more money than the crown, and he just can't understand why that doesn't make him more powerful than they are."

"Anyway, you can imagine how glad they were to see me in Palos. And then, to make sure both cheeks were well slapped, he issued a proclamation that any man who agreed to join my expedition would win a suspension of any civil and criminal actions pending against him."

"Oh, no."

"Oh, *yes*. You can imagine what that did to the *real* sailors of Palos. *They* weren't going to sail with a bunch of criminals and debtors—or run the risk of people thinking that *they* had needed such a pardon."

"His Majesty no doubt imagined that it would take such an incentive to persuade anyone to sail with you on your mad adventure."

"Yes, well, his 'help' nearly killed the expedition from the start."

"So—how many felons and paupers are there in your crew?"

"None, or at least none that we know of. Thank God for Martin Pinzón."

"Oh, yes, a man of legend."

"You know of him?"

"All the sailors' lore comes to the Canaries. We live by the sea."

"He caught the vision of the thing. But once he noised it about that he was going, we started to get recruits. And it was his friends who ended up risking their caravels on the voyage."

"Not free of charge, of course."

"They hope to be rich, at least by their standards."

"As you hope to be rich by yours."

"No, my lady. I hope to be rich by *your* standards."

She laughed and touched his arm. "Cristóbal, how good it is to see you again. How glad I am that God chose you to be his champion in this war against the Ocean Sea and the court of Spain."

Her remark was light, but it touched on a matter quite tender: She was the only one who knew that he had undertaken his voyage at the command of God. The priests of Salamanca thought him a fool, but if he had ever breathed a word of his belief in God's having spoken to him, they would have branded him a heretic and that would have brought an end to more than Columbus's plan for an expedition to the Indies. He had not meant to tell *her*, either; he had not meant to tell anyone, had not even told his brother Bartholomew, nor his wife Felipa before she died, nor even Father Perez at La Rábida. Yet after only an hour in the company of Lady Beatrice, he had told her. Not *all*, of course. But that God had chosen him, had commanded him to make this voyage, he told her that much.

Why had he told her? Perhaps because he knew implicitly that he could trust her with his life. Or perhaps because she looked at him with such piercing intelligence that he knew that no other explanation than the truth would convince her. Even so, he had not told her the half of it, for even *she* would have thought him mad.

And she did not think him mad, or if she did, she must have some special love of madmen. A love that continued even now, to a degree beyond his hopes. "Stay the night with me, my Cristóbal," she said.

"My lady," he answered, unsure if he had heard aright.

"You lived with a common woman named Beatrice in Córdoba. She had your child. You can't pretend to be living a monkish life."

"I seem doomed to fall under the spell of ladies named Beatrice. And none of them has been, by any stretch of the imagination, a common woman."

Lady Beatrice laughed lightly. "You managed to compliment your old lover and one who would be your new one, both at once. No wonder you were able to win your way past the priests and scholars. I daresay Queen Isabella fell in love with your red hair and the fire in your eyes, just as I did."

"More grey in the hair than red, I fear."

"Hardly any," she answered.

"My lady," he said, "it was your friendship I prayed for when I came to Gomera. I did not dare to dream of more."

"Are you beginning a long and gracefully convoluted speech that will, in the end, decline my carnal invitation?"

"Ah, Lady Beatrice, not decline, but perhaps postpone?"

She reached out, leaned forward, touched his cheek. "You're not a very handsome man, you know, Cristóbal."

"That has always been my opinion as well," he answered.

"And yet one can't take one's eyes from you. Nor can one purge one's thoughts of you when you're gone. I'm a widow, and you're a widower. God saw fit to remove our spouses from the torments of this world. Must we also be tormented by unfulfilled desires?"

"My lady, the scandal. If I stayed the night."

"Oh, is that all? Then leave before midnight. I'll let you over the parapet by a silken rope.

"God has answered my prayers," he said to her.

"As well he should, since you were on his mission."

"I dare not sin and lose his favor now."

"I knew I should have seduced you back in Santa Fé."

"And there's this, my lady. When I return, successful, from this great enterprise, then I'll not be a commoner, whose only touch of gentility is by his marriage into a not-quite-noble family of Madeira. I'll be Viceroy. I'll be Admiral of the Ocean Sea." He grinned. "You see, I took your advice and got it all in writing in advance."

"Well, Viceroy indeed! I doubt you'll waste a glance on a mere governor of a far-off island."

"Ah, no, Lady. I'll be Admiral of the Ocean Sea, and as I contemplate my realm—"

"Like Poseidon, ruler over all the shores that are touched by the waves of the sea—"

"I will find no more treasured crown than this island of Gomera, and no more lovely jewel in that crown than the fair Beatrice."

"You've been at court too long. You make your compliments sound rehearsed."

"Of course I've rehearsed it, over and over, the whole week I waited here in torment for your return."

"For the *Pinta*'s return, you mean."

"Both were late. Your rudder, however, was undamaged."

Her face reddened, and then she laughed.

"You complained that my compliments were too courtly. I thought you might appreciate a tavern compliment."

"Is that what that was? Do strumpets sleep with men for free if they say such pretty things?"

"Not strumpets, Lady. Such poetry is not for those who can be had for mere money."

"Poetry?"

"Thou art my caravel, with sails full-winded—"

"Watch your nautical references, my friend."

"Sails full-winded, and the bright red banners of thy lips dancing as thou speakest."

"You're very good at this. Or are you *not* making it up as you go along?"

"Making it all up. Ah, thy breath is the blessed wind that sailors pray for, and the sight of thy rudder leaves this poor sailor full-masted—"

She slapped his face, but it wasn't meant to hurt.

"I take it my poetry is a failure."

"Kiss me, Cristóbal. I believe in your mission, but if you never return I want at least your kiss to remember you by."

So he kissed her, and again. But then he took his leave of her, and returned to the last preparations for his voyage. It was God's work now; when it was done, then it was time to collect the worldly rewards. Though who was to say that she was not, after all, a reward from heaven? It was God, after all, who had made a widow of her, and perhaps God also who made her, against all probability, love this son of a Genovese weaver.

He saw her, or thought he saw her—and who else could it have been?—waving a scarlet handkerchief as if it were a banner from the parapet of the castle as his caravels at last set forth. He raised his hand in a salute to her, and then turned his face westward. He would not look again to the east, to Europe, to home, not until he had achieved what God had sent him to do. The last of the obstacles was past now, surely. Ten days' sailing and he would step ashore in Cathay or India, the Spice Islands or in Cipangu. Nothing could stop him now, for God was with him, as he had been with him since that day on the beach when God appeared to him and told him to forget his dreams of a crusade. "I have a greater work for you," God said then, and now Columbus was near the culmination of that work. It filled him like wine, it filled him like light, it filled him like the wind in the sails over his head.

2

Slaves

Though Tagiri did not put her own body back in time, it is still true to say that she was the one who stranded Christopher Columbus on the island of Hispaniola and changed the face of history forever. Though she was born seven centuries after Columbus's voyage and never left her birth continent of Africa, she found a way to reach back and sabotage the European conquest of America. It was not an act of malice. Some said that it was like correcting a painful hernia in a brain-damaged child: In the end, the child would still be severely limited, but it would not suffer as much along the way. But Tagiri saw it differently.

"History is not prelude," she said once. "We don't justify the suffering of people in the past because everything turned out well enough by the time we came along. Their suffering counts just as much as our peace and happiness. We look out of our golden windows and feel pity for the scenes of blood and blades, of plagues and famines that are played out in the surrounding country. When we believed that we could not go back in time and make changes, then we could be excused for shedding a tear for them and then going on about our happy lives. But once we know that it is in our power to help them, then, if we turn away and let their suffering go on, it is no golden age we live in, and we poison our own happiness. Good people do not let others suffer needlessly.'' What she asked was a hard thing, but some agreed with her. Not all, but in the end, enough.

Nothing in her parentage, her upbringing, or her education gave any hint that one day, by unmaking one world, she would create another. Like most young people who joined Pastwatch, Tagiri's first use of the Tempoview machine was to trace her own family back, generation before generation. She was vaguely aware that, as a novice, she would be observed during her first year. But hadn't they told her that as she learned to control and finetune the machine (''it's an art, not a science'') she could explore anything she wanted? It wouldn't have bothered her, anyway, to know that her superiors nodded knowingly when it became clear that she was following her matrilineal line back to a Dongotona village on the banks of the Koss River. Though she was as racially mixed as anyone else in the world these days, she had picked the one lineage that mattered most to her, the one from which she derived her identity. Dongotona was the name of her tribe and of the mountainous country where they lived, and the village of Ikoto was her foremothers' ancient home.

It was hard to learn to use the Tempoview. Even though it had extraordinarily good computer-assisted guidance, so that getting to the exact place and time you wanted was precise within minutes, there was no computer yet that could overcome what the pastwatchers called the "significance problem." Tagiri would pick a vantage point in the village—near the main path winding among the houses— and then set up a time frame, such as a week. The computer would then scan for human passage and record all that took place within range of the vantage point.

All this took only minutes—and enormous amounts of electricity, but this was the dawn of the twenty-third century, and solar energy was cheap. What ate up Tagiri's first weeks was sorting through the empty conversations, the meaningless events. Not that they seemed empty or meaningless at first. When she started, Tagiri could listen to any conversation and be enthralled. These were real people, from her own past! Some of them were bound to be ancestors of hers, and sooner or later she'd sort out which ones. In the meantime, she loved it all—the flirtatious girls, the complaining old men, the tired women snapping at the rude children; and oh, those children! Those fungus-covered, hungry, exuberant children, too young to know they were poor and too poor to know that not everyone in the world woke up hungry in the morning and went to bed hungry at night. They were so alive, so alert.

Within a few weeks, though, Tagiri had run into the significance problem. After watching a few dozen girls flirting, she knew that all girls of Ikoto flirted in pretty much the same way. After watching a few dozen teasings, tauntings, quarrels, and kindnesses among the children, she realized that she had seen pretty much every variation on teasing, taunting, quarreling, and kindness that she would ever see. No way had yet been found to program the Tempoview computers to recognize unusual, unpredictable human behavior. It had been hard enough to train them to recognize human movement in the first place; in the early days, pastwatchers had had to wade through endless landings and peckings of small birds and scamperings of lizards and mice in order to see a few human interactions.

Tagiri found her own solution—the minority solution, but those who observed her were not surprised that she was one of those who took this route. Where most pastwatchers began to resort to statistical approaches to their research, keeping counts of different behaviors and then writing papers on cultural patterns, Tagiri took quite the opposite route, beginning to follow one individual from the beginning to the end of life. She wasn't looking for patterns. She was looking for stories. Ah, said her observers. She will be a biographer; it is lives, not cultures, that she will find for us.

Then her research took a twist that her superiors had seen only a few times before. Tagiri had already worked her way seven generations deep into her mother's family when she abandoned the biographical approach and, instead of following each person from birth to death, she began to follow individual women backward, from death to birth.

Tagiri began doing this with an old woman named Amami, setting up her Tempoview to keep shifting vantage points to track Amami backward in time. It meant that except when she overrode her program, Tagiri was unable to make sense of the woman's conversations. And instead of cause and effect unfolding in the normal linear pattern, she was constantly seeing the effect first, then discovering the cause. In old age Amami walked with a pronounced limp; only after weeks of following her backward in time did Tagiri find the origin of the limp, as a much younger Amami lay bleeding on her mat, and then seemed to crawl backward away from the mat until she uncrumpled and rose to her feet to face her husband, who seemed to draw his walking stick sharply away from her body again and again.

And why had he beaten her? A few more minutes of backtracking brought the answer: Amami had been raped by two powerful men from a nearby village of Lotuko tribesmen when she went for water. But Amami's husband could not accept the idea that it was rape, for that would have meant that he was incapable of protecting his wife; it would have required him to take some kind of vengeance, which would have endangered the fragile peace between Lotuko and Dongotona in the Koss Valley. So for the good of his tribe and to salvage his own ego, he had to interpret his weeping wife's story as a lie, and assume that in fact she had been playing the whore. He was beating her to get her to give him the money she had been paid, even though it was obvious to Tagiri that he knew there was no money, that his beloved wife had not gone whoring, that in fact he was being unjust. His obvious sense of shame at what he was doing did not seem to make him go easier on her. He was more brutal than Tagiri had ever seen any man in the village—needlessly so, continuing to cane her long after she was screaming and pleading and confessing to all sins ever committed in the world. Since he was doing this beating, not because he believed in the justice of it, but so that he could convince the neighbors that he believed his wife deserved it, he overdid it. Overdid it, and then had to watch Amami limping through the rest of her life.

If he ever asked forgiveness, or even implied it, Tagiri had missed it. He had done what he thought a man had to do to maintain his honor in Ikoto. How could he be sorry for that? Amami might limp, but she had an honorable husband whose prestige was undiminished. Never mind that even the week before she died, some of the little children of the village had still been following after her, taunting her with the words they had learned from the previous batch of children a few years older: "Lotuko-whore!"

The more Tagiri began to care about and identify with the people of Ikoto, the more she began to live in the back-to-front timeflow. As she looked at other people's actions, in and out of the Tempoview, instead of waiting to see the results of actions, she waited to see the causes. To her the world was not a potential future awaiting her manipulation; to her, it was an irrevocable set of results, and all that could be found was the irrevocable causes that led to the present moment.

Her superiors noted this with much curiosity, for those few novices who had experimented with backward timeflow in the past usually gave it up quite soon, because it was so disorienting. But Tagiri did not give it up. She went back and back and back in time, taking old women into the womb, and then following their mothers, on and on, finding the cause of everything.

It was because of this that her novice period was allowed to extend long past those uncertain months when she was still gaining skill at handling the Tempoview and finding her own way past the significance problem. Instead of giving her an assignment in one of the ongoing projects, she was allowed to continue exploring her own past. This was a very practical decision, of course, for as a story-seeker instead of a pattern-seeker, she would not fit in with any of the ongoing projects anyway. Story-seekers were usually allowed to follow their own desires. However, Tagiri's continued backward watching made her, not just unusual, but unique. Her superiors were curious to discover where her research would lead her, and what she would write.

They were not like Tagiri herself. *She* would have watched herself in order to discover, not where her peculiar research approach would lead, but rather where it had come from.

If they had asked her, she would have thought for a moment and told them, for she was and always had been extraordinarily self-aware. It was my parents' divorce, Tagiri would have said. They had seemed perfectly happy to her all her life; then, when she was fourteen, she learned that they were divorcing, and suddenly all the idyll of her childhood turned out to be a lie, for her father and mother had been jockeying all those years in a vicious, deadly competition for supremacy in the household. It had been invisible to Tagiri because her parents hid their pernicious competitiveness even from each other, even from themselves, but when Tagiri's father was made head of Sudan Restoration, which would put him two levels higher than Tagiri's mother in the same organization, their hatred for each other's accomplishments finally emerged into the open, naked and brutal.

Only then was Tagiri able to think back to cryptic conversations over breakfast or supper, when her parents had congratulated each other for various accomplishments. Now, no longer naive, Tagiri could remember their words and realize that they had been digging knives into each other's pride. And so it was that at the cusp of her childhood, she suddenly reexperienced all of her life till then, only in reverse, with the result clear in her mind, thinking backward and backward, discovering the true causes of everything. That was how she had seen life ever since—long before she thought of using her university study in ethnology and ancient languages as an entrée to Pastwatch.

They did not ask her why her timeflow ran backward, and she did not tell them. Though she was vaguely uneasy that she had not yet been assigned to anything, Tagiri was also glad, for she was playing the greatest game of her life, solving puzzle after puzzle. Hadn't Amami's daughter been late to marry? And hadn't *her* daughter in turn married too young, and to a man who was far more strong-willed and selfish than her mother's kind but compliant husband? Each generation rejected the choices of the generation before, never understanding the reasons behind the mother's life. Happiness for this generation, misery for the next, but all traceable back to a rape and an unjust beating of an already miserable woman. Tagiri had heard all the reverberations before at last she came upon the ringing bell; she had felt all the waves before she came, at last, to the stone dropping into the pool. Just as it had been in her own childhood.

By all signs, she would have a strange and intriguing career, and her personnel file was given the rare status of a silver tag, which told anyone who had authority to reassign her that she was to be left alone or encouraged to go on with whatever she was doing.

In the meantime, unknown to her, a monitor would be permanently assigned to her, to track all her work, so that in case (as sometimes happened with these strange ones) she never published, upon her death a report on her life's work would be issued anyway, for whatever value it might then have. Only five other people had silver tags on their files when Tagiri achieved this status. And Tagiri was the strangest of them all.

Her life might have gone on that way, for nothing outside her was allowed to interfere with the course she naturally followed. But well into her second year of personal research, she came upon an event in the village of Ikoto that turned her away from one path and into another, with consequences that would change the world. She was backtracking through the life of a woman named Diko. More than any other woman she had studied, Diko had won Tagiri's heart, for there was from the day of her death on back an air of sadness to her that made her seem a figure of tragedy. The others around her sensed it, too—she was treated with great reverence, and often was asked for advice, even by men, though she was not one of the omen-women and performed no more priestly rites than any other Dongotona.

The sadness remained, year before year, back and back into her years as a young wife, until at last it gave way to something else: fear, rage, even weeping. I am close, thought Tagiri. I will find out the pain at the root of her sadness. Was this, too, some act of her husband's? That would be hard to believe, for unlike Amami's husband, Diko's was a mild and kind man, who enjoyed his wife's position of respect in the village while never seeming to seek any honor for himself. Not a proud man, or a brutal one. And they seemed, in their most private moments, to be genuinely in love; whatever caused Diko's sadness, her husband was a comfort to her.

Then Diko's fear and rage gave way to fear alone, and now the whole village was turned out, searching, hunting through the brush and the forest and along the riverbanks for something lost. Some*one* lost, rather, for there were no possessions among the Dongotona that would be worth searching for so intently, if lost—only human beings had such value, for only they were irreplaceable.

And then, suddenly, the search was unbegun, and for the first time Tagiri could see the Diko that might have been: smiling, laughing, singing, her face filled with perfect delight at the life the gods had given her. For there in Diko's house Tagiri now saw for the first time the one whose loss had brought Diko such deep sadness all her life: an eight-year-old boy, bright and alert and happy. She called him Acho, and she talked to him constantly, for he was her companion in work and play. Tagiri had seen good mothers and bad in her passage through the generations, but never such a delight of a mother in her son, and of a son in his mother. The boy also loved his father, and was learning all the manly things from him as he should, but Diko's husband was not as verbal as his wife and firstborn son, so he watched and listened and enjoyed them together, only occasionally joining in their banter.

Perhaps because Tagiri had watched with such suspense through so many weeks, searching for the cause of Diko's sadness, or perhaps because she had come to admire and love Diko so much during her long passage with her, Tagiri could not do as she had done before, and simply continue to move backward, to Acho's emergence from Diko's womb, back to Diko's childhood home and her own birth. Acho's disappearance had had too many reverberations, not just in his mother's life but, through her, in the lives of the whole village, for Tagiri to leave the mystery of his disappearance unsolved. Diko never knew what happened to her boy, but Tagiri had the means to find out. And besides, even though it meant changing direction and searching forward in time for a while, tracking, not a woman, but a boy, it was still a part of her backward search. She would find what it was that took Acho and caused Diko's endless grief.

There were hippos in the waters of the Koss in those days, though rarely this far upriver, and Tagiri dreaded seeing what the villagers assumed—poor Acho broken and drowned in the jaws of a surly hippopotamus.

But it was not a hippo. It was a man.

A strange man, who spoke a language unlike any that Acho had heard—though Tagiri recognized it at once as Arabic. The man's light skin and beard, his robe and turban, all were intriguing to the nearly naked Acho, who had seen only people with dark brown skin, except when a group of blue-black Dinkas came hunting up the river. How was such a creature as this possible? Unlike other children, Acho was not one to turn and flee, and so when the man smiled and talked his incomprehensible babble (Tagiri knew he was saying, "Come here, little boy, I won't hurt you") Acho stood his ground, and even smiled.

Then the man lashed out with his stick and knocked Acho senseless to the ground. For a moment the man seemed concerned that he might have killed the boy, and he was satisfied to find Acho was still breathing. Then the Arab folded the unconscious child into fetal position and jammed his small body into a bag, which he hoisted over his shoulder and carried back down the riverbank, where he joined two other companions, who also had full bags.

A slaver, Tagiri realized at once. She had thought they did not come this far. Usually they bought their slaves from Dinkas down at the White Nile, and the Dinka slavers knew better than to come into the mountains in groups so small. Their method was to raid a village, kill all the men, and take the small children and the pretty women off for sale, leaving only the old women behind to keen for them. Most of the Muslim slavers preferred to trade for slaves rather than to do their own kidnapping. These men had broken with the pattern. In the old marketeering societies that nearly ruined the world, thought Tagiri, these men would have been viewed as vigorous, innovative entrepreneurs, trying to make a bit more profit by cutting out the Dinka middlemen.

She meant to resume her backward watching then, returning to the life of Acho's mother, but Tagiri found that she could not do it. The computer was set to find new vantage points tracking Acho's movements, and Tagiri did not reach out and give the command that would have returned to the earlier program. Instead she watched and watched, moving forward through time to see, not what caused all this, but where it led. What would happen to this bright and wonderful boy that Diko loved.

What happened at first was that he was almost liberated—or killed. The slavers were stupid enough to have captured slaves on their way *up* the river, even though there was no way to return except by passing near the very villages where they had already kidnapped children. At a village farther downstream, some Lotuko men in full warrior dress ambushed them. The other two Arabs were killed, and since their sacks contained the only children the Lotuko villagers cared about—their own—they allowed the slaver who carried Acho on his back to escape.

The slaver eventually found his way to the village where two black slaves of his were keeping the camels. Strapping the bag containing Acho onto the camel, the surviving members of the slaving party got under way at once. To Tagiri's disgust, the man didn't so much as open the bag to see if the boy was still alive.

And so the journey down the Nile continued, all the way to the slave market of Khartoum. The slaver would open the bag containing Acho only once a day, to splash some water into the boy's mouth. The rest of the time the boy rode in darkness, his body cramped in fetal position. He was brave, for he never wept, and after the slaver brutally kicked the bag a few times, Acho stopped trying to plead. Instead he endured in silence, his eyes bright with fear. The bag no doubt stank of his urine by now, and since, like most children of Ikoto, Acho's bowels had always been loose from dysentery, the bag was certainly foul with fecal matter, too. But that soon grew old and dry in the desert, and since Acho was fed nothing, this pollution at least was not renewed. Of course the boy could not have been allowed out of the bag to void his bladder and bowel—he might have run off, and the slaver was determined to realize *some* profit from a trip that cost the lives of his two partners.

In Khartoum, it was no surprise that Acho could not walk for a whole day. Beatings, liberally applied, and a meal of sorghum gruel soon had him on his feet, however, and within a day or two he had been bought by a wholesaler for a price that made Acho's captor temporarily rich in the economy of Khartoum.

Tagiri followed Acho down the Nile, by boat and by camel, until he was finally sold in Cairo. Better fed now, well-washed, and looking quite exotic in the bustling Arab-African city that was the cultural center of Islam in those days, Acho fetched an excellent price and joined the household of a wealthy trader. Acho quickly learned Arabic, and his master discovered his bright mind and saw to his education. Acho eventually became the factotum of the house, tending to all while the master was off on voyages. When the master died, his eldest son inherited Acho along with everything else, and relied on him even more heavily, until Acho had de facto control of the entire business, which he ran very profitably, expanding into new markets and new trade goods until the family fortune was one of the greatest in Cairo. And when Acho died, the family sincerely mourned him and gave him an honorable funeral, for a slave.

Yet what Tagiri could not forget was that through all of this, through every hour of every day of every year of Acho's slavery, his face never lost that look of unforgotten longing, of grief, of despair. The look that said, I am a stranger here, I hate this place, I hate my life. The look that said to Tagiri that Acho grieved for his mother just as long and just as deeply as she grieved for him.

That was when Tagiri left her backward search through her own family's past and took on what she thought would be her lifelong project: slavery. Till now, all the story-seekers in Pastwatch had devoted their careers to recording the stories of great, or at least influential, men and women of the past. But Tagiri would study the slaves, not the owners; she would search throughout history, not to record the choices of the powerful, but to find the stories of those who had lost all choice. To remember the forgotten people, the ones whose dreams were murdered and whose bodies were stolen from themselves, so that they were not even featured players in their own autobiographies. The ones whose faces showed that they never forgot for one instant that they did not belong to themselves, and that there was no lasting joy possible in life because of that.

She found this look on faces everywhere. Oh, sometimes there was defiance—but the defiant ones were always singled out for special treatment, and the ones who didn't die from it were eventually brutalized into wearing the look of despair that the other faces bore. It was the slave look, and what Tagiri discovered was that for an enormous number of human beings in almost every age of history, that was the only face they could ever show to the world.

Tagiri was thirty years old, some eight years into her slavery project, with a dozen of the more traditional pattern-seeking pastwatchers working under her alongside two of the story-seekers, when her career took its final turn, leading her at last to Columbus and the unmaking of history. Though she never left Juba, the town where her Pastwatch observatory was located, the Tempoview could range anywhere over the Earth's surface. And when the TruSite II was introduced to replace the now-aging Tempoviews, she began to be able to explore farther afield, for rudimentary translation of ancient languages was now built into the system, and she did not have to learn each language herself in order to get the gist of what was going on in the scenes she saw.

Tagiri was often drawn to the TruSite station of one of her story-seekers, a young man named Hassan. She had not bothered to observe his station much when he was using the old Tempoview, because she didn't understand any of the Antillean languages that he was laboriously reconstructing by analogy with other Carib and Arawak languages. Now, however, he had trained the TruSite to catch the main drift of the dialect of Arawak being spoken by the particular tribe he was observing.

"It's a mountain village," he explained, as soon as he saw that she was watching. "Much more temperate than the villages near the coast—a different kind of agriculture."

"And the occasion?" she asked.

"I'm seeing the lives that were interrupted by the Spanish," he said. "This is only a few weeks before an expedition finally comes up the mountain to take them into slavery. The Spanish are getting desperate for labor down on the coast."

"The plantations are growing?"

"Not at all," said Hassan. "In fact, they're failing. But the Spanish aren't very good at keeping their Indie slaves alive."

"Do they even try?"

"Most do. The murder-for-sport attitude is here, of course, because the Spanish have absolute power and for some that power has to be tested to the limit. But by and large the priests have got control of things and they're really trying to keep the slaves from dying."

Priests in control, thought Tagiri, and yet slavery is unchallenged. But even though it always tasted freshly bitter in her mouth, she knew that there was no point in reminding Hassan of the irony of it—wasn't he on the slavery project with her?

"The people of Ankuash are perfectly aware of what's going on. They've already figured out that they're just about the last Indies left who haven't been enslaved. They've tried to stay out of sight, lighting no fires and making sure the Spanish don't see them, but there are too many Arawaks and Caribs of the lowlands who are saving some bit of their freedom by collaborating with the Spanish. *They* remember Ankuash. So there'll be an expedition, soon, and they know it. You see?''

What Tagiri saw was an old man and a middle-aged woman, squatting on opposite sides of a small fire, where a jar of water was giving off steam. She smiled at the new technology—to be able to see *steam* in the holographic display was amazing; she almost expected to be able to smell it.

''Tobacco water,'' said Hassan.

''They drink the nicotine solution?''

Hassan nodded. ''I've seen this sort of thing before.''

''Aren't they being careless? This doesn't look like a smokeless fire.''

''The TruSite may be enhancing the smoke too much in the holo, so there may be less of it than we're seeing,'' said Hassan. ''But smoke or not, there's no way to boil the tobacco water without fire, and at this point they're near despair. Better to risk their smoke being seen than to go another day without word from the gods.''

''So they drink . . .''

''They drink and dream,'' said Hassan.

''Don't they give greater trust to dreams that come of themselves?'' asked Tagiri.

''They know that most dreams mean nothing. They hope that their nightmares mean nothing—fear dreams instead of true dreams. They use the tobacco water to make the gods tell them the truth. Farther down the slopes, the Arawaks and Caribs would have offered a human sacrifice, or bled themselves the way the Mayas do. But this village has no tradition of sacrifice and never adopted it from their neighbors. They're a holdout from a different tradition, I think. Similar to some tribes in the upper Amazon. They don't need death or blood to talk to the gods.''

The man and the woman both tipped pipes into the water and then sucked liquid up into their mouths as if through a drinking straw. The woman gagged; the man was apparently inured to the liquid. The woman began to look very sick, but the man made her drink more.

"The woman is Putukam—the name means *wild dog*," said Hassan. "She's a woman noted for her visions, but she hasn't used tobacco water much before."

"I can see why not," said Tagiri. For now the woman named Putukam was puking and retching. For a moment or two the old man tried to steady her, but in moments he too was vomiting; their discharge mingled and flowed into the ashes of the fire.

"On the other hand, Baiku is a healer, so he uses the drugs more. All the time, actually. So he can send his spirit into the body of the sick person and find out what's wrong. Tobacco water is his favorite. Of course, it still makes him vomit. It makes everybody vomit."

"Making him a candidate for stomach cancer."

"He should live so long," said Hassan.

"Do the gods speak to them?"

Hassan shrugged. "Let's zip ahead and see."

He rushed the display for a few moments—Putukam and Baiku may have slept for hours, but to the pastwatchers it took only seconds. Whenever they stirred, the TruSite automatically slowed down a little; only when it was clear that the movements were signs of waking, not the normal wriggling of sleep, did Hassan bring the speed back to normal. Now he turned up the sound, and because Tagiri was there, he used the computer translator instead of just listening to the native speechsounds.

"I dreamed," said Putukam.

"And I," said Baiku.

"Let me hear the healing dream," said Putukam.

"There is no healing in it," he said, his face looking grave and sad.

"All slaves?"

"All except the blessed ones who are murdered or die from plagues."

"And then?"

"All dead."

"This is our healing, then," said Putukam. "To die. Better to have been captured by Caribs. Better to have our hearts torn out and our livers eaten. Then at least we would be an offering to a god."

"What was your dream?"

"My dream was madness," she said. "My dream had no truth in it."

"The dreamer does not know," said Baiku.

She sighed. "You will think I am a poor dreamer indeed, and the gods hate my soul. I dreamed of a man and woman watching us. They were full grown, and yet I knew in the dream that they are forty generations younger than us."

Tagiri interrupted. "Stop," she said.

He stopped.

"Was that translation correct?" she demanded.

Hassan spun the TruSite back a little, and ran the seen again, this time with the translator routine suppressed. He listened to the native speech, twice. "The translation is right enough," he said. "The words she used that were rendered as 'man' and 'woman' are from an older language, and I think there may be overtones that might make the words mean *hero-man* and *hero-woman*. Less than gods, but more than human. But they often use those words for talking about each other, as opposed to people from other tribes."

"Hassan," she said, "I'm not asking about the etymology. I'm asking about the meaning of what she said."

He looked at her blankly.

"Don't you think that it sounded very much as though she were seeing *us?*"

"But that's absurd," said Hassan.

"Forty generations. Isn't the time about right? A man and a woman, watching."

"Out of all possible dreams, can't there be dreams of the future?" asked Hassan. "And since Pastwatch scours all eras of history so thoroughly now, isn't it likely that eventually a watcher will witness the telling of a dream that seems to be a dream of the watcher himself?"

"Probability of coincidence," she said. She knew that principle, of course; it had been thoroughly covered in the later stages of training. But there was something else. Yes. As Hassan showed the scene yet a third time, it seemed to Tagiri that when Putukam spoke

of her dream, her gaze was steady in the direction from which
Hassan and Tagiri were watching, her eyes focused as if she could
actually see them, or some glimmer of them.

"It can be disorienting, can't it?" Hassan grinned at her.

"Show the rest," said Tagiri. Of course it was disorienting—
but scarcely less so than Hassan's grin. None of her other sub-
ordinates would ever have grinned at her like that, with such a
personal comment. Not that Hassan was being impertinent. Rather
he was simply . . . friendly, yes, that was it.

He started the TruSite viewing beyond what they had seen before.

"I dreamed that they watched me three times," Putukam was
saying, "and the woman seemed to know that I could see her."

Hassan slammed his hand onto the Pause button. "There is no
God but God," he muttered in Arabic, "and Muhammad is his
prophet."

Tagiri knew that sometimes when a Muslim says this, it is
because he has too much respect to curse the way a Christian
might.

"Probability of coincidence?" she murmured. "I was just
thinking that it seemed as though she could see us."

"If I go back and we watch the scene again," said Hassan,
"then it will be four times, not three."

"But it had been three times when we first heard her say how
many. That will never change."

"The TruSite has *no* effect on the past," said Hassan. "It can't
possibly be detected there."

"And how do we know that?" asked Tagiri.

"Because it's impossible."

"In theory."

"And because it never has."

"Till now."

"You *want* to believe that she really saw us in her nicotine
dream?"

Tagiri shrugged, feigning a nonchalance she didn't feel. "If she
saw us, Hassan, then let's go on and see what it means to her."

Hassan slowly, almost timidly, released the TruSite to continue
exploring the scene.

"This is prophecy, then," Baiku was saying. "Who knows what wonders the gods will bring in forty generations?"

"I always thought that time moved in great circles, as if all of us had been woven into the same great basket of life, each generation another ring around the rim," said Putukam. "But when in the great circles of time was there ever such horror as these white monsters from the sea? So the basket is torn, and time is broken, and all the world spills out of the basket into the dirt."

"What of the man and woman who watch us?"

"Nothing," said Putukam. "They watched us. They were interested."

"They see us now?"

"They saw all the suffering in your dream," said Putukam. "They were interested in it."

"What do you mean, interested?"

"I think they were sad," said Putukam.

"But . . . were they white, then? Did they watch the people suffer and care nothing for it, like the white men?"

"They were dark. The woman is very black. I have never seen a person of such blackness of skin."

"Then why don't they stop the white men from making us slaves?"

"Maybe they can't," said Putukam.

"If they can't save us," said Baiku, "then why do they look at us, unless they are monsters who enjoy the suffering of others?"

"Turn it off," said Tagiri to Hassan.

He paused the display again and looked at her in surprise. He saw something in her face that made him reach out and touch her arm. "Tagiri," he said gently, "of all people who have ever watched the past, you are the one who has never, even for a moment, forgotten compassion."

"She has to understand," murmured Tagiri. "I would help her if I could."

"How can she understand such a thing?" asked Hassan. "Even if she really saw us, somehow, in a true dream, she can't possibly comprehend the limitations on what we can do. To her, the ability to see into the past like this would be the power of the gods. So of course she will think we can do anything, and simply choose not

to. But you know and I know that we can't, and therefore choose
not at all.''

"The vision of the gods without the power of the gods," said
Tagiri. "What a terrible gift."

"A glorious gift," said Hassan. "You know that the stories
we've brought out of the slavery project have awakened great interest and compassion in the world around us. You can't change
the past, but you've changed the present, and these people are no
longer forgotten. They loom larger in the hearts of the people of our
time than the old heroes ever did. You have given these people the
only help that it was in your power to give. They're no longer
forgotten. Their suffering is seen.''

"It isn't enough," said Tagiri.

"If it's all that you can do," said Hassan, "then it *is* enough."

"I'm ready now," said Tagiri. "You can show the rest of it."

"Perhaps we should wait."

She reached down and pressed the button to resume the display.

Putukam and Baiku gathered the dirt where their vomit had
formed mud. They threw it into the tobacco water. The fire under
it had died, so no steam was rising, yet they put their faces over
the water as if to smell the steam of the dirt and the vomit and the
tobacco.

Putukam began a chant. "From my body, from the earth, from
the spirit water, I . . .''

The TruSite II paused automatically.

"It can't translate the word," said Hassan. "And neither can I.
It's not in the normally used vocabulary. They do use scraps of older
languages in their magicking, and this may be related to a root in the
old language that means shaping, like forming something out of mud.
So she's saying, 'I shape you,' or something related to that."

"Go on," said Tagiri.

Putukam's chant began again. "From my body, from the earth,
from the spirit water, I shape you, O children of forty generations
who look at me from inside my dream. You see the suffering of us
and all the other villages. You see the white monsters who make
us slaves and murder us. You see how the gods send plagues to

save the blessed ones and leave only the cursed ones to bear this terrible punishment. Speak to the gods, O children of forty generations who look at me from inside my dream! Teach them mercy! Let them send a plague to take us all, and leave the land empty for the white monsters, so they will hunt and hunt for us from shore to shore and find none of us, no people at all, not even the human-eating Caribs! Let the land be empty except for our dead bodies, so that we will die in honor as free people. Speak to the gods for us, O man, O woman!''

And so it went on like that, Baiku taking over the chant when Putukam wearied. Soon others from the village gathered around them and sporadically joined in the chant, especially when they were intoning the name they were praying to: Children-of-Forty-Generations-Who-Look-at-Us-from-Inside-the-Dream-of-Puthukam.

They were still chanting when the Spanish, led by two shame-faced Indie guides, shambled along the path, their muskets, pikes, and swords at the ready. The people made no resistance. They kept up the chant, even after they had all been seized, even as the old men, including Baiku, were being gutted with swords or spitted on pikes. Even as the young girls were being raped, all who could speak kept up the chanting, the prayer, the conjuration, until finally the Spanish commander, unnerved by it all, walked over to Putukam and drove his sword into the base of her throat, just above where the collarbones come together. With a gurgle, she died, and the chanting ended. For her, as for Baiku, the prayer was answered. She was not a slave before she died.

With all the villagers dead, Tagiri reached down again, but Hassan's hand was there before her, stopping the display.

Tagiri was trembling, but she pretended not to feel strong emotions. ''I have seen such terrible things before,'' said Tagiri. ''But this time she saw me. Saw *us*.''

''Or so it seems.''

''She saw, Hassan.''

''So it seems.'' Now the words admitted she might be right.

''Something from our time, from right now, was visible to her in her dream. Perhaps we were still visible when she awoke. It seemed to me that she was looking at us. I didn't think of her seeing us until after she awoke from her dream, and yet she saw that I knew she could see us. It's too much to be chance.''

"If this is true," said Hassan, "then why haven't other watchers using the TruSite II been seen?"

"Perhaps we're only visible to those who need so desperately to see us."

"It's impossible," said Hassan. "We were taught that from the beginning."

"No," said Tagiri. "Remember the course in the history of Pastwatch? The theorists weren't certain, were they? Only years of observation convinced them that their theory was right—but in the early days there was much talk of temporal backwash."

"So you paid more attention in class than I did," said Hassan.

"Temporal backwash," she said again. "Don't you see how dangerous this is?"

"If it's true, if they really saw us, then it can't be dangerous because, after all, nothing changed as a result of it."

"Nothing would ever *seem* to change," she said, "because we would then live in the version of the present created by the new past. Who knows how many changes, small and great, we might have made, and yet never knew it because the change made our present different and we couldn't remember it being any other way?"

"We can't have changed anything at all," said Hassan. "Or history would have changed, and even if Pastwatch itself still existed, certainly the circumstances where we decided to stand here together and watch this village would never have happened in just that way, and therefore the change we made in the past would have *unmade* our very making of that change, and therefore it couldn't happen. She didn't see us."

"I know the circularity argument as well as you do, Hassan," she said. "But this particular case proves it false. You can't deny that she saw us, Hassan. You can't call it coincidence. Not when she saw I was black."

He grinned. "If the devils of her time are white, then maybe she needed to invent a god as black as you."

"She also saw that there were two of us, that we watched her three times, that I knew she could see us. She even got our era approximately right. She saw and she understood. We changed the past."

Hassan shrugged. "I know," he said. Then he sat up, alert again, having found an argument. "It doesn't mean that circularity is proved false," he said. "The Spaniards behaved exactly as they would have anyway, so any change that came about because she saw us watching her made no difference in the future because she and all her people were so soon dead. Maybe that's the only time the TruSite II has a backwash effect. When it can't possibly make a difference. So the past is still safe from our meddling. Which means we're also safe."

Tagiri did not bother pointing out that even though the Spaniards had killed or enslaved everyone, it didn't change the fact that because of what Putukam saw in her vision, the people were chanting a prayer as they were taken. That had to have an effect on the Spaniards. It had to bend their lives, just a little bit, the sheer strangeness of it. No change in the past would fail to have some kind of reverberation. It was the butterfly's wing, just as they taught in school: Who knew whether or not a storm in the North Atlantic might not have been triggered, far back in the chain of cause-and-effect, by the flapping of a butterfly's wing in China? But there was no point in arguing this with Hassan. Let him believe in safety while he could. Nothing was safe now; but neither were the watchers powerless, either.

"She saw me," said Tagiri. "Her desperation made her believe I was a god. And her suffering makes me wish that she were right. To have the power to help these people—Hassan, if she could sense us, it means that we're sending something back. And if we're sending anything back at all, *anything,* then perhaps we could do something that would help."

"How could we save that village?" said Hassan. "Even if it were possible to travel back in time, what would we do? Lead an avenging army to destroy the Spanish who came to take this village? What would that accomplish? More Spanish would come later, or English or some other conquering nation from Europe. And in the meantime, our own time would have been destroyed. Undone by our own intervention. You can't change great sweeps of history by changing one small event. The forces of history go on anyway."

"Dear Hassan," she said, "you tell me now that history is such an inexorable force that we can't alter its onward march. Yet a moment ago you told me that any change, however small, would alter history by so much that it would undo our own time. Explain to me why this isn't a contradiction."

"It *is* a contradiction, but that doesn't mean it's untrue. History is a chaotic system. The details can shift endlessly, but the overall shape remains constant. Make a small change in the past, and it changes enough *details* in the present that we would not have come together at exactly this place and time to watch exactly this scene. And yet the great movements of history would be largely un-changed."

"Neither of us is a mathematician," said Tagiri. "We're just playing logic games. The fact is that Putukam saw us, you and me. There *is* some kind of sending from our time to the past. This changes everything, and soon the mathematicians will discover truer explanations for the workings of our time machines, and then we'll see what's possible and what isn't. And if it turns out that we *can* reach into the past, deliberately and purposefully, then we will do it, you and I."

"And why is that?"

"Because we're the ones she saw. Because she . . . *shaped* us."

"She prayed for us to send a plague to wipe out all the Indies before the Europeans ever came. Are you really going to take that seriously?"

"If we're going to be gods," said Tagiri, "then I think we have a duty to come up with better solutions than the people who pray to us."

"But we're not going to be gods," said Hassan.

"You seem sure of that," she said.

"Because I'm quite sure the people of our time won't relish the idea of our world being undone in order to ameliorate the suffering of one small group of people so long dead."

"Not undone," said Tagiri. "Remade."

"You're even crazier than a Christian," said Hassan. "*They* believe that one man's death and suffering was worth it because it saved all of humankind. But you, you're ready to sacrifice half the people who ever lived, just to save one village."

She glared at him. "You're right," she said. "For one village, it wouldn't be worth it."

She walked away.

It was real, she knew it. The TruSite II reached back into the past, and the watchers were somehow visible to the watched, if they knew how to look, if they were hungry to see. So what should they do? There would be those, she knew, who would want to shut down all of Pastwatch to avoid the risk of contaminating the past with unpredictable and possibly devastating results in the present. And there would be others who would trust complacently in the paradoxes, believing that Pastwatch could be seen by people of the past only under circumstances where it could not possibly affect the future. Fearful overreaction or smug negligence, neither was appropriate. She and Hassan had changed the past, and the change they introduced had in fact changed the present. Perhaps it had not changed all the intervening generations between then and now, but certainly it had changed Hassan and her. Neither of them would think or do or say anything that they would have thought or done or said without having heard the prayer of Putukam. They had changed the past, and the past had changed the future. It could be done. The paradoxes didn't stop it. The people of this golden time could do more than observe and record and remember.

If that was so, then what of all the suffering that she had seen over all these years? Could there be some way to change it? And if it could be changed, how could she refuse? They had shaped her. It was superstition, it meant nothing, and yet she could not eat that evening, could not sleep that night for thinking of their chanted prayer.

Tagiri got up from her mat and checked the time. After midnight, and she could not sleep. Pastwatch allowed its workers, wherever they dwelt, to live in the native manner, and the city of Juba had chosen to do so, as much as possible. So she was lying on woven reeds in a loose-walled hut cooled only by the wind. But there was a breeze tonight, and the hut was cool, so it wasn't heat that kept her awake. It was the prayer of the village of Ankuash.

She pulled a robe over her head and went to the laboratory, where others also worked late—there were no set working hours for people who played so loosely with the flow of time. She told her TruSite to show her Ankuash again, but after only a few seconds she could not bear it and switched to another view. Columbus, landing on the coast of Hispaniola. The wrecking of the *Santa Maria*. The fort he built to hold the crew that he could not take back home with him. It was a miserable sight to see again—the way the crew attempted to make slaves of the nearby villagers, who simply ran away; the kidnapping of young girls, the gang rapes until the girls were dead.

Then the Indies of several tribes began fighting back. This was not the ritual war to bring home victims for sacrifice. Nor was it the raiding war of the Caribs. It was a new kind of war, a punishing war. Or perhaps it was not so new, Tagiri realized. These oft-viewed scenes had been completely translated and it appeared that the natives already had a name for a war of annihilation. They called it "star-at-white-man's-village war." The crew awoke one morning to find pieces of their sentries' bodies scattered through the fort, and five hundred Indie soldiers in feathered splendor *inside* the stockade. Of course they surrendered.

The Indie villagers did not, however, adopt their captives preparatory to sacrifice. They had no intention of making these miserable rapists, thieves, and murderers into gods before they died. There was no formula declaration of "He is as my beloved son" when each Spanish sailor was taken into custody.

There would be no sacrifice, but there would still be blood and pain. Death, when it came, was a sweet relief. There were those, Tagiri knew, who relished this scene, for it was one of the few victories of the Indies over the Spanish, one of the first victories of a dark people over the arrogant whites. But she hadn't the stomach to watch it all the way through; she took no joy in torture and slaughter, even when the victims of it were monstrous criminals who had tortured and slaughtered others. Tagiri understood too well that in the minds of the Spaniards, their victims had not been human. It is our nature, she thought, that when we intend to enjoy being cruel, we must transform our victim into either a beast or a god. The Spanish sailors made the Indies into animals in their minds; all that the Indies proved, with their bitter vengeance, was that they were capable of the identical transformation.

Besides, there was nothing in this scene to tell her what she wanted to see. Instead she sent the TruSite to Columbus's cabin on the *Niña,* where he wrote his letter to the King of Aragon and the Queen of Castile. He spoke of vast wealth in gold and spices, rare woods, exotic beasts, vast new realms to be converted into Christian subjects, and plenty of slaves. Tagiri had seen this before, of course, if only to marvel at the irony that Columbus saw no contradiction between promising his sovereigns both slaves and Christian subjects out of the same populations. Now, though, Tagiri found something else to marvel at. She knew well enough that Columbus had seen no serious quantities of gold, beyond what might have been found in any Spanish village where the wealthiest household in town might have a few trinkets. He had understood almost nothing of what the Indies had said to him, though he convinced himself that he understood that they were telling him of gold farther inland. Inland? They were pointing west, across the Caribbean, but Columbus had no way of knowing that. He had seen no glimmer of the vast wealth of the Incas or the Mexica—those were not to be seen by Europeans for more than twenty years, and when the gold at last began to flow, Columbus would be dead. Yet as she watched him writing, then spun back and watched him write again, she thought: He isn't lying. He knows the gold is there. He is so *sure* of it, even though he has never seen it and will never see it in his life.

This is how he turned the eyes of Europe westward, Tagiri realized. By the force of his unshakable belief. If the king and queen of Spain had made their decision solely on the basis of the evidence that Columbus brought back with him, there would have been no follow-up to Columbus's voyage. Where were the spices? Where was the gold? His first discoveries had not begun to repay even the costs of his own expedition. Who would throw good money after bad?

Without real evidence, Columbus made these extravagant claims. He had found Cipangu; Cathay and the Spice Islands were close at hand. All false, or Columbus would have had a cargo to show for it. Yet anyone who looked at him, who heard him, who knew him, would recognize that this man was not lying, that he believed in his soul the things he said. On the strength of such a witness as this, new expeditions were financed, new fleets set sail; great civilizations fell, and the gold and silver of a continent flowed eastward while millions of people died of plagues and the survivors watched helplessly as strangers came to rule their land forever.

All because Columbus could not be doubted when he spoke of things he had not seen.

Tagiri played the recording of the scene in Ankuash, of the moment when Putukam told of her dream. She saw me and Hassan, thought Tagiri. And Columbus saw the gold. Somehow he saw the gold, even though it lay decades in the future. We with our machines can see only into the past. But somehow this Genovese man and this Indie woman saw what none can see, and they were right even though there was no way, no sensible way, no logical way they could be right.

It was four in the morning when Tagiri came to the door of Hassan's wind-cooled hut. If she clapped her hands or called to him, it would waken others. So she slipped inside and found that he, too, was still awake.

"You knew that I would come," she said.

"If I had dared," he answered, "I would have come to you."

"It can be done," she said, blurting it out at once. "We can change it. We can stop—something. Something terrible, we can make it go away. We can reach back and make it *better*."

He said nothing. He waited.

"I know what you're thinking, Hassan. We might also make it worse."

"Do you think I haven't been going through this in my mind tonight?" said Hassan. "Over and over. Look at the world around us, Tagiri. Humanity is finally at peace. There are no plagues. No children die hungry or live untaught. The world is healing. That was not inevitable. It might have ended up far worse. What change could we possibly make in the past that would be worth the risk of creating a history without this resurrection of the world?"

"I'll tell you what change would be worth it," she said. "The world would not have needed resurrecting if it had never been killed."

"What, do you imagine that there's some change we could make that would improve human nature? Undo the rivalry of nations? Teach people that sharing is better than greed?"

"Has human nature changed even now?" asked Tagiri. "I think not. We still have as much greed, as much power-lust, as much pride and anger as we ever had. The only difference now is that we know the consequences and we fear them. We control ourselves. We have become, at long last, civilized."

"So you think that we can civilize our ancestors?"

"I think," said Tagiri, "that *if* we can find some way to do it, some sure way to stop the world from tearing itself to pieces as it did, then we must do it. To reach into the past and prevent the disease is better than to take the patient at the point of death and slowly, slowly bring her back to health. To create a world in which the destroyers did not triumph."

"If I know you at all, Tagiri," said Hassan, "you would not have come here tonight if you didn't know already what the change must be."

"Columbus," she said.

"One sailor? Caused the destruction of the world?"

"There was nothing inevitable about his westward voyage at the time he sailed. The Portuguese were on the verge of finding a route to the Orient. No one imagined an unknown continent. The wisest ones knew that the world was large, and believed that an ocean twice the width of the Pacific stretched between Spain and China. Not until they had a sailing vessel they believed was capable of crossing such an ocean would they sail west. Even if the Portuguese bumped into the coast of Brasil, there was no profit there. It was dry and sparsely populated, and they would have ignored it just the way they largely ignored Africa and didn't colonize it for four long centuries after exploring its coast."

"You've been studying," he said.

"I've been thinking," she said. "I studied all this years ago. It was because Columbus came to America, with his relentless faith that he had found the Orient. Merely stumbling on the landmass meant nothing—the Norse did it, and where did that lead? Even a chance landing by someone else on Cuba or the eastern tip of Brasil would have meant no more than the meaningless landings on Vinland or the Guinea coast. It was only because of Columbus's reports of boundless wealth that never came true until after he was dead that other sailors followed him. Don't you see? It was not the fact that *somebody* sailed west that led to the European conquest of America and thus of the world. It was because *Columbus* did it."

"One man, then, was responsible for the devastation of our planet?"

"Of course not," said Tagiri. "I'm not talking about moral responsibility anyway, I'm talking about cause. Europe was already Europe. Columbus didn't make it that way. But it was the pillaging of America that financed the terrible religious and dynastic wars that swept Europe back and forth for generations. If Europe hadn't had possession of America, could it have imposed its culture on the world? Would a world dominated by Islam or ruled by Chinese bureaucracy have ever destroyed itself the way we did in a world where every nation tried to become as European as it could?"

"Of course it would," said Hassan. "Europeans didn't invent pillage."

"No, they invented the machines that made their pillaging so madly efficient. The machines that sucked all the oil out of the ground and let us carry war and famine across oceans and continents until nine-tenths of humankind was dead."

"So Columbus is responsible for the age of technology."

"Don't you see, Hassan, I'm not affixing blame?"

"I know, Tagiri."

"I'm finding the place where the smallest, simplest change would save the world from the most suffering. That would cause the fewest cultures to be lost, the fewest people to be enslaved, the fewest species to fall extinct, the fewest resources to be exhausted. It comes together at the point where Columbus returns to Europe with his tales of gold and slaves and nations to be converted into Christian subjects of the king and queen."

"So you would kill Columbus?"

Tagiri shuddered. "No," she said. "Who is to say that we could ever travel physically into the past in such a way that that would even be possible? We don't need to kill him, anyway. We only need to turn him away from his plan of sailing west. We have to find out what's possible before we decide how to do it. And murder—I could never agree to that. Columbus was no monster. We've all agreed to that, ever since the Tempoview showed the truth of him. His vices were the vices of his time and culture, but his virtues transcended the milieu of his life. He was a great man. I have no wish to undo the life of a great man."

Hassan nodded, slowly. "Let us say this: *If* we knew that we could turn Columbus away, and *if* after much research we were sure that stopping him would really stop the terrible course of the world from that time forward, then it might be worth undoing this age of healing on the firm chance of making it unnecessary."

"Yes," said Tagiri.

"It might be the work of lifetimes, finding the answers to those questions."

"It might," said Tagiri. "But it might not."

"And even after we were very sure, we might be wrong, and the world might end up worse off than before."

"With one difference," said Tagiri. "If we stop Columbus, we can be sure of this: Putukam and Baiku would never die under Spanish swords."

"I'm with you this far," said Hassan. "Let's find out if possible and desirable to do this thing. Let's find out if the people of our own time agree that it's worth it, that it's *right* to do it. And if they agree that it is, then I'll be with you when it's done."

His words were so confident—yet she felt a dizzying vertigo, as if she stood on the edge of a great chasm, and the ground had just shifted a little under her feet. What sort of arrogance did she have, even to imagine reaching back into the past and making changes? Who am I, she thought, if I dare to answer prayers intended for the gods?

Yet she knew even as she doubted herself that she had already made up her mind. The Europeans had had their future, had fulfilled their most potent dreams, and it was their future that now was the dark past of her world, the consequences of their choices that now were being scoured from the Earth.

European dreams led to this, to a deeply wounded world in convalescence, with a thousand years of physicking ahead, with so much irretrievably lost, to be recovered only on the holotapes of Pastwatch. So if it is in my power to undream their dreams, to give the future to another people, who is to say that it's wrong? How could it be worse? Christopher Columbus—Cristóbal Colón, as the Spanish called him; Cristoforo Colombo, as he was baptized in Genova—he would not discover America after all, if she could find a way to stop him. The prayer of the village of Ankuash would be answered.

And by answering that prayer, her own thirst would be slaked. She could never satisfy the hopeless longing in the faces of all slaves in all times. She could never wipe away the sadness in the face of her ancient great-grandmother Diko and her once-joyous little boy, Acho. She could never give their lives and bodies back to the slaves. But she could do this one thing, and by doing it, the burden that had been building up inside her all these years would finally be lifted. She would know that she had done all that was possible to heal the past.

The next morning Tagiri and Hassan reported what had happened. For weeks the most important leaders of Pastwatch and many leaders from outside Pastwatch, too, came to them to see the holotape, to discuss what it might mean. They listened to Tagiri and Hassan as they raised their questions and proposed their plans. In the end, they gave consent for a new project to explore what Putukam's vision might mean. They called it the Columbus Project, as much because it seemed the same kind of mad impossible journey that Columbus had embarked on in 1492 as because the project might lead to undoing his great achievement.

Tagiri kept the slavery project going, of course, but with Hassan she now launched the new project with a very different team of workers. Hassan led the group that studied history to see if stopping Columbus would have the effect that they desired, and to discover if some other change might be more desirable or more easily practicable. Tagiri divided her working hours between the slavery project and coordinating the work of a dozen physicists and engineers who were trying to find out exactly how it was that temporal backwash might work, and how to alter the time machines in order to enhance the effect enough to allow the alteration of the past.

Early on in their collaboration, Tagiri and Hassan married and had a daughter and a son. The daughter they named Diko, and Acho was the boy. Both children grew strong and wise, immersed in their parents' love and in the Columbus project from their infancy. Acho grew up to be a pilot, skimming over the surface of the Earth like a bird, fast and free. Diko did not stray so far from home. She learned the languages, the tools, the stories inherent in her parents' work, and spent her days beside them. Tagiri looked at her husband, her children, and more than once she thought, What if some stranger from a faraway place came and stole my son from me and made a slave of him, and I never saw him again? What if a conquering army from a place unheard of came and murdered my husband and raped my daughter? And what if, in some other place, happy people watched us as it happened, and did nothing to help us, for fear it might endanger their own happiness? What would I think of them? What kind of people would they be?

3

Ambition

Sometimes Diko felt as if she had grown up with Christopher Columbus, that he was her uncle, her grandfather, her older brother. He was always present in her mother's work, scenes from his life playing out again and again in the background.

One of her earliest memories was of Columbus giving orders for his men to capture several Indies to take back to Spain as slaves. Diko was so young she didn't realize the significance of what was happening, really. She knew, however, that the people in the holoview weren't real, so when her mother said, with deep, bitter anger, "I will stop you," Diko thought that Mother was speaking to her and she burst into tears.

"No, no," said Mother, rocking her back and forth. "I wasn't talking to you, I was talking to the man in the holoview."

"He can't hear you," said Diko.

"He will someday."

"Papa says he died a hundred years ago."

"Longer than that, my Diko."

"Why are you so mad at him? Is he bad?"

"He lived in a bad time," said Mother. "He was a great man in a bad time."

Diko couldn't understand the moral subtleties of this. The only lesson she learned from the event was that somehow the people in the holoview were real after all, and the man called variously Cristoforo Colombo and Cristóbal Colón and Christopher Columbus was very, very important to Mother.

He became important to Diko, too. He was always in the back of her mind. She saw him playing as a child. She saw him arguing endlessly with priests in Spain. She saw him kneel before the King of Aragon and the Queen of Castile. She saw him trying vainly to talk to Indies in Latin, Genovese, Spanish, and Portuguese. She saw him visiting his son at a monastery in La Rábida.

When she was five, Diko asked her mother, "Why doesn't his son live with him?"

"Who?"

"Cristoforo," said Diko. "Why does his little boy live at the monastery?"

"Because Colombo has no wife."

"I know," said Diko. "She died."

"So while he's struggling to try to get the king and queen to let him make a voyage west, his son has to stay somewhere safe, where he can get an education."

"But Cristoforo has another wife the whole time," said Diko.

"Not a wife," said Mother.

"They sleep together," said Diko.

"What have you been doing?" asked Mother. "Have you been running the holoview when I wasn't here?"

"You're always here, Mama," said Diko.

"That's not an answer, you sly child. What have you been watching?"

"Cristoforo has another little boy with his new wife," said Diko. *"He* never goes to live in the monastery."

"That's because Colombo isn't married to the new baby's mother."

"Why not?" asked Diko.

"Diko, you're five years old and I'm very busy. Is it such an emergency that I have to explain all this to you right now?"

Diko knew that this meant that she would have to ask Father. That was all right. Father wasn't home as much as Mother, but when he was, he answered all her questions and never made her wait till she grew up.

Later that afternoon, Diko stood on a stool beside her mother, helping her crush the soft beans for the spicy paste that would be supper. As she stirred the mashed beans as neatly but vigorously as she could manage, another question occurred to her. "If you died, Mama, would Papa send me to a monastery?"

"No," said Mother.

"Why not?"

"I'm not going to die, not till you're an old woman yourself."

"But if you did."

"We're not Christians and it's not the fifteenth century," said Mother. "We don't send our children to monasteries to be educated."

"He must have been very lonely," said Diko.

"Who?"

"Cristoforo's boy in the monastery."

"I'm sure you're right," said Mother.

"Was Cristoforo lonely, too?" asked Diko. "Without his little boy?"

"I suppose," said Mother. "Some people get very lonely without their children. Even when they're surrounded by other people all the time, they miss their little ones. Even when their little ones get older and turn into big ones, they miss the little ones that they'll never see again."

Diko grinned at that. "Do you miss the two-year-old me?"

"Yes."

"Was I cute?"

"Actually, you were annoying," said Mother. "Always into everything, never at rest. You were an impossible child. Your father and I could hardly get anything done for looking after you."

"Wasn't that cute?" asked Diko. She was a little disappointed.

"We kept you, didn't we?" said Mother. "You must have been at least a little bit cute. Don't splash the beans like that, or we'll end up eating dinner off the walls."

"Papa makes bean mash better than you do," said Diko.

"How kind of you to say so," said Mother.

"But when you go to work, you're Papa's boss."

Mother sighed. "Your father and I work together."

"You're head of the project. Everybody says so."

"Yes, that's true."

"If you're the head, is Papa the elbow or what?"

"Papa is the hands and feet, the eyes and heart."

Diko started to giggle. "Are you sure Papa isn't the stomach?"

"I think your father's little pot belly is sweet."

"Well it's a good thing Papa isn't the *bottom* of the project."

"That's enough, Diko," said Mother. "Have a little respect. You really are not young enough anymore for that sort of thing to be cute."

"If it's not cute, what is it?"

"Nasty."

"I'm going to be nasty my whole life," said Diko defiantly.

"I have no doubt of it," said Mother.

"I'm going to stop Cristoforo," she said.

Mother looked at her oddly. "That's *my* job, if it can be done at all."

"You'll be too old," said Diko. "I'm going to grow up and stop him for you."

Mother didn't argue.

By the time Diko was ten, she spent all her afternoons in the lab, learning to use the old Tempoview. Technically she wasn't supposed to use it, but the whole installation at Ileret was now devoted to Mother's project, and so it was Mother's attitudes toward the rules that prevailed. This meant that everyone followed scientific procedures rigorously, but the boundary line between work and home wasn't very carefully observed. Children and relatives were often about, and as long as they were quiet, no one worried. It wasn't as if anything secret were going on. Besides, nobody was using the outdated Tempoviews except to replay old recordings, so Diko wasn't interfering with anybody's work. Everyone knew that Diko was careful. So no one even commented on the fact that an unauthorized, half-educated child was browsing through the past unsupervised.

At first, Father rigged the Tempoview that Diko used so that it would only replay previously recorded views. Diko soon became annoyed with this, however, because the Tempoview had such a restricted perspective. She always longed to see things from another angle.

Just before her twelfth birthday, she figured out how to bypass Father's cursory attempt at blocking her from full access. She wasn't particularly deft about it; Father's computer must have told him what she had done, and he came to see her almost within the hour.

"So you want to go looking into the past," he said.

"I don't like the views that other people recorded," she said. "They're never interested in what I'm interested in."

"What we're deciding right now," said Father, "is whether to banish you from the past entirely, or to give you the freedom that you want."

Diko felt suddenly ill. "Don't banish me," she said. "I'll stay with the old views but don't make me leave."

"I know that all the people you look at are dead," said Father. "But that doesn't mean that it's right for you to spy on them just out of curiosity."

"Isn't that what Pastwatch is all about?" asked Diko.

"No," said Father. "Curiosity yes, but not *personal* curiosity. We're scientists."

"I'll be a scientist too," said Diko.

"We look at people's lives to find out why people do what they do."

"Me too," said Diko.

"You'll see terrible things," said Father. "Ugly things. Very private things. Disturbing things."

"I already have."

"That's what I mean," said Father. "If you thought the things we've allowed you to see up to now were ugly, private, or disturbing, what will you do when you see things that are *really* ugly, private, and disturbing?"

"Ugly, Private, and Disturbing. Sounds like a firm of solicitors," said Diko.

"If you're going to have the privileges of a scientist, then you have to act like a scientist," said Father.

"Meaning?"

"I want daily reports of what places and times you've watched. I want weekly reports of what you've been examining and what you've learned. You must maintain a log just like everybody else. And if you see something disturbing, talk to me or your mother."

Diko grinned. "Got it. Ugly and Private I deal with myself, but Disturbing I discuss with the Ancient Ones."

"You are the light of my life," said Father. "But I think I didn't yell at you enough when you were young enough for it to do any good."

"I'll turn in all the reports you asked for," she said. "But *you* have to promise to read them."

"On exactly the same basis as anybody else's reports," said Father. "So you'd better not show me any second-rate work."

Diko explored, reported, and began to look forward to her weekly interviews with Father concerning the work she did. Only gradually did she realize how childish and elementary those early reports were, how she skimmed over the surface of issues resolved long before by adult watchers; she marveled that Father never gave her a clue that she wasn't on the cutting edge of science. He always listened with respect, and within a few years Diko was doing things that merited it.

It was old Cristoforo Colombo, of all people, who got her away from the Tempoview and onto the far more sensitive TruSite. She had never forgotten him, because Mother and Father never forgot him, but her early explorations with the Tempoview never involved him. Why should they? She had seen practically every moment of Colombo's life in the old recordings that Mother and Father had been looking at more or less continuously all her life. What brought her back to Colombo was the question she had set for herself: When do the great figures of history make the decisions that set them on the path of greatness? She eliminated from her study all the people who simply drifted into fame; it was the ones who struggled against great obstacles and never gave up who intrigued her. Some of them were monsters and some were noble; some were self-serving opportunists and some were altruists; some of their achievements crumbled almost at once, and some changed the world in ways that had reverberations down to the present. To Diko, that hardly mattered. She was searching for the moment of decision, and, after she had written reports on several dozen great figures, it occurred to her that in all her watching of Cristoforo, she had never actually sat down and studied him in a linear way, seeing what caused this son of an ambitious Genovese weaver to take to the sea and tear up all the old maps of the world.

That Cristoforo was one of the great ones could not be doubted, whether Mother and Father approved of him or not. So . . . when was the decision made? When did he first set foot on the course that made him one of the most famous men in history?

She thought she found the answer in 1459, when the rivalry between the two great houses of Genova, the Fieschi and the Adorno, was coming to a head. In that year a man named Domenico Colombo was a weaver, a supporter of the Fieschi party, the former keeper of the Olivella Gate, and the father of a little redheaded boy who had within him the power to change the world.

Cristoforo was eight years old the last time Pietro Fregoso came to visit his father. Cristoforo knew the man's name, but he also knew that in Domenico Colombo's house, Pietro Fregoso was always called by the title that had been wrested from him by the Adorno party: the Doge. Pietro Fregoso had decided to make a serious play for power again, and since Cristoforo's father was one of the most fiery partisans in the Fieschi cause, it was not too surprising that Pietro chose to honor the Colombo house by holding a secret meeting there.

Pietro arrived in the morning, accompanied by only a couple of men—he had to move inconspicuously through the city, or the Adornos would know he was plotting something. Cristoforo saw his father kneel and kiss Pietro's ring. Mother, who was standing in the doorway between the weaving shop and the front room, muttered something about the Pope under her breath. But Pietro was the Doge of Genova, or rather the former Doge. No one called him the Pope. "What did you say, Mama?"

"Nothing," she said. "Come in here."

Cristoforo found himself being dragged into the weaving shop, where the journeymen's looms rocked and banged as the apprentices carried thread back and forth or crawled under the loom to fold the cloth that the journeymen were weaving. Cristoforo had a vague awareness that someday soon his father would expect him to take his place as an apprentice in the shop of some other member of the weavers' guild. He did not look forward to it. The life of the apprentice was one of drudgery and meaningless labor, and the journeymen's teasing turned into serious torment when Father and Mother were not in the room. In another weavers' shop, Cristoforo knew, he would not have the protected status he had here, where his father was master.

Soon Mother lost interest in Cristoforo and he was able to drift back to the doorway and watch the goings-on in the front room, where the bolts of cloth had been cleared from the display table and the great spools of thread pulled up like chairs. Several other men had drifted in during the past few minutes. It was to be a meeting, Cristoforo saw Pietro Fregoso was holding a council of war, and in Father's house.

At first it was the great men that Cristoforo watched. They were dressed in the most dazzling, extravagant clothing he had ever seen. None of Father's customers came into the shop dressed like this, but some of their clothing was made from Father's finest cloth. Cristoforo recognized the rich brocade one gentleman was wearing as a cloth made not a month ago by Carlo, the best of the journeymen. It had been picked up by Tito, who always wore a green uniform. Only now did Cristoforo realize that when Tito came to buy, he was not buying for himself, but rather for his master. Tito was not a customer, then. He merely did what he was sent to do. Yet Father treated him like a friend, even though he was a servant.

This got Cristoforo thinking about the way Father treated his friends. The joking, the easy affection, the shared wine, the stories. Eye to eye they spoke, Father and his friends.

Father always said that his greatest friend was the Doge—was Pietro Fregoso. Yet now Cristoforo saw that this was not the truth, for Father did not joke, showed no easiness in his manner, told no stories, and the wine he poured was for the gentlemen at the table, and not for himself at all. Father hovered at the edges of the room, watching to see if any man needed more wine, pouring it immediately if he did. And Pietro did not include Father in his glance when he met the eyes of the men around the table. No, Pietro was not Father's friend; by all appearances, Father was Pietro's servant.

It made Cristoforo feel a little sick inside, for he knew that Father took great pride in having Pietro for a friend. Cristoforo watched the meeting, seeing the graceful movements of the rich men, listening to the elegance of their language. Some of the words Cristoforo didn't even understand, and yet he knew the words were Genovese and not Latin or Greek. Of course Father has nothing to say to these men, Cristoforo thought. They speak another language. They were foreigners as surely as the strange men Cristoforo saw down at the docks one day, the ones from Provence.

How did these gentlemen learn to speak this way? Cristoforo wondered. How did they learn to say words that are never spoken in our house or on the street? How can such words belong to the language of Genova, and yet none of the common Genovese know them? Is this not one city? Are these men not of the Fieschi as Father is? The Adorno braggarts who pushed over Fieschi carts in the market, Father spoke more like *them* than like these gentlemen who were supposedly of his own party.

There is more difference between gentlemen and tradesmen like Father than there is between Adorno and Fieschi. Yet the Fieschi and the Adorno often come to blows, and there are stories of killings. Why are there no quarrels between tradesmen and gentlemen?

Only once did Pietro Fregoso include Father in the conversation. "I'm impatient with all this biding our time, *biding* our time!" he said. "Look at our Domenico here." He gestured toward Cristoforo's father, who stepped forward like a tavernkeeper who had been called upon. "Seven years ago he was keeper of the Olivella Gate. Now he has a house half the size of the one he had then, and only three journeymen instead of the six from before. Why? Because the so-called Doge steers all the business to Adorno weavers. Because I am out of power and I can't protect my friends!"

"It is not all a matter of Adorno patronage, my lord," said one of the gentlemen. "The whole city is poorer, what with the Turk in Constantinople, the Muslims harrying us at Chios, and the Catalonian pirates who boldly raid our very docks and loot the houses near the water."

"My point exactly!" said the Doge. "Foreigners put this puppet into power—what do they care how Genova suffers? It is time to restore true Genovese rule. I will not hear a contradiction.''

One of the gentlemen spoke quietly into the silence that followed Pietro's speech. "We are not ready," he said. "We will pay in precious blood for a foolhardy attack now."

Pietro Fregoso glowered at him. "So. I say I will not hear a contradiction, and then you contradict me? What party are you in, de Portobello?"

"Yours to the death, my lord," said the man. "But you were never one who punished a man for saying to you what he believed to be the truth."

"Nor will I punish you now," said Pietro. "As long as I can count on you standing beside me."

De Portobello rose to his feet. "In front of you, my lord, or behind you, or wherever I must stand to protect you when danger threatens."

At that, Father stepped forward, unbidden. "I too will stand beside you, my lord!" he cried. "Any man who would raise a hand against you must first strike down Domenico Colombo!"

Cristoforo saw how the others reacted. Where they had nodded when de Portobello made his promise of loyalty, they only looked silently at the table when Father spoke. Some of them turned red— in anger? Embarrassment? Cristoforo wasn't sure why they would not want to hear Father's promise. Was it because only a gentleman could fight well enough to protect the rightful Doge? Or was it because Father should not have been so bold as to speak at all in such exalted company?

Whatever the reason, Cristoforo could see that their silence had struck Father like a blow. He seemed to wither as he shrank back against the wall. Only when his humiliation was complete did Pietro speak again. "Our success depends on all the Fieschi fighting with courage and loyalty." His words were gracious, but they were too late to spare Father's feelings. They came, not as an honorable acceptance of Father's offer, but rather as a consolation, the way a man might pet a loyal dog.

Father doesn't matter to them, thought Cristoforo. They meet in his house because they must keep their meeting secret, but he himself is nothing to them.

The meeting ended soon after; the decision was to go on the attack in two days. As soon as the gentlemen had left and Father closed the door, Mother sailed past Cristoforo and pushed herself into Father's face. "What do you mean, you fool? If anyone wants to harm the rightful Doge, they'll have to strike down Domenico Colombo first!—what nonsense! When did you become a soldier? Where is your fine sword? How many duels have you fought? Or are you thinking this will be a brawl in a tavern, and you have only to knock together the heads of a couple of drunks, and the battle will be won? Do you care nothing for our children, that you plan to leave them fatherless?"

"A man has honor," said Father.

Cristoforo wondered, What is Father's honor, when his greatest friend despises the offer of his life?

"Your honor will have your children on the street in rags."

"My honor made me keeper of the Olivella Gate for four years. You liked living in our fine house then, didn't you?"

"That time is over," said Mother. "Blood will flow, and it will not be Adorno blood."

"Don't be too sure of that," said Father. He stormed upstairs. Mother burst into tears of rage and frustration. The argument was over.

But Cristoforo wasn't satisfied. He waited as Mother calmed herself by pulling the extra spools away from the table and putting the cloth back on it, so customers could look at it and so it would stay clean. When he judged he could speak without being screamed at, he said, "How do gentlemen learn to be gentlemen?"

She glared at him. "They're born that way," she said. "God made them gentlemen."

"But why can't we learn to talk the way they do?" Cristoforo asked. "I don't think it would be hard." Cristoforo imitated the refined voice of de Portobello, saying, "You were never one who punished a man for saying what he believed to be the truth."

Mother came to him and slapped him hard across the face. It stung, and even though Cristoforo had long since stopped crying when he was punished, the sheer surprise of it more than the sting made tears leap from his eyes.

"Don't ever let me hear you putting on airs like that again, Cristoforo!'' she shouted. ''Are you too good for your father? Do you think that honking like a goose will make you grow feathers?''

In his anger, Cristoforo shouted back at her. ''My father is as good a man as any of *them*. Why shouldn't his son learn to be a gentleman?''

Almost she slapped him again, for having dared to answer her back. But then she caught herself, and actually heard what he had said. ''Your father *is* as good as any of them,'' she said. ''Better!''

Cristoforo gestured toward the fine fabrics spread across the table. ''There is the cloth—why can't Father dress like a gentleman? Why can't he speak the way they do, and dress like them, and *then* the Doge would honor him!''

''The Doge would laugh at him,'' said Mother. ''And so would everyone else. And then if he kept on trying to act the gentleman, one of them would come along and put a rapier through your father's heart, for daring to be such an upstart.''

''Why would they laugh at him, if they don't laugh at these other men for dressing and talking the way they do?''

''Because they really *are* gentlemen, and your father is not.''

''But if it isn't their clothing and their language . . . Is there something in their blood? They didn't look *stronger* than Father. They had weak arms, and most of them were fat.''

''Father is stronger than they are, of course. But *they* carry swords.''

''Then Father should buy a sword!''

''Who would sell a sword to a weaver!'' said Mother, laughing. ''And what would Father do with it? He has never wielded a sword in his life. He'd cut off his own fingers!''

''Not if he practiced,'' said Cristoforo. ''Not if he *learned*.''

''It isn't the sword that makes a man a gentleman,'' said Mother. ''Gentlemen are born as the children of gentlemen, that's all. Your father's father wasn't a gentleman, and so *he* isn't.''

Cristoforo thought about this for a moment. ''Aren't we all descended from Noah, after the flood? Why are the children of one family gentlemen, and the children of Father's family aren't? God made us all.''

Mother laughed bitterly. ''Oh, is that what the priests taught you? Well, you should see them bowing and scraping to the gentlemen while they piss on the rest of us. *They* think that God likes gentlemen better, but Jesus Christ didn't act that way. He cared nothing for gentlemen!''

"So what gives them the right to look down at Father?" demanded Cristoforo, and against his will his eyes again filled with tears.

She regarded him for a moment, as if deciding whether to tell him the truth. "Gold and dirt," she said.

Cristoforo didn't understand.

"They have gold in their treasure boxes," said Mother, "and they own land. That's what makes them gentlemen. If we had huge swatches of land out in the country, or if we had a box filled with gold in the attic, then your father would be a gentleman and no one would laugh at you if you learned to talk the fancy way they do and wore clothing made of *this*." She held the trailing end of a bolt of cloth against Cristoforo's chest. "You'd make a fine gentleman, my Cristoforo." Then she dropped the fabric and laughed and laughed and laughed.

Finally Cristoforo left the room. Gold, he thought. If Father had gold, then those other men would listen to him. Well, then—I will get him gold.

One of the men at the meeting must have been a traitor, or perhaps one of them spoke carelessly, where a traitorous servant overheard, but somehow the Adornos got word of the plans of the Fieschi, and when Pietro and his two bodyguards showed up beside the cylindrical towers of the Sant'Andrea Gate where the rendezvous was supposed to take place, they were set upon by a dozen of the Adornos. Pietro was dragged from his horse and struck in the head with a mace. They left him for dead as they ran away.

The shouting could be heard in the Colombo house as clearly as if it had happened next door, which it almost had—they lived scarcely a hundred yards from the Sant'Andrea Gate. They heard the first shouts of the men, and Pietro's voice as he cried out, "Fieschi! To me, Fieschi!"

At once Father took his heavy staff from its place by the fire and ran into the street. Mother got to the front of the house too late to stop

him. Screaming and crying, she gathered the children and the apprentices into the back of the house while the journeymen stood
guard at the front door. There in the gathering darkness they heard
the tumult and shouting, and then Pietro's screaming. For he had not
been killed outright, and now in his agony he howled for help in the
night.

"Fool," whispered Mother. "If he keeps screeching like that,
he'll tell all the Adornos that they didn't kill him and they'll come
back and finish him off."

"Will they kill Father?" asked Cristoforo.

The younger children began to cry.

"No," said Mother, but Cristoforo could tell that she was not
sure.

Perhaps she could sense his skepticism. "All fools," she said.
"All men are fools. Fighting over who gets to rule Genova—what does
that matter? The Turk is in Constantinople! The heathens have the
Holy Sepulchre in Jerusalem! The name of Christ is no longer spoken
in Egypt, and these little boys are squabbling over who gets to sit on
a fancy chair and call himself the Doge of Genova? What is the honor
of Pietro Fregoso compared to the honor of Jesus Christ? What is it to
possess the palace of the Doge when the land where the Blessed Virgin walked in her garden, where the angel came to her, is in the
hands of circumcised dogs? If they want to kill somebody, let them
liberate Jerusalem! Let them free Constantinople! Let them shed
blood to redeem the honor of the Son of God!"

"That's what *I* will fight for," said Cristoforo.

"Don't fight!" said one of his sisters. "They'd kill you."

"I'd kill them first."

"You're very small, Cristoforo," his sister said.

"I won't always be small."

"Hush," said Mother. "This is all nonsense. The son of a
weaver doesn't go on Crusade."

"Why not?" said Cristoforo. "Would Christ refuse my sword?"

"What sword?" said Mother scornfully.

"I'll have a sword one day," said Cristoforo. "I'll be a gentleman!"

"How, when you have no gold?"

"I'll *get* gold!"

"In Genova? As a weaver? As long as you live, you'll be the son of Domenico Colombo. No one will give you gold, and no one will call you a gentleman. Now be silent, or I'll pinch your arm."

It was a worthy threat, and all the children knew well enough to obey when Mother uttered it.

A couple of hours later, Father came home. The journeymen almost didn't let him in, just from his knocking. Not until he cried out in anguish "My lord is dead! Let me in!" did they unbar the door.

He staggered inside just as the children raced after Mother into the front room. Father was covered with blood, and Mother screamed and embraced him and then searched him for wounds.

"It's not my blood," he said in anguish. "It's the blood of my Doge! Pietro Fregoso is dead! The cowards set on him and pulled him from his horse and struck him in the head with a mace!"

"Why are you covered with his blood, Nico!"

"I carried him to the doors of the palace of the Doge. I carried him to the place where he ought to be!"

"Why would you do that, you fool!"

"Because he told me to! I came to him and he was crying out and covered with blood and I said, 'Let me take you to your physicians, let me take you to your house, let me find the ones who did this and kill them for you,' and he said to me, 'Domenico, take me to the palace! That's where the Doge should die—in the palace, like my father!' So I carried him there, in my own arms, and I didn't care if the Adornos saw us! I carried him there and he was in my arms when he died! I was his true friend!"

"If they saw you with him, they'll find you and kill you!"

"What does it matter?" said Father. "The Doge is dead!"

"It matters to me," said Mother. "Get those clothes off." She turned to the journeymen and began giving orders. "You—get the children to the back of the house. You—have the apprentices draw water and heat it for a bath. You—when I get these clothes off him, burn them."

The other children obeyed the journeyman and fled to the back of the house, but Cristoforo did not. He watched as his mother undressed his father, covering him with kisses and curses the whole time. Even after she led him into the courtyard for his bath, even as the stench of the burning bloody clothing came into the house, Cristoforo stayed there in the front room. He was on watch, guarding the door.

Or so the old accounts of that night all said. Columbus was on watch, to keep his family safe. But Diko knew that this was not all that was going through Cristoforo's mind. No, he was making his decision. He was setting before himself the terms of his future greatness. He would be a gentleman. Kings and queens would treat him with respect. He would have gold. He would conquer kingdoms in the name of Christ.

He must have known even then that to accomplish all of this, he would have to leave Genova. As his mother had said: As long as he lived in this city, he would be the son of Domenico the weaver. From the next morning he bent his life toward achieving his new goals. He began to study—languages, history—with such vigor that the monks who were teaching him commented on it. "He has caught the spirit of scholarship," they said, but Diko knew that it wasn't learning for its own sake. He had to know languages to travel abroad in the world. He had to know history to know what was in the world when he ventured into it.

And he had to know how to sail. Every chance he got, Cristoforo was down at the docks, listening to the sailors, questioning them, learning what all the crewmen did. Later he focused on the navigators, plying them with wine when he could afford it, simply demanding answers when he could not. Eventually it would get him aboard a ship, and then another; he turned down no chance to sail, and did any work that was asked of him, so that he would know all that a weaver's son could hope to learn about the sea.

Diko made her report on Cristoforo Colombo, on the moment when he made his decision. As always, her father praised it, criticizing only minor points. But she knew by now that his praise could conceal serious criticism. When she challenged him, he wouldn't tell her what his criticism was. "I say that this report is a good one," he told her. "Now leave me alone."

"There's something wrong with it," Diko said, "and you're not telling me."

"It's a well-written report. It has nothing wrong except the points I told you."

"Then you disagree with my conclusion. You don't think this was what made Cristoforo decide to be great."

"Decide to be great?" asked Father. "Yes, I think this is almost certainly the point in his life where he made that decision."

"Then what's *wrong* with it!" she shouted.

"Nothing!" he shouted back.

"I'm not a child!"

He looked at her in consternation. "You aren't?"

"You're humoring me and I'm tired of it!"

"All right," he said. "Your report is excellent and observant. He certainly decided on the night you pinpointed, and for the reasons that you laid out, that he would pursue gold and greatness and the glory of God. All that is very good. But there is not one breath of a hint in anything you reported on that would tell us why and how he decided that he would achieve those goals by sailing west into the Atlantic."

It struck as brutally as the slap that Cristoforo's mother had given him, and it brought the same tears to her eyes, even though there was no physical blow involved.

"I'm sorry," said Father. "You said you were not a child."

"I'm not," she said. "And you're wrong."

"I am?"

"*My* project is to find when the decision for greatness was made, and that's what I found. It's *your* project and *Mother's* project to figure out when Columbus decided to go west."

Father looked at her in surprise. "Well, yes, I suppose so. It's certainly something we need to know."

"So there's nothing wrong with my report for *my* project, just because it doesn't happen to answer the question that's bothering you in *yours*."

"You're right," said Father.

"I know!"

"Well, now I know, too. I withdraw the criticism. Your report is complete and acceptable and I accept it. Congratulations."

But she didn't go away.

"Diko, I'm working," he said.

"I'll find it for you," she said.

"Find what?"

"Whatever it was that caused Cristoforo to sail west."

"Finish your own project, Diko," said Father.

"You don't think I can, do you?"

"I've been over the recordings of Columbus's life, and so has your mother, and so have countless other scholars and scientists. You think you'll find what none of them ever found?"

"Yes," said Diko.

"Well," said Father. "I think we've just isolated *your* decision for greatness."

He smiled at her, a crooked little smile. She assumed that he was teasing her. But she didn't care. He might think he was joking, but she would make his joke turn real. Had he and Mother and countless others pored over all the old Tempoview recordings of Columbus's life? Very well, then, Diko would stop looking at recordings at all. She would go and look directly at his life, and not with the Tempoview, either. The TruSite II would be her tool. She didn't ask for permission, and she didn't ask for help. She simply took over a machine that wasn't used at night, and adjusted the schedule of her life to fit the hours when the machine was hers to use. Some wondered whether she really ought to be using the most up-to-date machines—after all, she wasn't actually a member of Pastwatch. Her training was at best informal. She was merely the child of watchers, and yet she was using a machine that one normally got access to after years of study.

Those who had those doubts, however, seeing the set of her face, seeing how hard she worked and how quickly she learned to use the machine, soon lost any desire to question her right to do it. It occurred to some of them that this was the human way, after all. You went to school to learn to do a trade that was different from your parents' work. But if you were going into the family business, you learned it from childhood up. Diko was as much a watcher as anyone else, and by all indications a good one. And those who had at first thought of questioning her or even stopping her instead notified the authorities that here was a novice worth observing. A recording was started, watching all that Diko did. And soon she had a silver tag on her file: Let this one go where she wants.

4

Kemal

The *Santa Maria* sank on a reef on the north shore of Hispaniola, due to Columbus's foolhardiness in sailing at night and the inattention of the pilot. But the *Niña* and the *Pinta* did not sink; they sailed home to report to Europe on the vast lands awaiting them to the west, triggering a westward flood of immigrants, conquerors, and explorers that wouldn't stop for five hundred years. If Columbus was to be stopped, the *Niña* and the *Pinta* could not return to Spain.

The man who sank them was Kemal Akyazi, and the path that brought him to Tagiri's project to change history was a long and strange one.

Kemal Akyazi grew up within a few miles of the ruins of Troy; from his boyhood home above Kumkale he could see the waters of the Dardanelles, the narrow strait that connects the waters of the Black Sea with the Aegean. Many a war had been fought on both sides of that strait, one of which had produced the great epic of Homer's *Iliad*.

This pressure of history had a strange influence on Kemal as a child. He learned all the tales of the place, of course, but he also knew that the tales were Greek, and the place was of the Greek

Aegean world. Kemal was a Turk; his own ancestors had not come
to the Dardanelles until the fifteenth century. He felt that it was a
powerful place, but it did not belong to him. So the *Iliad* was not
the story that spoke to Kemal's soul. Rather it was the story of
Heinrich Schliemann, the German explorer who, in an era when
Troy had been regarded as a mere legend, a myth, a fiction, had
been sure not only that Troy was real but also that he could find
it. Despite all scoffers, he mounted an expedition and located it and
unburied it. The old stories turned out to be true.

In his teens Kemal thought it was the greatest tragedy of his life
that Pastwatch was using machines to look through the the millennia of human history. There would be no more Schliemanns, studying and pondering and guessing until they found some artifact,
some ruin of a long-lost city, some remnant of a legend made true
again. Thus Kemal had no interest in joining Pastwatch, though
they tried to recruit him for it as he entered college. It was not
history but exploration and discovery that he hungered for; what
was the glory in finding the truth through a machine?

So, after an abortive try at physics, he studied to become a
meteorologist. At the age of eighteen, heavily immersed in the study
of climate and weather, he touched again on the findings of Pastwatch. No longer did meteorologists have to depend on only a few
centuries of weather measurements and fragmentary fossil evidence
to determine long-range patterns. Now they had accurate accounts
of storm patterns for millions of years. Indeed, in the earliest years
of Pastwatch, the machinery of the TruSite I had been so coarse
that individual humans could not be seen. It was like time-lapse
photography in which people don't remain in place long enough to
be on more than a single frame of the film, making them invisible.
So in those days Pastwatch recorded the weather of the past,
erosion patterns, volcanic eruptions, ice ages, climatic shifts.

All that data was the bedrock on which modern weather prediction and control rested. Meteorologists could see developing
patterns and, without disrupting the overall flow, could make tiny
changes that prevented any one area from going completely rainless
during a time of drought, or sunless during a wet growing season.
They had taken the sharp edge off the relentless scythe of climate,
and now the great project was to determine how they might make

a more serious change, to bring a steady pattern of light rain to the desert regions of the world, to restore the prairies and savannas that had once been there. That was the work that Kemal wanted to be a part of.

Yet he could not bring himself out from the shadow of Troy, the memory of Schliemann. Even as he studied the climatic shifts involved with the waxing and waning of the ice ages, his mind contained fleeting images of lost civilizations, legendary places that waited for a Schliemann to uncover them.

His project for his degree in meteorology was part of the effort to determine how the Red Sea might be exploited to develop dependable rains for the Sudan and central Arabia; Kemal's immediate target was to study the difference between weather patterns during the last ice age, when the Red Sea had all but disappeared, and the present, with the Red Sea at its fullest. Back and forth he went through the coarse old Pastwatch recordings, gathering data on sea level and on precipitation at selected points inland. The old TruSite I had been imprecise at best, but good enough for counting rainstorms.

Time after time Kemal would cycle through the up-and-down fluctuations of the Red Sea, watching as the average sea level gradually rose toward the end of the Ice Age. He always stopped, of course, at the abrupt jump in sea level that marked the rejoining of the Red Sea and the Indian Ocean. After that, the Red Sea was useless for his purposes, since its sea level was tied to that of the great world ocean.

The echo of Schliemann inside Kemal's mind made him think: What a flood that must have been.

What a flood. The Ice Age had locked up so much water in glaciers and ice sheets that the sea level of the whole world fell. It eventually reached a low enough point that land bridges arose out of the sea. In the north Pacific, the Bering land bridge allowed the ancestors of the Indies to cross on foot into their great empty homeland. Britain and Flanders were joined. The Dardanelles were closed and the Black Sea became a salty lake. The Persian Gulf disappeared and became a great plain cut by the Euphrates. And the Bab al Mandab, the strait at the mouth of the Red Sea, became a land bridge.

But a land bridge is also a dam. As the world climate warmed and the glaciers began to release their pent-up water, the rains fell heavily everywhere; rivers swelled and the seas rose. The great south-flowing rivers of Europe, which had been mostly dry during the peak of glaciation, now were massive torrents. The Rhone, the Po, the Strimon, the Danube poured so much water into the Mediterranean and the Black Sea that their water level rose at about the same rate as that of the great world ocean.

The Red Sea had no great rivers, however. It was, in geological terms, a new sea, formed by rifting between the new Arabian plate and the ancient African, which meant it had uplift ridges on both coasts. Many rivers and streams flowed from those ridges down into the Red Sea, but none of them carried much water compared to the rivers that drained vast basins and carried the melt-off of the glaciers of the north. So, while the Red Sea gradually rose during this time, it lagged far, far behind the great world ocean. Its water level responded to the immediate local weather patterns rather than to worldwide weather. Until one day the Indian Ocean rose so high that tides began to spill over the Bab al Mandab. The water cut new channels in the grassland there. Over a period of several years, the leakage grew, creating a series of large new tidal lakes on the Hanish Plain. And then one day, some fourteen thousand years ago, the flow cut a channel so deep that it didn't dry up at low tide. The water kept running through it, cutting the channel deeper and deeper, until those tidal lakes were full, and brimmed over. With the weight of the Indian Ocean behind it the water gushed into the basin of the Red Sea in a vast flood that in a few hours brought the Red Sea up to the level of the world ocean.

This isn't just the boundary marker between useful and useless water level data, thought Kemal. This is a cataclysm, one of the rare times when a single event changes a vast area in a period of time short enough that human beings could notice it. And, for once, this cataclysm happened in an era when human beings were there. It was not only possible but likely that someone saw this flood—indeed, that it killed many, for the southern end of the Red Sea basin was rich savanna and marshland up to the moment when the ocean broke through, and surely the humans of fourteen thousand years ago would have hunted there. Would have gathered seeds and fruits and berries there. Some hunting party must have seen, from the peaks of the Dehalak Mountains, the great walls of water that roared up the plain, breaking and parting around the slopes of the Dehalaks, making islands of them.

Such a hunting party would have known that their families had been killed by this water. What would they have thought? Surely that some god was angry with them. That the world had been done away, buried under the sea. And if they survived, if they found a way to the Eritrean shore after the great turbulent waves settled down to the more placid waters of the new, deeper sea, they would tell the tale to anyone who would listen. And for a few years they could take their hearers to the water's edge, show them the treetops barely rising above the surface of the sea, and tell them tales of all that had been buried under the waves.

Noah, thought Kemal. The immortal Utnapishtim, the flood survivor that Gilgamesh visited. Ziusudra of the Sumerian flood story. Atlantis. The stories were believed. The stories were remembered. In time the tellers of the tale forgot where it happened—they naturally transposed the events to locations that they knew. But they remembered the things that mattered. What did the flood story of Noah say? Not just rain, no, it wasn't a flood caused by rain alone. The "fountains of the great deep" broke open. No local flood on the Mesopotamian plain would cause that image to be part of the story. But the great wall of water from the Indian Ocean, coming on the heels of years of steadily increasing rain—*that* would bring those words to the storytellers' lips, generation after generation for ten thousand years until they could be written down.

As for Atlantis, everyone was so sure they had found it years ago. Santorini—Thios—the Aegean island that blew up. But the oldest stories of Atlantis said nothing of blowing up in a volcano. They spoke only of the great civilization sinking into the sea. The supposition was that later visitors came to Santorini and, seeing water where an island city used to be, assumed that it had sunk, knowing nothing of the volcanic eruption. To Kemal, however, this now seemed far-fetched indeed, compared to the way it would have looked to the people of Atlantis themselves, somewhere on the Massawa Plain, when the Red Sea seemed to leap up in its bed, engulfing the city. *That* would be sinking into the sea! No explosion, just water. And if the city were in the marshes of what was now the Massawa Channel, the water would have come not just from the southeast but from the northeast and the north as well, flowing among and around the Dehalak mountains, making islands of them and swallowing up the marshes and the city with them.

Atlantis. They were not beyond the pillars of Hercules, but Plato was right to associate the city with a strait. He, or whoever told the tale to him, simply replaced the Bab al Mandab with the greatest strait that he had heard of. The story might well have reached Plato by way of Phoenicia, where Mediterranean sailors would have made the story fit the sea they knew. They learned it from Egyptians, perhaps, or nomad wanderers from the hinterlands of Arabia, or perhaps it was already latent within every old-world culture by then; and "within the straits of Mandab" would have become "within the pillars of Hercules," and then, because the Mediterranean itself was not strange and exotic enough, the locale was moved outside even that strait.

All these suppositions came to Kemal with the absolute certainty that they were true, or nearly true. He rejoiced at the thought of it: There was still an ancient civilization left to discover.

But if it was there, why hadn't Pastwatch found it? The answer was simple enough. The past was huge, and while the TruSite I had been used to collect climatological information, the new machines that were precise enough to track individual human beings would never have been used to look at oceans where nobody lived. Yes, the Tempoview had explored the Bering Strait and the English Channel, but that was to track long-known-of migrations. There was no such migration in the Red Sea. Pastwatch had simply never looked through their precise new machines to see what was under the water of the Red Sea in the waning centuries of the last Ice Age. And they never *would* look, either, unless someone gave them a compelling reason.

Kemal understood bureaucracy enough to know that he, a student meteorologist, would hardly be taken seriously if he brought an Atlantis theory to Pastwatch—particularly a theory that put Atlantis in the Red Sea of all places, and fourteen thousand years ago, long before civilizations arose in Sumeria or Egypt, let alone China or the Indus Valley or among the swamps of Tehuantepec.

Yet Kemal also knew that the setting would have been right for a civilization to grow in the marshy land of the Massawa Channel. Though there weren't enough rivers flowing into the Red Sea to fill it at the same rate as the world ocean, there were still rivers. For instance, the Zula, which still had enough water to flow even today, once watered the whole length of the Massawa Plain and flowed down into the rump of the Red Sea near Mersa Mubarek. And, because of the different rainfall patterns of that time, there was a large and dependable river flowing out of the Assahara basin. Assahara was now a dry rift valley below sea level, but then it would have been a freshwater lake fed by many streams and spilling over the lowest point into the Massawa Channel. The river meandered along the nearly level Massawa Plain, with some branches of it joining the Zula River, and some wandering east and north to form several mouths in the Red Sea.

Thus dependable sources of fresh water fed the area, and in rainy season the Zula, at least, would have brought new silt to freshen the soil, and in all seasons the wandering flatwater rivers would have provided a means of transportation through the marshes. The climate was also dependably warm, with plenty of sunlight and a long growing season. There was no early civilization that did not grow up in such a setting. There was no reason a civilization might not have grown up then.

Yes, it was six or seven thousand years too early. But couldn't it be that the very destruction of Atlantis convinced the survivors that the gods did not want human beings to gather together in cities? Weren't there hints of that anti-civilization bias lingering in many of the ancient religions of the Middle East? What was the story of Cain and Abel, if not a metaphorical expression of the evil of the city-dweller, the farmer, the brother-killer who is judged unworthy by the gods because he does not wander with his sheep? Couldn't such stories have circulated widely in those ancient times? That would explain why the survivors of Atlantis hadn't immediately begun to rebuild their civilization at another site: They knew that the gods forbade it, that if they built again their city would be destroyed again. So they remembered the stories of their glorious past, and at the same time condemned their ancestors and warned everyone they met against people gathering together to build a city.

It would have made people yearn for such a place and fear it, both at once.

Not until a Nimrod came, a tower-builder, a Babel-maker who defied the old religion, would the ancient proscription be overcome at last and another city rise up, in another river valley far in time and space from Atlantis, but remembering the old ways that had been memorialized in the stories and, as far as possible, replicating them. We will build a tower so high that it *can't* be immersed. Didn't Genesis link the flood with Babel in just that way, complete with the nomads' stern disapproval of the city? This was the story that survived in Mesopotamia—the tale of the beginning of city life there, but with clear memories of a more ancient civilization that had been destroyed in a flood.

A more ancient civilization. The golden age. The giants who once walked the earth. Why couldn't all these stories be remembering the first human civilization, the place where the city was invented? Atlantis, the city of the Massawa Plain.

But how could he prove it without using the Tempoview? And how could he get access to one of those machines without first convincing Pastwatch that Atlantis was really in the Red Sea? It was circular, with no way out.

Until he thought: Why do large cities form in the first place? Because there are public works to do that require more than a few people to accomplish them. Kemal wasn't sure what form the public works might take, but surely they would have made something that would change the face of the land plainly enough that the old TruSite I recordings would show it, though it wouldn't be noticeable unless someone was looking for it.

So, putting his degree at risk, Kemal set aside the work he had been assigned to do and began poring over the old TruSite I recordings. He concentrated on the last century before the Red Sea flood—there was no reason to suppose that the civilization had lasted very long before it was destroyed. And within a few months he had collected data that was irrefutable. There were no dikes and dams to prevent flooding—that kind of structure would have been large enough that no one would have missed it on the first go-round. Instead there were seemingly random heaps of mud and earth that grew between rainy seasons, especially in the drier years when the rivers were lower than usual. To people looking only for weather patterns, these unstructured, random piles would mean nothing. But to Kemal they were obvious: In the shallowing water, the Atlanteans were dredging channels so that their boats could continue to traffic from place to place. The piles of earth were simply the dumping-places for the muck they dredged from the water. None of the boats showed up on the TruSite I, but now that Kemal knew where to look, he began to catch fleeting glimpses of reed huts. Every year when the floods came, the houses disappeared, so they were only visible for a moment or two in the Trusite I: flimsy mud-and-reed structures that must have been swept away in every flood season and rebuilt again when the waters receded. But they were there, close by the hillocks that marked the channels. Plato was right again—Atlantis grew up around its canals. But Atlantis was the people and their boats; the buildings were washed away and built again every year.

When Kemal presented his findings to Pastwatch he was not yet twenty years old, but his evidence was impressive enough that Pastwatch immediately turned, not a Tempoview, but the still-newer TruSite II machine to look under the waters of the Red Sea in the Massawa Channel during the hundred years before the Red Sea flood. They found that Kemal was gloriously, spectacularly right. In an era when other humans were still following game animals and gathering berries, the Atlanteans were planting amaranth and ryegrass, melons and beans in the rich wet silt of the receding rivers, and carrying food in baskets and on reed boats from place to place. The only thing that Kemal had missed was that most of the buildings weren't houses at all. They were floating silos for the storage of grain. The Atlanteans slept under the open air during the dry season, and in the rainy season they lived on their tiny reed boats.

Kemal was brought into Pastwatch and made head of the vast new Atlantis project. At first he loved the work, because, like Schliemann, he could search for the originals of the great events. Most important to Kemal was when he found Noah, though he had a different name—Yewesweder when he was a child, Naog when he became an adult. For his trial of manhood, this Yewesweder, already tall for his age, made the perilous journey to the land bridge at the Bab al Mandab to see the "Heaving Sea." He saw it, all right, but also saw that this arm of the Indian Ocean was only a few meters below the level of the bench that marked the old shore-line of the Red Sea before the last ice age. Yewesweder knew noth-ing of ice ages, but he knew that the shelf of land was absolutely level—he had loped along that route during his entire journey. Yet that level shelf was hundreds of meters above the plain where the "Salty Sea"—the rump of the Red Sea—was slowly, slowly rising. Already the Heaving Sea was cutting a channel that during the storm tides of seasonal hurricanes poured saltwater into several lakes, occasionally spilling over and sending a river of saltwater down to the Red Sea. Sometime—the next storm, or the storm after that—the Heaving Sea would crash through and an entire ocean would be poured in on top of Atlantis.

Yewesweder decided that he had earned his man-name, Naog, the day he made this discovery, and at once he set out for home. He had married a wife from among the tribe that lived at the Bab al Mandab, and it was only with great difficulty that she followed him so far that he was given no choice but to bring her home with him. When he reached the land of the Derku, as the Atlanteans called themselves, he learned that what had seemed plain to him at the shores of the Heaving Sea sounded like a far-fetched lie to the elders of his clan, and of all the clans. A huge flood? They had a flood every year, and simply rode it out on their boats. *If* Naog's flood actually happened, they'd ride it out, too.

But Naog knew that they would not. So he began experimenting with logs lashed together, and within a few years had learned how to build a boxy, watertight house-on-a-raft that might withstand the pressures of the flood that only he believed in. Others realized after the normal seasonal floods that his tight, dry wooden box was a superior seedboat, and eventually half of his clan's stored grain and beans ended up in his ark for safekeeping. Other clans also built wooden seedboats, but not to Naog's exacting specifications for strength and watertightness. In the meantime Naog was ridiculed and threatened because of his constant warnings that the whole land would be covered in water.

When the flood came, Naog had a little advance notice: The first torrent to break through the Bab al Mandab caused the Salty

Sea to rise rapidly, backing up in the canals of the Derku people
for several hours before the pressure of the ocean burst through in
earnest, sending a wall of water dozens of meters high scouring the
entire width of the Red Sea basin. By the time the flood reached
Naog's boat, it was sealed tight, bearing a cargo of seed and food,
along with his two wives, their small children, the three slaves that
had helped him with the construction of the boat, and the slaves'
families. They were tossed unmercifully in the turbulent waves,
and the ark was often immersed, but it held, and eventually they
came to shore not far from Gibeil on the southern tip of the Sinai
peninsula.

They set up farming for a brief time in the El Qa' Valley in the
shadows of the mountains of Sinai, telling all comers of the flood
sent by God to destroy the unworthy Derku people, and how this
handful of people alone had been saved because God had shown
Naog what he intended to do. Eventually, though, Naog became a
wandering herdsman, spreading his story wherever he went. As
Kemal had expected, Naog's story, with his anti-urban interpretation, had enormous influence in stopping people from gathering together in large communities that might become cities.

There was also a strong element of opposition to human sacrifice
in his story, for Naog's own father had been sacrificed to the crocodile god of the Derku people while he was gone on his manhood
journey, and Naog believed that the main reason the powerful god
of storms and seas had destroyed the Derku was their practice of
offering living victims to the large crocodile they penned up to represent their god every year after the flood season. In a way this
linkage between human sacrifice and city-building was unfortunate,
because when city-building was resumed by deliberate heretics re-
jecting the old wisdom of Naog many generations later, human sacrifice came along as part of the package. In the long run, though,
Naog got his way, for even those societies that gave human offerings
to their gods felt they were doing something dark and dangerous,
and eventually human sacrifice became regarded first as barbaric,
then as an unspeakable atrocity throughout the lands touched by
the story of Naog.

Kemal had found Atlantis; he had found the original of Noah
and Utnapishtim and Ziusudra. His childhood dream had been ful-

filled; he had played the Schliemann role and made the greatest discovery of them all. What remained now seemed to him to be clerical work.

He withdrew from the project, but not from Pastwatch. At first he simply dabbled at whatever work he fitfully began; mostly he concentrated on raising a family. But gradually, as his children grew up, his desultory efforts took shape and became more intense. He had found an even greater project: discovering why civilization arose in the first place. As far as he was concerned, all old-world civilizations after Atlantis were dependent on that first civilization. The *idea* of the city was already with the Egyptians and the Sumerians and the people of the Indus and even the Chinese, because the story of the Golden Age of Atlantis had spread far and wide.

The only civilization that grew up out of nothing, without the Atlantis legend, was in the Americas, where the story of Naog had not reached, except in legends borne by the few seafarers who crossed the barrier oceans. The land bridge to America had been buried in water for ten generations before the Red Sea basin was flooded. It took ten thousand years after Atlantis for civilization to arise there, among the Olmecs of the marshy land on the southern shores of the Gulf of Mexico. Kemal's new project was to study the differences between the Olmecs and the Atlanteans and, by seeing what elements they had in common, determine what civilization actually was: why it arose, what it consisted of, and how human beings adapted to giving up the tribe and living in the city.

He was in his early thirties when he began his Origin project. He was almost forty when word of the Columbus project reached him and he came to Tagiri to offer her all that he had learned so far.

Juba was one of those annoying cities where the locals tried to pretend that they had never heard of Europe. The Nile Rail brought Kemal into a station as modern as anywhere else, but when he came outside, he found himself in a city of grass huts and mud fences, with dirt roads and naked children running around and the adults scarcely better clothed. If the idea was to make the visitor think he had stepped back in time into primitive Africa, then for a moment it worked. The open houses clearly could not be air-conditioned, and wherever their power station and solar collectors were located, Kemal certainly couldn't see them. And yet he knew they were somewhere, and not far away, just like the water-purification system and the satellite dishes. He knew that these naked children went to a clean, modern school and used the latest computer equipment. He knew that the bare-breasted young women and the thong-clad young men went somewhere at night to watch the latest videos, or not watch them; to dance, or not dance, to the same new music that was all the rage in Recife, Madras, and Semarang. Above all, he knew that somewhere—probably underground—was one of Pastwatch's major installations, housing as it did both the slavery project and the Columbus project.

So why pretend? Why make your lives into a perpetual museum of an era when life was nasty, brutish, and short? Kemal loved the past as much as any man or woman now alive, but he had no desire to live in it, and he thought sometimes that it was just a bit sick for these people to reject their own era and raise their kids like primitive tribesmen. He thought of what it might have been like to grow up like a primitive Turk, drinking fermented mare's milk or, worse, horse's blood, while dwelling in a yurt and practicing with a sword until he could cut off a man's head with a single blow from horseback. Who would want to live in such terrible times? Study them, yes. Remember the great accomplishments. But not live like those people. The citizens of Juba of two hundred years before had got rid of the grass huts and built European-style dwellings as quickly as they could. *They* knew. The people who had *had* to live in grass huts had no regrets about leaving them behind.

Still, despite the masquerade, there were a few visible concessions to modern life. For instance, as he stood on the portico of the Juba station, a young woman drove up on a small lorry. "Kemal?" she asked.

He nodded.

"I'm Diko," she said. "Tagiri's my mom. Toss your bag on and let's go!"

He tossed his bag into the small cargo area and then perched beside her on the driving bench. It was fortunate that this sort of lorry, designed for short hauls, couldn't go faster than about thirty kilometers an hour, or he was sure he would have been pitched out in no time, the way this insane young woman rattled headlong over the rutted road.

"Mother keeps saying we should pave these roads," said Diko, "but then somebody always says that hot pavement will blister the children's feet and so the idea gets dropped."

"They could wear shoes," suggested Kemal. He spoke Simple as clearly as he could, but it still wasn't good, what with his jaws getting smacked together as the lorry bumped through rut after rut.

"Oh, well, they'd look pretty silly, stark naked with sneakers on." She giggled.

Kemal refrained from saying that they looked pretty silly *now*. He would merely be accused of being a cultural imperialist, even though it wasn't *his* culture he was advocating. These people were apparently happy living as they did. Those who didn't like it no doubt moved to Khartoum or Entebbe or Addis Ababa, which were modern with a vengeance. And it did make a kind of sense for the Pastwatch people to live in the past even as they watched it.

He wondered vaguely if they used toilet paper or handfuls of grass.

To his relief, the grass hovel where Diko stopped was only the camouflage for an elevator down into a perfectly modern hotel. She insisted on carrying his bag as she led him to his room. The underground hotel had been dug into the side of a bluff overlooking the Nile, so the rooms all had windows and porches. And there was air-conditioning and running water and a computer in the room.

"All right?" asked Diko.

"I was hoping to live in a grass hut and relieve myself in the weeds," said Kemal.

She looked crestfallen. "Father said that we ought to give you the full local experience, but Mother said you wouldn't want it."

"Your mother was right. I was only joking. This room is excellent."

"Your journey was long," said Diko. "The Ancient Ones are eager to talk to you, but unless you prefer otherwise, they'll wait till morning."

"Morning is excellent," said Kemal.

They set a time. Kemal called room service and found that he could get standard international fare instead of puréed slug and spicy cow dung, or whatever was involved in the local cuisine.

The next morning he found himself in the shade of a large tree, sitting in a rocking chair and surrounded by a dozen people who sat or squatted on mats. "I can't possibly be comfortable having the only chair," he said.

"I told you he would want a mat," said Hassan.

"No," said Kemal. "I don't want a mat. I just thought you might be more comfortable . . ."

"It's our way," said Tagiri. "When we work at our machines, we sit in chairs. But this is not work. This is joy. The great Kemal asked to meet with us. We never dreamed that you would be interested in our projects."

Kemal hated it when he was called "the great Kemal." To him, the great Kemal was Kemal Ataturk, who re-created the Turkish nation out of the wreckage of the Ottoman Empire centuries before. But he was weary of giving that speech, too, and besides, he thought there might have been just a hint of irony in the way Tagiri said it. Time to end pretenses.

"I'm not interested in your projects," said Kemal. "However, it seems that you are capturing the attention of a growing number of people outside Pastwatch. From what I hear, you're thinking of taking steps with far-reaching consequences, and yet you seem to be basing your decisions on . . . incomplete information."

"So you're here to correct us," said Hassan, reddening.

"I'm here to tell you what I know and what I think," said Kemal. "I didn't ask you to make this a public gathering. I would just as happily speak to you and Tagiri alone. Or, if you prefer, I'll go away and let you proceed in ignorance. I've offered you what I know, and I see no need to pretend that we are equals in those areas. I'm sure that there are many things you know that *I* don't— but *I'm* not trying to build a machine to change the past, and therefore there is no urgency about alleviating *my* ignorance."

Tagiri laughed. "It's one of the glories of Pastwatch, that it's not the smooth-talking bureaucrats who head the major projects." She leaned forward. "Do your worst to us, Kemal. We aren't ashamed to learn that we might be wrong."

"Let's start with slavery," said Kemal. "After all, that's what *you* did. I've read some of the softhearted, sympathetic biographies and the analytical papers that have emerged from your slavery project, and I get the clear impression that if you could, you would find the person who thought of slavery and stop him, so that no human being would ever have been bought or sold on this planet. Am I right?''

"Are you saying that slavery was *not* an unmitigated evil?" asked Tagiri.

"Yes, that's what I'm saying," said Kemal. "Because you're looking at slavery from the wrong end—from the present, when we've abolished it. But back at the beginning, when it started, doesn't it occur to you that it was infinitely better than what it replaced?"

Tagiri's veneer of polite interest was clearly wearing thin. "I've read your remarks about the origin of slavery."

"But you're not impressed."

"It's natural, when you make a great discovery, to assume that it has wider implications than it actually has," said Tagiri. "But there is no reason to think that human bondage originated exclusively with Atlantis, as a replacement for human sacrifice."

"But I never said that," said Kemal. "My opponents said that I said that, but I thought *you* would have read more carefully."

Hassan spoke up, trying to sound mild and forceful, both at once. "I think that this seems to be getting too personal. Did you come all this way, Kemal, to tell us that we're stupid? You could have done that by mail."

"No," said Kemal, "I came for Tagiri to tell me that I have a pathological need to think that Atlantis is the cause of everything." Kemal rose out of his chair, turned around, picked it up, and hurled it away. "Give me a mat! Let me sit down with you and tell you what I know! If you want to reject it afterward, go ahead. But don't waste my time or yours by defending yourselves or attacking me!"

Hassan stood up. For a moment Kemal wondered if he was going to strike him. But then Hassan bent down, picked up his mat from the grass, and held it out to Kemal. "So," said Hassan. "Talk."

Kemal laid out the mat and sat down. Hassan shared his daughter's mat, in the second row.

"Slavery," said Kemal. "There are many ways that people have been held in bondage. Serfs were bound to the land. Nomad tribes adopted occasional captives or strangers, and made them second-class members of the tribe, without the freedom to leave. Chivalry originated as a sort of dignified mafia, sometimes even a protection racket, and once you accepted an overlord you were his to command. In some cultures, deposed kings were kept in captivity, where they had children born in captivity, and grandchildren, and great-grandchildren who were never harmed, but never allowed to leave. Whole populations have been conquered and forced to work under foreign overlords, paying unpayable tribute to their masters. Raiders and pirates have carried off hostages for ransom. Starving people have bound themselves into service. Prisoners have been forced into involuntary labor. These kinds of bondage have shown up in many human cultures. But none of these is slavery."

"By a narrow definition, that's right," said Tagiri.

"Slavery is when a human being is made property. When one person is able to buy and sell, not just someone's labor, but his actual body, and any children he has. Movable property, generation after generation." Kemal looked at them, at the coldness still visible in their faces. "I know that you all know this. But what you seem not to realize is that slavery was not inevitable. It was invented, at a specific time and place. We know when and where the first person was turned into property. It happened in Atlantis, when a woman had the idea of putting the sacrificial captives to work, and then, when her most valued captive was going to be sacrificed, she paid her tribal elder to remove him permanently from the pool of victims."

"That's not exactly the slave block," said Tagiri.

"It was the beginning. The practice spread quickly, until it became the main reason for raiding other tribes. The Derku people began buying the captives directly from the raiders. And then they started trading slaves among themselves and finally buying and selling them."

"What an achievement," said Tagiri.

"It became the foundation of their city, the fact that the slaves were doing the citizens' duty in digging the canals and planting and tending the crops. Slavery was the reason they could afford the leisure time to develop a recognizable civilization. Slavery was so profitable to them that the Derku holy men wasted no time in finding that the dragon-god no longer wanted human sacrifices, at least for a while. That meant that *all* their captives could be made into slaves and put to work. It's no accident that when the great flood destroyed the Derku, the practice of slavery didn't die with them. The surrounding cultures had already picked it up, because it *worked*. It was the only way that had yet been found to get the use of the labor of strangers. All the other instances of genuine slavery that we've found can be traced back to that Derku woman, Nedz-Nagaya, when she paid to keep a useful captive from being fed to the crocodile."

"Let's build her a monument," said Tagiri. She was very angry.

"The concept of buying and selling people was invented *only* among the Derku," said Kemal.

"It didn't *have* to be invented anywhere else," said Tagiri. "Just because Agafna built the first wheel doesn't mean that someone else wouldn't have built another one later."

"On the contrary. We *do* know that slavery—commerce in human beings—was *not* discovered in the one place where the Derku had no influence," said Kemal. He paused.

"America," said Diko.

"America," said Kemal. "And in the place where people weren't conceived of as property, what did they have?"

"There was plenty of bondage in America," said Tagiri.

"Of those other kinds. But humans as property, humans with a cash value—it wasn't there. And that's one of the things you love best about your idea of stopping Columbus. Preserve the one place on earth where slavery never developed. Am I right?"

"That's not the primary reason for looking at Columbus," said Tagiri.

"I think you need to look again," said Kemal. "Because slavery was a direct replacement for human sacrifice. Are you actually telling me that you prefer the torture and murder of captives, as the Mayas and Iroquois and Aztecs and Caribs practiced it? Do you find that more civilized? After all, those deaths were offered to the *gods*."

"You will never make me believe that there was a one-for-one trade, slavery for human sacrifice."

"I don't care whether you *believe* it," said Kemal. "Just admit the possibility. Just admit that there are some things worse than slavery. Just admit that maybe your set of values is as arbitrary as any other culture's values, and to try to revise history in order to make your values triumph in the past as well as the present is pure—"

"Cultural imperialism," said Hassan. "Kemal, we have this argument ourselves every week or so. And if we were proposing to go back and stop that Derku woman from inventing slavery, your point would be well taken. But we aren't trying to do anything of the kind. Kemal, we aren't sure we want to do *anything!* We're just trying to find out what's possible."

"That's so disingenuous it's laughable. You've known from the beginning that it was Columbus you were going after. Columbus you were going to *stop*. And yet you seem to forget that along with the evil that European ascendancy brought to the world, you will also be throwing away the good. Useful medicine. Productive agriculture. Clean water. Cheap power. The industry that gives us the leisure to have this meeting. And don't dare to tell me that all the goods of our modern world would have been invented anyway. Nothing is inevitable. You're throwing away too much."

Tagiri covered her face with her hands. "I know," she said.

Kemal had expected argument. Hadn't she been sniping at him all along? He found himself speechless, for a moment.

Tagiri took her hands away from her face, but still she looked at her lap. "Any change would have a cost. And yet not changing also has a cost. But it's not my decision. We will lay all our arguments before the world." She lifted her face, to look at Kemal. "It's easy for you to be sure that we should *not* do it," she said. "You haven't looked into their faces. You're a *scientist*."

He had to laugh. "I'm not a scientist, Tagiri. I'm just another one like you—somebody who gets an idea in his head sometimes and can't let it go."

"That's right," said Tagiri. "I can't let it go. Somehow, when we're through with all our research, if we have a machine that lets us touch the past, then there'll be something we can do that's worth doing, something that will answer the . . . hunger . . . of an old woman who dreamed.''

''The prayer, you mean,'' said Kemal.

''Yes,'' she said defiantly. ''The prayer. There is something we can do to make things better. Somehow.''

''I see that I'm not dealing with science, then.''

''No, Kemal, you're not, and I've never said so.'' She smiled ruefully. ''I was shaped, you see. I was given the charge to look at the past as if I were an artist. To see if it could be given a new shape. A better shape. If it can't, then I'll do nothing. But if it can . . .''

Kemal was not expecting such frankness. He had come expecting to find a group of people committed to a course of madness. What he found instead was a commitment, yes, but no course, and therefore no madness. ''A better shape,'' he said. ''That really comes down to three questions, doesn't it. First is whether the shape is better or not—a question that's impossible to answer except with the heart, but at least you have the sense not to trust your own desires. And the second question is whether it's technically possible—whether we can devise a way to change the past. That's up to the physicists and mathematicians and engineers.''

''And the third question?'' asked Hassan.

''Whether you can determine exactly what change or changes must be made in order to get exactly the result you want. I mean, what are you going to do, send an abortificant back and slip it into Columbus's mother's wine?''

''No,'' said Tagiri. ''We're trying to save lives, not murder a great man.''

''Besides,'' said Hassan, ''as you said, we don't want to stop Columbus if by doing so we'd make the world worse. It's the most impossible part of the whole problem—how can we guess what would have happened without Columbus's discovery of America? That's something the TruSite II still can't show us. What *might* have happened.''

Kemal looked around at the people who had gathered for this meeting, and he realized that he had been completely wrong about them. These people were even more determined than he was to avoid doing anything foolish.

"That's an interesting problem," he said.

"It's an impossible one," said Hassan. "I don't know how happy this will make you, Kemal, but you gave us our only hope."

"How did I do that?"

"Your analysis of Naog," said Hassan. "If there's anyone who was like Columbus in all of history, it was him. He changed history by the sheer force of his will. The only reason his ark was built at all was because of his grim determination. Then because his boat carried him through the flood, he became a figure of legend. And because his father was a victim of the Derku's brief return to human sacrifice just before the flood, he told everyone who would listen that cities were evil, that human sacrifice was an unforgivable crime, that God had destroyed a world because of their sins."

"If only he had told people slavery was evil, too," said Diko.

"He told them the opposite," said Kemal. "He was a living example of how beneficial slavery could be—because he kept with him his whole life the three slaves who built his boat for him, and everyone who came to meet the great Naog saw how his greatness depended on his ownership of these three devoted men." Turning to Hassan, Kemal added, "I don't see how Naog's example inspired you with any kind of hope."

"Because one man, alone, reshaped the world," said Hassan. "And you were able to see exactly where he turned onto the path that led to those changes. You found that moment where he stood on the shore of the new channel that was being carved into the Bab al Mandab, and he looked up at the shelf of the old coastline and realized what was going to happen."

"It was easy to find," said Kemal. "He immediately started for home, and to his wife he explained exactly what he had thought of and when he had thought of it."

"Yes, well, it was certainly clearer than anything we've found with Columbus," said Hassan. "But it gives us the hope that perhaps we can find such a moment. The event, the thought that turned him west. Diko found the moment when he determined on being a great man. But we haven't found the point where he became so unrelentingly monomaniacal about a westward voyage. Yet because of Naog, we still have hope that someday we'll find it."

"But I *have* found it, Father," said Diko.

Everyone turned to her. She seemed flustered. "Or at least I think I have. But it's very strange. I was working on it last night. It's so silly, isn't it? I thought—wouldn't it be wonderful if I found it while . . . while Kemal was here. And then I did. I think."

No one said anything for a long moment. Until Kemal rose to his feet and said, "What are we doing here, then? Show us!"

5

Vision

It was more than Cristoforo could have hoped for, to be included on the Spinola convoy to Flanders. True, it was just the sort of opportunity that he had been preparing for all his life till now, begging his way onto any ship that would carry him until he knew the coast of Liguria better than he knew the lumps in his own mattress. And hadn't he turned his "observational" trip to Chios into a commercial triumph? Not that he had come back rich, of course, but starting with relatively little he had traded in mastic until he came home with a hefty purse—and then had wit enough to contribute much of it, quite publicly, to the Church. And he did it in the name of Nicoló Spinola.

Spinola sent for him, of course, and Cristoforo was the picture of gratitude. "I know that you gave me no duties in Chios, my lord, but it was nevertheless you who allowed me to join the voyage, and at no charge. The tiny sums I was able to earn in Chios were not worth offering to you—you give more to your servants when they go to market to buy the day's food for your household." A ludicrous exaggeration, they would both know. "But when I gave them to Christ, I couldn't pretend that the money, meager as it was, came from me, when it came entirely from your kindness."

Spinola laughed. "You're very good at this," he said. "Practice a little more, so it doesn't sound memorized, and speeches like that will make your fortune, I promise you."

Cristoforo thought that he meant he had failed, until Spinola invited him to take part in a commercial convoy to Flanders and England. Five ships, sailing together for safety, and one of them devoted to a cargo that Cristoforo himself was in charge of trading. It was a serious responsibility, a good-sized chunk of the Spinola fortune, but Cristoforo had prepared himself well. What he hadn't done himself, he had watched others do with a close eye to detail. He knew how to supervise the loading of the ship and how to drive a hard bargain without making enemies. He knew how to talk to the captain, how to remain at once aloof and yet affable with the men, how to judge from the wind and the sky and the sea how much progress they would make. Even though he had actually done very little of the work of a sailor, he knew what all the jobs were, from watching, and he knew whether the jobs were being done well. When he was young, and they were not yet suspicious that he might get them in trouble, the sailors had let him watch them work. He had even learned to swim, which most sailors never bothered to do, because he had thought as a child that this was one of the requirements of life at sea. By the time the ship set sail, Cristoforo felt himself completely in control.

They even called him "Signor Colombo." That hadn't happened much before. His father was only rarely called "signor," despite the fact that in recent years Cristoforo's earnings had allowed Domenico Colombo to prosper, moving the weaving shop to larger quarters and wearing finer clothing and riding a horse like a gentleman and buying a few small houses outside the city walls so he could play the landlord. So the title was certainly not one that came readily to one of Cristoforo's birth. On this voyage, however, it was not just the sailors but also the captain himself who gave Colombo the courtesy title. It was a sign of how far he had come, this basic respect—but not as important a sign as having the trust of the Spinolas.

The voyage wasn't easy, even at the outset. The seas weren't rough, but they weren't placid, either. Cristoforo noticed with secret enjoyment that he was the only one of the commercial agents who wasn't sick. Instead he passed the time as he did on all his voyages—poring over the charts with the navigator or conversing with the captain, pumping them for all the information they knew, for everything they could teach him. Though he knew his destiny lay to the east, he also knew that he would someday have a ship— a fleet—that might need to voyage through every known sea. Liguria he knew; the voyage to Chios, his first open-sea journey, his first that ever lost sight of land, his first that relied on navigation and calculation, had given him a glimpse of eastern seas. And now he would see the west, going through the straits of Gibraltar and then veering north, coasting Portugal, crossing the Bay of Biscay—names he had heard of only in sailors' lore and brag. The gentlemen—the *other* gentlemen—might puke their way across the Mediterranean, but Cristoforo would use every moment, preparing himself, until at last he was ready to be the servant in the hands of God who would . . .

He dared not think of it, or God would know the awful presumption, the deadly pride that he concealed within his heart.

Not that God didn't already know, of course. But at least God also knew that Cristoforo did his best not to let his pride possess him. Thy will, O Lord, not mine be done. If I am the one to lead thy triumphant armies and navies on a mighty crusade to liberate Constantinople, drive the Muslims from Europe, and once again raise the Christian banner in Jerusalem, then so be it. But if not, I will do any task thou hast in mind for me, great or humble. I will be ready. I am thy true servant.

What a hypocrite I am, thought Cristoforo. To pretend that my motives are pure. I laid my purse from Chios into the bishop's own hands—but then used it to advance my cause with Nicoló Spinola. And even then, it wasn't the *whole* purse. I'm wearing a good part of it; a gentleman has to have the right clothes or people don't call him Signor. And much more of it went to Father, to buy houses and dress Mother like a lady. Hardly the perfect offering of faith. Do I want to become rich and influential in order to serve God? Or do I serve God in hopes that it will make me rich and influential?

Such were the doubts that plagued him, between his dreams and plans. Most of the time, though, he spent pumping the captain and the navigator or studying the charts or staring at the coasts

they passed, making his own maps and calculations, as if he were
the first ever to see this place.

"There are plenty of charts of the Andalusian coast," said the
navigator.

"I know," said Cristoforo. "But I learn more by charting them
myself than I ever would by studying them. And I have the charts
to check against my own maps."

The truth was that the charts were full of errors. Either that or
some supernatural power had moved the capes and bays, the
beaches and promontories of the Iberian coast, so that now and then
there was an inlet that wasn't shown on any chart. "Were these
charts made by pirates?" he asked the captain one day. "They
seem designed to make sure that a corsair can dodge out to engage
us in battle without any warning."

The captain laughed. "They *are* Moorish charts, or so I've
heard. And the copyists aren't always perfect. They miss a feature
now and then. What do they know, sitting at their tables, far from
any sea? We follow the charts generally and learn where the mistakes are. If we sailed these coasts all the time, as the Spanish
sailors do, then we'd rarely need these charts at all. And *they* aren't
about to issue corrected charts, because they have no wish to help
the ships of other nations to sail safely here. Every nation guards
its charts. So keep to your mapmaking, Signor Colombo. Someday
your charts may have value to Genova. If this voyage is a success,
there'll be others."

There was no reason to think it would *not* be a success, until
two days after they passed through the straits of Gibraltar, when a
cry went up: "Sails! Corsairs!"

Cristoforo rushed to the gunwale, where shortly the sails became visible. The pirates were not Moorish, by the look of them.
And they had not been daunted by the five merchant ships sailing
together. Why should they? The pirates had five corsairs of their
own.

"I don't like this," said the captain.

"We're evenly matched, aren't we?" asked Cristoforo.

"Hardly," said the captain. "We're loaded with cargo; they're
not. They know these waters; we don't. And they're used to

bloody-handed fighting. What do we have? Sword-bearing gentlemen and sailors who are terrified of battle on the open sea."

"Nevertheless," said Cristoforo, "God will fight on the side of just men."

The captain gave him a withering look. "I don't know that we're any more righteous than others who've had their throats slit. No, we'll outrun them if we can, or if we can't, we'll make them pay so dear that they'll give up and leave us. What are you good for, in a battle?"

"Not much," said Cristoforo. It would do no good to promise more than he could deliver. The captain deserved to know whom he could and could not count on. "I carry the sword for the respect of it."

"Well, these pirates will respect the blade only if it's well blooded. Have you an arm for throwing?"

"Rocks, as a boy," said Cristoforo.

"Good enough for me. If things look bad, then this is our last hope—we'll have pots filled with oil. We set them afire and hurl them onto the pirate ships. They can't very well fight us if their decks are afire."

"They have to be awfully close, then, don't they?"

"As I said—we only use these pots if things look bad."

"What's to keep the flames from spreading to our own ships, if theirs are in flames?"

The captain looked coldly at him. "As I said—we want to make our fleet a worthless conquest for them." He looked again at the corsairs' sails, which were well behind them and farther off the coast. "They want to pinch us against the shore," he said. "If we can make it to Cape St. Vincent, where we can turn north, then we'll lose them. Till then they'll try to intercept us as we tack outward, or run us aground on the shoreward tack."

"Then let's tack outward now," said Cristoforo. "Let's establish ourselves as far from shore as possible."

The captain sighed. "The wisest course, my friend, but the sailors won't stand for it. They don't like being out of sight of land if there's a fight."

"Why not?"

"Because they can't swim. Their best hope is to ride some flot-
sam in, if we do badly."

"But if we don't sail out of sight of shore, how can we do well?"

"This isn't a good time to expect sailors to be rational," said
the captain. "And one thing's sure—you can't lead sailors where
they don't want to go."

"They wouldn't mutiny."

"If they thought I was leading them to drown, they'd put this
ship to shore and leave the cargo for the pirates. Better than drowning, or being sold into slavery."

Cristoforo had not realized this. It hadn't come up on any of
his voyages before, and the sailors didn't speak of this when they
were ashore in Genova. No, *then* they were all courage, full of
fight. And the idea that the captain couldn't lead wherever he
might wish to command . . . Cristoforo brooded about that idea
for days, as the corsairs paced them, squeezing them ever closer to
the shore.

"French," said the navigator.

As soon as he said the word, a sailor near him said, "Coullon."

Cristoforo started at the name. In Genova he had heard enough
French, despite the hostility of the Genovese for a nation that had
more than once raided their docks and tried to burn the city, to
know that *coullon* was the French version of his own family's name:
Colombo, or, in Latin, Columbus.

But the sailor who said it was not French, and seemed to have
no idea that the name would mean anything to Cristoforo.

"Might be Coullon," said the navigator. "Bold as he is, it's
more likely to be the devil—but then they say that Coullon *is* the
devil."

"And everyone knows the devil is French!" said a sailor.

They laughed, all who could hear, but there was little real mirth
in it. And the captain made a point of showing Cristoforo where the
firepots were, once the ship's boy had filled them. "Make sure you
keep fire in your hands," he said to Cristoforo. *"That* is your
blade, Signor Colombo, and they *will* respect you."

Was the pirate Coullon toying with them? Was that why he let
them stay just out of reach until Cape St. Vincent was tantalizingly
in view? Certainly Coullon had no trouble *then,* closing the gap,

cutting them off before they could break to the north, around the cape, into the open Atlantic.

There was no hope of coordinating the defense of the fleet now. Each captain had to find his own way to victory. The captain of Cristoforo's ship realized at once that if he kept his current course he'd be run aground or boarded almost at once. "Come around!" he cried. "Get the wind behind us!"

It was a bold strategy, but the sailors understood it, and the other ships, seeing what Cristoforo's old whaler was doing, followed suit. They'd have to pass among the corsairs, but if they did it right, they'd end up with the open sea ahead of them, the corsairs behind them, and the wind with them. But Coullon was no fool, and brought his corsairs around in time to throw grappling hooks at the passing Genovese merchantmen.

As the pirates pulled the ropes hand over hand, forcing the boats together, Cristoforo could see that the captain had been right: Their own crew would have little hope in a fight. Oh, they'd give such a battle as they could, knowing that it was their lives at stake. But there was despair in all their eyes, and they visibly shrank from the bloodshed that was coming. He heard one burly sailor saying to the ship's boy, "Pray that you'll die." It wasn't encouraging; nor was the obvious eagerness on the part of the pirates.

Cristoforo reached down, took the match from the cinderpot, touched it to two of the firepots, and then, holding them tight though they singed his doublet, he stepped atop the forecastle, where he could get a clear throw at the nearest corsair. "Captain!" he cried. "Now?"

The captain didn't hear him—there was too much shouting at the helm. Never mind. Cristoforo could see that things were desperate, and the closer the corsairs got, the likelier the chance of the flames taking both ships. He threw the pot.

His arm was strong, his aim true, or true enough. The pot shattered on the corsair's deck, splashing flames like a spill of bright orange dye across the wood. In moments it was dancing up the sheets to the sails. For the first time, the pirates weren't grinning and hooting. Now they pulled all the more grimly on the grappling lines, and Cristoforo realized that of course their only hope, with their own ship afire, was to take the merchant vessel.

Turning, he could see that another corsair, also grappling with a Genovese ship, was close enough that he could visit a bit of fire on *it,* too. His aim was not as good—the pot splashed harmlessly into the sea. But now the ship's boy was lighting the pots and handing them up to him, and Cristoforo managed to put two onto the deck of the farther corsair, and another pair onto the deck of the pirate ship that was preparing to board his own. "Signor Spinola," he said, "forgive me for losing your cargo."

But Signor Spinola would not hear his prayers, he knew. And it wasn't a matter of his career as a trader now. It was a matter of saving his life. Dear God, he said silently, am I to be your servant or not? I give my life to you, if you spare it now. I will free Constantinople. "The Hagia Sophia will once again hear the music of the holy mass," he murmured. "Only save me alive, dear God."

"This is his moment of decision?" asked Kemal.

"No, of course not," said Diko. "I just wanted you to see what I was doing. This scene has been shown a thousand times, of course. Columbus against Columbus, they called it, since he and the pirate had the same name. But all the recordings were from the days of the Tempoview, right? So we saw his lips move, but in the chaos of battle there was no hope of hearing what he said. He was speaking too softly, his lips moved too slightly. And this bothered no one, because after all, what does it matter how a man prays in the midst of battle?"

"But this does matter, I think," said Hassan. "The Hagia Sophia?"

"The holiest shrine in Constantinople. Perhaps the most beautiful Christian place in all the world, in these days before the Sistine Chapel. And when Columbus is praying for God to spare his life, what does he vow? An eastern crusade. I found this several days ago, and it kept me awake night after night. Everyone had always looked for the origin of his westward voyage back farther, on Chios, perhaps, or in Genova. But he has already left Genova now for the last time. He'll never turn back. And he's only a week away from the beginning of his time in Lisbon, when it's clear that he has already turned his eyes irrevocably, resolutely to the west. And yet here, at this moment, *he vows to liberate Constantinople.*"

"Unbelievable," said Kemal.

"So you see," said Diko, "I knew that whatever it was that turned him to his obsession with the western voyage, with the Indies, it must have happened between this moment on board this ship whose sails are already burning, and his arrival in Lisbon a week later."

"Excellent," said Hassan. "Fine work, Diko. This narrows it down considerably."

"Father," said Diko. "I discovered this days ago. I told you that I found the moment of decision, not that I had found the *week.*"

"Then show us," said Tagiri.

"I'm afraid to," said Diko.

"And why is that?"

"Because it's impossible. Because . . . because as far as I can tell, God speaks to him."

"Show us," said Kemal. "I've always wanted to hear the voice of God."

Everyone laughed.

Except Diko. She didn't laugh. "You're about to," she said.

They stopped laughing.

The pirates were aboard, and along with them came the fire, leaping from sail to sail. It was obvious to all that even if they somehow repulsed the pirates, both ships were doomed. Those sailors who weren't already engaged in bloody-handed combat began throwing kegs and hatch covers into the water, and several managed to get the ship's boat into the water on the side opposite the pirates' ship. Cristoforo saw how the captain disdained to abandon his ship—he was fighting bravely, his sword dancing. And then the sword wasn't there, and through the smoke swirling across the deck Cristoforo could no longer see him.

Sailors were leaping into the sea, striking out for bits of floating debris. Cristoforo caught a glimpse of one sailor pushing another from a hatch-cover; he saw another go under the water without having found anything to cling to. The only reason pirates hadn't yet reached Cristoforo himself was that they were making some effort to cut loose the burning masts of the Genovese ship before the fire spread down to the deck. It looked to Cristoforo as though they might succeed, saving themselves and the cargo at the expense of the Genovese. That was intolerable. The Genovese would fail in any case—but Cristoforo could at least make certain that the pirates also failed.

Taking two more flaming pots in his hands, he lobbed one out onto the deck of his own ship, and then the second even farther, so that the helm was soon engulfed in flames. The pirates cried out in rage—those who weren't screaming in pain or terror—and their eyes soon found Cristoforo and the ship's boy on the forecastle.

"I think now's the time for us to leap into the sea," said Cristoforo.

"I can't swim," said the ship's boy.

"I can," said Cristoforo. But first he pulled up the hatch cover from the forecastle, dragged it to the gunwale, and heaved it over the side. Then, taking the boy by the hand, he jumped into the water just as the pirates swarmed up from the deck.

The boy was right about his inability to swim, and it took Cristoforo considerable effort just to get him up onto the hatch cover. But once the boy was safely atop the floating wood, he calmed down. Cristoforo tried to get part of his own weight onto the tiny raft, but it made it tilt dangerously down into the water, and the boy panicked. So Cristoforo let himself back down into the water. It was five leagues to shore, at least—more likely six. Cristoforo was a strong swimmer, but not that strong. He needed to cling to something to help bear his weight so he could rest in the water from time to time, and if it couldn't be this hatch cover, he would have to leave it and find something else. "Listen, boy!" shouted Cristoforo. "The shore is that way!" He pointed.

Did the boy understand? His eyes were wide, but at least he looked at Cristoforo as he spoke.

"Paddle with your hands," said Cristoforo. "That way!"

But the boy just sat there, terrified, and then he looked away from Cristoforo toward the burning ship.

It was too tiring, treading water while trying to communicate with this boy. He had saved the boy's life, and now he had to get about the business of saving his own.

What he finally found, as he swam toward the invisible shore, was a floating oar. It wasn't a raft and couldn't lift him entirely out of the water, but by straddling the handle and keeping the blade of the oar flat under his chest and face he was able to get some respite when his arms grew weary. Soon he left the smoke of the fires behind him, and then the sound of screaming men, though whether he ceased hearing that awful noise because he had swum so far or because all had drowned, he could not guess. He did not look back; he did not see the burning hulks finally slip down under the water. Already the ships were forgotten, and his commercial mission. All he thought of now was moving his arms and legs, struggling through the heaving waters of the Atlantic toward the ever-receding shore.

Sometimes Cristoforo was sure that there was a current running away from shore, that he was caught in it and would be carried away no matter what he did. He ached, his arms and legs were exhausted and could move no more, and yet he kept them moving, however weakly now, and at last, at last he could see that he was indeed much closer to shore than before. It gave him hope enough to keep going, though the pain in his joints made him feel as though the sea were tearing his limbs off.

He could hear the crashing of waves against the shore. He could see scruffy-looking trees on low bluffs. And then a wave broke around him, and he could see the beach. He swam farther, then tried to stand. He could not. Instead he collapsed back into the water, only now he had lost the oar and for a moment he went under the water, and it occurred to him that it would be such a foolish thing for him to swim so far only to drown on the beach because his legs were too weary to hold him.

Cristoforo decided not to do anything so foolish as to die here and now, though the idea of giving up and resting did have a momentary appeal. Instead he pushed against the bottom with his legs, and because the water was, after all, not deep, his head rose above the surface and he breathed again. Half swimming, half walking, he forced his way to shore and then crept across the wet until he reached dry sand. Nor did he stop then—some small rational part of his mind told him that he must get above the high tide, marked by the line of dried-up sticks and seaweed many yards beyond him. He crawled, crept, finally dragged himself to that line and beyond it; then he collapsed into the sand, unconscious at once.

It was the high tide that woke him, as several of the highest-reaching waves cast thin riffs of water up to the old high-tide line, tickling his feet and then his thighs. He woke up with a powerful thirst, and when he tried to move he found that all his muscles were on fire with pain. Had he somehow broken his legs and arms? No, he quickly realized. He had simply drawn from them more work than they had been designed to give, and he was paying for it now with pain.

Pain, though, was not going to make him stay on the beach to die. He got up onto all fours and crawled ahead until he reached the first tufts of shoregrass. Then he looked about for some sign of water he could drink. This close to shore it was almost too much to hope for, but how could he regain his strength without something to drink? The sun was setting. Soon it would be too dark to see, and while the night would cool him, it might as easily chill him, and weak as he was, it might kill him.

"Oh God," he whispered through parched lips. "Water."

Diko stopped the playback. "You all know what happens here, yes?"

"A woman from the village of Lagos comes and finds him," said Kemal. "They nurse him back to health and then he leaves for Lisbon."

"We've seen this in the Tempoview a thousand times," said Hassan. "Or at least thousands of people have seen it at least once."

"That's exactly right," said Diko. "You've seen it in the Tempoview." She went over to one of the older machines, kept now only for playing back old recordings. She ran the appropriate passage at high speed; looking like a comical, jerky puppet, Columbus peered in one direction, and then fell back into the sand for a while, perhaps praying, until he knelt up again and crossed himself and said, "The Father, the Son, and the Holy Spirit." It was in that posture that the woman of Lagos—Maria Luisa, daughter of Simão o Gordo, to be precise—found him. Also looking like a marionette in the fast Tempoview playback, she ran back to the village for help.

"Is this what you've all seen?" she asked.

It was.

"Obviously nothing happens," she said. "So who would have bothered to come back to look at this with the TruSite II? But that is what I did, and here is what I saw." She returned to the Tru-Site II and resumed the playback. They all watched as Columbus looked about for water, turning his head slowly, obviously exhausted and in pain. But then, to their shock, they heard a soft voice.

"Cristoforo Colombo," said the voice.

A figure, then two figures, shimmered in the darkening air before Columbus. Now as he peered in that direction, all the watchers could see that he was not looking for water, but rather staring at the image that formed itself in the air.

"Cristóbal Colón. Coullon. Columbus." The voice went on, calling his name in language after language. It was barely, barely audible. And the image never quite resolved itself into clarity.

"So tenuous," murmured Hassan. "The Tempoview would never have been able to detect this. Like smoke or steam. A slight excitation of the air."

"What are we seeing?" demanded Kemal.

"Be still and listen," said Tagiri, impatient. "What conclusion can you reach before you've seen the data?"

They fell silent. They watched and listened.

The vision resolved itself into two men, shining with a faint nimbus all around them. And on the shoulder of the smaller of the two men there sat a dove. There could be no doubt in the mind of any medieval man, especially one who had read as much as Cristoforo, what this vision was supposed to represent. The Holy Trinity. Almost he spoke their names aloud. But they were still speaking, calling him by name in languages he had never heard.

Then, finally: "Columbus, you are my true servant."

Yes, with all my heart I am.

"You have turned your heart to the east, to liberate Constantinople from the Turk."

My prayer, my promise was heard.

"I have seen your faith and your courage, and that is why I spared your life on the water today. I have a great work for you to do. But it is not Constantinople to which you must bring the cross."

Jerusalem, then?

"Nor is it Jerusalem, or any other nation touched by the waters of the Mediterranean. I saved you alive so you could carry the cross to lands much farther east, so far to the east that they can be reached only by sailing westward into the Atlantic."

Cristoforo could hardly grasp what they were telling him. Nor could he bear to look upon them anymore—what mortal man had the right to gaze directly upon the face of the resurrected Savior, let alone the Almighty or the dove of the Holy Spirit? Never mind that this was only a vision; he could not look at them anymore. He lowered his head forward into the sand so he could not see them anymore, but listened all the more intently.

"There are great kingdoms there, rich in gold and powerful in armies. They have never heard the name of my Only Begotten, and they die unbaptized. It is my will that you carry salvation to them, and bring back the wealth of these lands."

Cristoforo heard this and his heart burned within him. God had seen him, God had noticed him, and he was being given a mission far greater than the mere liberation of an ancient Christian capital. Lands so far to the east that he must sail west to reach them. Gold. Salvation.

"Your name will be great. Kings will make you their viceroy, and you will be the ruler of the Ocean. Kingdoms will fall at your feet, and millions whose lives are saved will call you blessed. Sail westward, Columbus, my son, a voyage easily within the reach of your ships. The winds of the south will carry you west, and then the winds farther to the north will return you easily to Europe. Let the name of Christ be heard in these nations, and you will save your own soul along with theirs. Take a solemn oath that you will make this voyage, and after many obstacles you will succeed. But do not break this oath, or it will be better for the men of Sodom than for you in the day of judgment. No greater mission has ever been given to mortal man than the one I give to you, and whatever honors you receive on earth will be multiplied a thousandfold in heaven. But if you fail, the consequences to you and all of Christianity will be terrible beyond your imagining. Now take the oath, in the name of the Father, the Son and the Holy Spirit.''

Columbus struggled back up to his knees. "The Father, the Son, and the Holy Spirit," he murmured.

"I have sent a woman to you, to nurse you back to health. When your strength is restored to you, you must begin your mission in my name. Tell no one that I have spoken to you—it is not my will that you perish like the prophets of old, and if you say that I have spoken to you the priests will surely burn you as a heretic. You must persuade others to help you undertake this great voyage for its own sake, and not because I have commanded it. I care not whether they do it for gold or for fame or for love of me, just so they fulfill this mission. Just so you fulfill it. You. Carry out my mission.''

The image faded, and was gone. Almost weeping with exhaustion and glorious hope, Cristoforo—no, he was Columbus now, God had called him Columbus, his name in Latin, the language of the Church—Columbus waited in the sand. And, as the vision had promised, within minutes a woman came and, seeing him, immediately ran for help. Before night had fully come, he was being carried in the strong arms of fishermen to the village of Lagos, where gentle hands put wine to his lips and took his salt- and sand-caked clothing from him and bathed the salt from his chafed skin. Thus am I newly baptized, thought Columbus, born again on the mission of the Holy Trinity.

He uttered no word of what had transpired on the beach, but already his mind churned with thoughts of what he had to do. The great kingdoms of the east—immediately he thought of the tales of Marco Polo, of the Indies, of Cathay, of Cipango. Only to reach them he would not sail east, nor south along the coast of Africa as the Portuguese were said to be doing. No, he would sail west. But how would he get a ship? Not in Genova. Not after the ship he had been entrusted with was sunk. Besides, the ships of Genova were not fast enough, and they wallowed too low in the open water of the ocean.

God had brought him to the Portuguese shore, and the Portuguese were the great sailors, the daring explorers of the world. Would he not be the viceroy of kings? He would find a way to win the sponsorship of the King of Portugal. And if not him, then another king, or some other man and not a king at all. He would succeed, for God was with him.

Diko stopped the playback. "Do you want to see it again?" she asked.

"We'll want to see it many times," said Tagiri. "But not at this moment."

"That was not God," said Kemal.

"I hope not," said Hassan. "I didn't like seeing that Christian trinity. I found it—disappointing."

"Show this anywhere in the Muslim world," said Kemal, "and the rioting would not stop until every Pastwatch installation within their reach was destroyed."

"As you said, Kemal," said Tagiri, "it was not God. Because this vision was not visible to Columbus alone. All the other great visions of history have been utterly subjective. This one we saw, but not on the Tempoview. Only the TruSite II was able to detect it, and we already know that when the TruSite II is used, it can cause people in the past to see those who are watching."

"One of us? That message was sent by Pastwatch?" asked Kemal, already angry at the thought of one of them meddling with history.

"Not one of *us*," said Diko. "*We* live in the world in which Columbus sailed west and brought Europe to destroy or dominate all of America. In the hours since I saw this, I realized: This vision created our time. We already know that Columbus's voyage changed everything. Not just because he reached the West Indies, but because when he returned he was full of absolutely believable stories of things he had *not* seen. Of gold, of great kingdoms. And now we now why. He had sailed west at the command of God, and God had told him he would find these things. So he had to report finding them, he had to *believe* that gold and great kingdoms were there to be found, even though he had no evidence for them, because God had told him they were there.''

"If not one of us, then who did this?" asked Hassan.

Kemal laughed nastily. "It *was* one of us, obviously. Or rather, one of *you.*"

"Are you saying we created this as a hoax?" said Tagiri.

"Not at all," said Kemal. "But look at you. You are the people in Pastwatch who are determined to reach back into the past and make things better. So let's say that in another version of history, another group within a previous iteration of Pastwatch discovered they could change the past, and they did it. Let's say that they decided that the most terrible event in all of history was the last crusade, the one led by the son of a Genovese weaver. Why not? In that history, Columbus turned his unrelenting ambition toward the goal he had right *before* this vision. He comes to shore and interprets his survival as God's favor. He pursues the crusade to liberate Constantinople with the same charm, the same relentlessness that we have seen in him on his other mission. Eventually he leads an army in a bloody war against the Turk. What if he wins? What if he destroys the Seljuk Turks, and then sweeps on into all the Muslim lands, wreaking blood and carnage in the normal European Christian manner? The great Muslim civilization might be destroyed, and with it who knows what treasures of knowledge. What if Columbus's crusade was seen as the worst event in all of history—and the people of Pastwatch decided, as you have, that they *must* make things better? The result is *our* history. The devastation of the Americas. And the world is dominated by Europe all the same."

The others looked at him, unable to think of anything to say.

"Who is to say that the change these people made didn't end up with a worse result than the events they tried to avoid?" Kemal grinned at them wickedly. "The arrogance of those who wish to play God. And that's exactly what they did, isn't it? They played God. The Trinity, to be exact. The dove was such a nice touch. Yes, by all means, look at this scene a thousand times. And every time you see those poor actors pretending to be the Trinity, fooling Columbus into turning away from his crusade and embarking on a

westward voyage that devastated a world, I hope you see yourselves. It was people just like you who caused all that suffering."

Hassan took a step toward Kemal, but Tagiri interposed herself
between them. "Perhaps you're right, Kemal," she said. "But perhaps not. For one thing, I don't think their purpose was just to turn
Columbus away from his crusade. For that, all they would have
needed to do was command him to abandon the idea. And they
said that if he failed, the consequences would be terrible *for Christianity*. A far cry from trying to undo the Christian conquest of the
Muslim world."

"They could easily have been lying," said Kemal. "Telling him
what they thought he needed to hear to get him to act as they
wanted."

"Perhaps," said Tagiri. "But I think they were doing something else. There was something else that would have happened if
Columbus had not received this vision. And we must find out what
it was."

"How can we find out what *would* have happened?" asked
Diko.

Tagiri smiled nastily at Kemal. "I know one man of unflagging
persistence and great wisdom and quick judgment. He is just the
man to undertake the project of determining what it was that this
vision was meant to avoid, or what it was meant to accomplish. For
some reason the people of that other future determined to send
Columbus west. Someone must head the project of finding out why.
And you, Kemal, you're doing nothing productive at all, are you?
Your great days are behind you, and now you're reduced to going
about telling other people that *their* dreams are not worth accomplishing."

For a moment it seemed that Kemal might strike her, so cruel
was her assessment of him. But he did not raise his hand, and after
a long moment he turned and left the room.

"Is he right, Mother?" asked Diko.

"More to the point," said Hassan, "will he make trouble for
us?"

"I think he'll head the project of finding out what would have
happened," said Tagiri. "I think the problem will take hold of him
and won't let go and he'll end up working with us."

"Oh good," murmured someone dryly, and they all laughed.

"Kemal as an enemy is formidable, but Kemal as a friend is irreplaceable," said Tagiri. "He found Atlantis, didn't he, when no one believed it even needed to be discovered? He found the great flood. He found Yewesweder. And if anyone can, he'll find what history would have been, or at least a plausible scenario. And we'll be glad to be working with him." She grinned. "We mad people, we're stubborn and unreasonable and impossible to deal with, but there is a certain breed of willing victim that chooses to work with us anyway."

The others laughed, but few of them thought that Kemal was anything like their beloved Tagiri.

"And I think we've all missed one of the biggest points of all in Diko's great discovery. Yes, Diko, *great*." Tagiri looked around at them. "Can't you see what it is?"

"Of course," said Hassan. "Seeing that little performance by actors pretending to be the Trinity lets us know one fact beyond doubting: We *can* reach back into the past. If they can send a vision, a deliberately controlled vision, then so can we."

"And maybe," said Tagiri, "maybe we can do better."

6

Evidence

According to the Popul Vuh, the holy book of the Mayan people, Xpiyacoc and Xmucane gave birth to two sons, named One Hunahpu and Seven Hunahpu. One Hunahpu grew to be a man, and he married, and his wife, Xbaquiyalo, gave birth to two sons, One Monkey and One Artisan. Seven Hunahpu never grew up; before he could become a man he and his brother were sacrificed at the ball court when they lost to One and Seven Death. Then One Hunahpu's head was put in the crotch of a calabash tree, which had never before borne fruit. And when it did bear, the fruit looked like a head, and One Hunahpu's head came to look like the fruit, so they were the same.

Then a young virgin named Blood Woman came to the ball court of sacrifice to see the tree, and there she spoke to the head of One Hunahpu, and the head of One Hunahpu spoke to her. When she touched the bone of his head, his spittle came out onto her hand, and soon she conceived a child. Seven Hunahpu consented to this, and so he was also the father of what filled her belly.

Blood Woman refused to tell her father how the child came to be in her womb, since it was forbidden to go to the calabash tree where One Hunahpu's head had been perched. Disgusted that she had conceived a bastard, her father sent her away to be sacrificed. But to save her life, she told the Military Keepers of the Mat, who were sent to kill her, that the child in her came from One Hunahpu's head. Then they didn't want to kill her, but they had to bring her heart back to show her father, Blood Gatherer. So Blood Woman fooled her father by filling a bowl with the red sap of the croton tree, which congealed to look like a bloody heart. All the gods of Xibalba were fooled by her false heart.

Blood Woman went to the house of One Hunahpu's widow, Xbaquiyalo, to bear her child. When the child was born, it was two children, two sons, whom she named Hunahpu and Xbalanque. Xbaquiyalo didn't like the noise the babies made, and she had them thrown out of the house. Her sons, One Monkey and One Artisan, had no wish for new brothers, so they put them out on an anthill. When the babies didn't die there, the older brothers put them in brambles, but still they thrived. The hatred between the older brothers and the younger brothers continued through all the years as the babies grew to be men.

The older brothers were flutists, singers, artists, makers, and knowers. Above all, they were knowers. They knew when their brothers were born exactly who and what they were, and what they would become, but out of jealousy they told no one. So it was justice when Hunahpu and Xbalanque tricked them into climbing a tree and trapped them there, where the two older brothers turned into monkeys and never touched the ground again. Then Hunahpu and Xbalanque, great warriors and ball players, went to contest the quarrel between their fathers, One and Seven Hunahpu, and the gods of Xibalba.

At the end of the game, Xbalanque was forced to sacrifice his brother Hunahpu. He wrapped his brother's heart in a leaf, and then he danced alone in the ball court until he cried out his brother's name and Hunahpu rose up from the dead and took his place beside him. Seeing this, their two opponents in the game, the great lords One and Seven Death, demanded that they, too, be sacrificed. So Hunahpu and Xbalanque took the heart from One Death; but he didn't rise from the dead. Seeing this, Seven Death was terrified and begged to be released from his sacrifice. Thus, in shame, his heart was taken without courage and without consent. And this was how Hunahpu and Xbalanque avenged their fathers, One and Seven Hunahpu, and broke the great power of the lords of Xibalba.

Thus it says in the Popol Vuh.

When a third son was born to Dolores de Cristo Matamoro, she remembered her studies in Mayan culture when she was growing up back in Tekax in the Yucatán, and since she was unsure who the father of this child was, she named him for Hunahpu. If she had had yet another son, no doubt she would have named him Xbalanque, but instead when Hunahpu was still a toddler she was jostled off a platform in the station at San Andrés Tuxtla and the train mangled her.

Hunahpu Matamoro had nothing of her, really, but the name she gave him, and perhaps that was what steered him into his obsession with the past of his people. His older brothers became normal men of San Andrés Tuxtla: Pedro became a policeman and Josemaria became a priest. But Hunahpu studied the history of the Maya, of the Mexica, of the Toltecs, of the Zapotecs, of the Olmecs, the great nations of Mesoamerica, and when his test scores proved high enough on his second try, he was admitted to Pastwatch and began his studies in earnest.

This was his project from the beginning: to find out what would have happened in Mesoamerica if the Spanish had not come. Unlike Tagiri, whose file had a silver tag that meant her oddities were to be indulged, Hunahpu met resistance every step of the way. "Pastwatch watches the past," he was told again and again. "We don't speculate on what might have been if the past had not happened the way it happened. There's no way to test it, and it would have no value even if you got it right."

But despite the resistance, Hunahpu continued. No team of coworkers grew up around him. In fact he belonged to another team, one that was researching the Zapotecan cultures of the northern coast of the Isthmus of Tehuantepec in the years prior to the coming of the Spanish. He was assigned to this team because it was the legitimate project that came closest to Hunahpu's interest. His supervisors were well aware that he spent at least as much time on his speculative research as on the observations that would contribute to real knowledge. They were patient. They hoped he would grow out of his obsession with trying to know the unknowable, if they left him long enough. As long as his work on the Zapotec project remained adequate—which it did, barely.

Then came the news of the discovery of the Intervention. A Pastwatch from another future had sent a vision to Columbus, which turned him away from his dream of leading a crusade to liberate Constantinople and brought him, eventually, to America. It was astonishing; to an Indie like Hunahpu it was also appalling. How dared they! For he knew at once what it was that the Interveners had been trying to avoid, and it wasn't the Christian conquest of Islam.

Rumors began circulating a few weeks later, and repetition made them believable. The great Kemal was setting up a new project. For the first time, Pastwatch was trying to extrapolate from the past what *would* have happened in the future if a particular event hadn't happened. Why are they forming a project to study this, Hunahpu wondered. He knew that he could answer all of Kemal's questions in a moment. He knew that if anyone in Kemal's new project read a single paper he had written and posted on the nets, they would realize that the answer was right before them, the work was already laid out, it was just a matter of applying a few man-years to filling in the details.

Hunahpu waited for Kemal to write to him, or for one of the Pastwatch supervisors to recommend that Kemal look into Hunahpu's research, or even—as must inevitably happen—for Hunahpu's reassignment to Kemal's project. But the reassignment didn't come, the letter didn't come, and Hunahpu's superiors seemed not to realize that Kemal's most valuable assistant would be this sluggish young Maya who had worked dispiritedly on their tedious data-gathering project.

That was when Hunahpu realized that it wasn't just the resistance of others that he faced: It was their disdain as well. His work was so despised that no one thought of it at all, no rumors of it had circulated, and when he looked into it he found out that none of the papers he had posted on the networks had been downloaded and read, not one, not once.

But it was not in Hunahpu's nature to despair. Instead he

grimly redoubled his efforts, knowing that the only way to surmount the barrier of contempt was to produce a body of evidence so compelling that Kemal would be forced to respect it. And if he had to, Hunahpu would carry that evidence to Kemal directly, bypassing all the regular channels, the way that Kemal had come to Tagiri in that already-legendary meeting. Of course, there was a difference. Kemal had come as a famous man, with known achievements, so that he was courteously received even when his message was unwelcome. Hunahpu had no achievements whatsoever, or none that were recognized by anybody, and so it was unlikely that Kemal would ever agree to see him or look at his work. Yet this did not stop him. Hunahpu continued, patiently assembling evidence and writing careful analyses of what he had found and loathing every moment he had to spend recording the details of the building of seagoing ships among the coastal Zapotecs during the years from 1510 to 1524.

His older brothers, the policeman and the priest, who were not bastards and therefore always looked down on him, became worried about him. They came to see him at the Pastwatch station at San Andrés Tuxtla, where Hunahpu was allowed to use a conference room to meet with them, since there was no privacy in his cubicle. "You're never home," the policeman said. "I call and you never answer."

"I'm working," said Hunahpu.

"You don't look healthy," said the priest. "And when we spoke to your supervisor about you, she said you weren't very productive. Always working on your own useless projects."

"You asked my supervisor about me?" asked Hunahpu. He wasn't sure whether to be annoyed at the intrusion or pleased that his brothers had cared enough to check up on him.

"Well, actually, she came to us," said the policeman, who always told the truth even when it was slightly embarrassing. "She wanted to see if we could encourage you to abandon your foolish obsession with the lost future of the Indies."

Hunahpu looked at them sadly. "I can't," he said.

"We didn't think so," said the priest. "But when you're dropped from Pastwatch, what will you do? What are you qualified for?"

Don't think either of us has any money to help you,'' said the
policeman. ''Or even to feed you more than a few meals a week,
though you're welcome to that much, for our mother's sake.''

''Thank you,'' said Hunahpu. ''You've helped me clarify my
thinking.''

They got up to leave. The policeman, who was older and hadn't
beaten him up as a child half so often as the priest, stopped in the
doorway. His face was tinged with regret. ''You aren't going to
change a thing, are you?'' he said.

''Yes, I am,'' said Hunahpu. ''I'm going to hurry and finish
sooner. Before I'm dropped from Pastwatch.''

The policeman shook his head. ''Why do you have to be so . . .
Indie?''

Hunahpu didn't understand the question for a moment. ''Because I *am*.''

''So are we, Hunahpu.''

''You? Josemaria and Pedro?''

''So our names are Spanish.''

''And your veins are thinned with Spanish blood, and you live
with Spanish jobs in Spanish cities.''

''Thinned?'' asked the policeman. ''Our veins are—''

''Whoever my father was,'' said Hunahpu, ''he was Maya, like
Mother.''

The policeman's face darkened. ''I see that you wish not to be
my brother.''

''I'm proud to be your brother,'' said Hunahpu, dismayed at
the way his words had been taken. ''I have no quarrel with you.
But I also have to know what my people—our people—would have
been without the Spanish.''

The priest reappeared in the doorway behind the policeman.
''They would have been bloody-handed human sacrificers, tortur-
ers, and self-mutilators who never heard the name of Christ.''

''Thank you for caring enough to come to me,'' said Hunahpu.
''I'll be fine.''

''Come to my house for dinner,'' said the policeman.

''Thank you. Another day I will.''

His brothers left, and Hunahpu turned to his computer and
addressed a message to Kemal. There was no chance that Kemal

would read it—there were too many thousands of people on the Pastwatch net for a man like Kemal to pay attention to what would end up as a third-tier message from an obscure data-collector on the Zapotec project. Yet he had to get through, somehow, or his work would come to nothing. So he wrote the most provocative message he could think of, and then sent it to everybody involved in the whole Columbus project, hoping that one of them would glance at third-tier e-mail and be intrigued enough to bring his words to the attention of Kemal.

This was his message:

Kemal: Columbus was chosen because he was the greatest man of his age, the one who broke the back of Islam. He was sent westward in order to prevent the worst calamity in all of human history: The Tlaxcalan conquest of Europe. I can prove it. My public papers have been posted and ignored, as surely as yours would have been if you had not found evidence of Atlantis in the old TruSite I weather recordings. There ARE no recordings of the Tlaxcalan conquest of Europe, but the proof is still there. Talk to me and save yourself years of work. Ignore me and I will go away.

—Hunahpu Matamoros

Columbus was not proud of the reason he had married Felipa. He had known from the moment he arrived that as a foreign merchant in Lisbon he would get no closer to his goal. There was a colony of Genovese merchants in Lisbon, and Columbus immediately became involved in their traffic. In the winter of 1476 he joined a convoy that sailed north to Flanders, to England, and on to Iceland. It was less than a year since he had set out on a similar voyage full of high hopes and expectations; now that he actually found himself in those ports, he could hardly concentrate on the business that brought him there. What good was it for him to be involved in the merchant trade among the cities of Europe? God had a higher work for him to do. The result was that, while he made some money on these voyages, he did not distinguish himself. Only in Iceland, where he heard sailors' tales of lands not all that far to the west that had once held flourishing colonies of Northmen, did he learn anything that seemed useful to him, but even then, he could not help but remember that God had told him to use a southern route for sailing west, and only return in the north. These lands the Icelanders knew of were not the great kingdoms of the east, that much was obvious.

Somehow he had to put together an expedition to explore the ocean to the west. Several of his trading voyages took him to the Azores and Madeira—the Portuguese would never let a foreigner go beyond that point, into African waters, but they were welcome to come to Madeira to buy African gold and ivory, or to the Azores to take on supplies at highly inflated prices. Columbus knew from his contacts in those places that great expeditions passed through Madeira every few months, bound for Africa. Columbus knew that Africa led nowhere useful—but he coveted the fleets. Somehow he had to win command of one of them, bound westward instead of southward. And yet what hope did he have of ever achieving this?

At least in Genova his father had ties of loyalty to the Fieschi, which had been an exploitable connection. In Portugal, all navigation, all expeditions were under the direct control of the king. The only way to get ships and sailors and funding for a voyage of exploration was by appealing to the king, and as a Genovese and a commoner there was scant hope of this.

Since he had been born with no family connections in Portugal, there was only one way to acquire them. And marriage into a well-connected family, when he had neither fortune nor prospects, was a difficult project indeed. He needed a family on the fringes of nobility, and one that was not on the way up. A rising family would be looking to improve its station by marrying above themselves; a sinking family, especially a junior branch with unlikely daughters and little fortune, might look upon such a foreign adventurer as Columbus with—well, not favor, exactly, but at least tolerance. Or perhaps resignation.

Whether because of his near death in the ocean or because God wished him to have a more distinguished appearance, Columbus found his red hair rapidly turning white. Since he was still youthful in the face and vigorous in the body, the whitening hair turned many heads his way. Whenever he wasn't voyaging on business, attempting to make headway in a trade that was always tilted in favor of the native Portuguese, he made it a point to attend All

Saints' Church, where the marriageable ladies of families not rich enough to have their own household priest in attendance were brought forth, heavily supervised, to hear mass, take communion, and make confession.

It was there that he saw Felipa, or rather made sure that she saw *him*. He had made discreet inquiries about several young ladies, and learned much that was promising about her. Her father, Governor Perestrello, had been a man of some distinction and influence, with a tenuous claim on nobility that no one contested during his lifetime because he had been one of the young seafarers trained by Prince Henry the Navigator and had taken part with distinction in the conquest of Madeira. As a reward, he had been made governor of the small island of Porto Santo, a nearly waterless place of little value except for the prestige it gave him back in Lisbon. Now he was dead, but he was not forgotten, and the man who married his daughter would be able to meet seafarers and make contacts in court that could eventually bring him before the king.

Felipa's brother was still governor of the island, and Felipa's mother, Dona Moniz, ruled over the family—including the brother— with an iron hand. It was she, not Felipa, whom Columbus had to impress; but first he had to catch Felipa's eye. It was not hard to do. The story of Columbus's long swim to shore after the famous battle between the Genovese merchant fleet and the French pirate Coullon was often told. Columbus made it a point to deny any heroism. "All I did was throw pots and set ships afire, including my own. Braver and better men than I fought and died. And then . . . I swam. If the sharks had thought I looked appetizing I wouldn't be here. Is this a hero?" But such self-deprecation in a society much given to boasting was exactly the pose that he knew he had to take. People love to hear the brag of the local boy, because they want him to be great, but the foreigner must deny that he has any outstanding virtue—this is what will endear him to the locals.

It worked well enough. Felipa had heard of him, and in church he caught her looking at him and bowed. She blushed and turned away. A rather homely girl. Her father was a warrior and her mother was built like a fortress—the daughter had her father's fierceness and her mother's formidable thickness. Yet there was a glint of grace and humor in her smile when she glanced back at

him, once the obligatory blush had passed. She knew it was a game
they were playing, and she didn't mind. After all, she was not a
prime prospect, and if the man who wooed her was an ambitious
Genovese who wanted to use her family connections, how was that
different from the daughters of more fortunate families who were
wooed by ambitious lords who wanted to use their families' wealth?
A woman of rank could hardly expect to be married for her own
virtues—those had only a minor effect on the asking price, as long
as she was a virgin, and *that* family asset, at least, had been well
protected.

Glances in church led to a call on the Perestrello household,
where Dona Moniz received him five times before agreeing to let
him meet Felipa, and then only after the marriage was all but
agreed upon. It was established that Columbus would have to give
up openly practicing a trade—his voyages could no longer be so
obviously commercial, and his brother Bartholomew, who had
joined him from Genova, would become the proprietor of the chart
shop that Columbus had started. Columbus would merely be a gentleman who occasionally stopped by to advise his tradesman
brother. This suited both Columbus and Bartholomew.

At last Columbus met Felipa, and not long afterward they were
married. Dona Moniz knew perfectly well what this Genovese adventurer was after, or thought she did, and she was quite certain
that no sooner would he have gained entrée into courtly society than
he would immediately begin to establish liaisons with prettier—and
richer—mistresses, angling for ever more advantageous connections
in court. She had seen his type a thousand times before, and she
saw through him. So, just before the wedding, she surprised everyone by announcing that her son, the governor of Porto Santo, had
invited Felipa and her new husband to come live with him on the
island. And Dona Moniz herself would of course come with them,
since there was no reason for her to stay in Lisbon when her dear
daughter Felipa and her precious son the governor—her *whole family,* and never mind the other married daughters—were hundreds
of miles away out in the Atlantic Ocean. Besides, the Madeira Islands had a warmer and more healthful climate.

Felipa thought it was a wonderful idea, of course—she had always loved the island—but to Dona Moniz's surprise, Columbus

also accepted the invitation with enthusiasm. He managed to hide his amusement at her obvious discomfiture. If he *wanted* to go, then there must be something wrong with the plan—he knew that was how she was thinking. But that was because she had no notion of what mattered to him. He was in the service of God, and while eventually he would have to present himself in court to win approval for a westward voyage, it would be years before he was prepared to make his case. He needed experience; he needed charts and books; he needed time to think and plan. Poor Dona Moniz—she didn't realize that Porto Santo put him directly on the sailing route of the Portuguese expeditions along the African coast. They all put in at Madeira, and there Columbus would be able to learn much about how to lead expeditions, how to chart unknown territories, how to navigate long distances in unknown seas. Old Perestrello, Felipa's late father, had kept a small but valuable library at Porto Santo, and Columbus would have access to it. Thus, if he could learn some of the Portuguese skills in navigation, if God led him to hidden information in his studies of the old writings, he might learn something encouraging about his coming voyage to the west.

The voyage was brutal for Felipa. She had never been seasick before, and by the time they arrived at Porto Santo, Dona Moniz was sure that she and Columbus had already conceived a child. Sure enough, nine months later Diego was born. Felipa took a long time recovering from the pregnancy and birth, but as soon as she was strong enough she devoted herself to the child. Her mother viewed this with some distaste, since there were nurses for that kind of thing, but she could hardly complain, for it soon became obvious that Diego was all that Felipa had; her husband did not seem hungry for her company. Indeed, he seemed eager to get off the island at every opportunity—but *not* for the sake of getting to court. Instead, he kept begging for chances to get onto a ship sailing along the African coast.

The more he begged, the less likely it seemed that he would get a chance to join a voyage. He was, after all, Genovese, and it occurred to more than one ship's captain that Columbus might have married into a sailing family as a ploy to learn the African coast and then return to Genova and bring Italian ships into competition with the Portuguese. That would be intolerable, of course. So there was never a question of Columbus getting what he *really* wanted.

With her husband so frustrated, Felipa began to pressure her mother to do something for her Cristovão. He loves the sea, Felipa said. He dreams of great voyages. Can't you do something for him?

So she brought her son-in-law into her late husband's library and opened for him the boxes of charts and maps, the cases of precious books. Columbus's gratitude was palpable. For the first time it occurred to her that perhaps he was sincere—that he had little interest in the African coast, that it was navigation that inspired him, voyaging for its own sake that he longed for.

Columbus began to spend almost every waking moment poring over the books and charts. Of course there were no charts for the western ocean, for no one who had sailed beyond the Azores or the Canaries or the Cape Verde Islands ever returned. Columbus learned, though, that the Portuguese voyagers had disdained to hug the coast of Africa. Instead, they sailed far out to sea, using better winds and deeper waters until their instruments told them that they had sailed as far south as the last voyage had reached. Then they would sail landward, eastward, hoping that this time they were farther south than the southernmost tip of Africa, that they would find a route leading eastward to India. It was that deep-sea sailing that had first brought Portuguese sailors to Madeira and then to the Cape Verde Islands. Some adventurers of the time had imagined that there might be chains of islands stretching farther to the west, and had sailed to see, but such voyages always ended in either disappointment or tragedy, and no one believed anymore that there were more islands to the west or south.

But Columbus could not disregard the records of old rumors that once had led sailors to search for westward islands. He devoured the rumors of a dead sailor washed ashore in the Azores or Canaries or Cape Verdes, a waterlogged chart tucked into his clothing showing western islands reached before his ship sank, the stories of floating logs from unknown species of tree, of flocks of land birds far away to the south or west, of corpses of drowned men with rounder faces than any seen in Europe, dark and yet not as black of skin as Africans, either. These all dated from an earlier time, and Columbus knew they represented the wishful thinking of a brief era. But he knew what none of them could know—that God intended Columbus to reach the great kingdoms of the east by sailing west, which meant that perhaps these rumors were not all wishful thinking, that perhaps they were true.

Even if they were, however, they would be unconvincing to those who would decide whether to fund a westward expedition. To persuade the king would mean first persuading the learned men of his court, and that would require serious evidence, not sailors' lore. For that purpose the real treasure of Porto Santo were the books, for Perestrello had loved the study of geography, and he had Latin translations of Ptolemy.

Ptolemy was cold comfort for Columbus—he had it that from the westernmost tip of Europe to the easternmost tip of Asia was 180 degrees, half the circumference of the earth. Such a voyage over open ocean would be hopeless. No ship could carry enough supplies or keep them fresh long enough to cover even a quarter of that distance.

Yet God had told him that he could reach the Orient by sailing west. Therefore Ptolemy must be wrong, and not just slightly wrong, either. He must be drastically, hopelessly wrong. And Columbus had to find a way to prove it, so that a king would allow him to lead ships to the west to fulfill the will of God.

It would be simpler, he said in his silent prayers to the Holy Trinity, if you sent an angel to tell the King of Portugal. Why did you choose *me?* No one will listen to me.

But God didn't answer him, and so Columbus continued to think and study and try to figure out how to prove what he knew must be true and yet no one had ever guessed—that the world was much, much smaller, the west and east much closer together than any of the ancients had ever believed. And since the only authorities that the scholars would accept were the books written by the ancients, Columbus would have to find, somewhere, ancient writers who had discovered what Columbus knew had to be the truth about the world's size. He found some useful ideas in Cardinal d'Ailly's *Imago Mundi,* a compendium of the works of ancient writers, where he learned that Marinus of Tyre had estimated that the great landmass of the world was not 180 degrees, but 225, leaving the ocean to take up only 135 degrees. That was still much too far, but it was promising. Never mind that Ptolemy lived and wrote *after* Marinus of Tyre, that he had examined Marinus's figures and refuted them. Marinus offered a picture of the world that helped build Columbus's case for sailing west, and so Marinus was the better authority. There were also helpful references from Aristotle, Seneca, and Pliny.

Then he realized that these ancient writers had been unaware of Marco Polo's discoveries on his journey to Cathay. Add 28 degrees of land for *his* findings, and then add another 30 degrees to account for the distance between Cathay and the island nation of Cipangu, and there were only 77 degrees of ocean left to cross. Then subtract another 9 degrees by starting his own voyage in the Canaries, the southwestern islands that seemed the likeliest jumping-off point for the sort of voyage God had commanded, and now Columbus's fleet would only have to cross 68 degrees of ocean.

It was still too far. But surely there were errors in Marco Polo's account, in the calculations of the ancients. Take off another 8 degrees, round it down to a mere 60! Yet it was still impossibly far. One-sixth of the Earth's circumference between the Canaries and Cipangu, and yet that still meant a voyage of more than 3,000 miles without a port of call. Bend or twist them as he might, Columbus couldn't make the writings of the ancients support what he knew to be true: that it was a matter of days or at most weeks to sail from Europe to the great kingdoms of the east. There had to be more information. Another writer, perhaps. Or some fact that he had overlooked. Something that would persuade the scholars of Lisbon to respect his request and recommend to King João that he give Columbus command of an expedition.

Through all of this, Felipa was obviously baffled and frustrated. Columbus was vaguely aware that she wanted more of his time and thought, but he couldn't concentrate on the silly things that interested her, not when God had set such a Herculean labor for him to accomplish. He hadn't married her to play at housekeeping, and he said so. He had great works to accomplish. But he couldn't explain what that great work was, or who had given it to him to accomplish, because he had been forbidden to tell. So he watched Felipa grow more and more hurt even as he grew more and more impatient with her obvious hunger for his company.

Felipa had been warned countless times that men were demanding and unfaithful, and she was prepared for that. But what was wrong with her husband? She was the only lady available to him, and Diego should have a brother or sister, but Columbus hardly seemed to want her. "He cares for nothing but charts and maps and old books," she complained to her mother. "That and meeting pilots and navigators and men who have ever had or might someday have the ear of the king."

At first Dona Moniz counseled her to be patient, that the insatiable lusts of men would eventually conquer Columbus's seeming indifference. But when that did not happen, she eventually gave her consent for them to move from isolated Porto Santo to a house the family owned on Funchal, the largest city on the main island of the Madeiras. The theory was that if Columbus could satisfy more of his hunger for the sea, he might, in his satisfaction, turn to Felipa.

Instead he turned even more devotedly to the sea, until he became one of the best-known men in the port of Funchal. No ship came into port without Columbus soon finding his way aboard, befriending captains and navigators, noticing the amounts of supplies taken aboard and how long they were expected to last, noticing, in fact, *everything*.

"If he's a spy," said one ship's captain to Dona Moniz, the widow of his old friend Perestrello, "then he's a clumsy one indeed, since he gathers his information so openly, so eagerly. I think he simply loves the sea and wishes he had been born Portuguese so he could join with the great expeditions."

"But he wasn't, and so he can't," said Dona Moniz. "Why can't he be content? He has a good life with my daughter, or he would have, if he simply paid attention to her."

The old fellow merely laughed. "When a man gets the sea in his blood, what does a woman have to offer him? What is a child? The wind is his woman, the birds his children. Why do you keep him here on these islands? He is surrounded by the sea all the time, and yet can't sail free. He's Genovese, and so he won't get to sail into the new African waters. But why not let him—no, *help* him—join with merchant voyages to other places?"

"I see that you actually like this white-haired man who makes my daughter feel like a widow."

"A widow? Perhaps a half-widow. For there are three types of men in the world—the living, the dead, and sailors. You should remember. Your husband was one of us."

"But he gave up the sea and stayed home."

"And died," said the gentleman, with brutal candor. "Your Felipa has a son, hasn't she? So now let her husband go out and earn the fortune that he will pass on to that grandson of yours someday. It's plain that you're killing him by keeping him here."

So it was that two years after coming to the Madeira Islands, Dona Moniz at last suggested that it was time for them to return to Lisbon. Columbus packed up his father-in-law's books and charts and eagerly prepared for the voyage. Yet he knew even as he did so that for Felipa there was far less hope. The voyage to Porto Santo had been a dreadful one for her, even filled with hope in her new marriage as she was at the time. Now she would not be pregnant— but she had also despaired of finding happiness with Columbus. What made it all the more unbearable was that the more aloof he became, the more hopelessly she loved him. She could hear him speaking to other men and his voice, his passion, his manner were captivating; she watched him poring over books that she could barely understand and she marveled at the brilliance of his mind. He wrote in the margins of the books—he dared to add his words to the words of the ancients! He dwelt in a world that she could never enter, and yet she longed to. Take me with you into these strange places, she said to him silently. But the silence with which he answered her was not filled with longing, or if it was, his long- ings did not include her or little Diego. So she knew that the voyage back to Lisbon would not bring her closer to her husband, or far- ther. She would never touch him, not really. She had his child, but the more she hungered for the man himself, the more she reached out to him, the more he would push her away; and yet if she did not reach out, he would ignore her completely; there was no path she could see that would lead her to happiness.

Columbus saw this in her. He was not as blind to her needs as she supposed. He simply had no time to make her happy. If she could have been content to share his bed and let him be with her whenever he was weary of his study, then he might have been able to give her something. But she demanded so much more: that he be interested in—no, delighted about—every clever childish thing that the incomprehensible Diego did! That he care about the gossip of women, that he admire her needlework, that he care what fabrics she had chosen for her new gown, that he intervene with a servant who was being lazy and impertinent. He knew that if he took interest in these things it would make her happy—but it would also encourage her to bring even more of this kind of nonsense to distract him, and he simply had no time for it. So he turned away, not wishing to hurt her and yet hurting her all the same, because he had to find a way to accomplish what God had given him to do.

During the voyage back to Portugal, Felipa was not so terribly seasick, but she nevertheless stayed in her bed, bleakly staring at the walls of her tiny cabin. And from this sickness of heart she would never recover. Even in Lisbon, where Dona Moniz hoped that her old friends would cheer her up, Felipa only rarely consented to go out. Instead she devoted herself to little Diego and spent the rest of her time haunting her own house. When Columbus was away on a voyage or on business in the city, she wandered about as if searching for him; when he was there, she would spend days working up the courage to try to engage him in conversation. Whether he politely listened or curtly asked her to let him alone so he could concentrate on his work, the end was the same. She went to her bed and wept, for she was not part of his life at all, and she knew no way to enter it, and so she loved him all the more desperately, and knew all the more surely that it was some failing in her that made her unlovable to her husband.

The worst agony was when he brought her along to some musical performance or to mass or to dine at court, for she knew that the only reason he was accepted among the aristocrats of Lisbon was because he was married to her, and so he needed her on these occasions and they both had to act as though they were husband and wife, and all the while she could barely keep herself from bursting into tears and screaming to everyone that her husband did not love her, that he slept with her perhaps once in a week, twice in a month, and that even that was without genuine affection. If she had ever allowed herself such an outburst, she might have been surprised at how surprised the other women would have been—not that she had such a relationship with her husband, but that she found anything wrong with it. It was very nearly the relationship that most of them had with their husbands. Women and men lived in separate worlds; they met only on the bed to produce heirs and on public occasions to enhance each other's status in the world. Why was she so upset about this? Why didn't she simply live as they did, a pleasant life of ease among other women, occasionally indulging their children and always relying upon servants to make things go easily?

The answer was, of course, that none of their husbands was Cristovão. None of them burned with his inner fire. None of them had such a deep gravity of passion in his heart, drawing a woman ever closer, even though that deep well in him would drown her and never yield anything, never give off anything that might nourish her or slake her thirst for his love.

And Columbus, for his part, looked at Felipa as the years of marriage aged her, as her lips turned downward into a permanent frown, as she spent more and more of her time in bed with nameless illnesses, and he knew that he was somehow causing this, that he was harming her, and that there was nothing he could do about it, not if he was going to fulfil his mission in life.

Almost as soon as Columbus returned to Lisbon, he found the book that he was looking for. The geographic work of an Arab named Alfragano had been translated into Latin, and Columbus found in it the perfect tool to shrink those last 60 degrees to a reasonable voyaging distance. If Alfragano's calculations were assumed to be in Roman miles, then the 60 degrees of distance between the Canaries and Cipangu would amount to as little as 2,000 nautical miles at the latitudes he would be sailing. With reasonably favorable winds, which God would surely provide for him, the voyage could be made in as few as eight days; two weeks at the most.

He had his proofs now in terms the scholars would understand. He wouldn't come before them with nothing but his own faith in a vision he couldn't tell them about. Now he had the ancients on his side, and never mind that one of them was a Muslim, he could still build a case for his expedition.

At last his marriage to Felipa paid off. He used every contact he had made, and won the chance to present his ideas at court. He stood boldly before King João, knowing that God would touch his heart and make him understand that it was God's will that he mount this expedition with Columbus at its head. He laid out his maps, with all his calculations, showing Cipangu within easy reach, and Cathay but a short voyage beyond that. The scholars listened; the King listened. They asked questions. They mentioned the ancient authorities that contradicted Columbus's view of the size of the earth and the ratio of land to water, and Columbus answered them patiently and with confidence. This is the truth, he said. Until one of them said, "How do you *know* that Marinus is right and Ptolemy is wrong?"

Columbus answered, "Because if Ptolemy is right then this voyage would be impossible. But it is not impossible, it *will* succeed, and so I know that Ptolemy is wrong."

Even as he said it, he knew that it was not an answer that would persuade them. He knew, seeing their polite nods, their not-so-covert glances at the King, that their recommendation would be squarely against him. Well, he thought, I have done all I could. Now it is up to God. He thanked the King for his kindness, reaffirmed his certainty that this expedition would cover Portugal in glory and make it the greatest kingdom of Europe and bring Christianity to countless souls, and took his leave.

He took it as an encouraging sign that, as he waited for the King's answer, he was given permission to join a trading expedition to the African coast. It wasn't a voyage of exploration, so no great secrets of the Portuguese crown were being laid before him. Still, it was a sign of trust and favor that he was allowed to sail as far as the fortress of São Jorge at La Mina. The King is preparing me to lead an expedition by letting me become acquainted with the great achievements of Portuguese navigation.

Upon his return he eagerly awaited the King's answer, expecting to be told any day that he would be given the ships, the crew, the supplies that he needed.

The King said no.

Columbus was devastated. For days he hardly ate or slept. He did not know what to think. Wasn't this God's plan? Didn't God tell kings and princes what to do? How, then, could King João have refused him?

It was something I did wrong. I shouldn't have spent so much time trying to prove that the voyage was possible; I should have spent more time trying to help the King catch the vision of why the voyage was desirable, necessary. Why God wanted this to be achieved. I acted foolishly. I prepared insufficiently. I was unworthy. All the explanations he could think of left him spiraling downward into despair.

Felipa saw her husband suffering and she knew that in the one thing that she had ever provided him that he desired, she had failed. He had needed a connection at court, and the influence of her family name was not enough. Why, then, was he married to her? She was now an intolerable burden to him. She had nothing that he could possibly desire or need or love. When she brought five-year-old Diego to him, to try to cheer him up, he sent the boy away so gruffly that the child cried for an hour and refused to go to his father again. It was the last straw. Felipa knew that Columbus hated her now, and that she deserved his hatred, having given him nothing that he wanted.

She went to bed, turned her face to the wall, and soon became exactly as ill as she declared herself to be.

In her last days, Columbus became as solicitous of her as she had ever desired. But she knew in her heart that this did not mean that he loved her. Rather he was doing his duty, and when he talked to her of how sorry he was for his long neglect, she knew that this was said not because he wished her to live so he could do better in the future, but rather because he wanted her forgiveness so that his conscience could be free when at last her death freed him in every other way.

"You will have your greatness, Cristovão, one way or another," she said.

"And you'll be there beside me to see it, my Felipa," he said.

She wanted to believe it, or rather wanted to believe that he actually desired it, but she knew better. "I ask only this promise: Diego will inherit everything from you."

"Everything," said Columbus.

"No other sons," she said. "No other heirs."

"I promise," he said.

Soon afterward she died. Columbus held Diego's hand as they followed her coffin to the family tomb, and as they walked, side by side, he suddenly lifted up his son and held him in his arms and said, "You are all I have left of her. I treated your mother unfairly, Diego, and you as well, and I can't promise to do any better in the future. But I made her this promise, and I make it to you. All that I ever have, all that I ever achieve, every title, every bit of property, every honor, every scrap of fame, it will be yours."

Diego heard this and remembered it. His father loved him after all. And his father had loved his mother, too. And someday, if his father became great, Diego would be great after him. He wondered if that meant that someday he would own an island, the way Grandmother did. He wondered if it meant that someday he would sail a ship. He wondered if it meant that someday he would stand before kings. He wondered if it meant that his father would leave him now and he would never see him again.

The following spring, Columbus left Portugal and crossed the border into Spain. He took Diego to the Franciscan monastery of La Rábida, near Palos. "I was taught by Franciscan fathers in Genova," he told his son. "Learn well, become a scholar and a Christian and a gentleman. And I will be about the business of serving God and making our fortune in the process."

Columbus left him there, but he visited from time to time, and in his letters to the prior, Father Juan Perez, he never failed to mention Diego and ask after him. Many sons had less of their fathers than that, Diego knew. And a small part of his dear father was far greater than all the love and attention of many lesser men. Or so he told himself to stave off the humiliation of tears during the loneliness of those first months.

Columbus himself went on to the court of Spain, where he would present a much more carefully refined version of the same unprovable calculations that had failed in Portugal. This time, though, he would persist. Whatever Felipa had suffered, whatever Diego was suffering now, deprived of family and left among strangers in a strange place, it would all be justified. For in the end Columbus would succeed, and the triumph would be worth the price.

He would not fail, he was sure of it. Because even though he had no proof, he knew that he was right.

"I have no proof," said Hunahpu, "but I know that I'm right."

The woman on the other end of the line sounded young. Too young to be influential, surely, and yet she was the only one who had answered his message, and so he would have to speak to her as if she mattered because what other choice did he have?

"How do you know you're right without evidence?" she asked mildly.

"I didn't say I have no evidence. Just that there can never be *proof* of what would have happened."

"Fair enough," she answered.

"All I ask is a chance to present my evidence to Kemal."

"I can't guarantee you that," she said. "But you can come to Juba and present your evidence to me."

Come to Juba! As if he had an unlimited budget for travel, he who was on the verge of being dismissed from Pastwatch altogether. "I'm afraid that such a journey would be beyond my means," he said.

"Of course we'll pay for your travel," she said, "and you can stay here as our guest."

That startled him. How could someone so young have authority to promise him *that*? "Who did you say you were?"

"Diko," she said.

Now he remembered the name; why hadn't he made the connection in the first place? Though it was Kemal's project to which he was determined to contribute, it was not Kemal who had found the Intervention. "Are you the Diko who—"

"Yes," she said.

"Have you read my papers? The ones I've been posting and—"

"And which no one has paid the slightest attention to? Yes."

"And do you believe me?"

"I have questions for you," she said.

"And if you're satisfied with my answers?"

"Then I'll be very surprised," she said. "Everyone knows that the Aztec Empire was on the verge of collapse when Cortés arrived in the 1520s. Everyone also knows that there was no possibility of Mesoamerican technology rivaling European technology in any way. Your speculations about a Mesoamerican conquest of Europe are irresponsible and absurd.''

"And yet you called me.''

"I believe in leaving no stone unturned. You're a stone that nobody's turned yet, and so . . .''

"You're turning me.''

"Will you come?''

"Yes,'' he said. A faint hope was better than no response at all.

"Send copies of all pertinent files beforehand, so I can look them over on my own computer.''

"Most of them are already in the Pastwatch system,'' he said.

"Then send me your bibliography. When can you come? I need to request a leave of absence on your behalf so you can consult with us.''

"You can do that?''

"I can request it,'' she said.

"Tomorrow,'' he said.

"I can't read everything by tomorrow. Next week. Tuesday. But send me all the files and lists I need immediately.''

"And you'll request my leave of absence . . . when I send the files?''

"No, I'll request it in the next fifteen minutes. Nice talking to you. I hope you aren't a crackpot.''

"I'm not,'' he said. "Nice talking to you, too.''

She broke the connection.

An hour later, his supervisor came to see him. "What have you been doing?'' she demanded.

"What I've always been doing,'' he answered.

"I was in the middle of writing a recommendation that you be steered to another line of work,'' she said. "Then this comes in. A request from the Columbus project for your presence next week. Will I grant you a paid leave of absence.''

"It would be cheaper for you to fire me,'' he said, "but it'll be harder for me to help them in Juba if I lose my access to the Past-watch computer system.''

She looked at him with thinly veiled consternation. ''Are you telling me that you aren't a crazy, self-willed, time-wasting, don-key-headed fool after all?''

''No guarantees,'' he said. ''That may end up being the list that everybody agrees to.''

''No doubt,'' she said. ''But you've got your leave, and you can stay with us until it's over.''

''I hope it turns out to be worth the cost,'' he said.

''It will,'' she said. ''Your salary during this leave is coming out of their budget.'' She grinned at him. ''I actually do like you, you know,'' she pointed out. ''I just don't think you've caught the vision of what Pastwatch is all about.''

''I haven't,'' said Hanahpu. ''I want to change the vision.''

''Good luck. If you turn out to be a genius after all, remember that I never once for a moment believed in you.''

''Don't worry,'' he said, smiling. ''I'll never forget that.''

7

What Would Have Been

Diko met Hunahpu at the station in Juba. He was easy to recognize, since he was small with light brown skin and Mayan features. He seemed placid, standing calmly on the platform, looking slowly across the crowd from side to side. Diko was surprised at how young he looked, though she was aware that the smooth-skinned Indies often seemed young to eyes accustomed to the look of other races. And, especially for one so young-looking, it was also surprising that there was no hint of tension in the man. He might have come here a thousand times before. He might be surveying an old familiar sight, to see how it had changed, or not changed, in the years since he had been away. Who could guess, looking at him, that his career was on the line, that he had never traveled farther than Mexico City in his life, that he was about to make a presentation that might change the course of history? Diko envied him the inner peace that allowed him to deal with life so . . . so steadily.

She went to him. He looked at her, his face betraying not even a flicker of expectation or relief, though he must have recognized her, must have looked up her picture in the Pastwatch roster before he came. "I'm Diko," she said, extending both hands. He clasped them briefly. "I'm Hunahpu," he said. "It was kind of you to greet me."

"We have no street signs," she said, "and I'm a better driver than the taxis. Well, maybe not, but I charge less."

He didn't smile. A cold fish, she thought. "Have you any bags?" she asked.

He shook his head. "Just this." He shrugged to indicate the small shoulder bag. Could it possibly carry so much as a change of clothes? But then, he was traveling from one tropical climate to another, and he wouldn't need a shaving kit—beardlessness was part of what made Indie men seem younger than their years—and as for papers, those would all have been transmitted electronically. Most people, though, brought much more than this when they traveled. Perhaps because they were insecure, and needed to surround themselves with familiar things, or to feel that they had many choices to make each day when they dressed, so they didn't have to be so frightened or feel so powerless. Obviously that was not Hunahpu's problem. He apparently never felt fear at all, or perhaps never regarded himself as a stranger. How remarkable it would be, thought Diko, to feel at home in any place. I wish I had that gift. Quite to her surprise, she found herself admiring him even as she felt put off by his coldness.

The ride to the hotel was wordless. He offered no comment on the accommodation. "Well," she said, "I assume you'll want to rest in order to overcome jet lag. The best advice is to sleep for three hours or so, and then get up and eat immediately."

"I won't have jet lag," he said. "I slept on the plane. And on the train."

He *slept?* On the way to the most important interview of his life?

"Well, then, you'll want to eat."

"I ate on the train," he said.

"Well, then," she said. "How long will you need before we start?"

"I can start now," he said. He took off his shoulder bag and laid it on the bed. There was an economy of movement in the way he did it. He neither tossed it carelessly nor placed it carefully.

Instead he moved so naturally that the shoulder bag seemed to have gone to the bed of its own free will.

Diko shuddered. She couldn't think why. Then she realized that it was because of Hunahpu, the way he was standing there with nothing in his hands, nothing on his shoulder, no *thing* that he could hold or fiddle with or clutch to himself. He had set aside the one accessory he carried, and yet seemed as calm and relaxed as ever. It made her feel the way she felt when someone else stood too close to the edge of a precipice, a sort of empathetic horror. She could never have done that. In a strange place, alone, she would have had to cling to *something* familiar. A notebook. A bag. Even a bracelet or ring or watch that she could fiddle with. But this man—he seemed perfectly at ease without anything. No doubt he could fling away his clothes and walk naked through life and never show a sign of feeling vulnerable. It was unnerving, his perfect self-possession.

"How do you do it?" she asked, unable to stop herself.

"Do what?" he asked.

"Stay so . . . so *calm.*"

He thought about that for a moment. "Because I don't know what else to do."

"I'd be terrified," she said. "Coming to a strange place like this. Putting my life's work into the hands of strangers."

"Yes," he said. "Me too."

She looked at him, unsure what he meant. "You're terrified?"

He nodded. But his face seemed just as placid as before, his body just as relaxed. In fact, even as he agreed that he was terrified, his manner, his expression radiated the opposite message—that he was at ease, perhaps a little bored, but not yet impatient. As if he were a disinterested spectator at the events that were about to take place.

And suddenly the comments of Hunahpu's supervisor began to make sense. She had said something about how he never seemed to care about anything, not even the things he cared most about. Impossible to work with, but good luck, the supervisor had said. Yet it was not as if Hunahpu were autistic, unable to respond. He looked at what was around him and clearly registered what he saw. He was polite and attentive when she spoke.

Well, no matter. He was strange, that was obvious. But he had come to make a presentation, and now was as good a time as any. "What do you need?" she asked. "To make your case? A Tru-Site?"

"And a network terminal," he answered.

"Then let's go to my station," she said.

"I was able to convince Don Enrique de Guzmán," said Columbus. "Why is it that only kings are immune to my arguments?"

Father Antonio only smiled and shook his head. "Cristóbal," he said, "all educated men are immune to your arguments. They are flimsy, they are meaningless. You are opposed by mathematics and by all the ancients who matter. Kings are immune to your arguments because kings have access to learned men who rip your arguments to shreds."

Columbus was shocked. "If you believe this, Father Antonio, then why do you support me? Why am I welcome here? Why did you help me persuade Don Enrique?"

"I was not convinced by your arguments," said Father Antonio. "I was convinced by the light of God within you. You are on fire inside. I believe only God can put such a fire in a man, and so even though I believe that your arguments are nonsense, I also believe that God wants you to sail west, and so I will help you all I can because I also love God and I also have a tiny spark of that fire in me."

At these words tears sprang into Columbus's eyes. In all the years of study, all the arguments in Portugal, and more recently in Don Enrique's house, no one had shown a sign of having been touched by God in support of his cause. He had begun to think that God had given up on him and was no longer helping him in any way. But now he heard words from Father Antonio—who was, after all, a greatly learned man with much respect among scholars throughout Europe—that confirmed that God was, in fact, touching the hearts of good men to make them believe in Columbus's mission.

"Father Antonio, if I did not know what I know, I would not have believed my arguments either," said Columbus.

"Enough of that," said Father Perez. "Never say that again."
Columbus looked at him, startled. "What do you mean?"

"Here at La Rábida, behind closed doors, you can say such a thing, and we will understand. But from now on you must never give anyone even the slightest hint that it is *possible* to doubt your arguments."

"It *is* possible to doubt them," said Father Antonio.

"But Columbus must never give a sign that he *knows* it is possible to doubt them. Don't you understand? If it is God's will that this voyage occur, then you must inspire others with confidence in it. That is what will bring you victory, Columbus. Not reason, not arguments, but faith, courage, persistence, certainty. Those who are touched by the Spirit of God will believe in you no matter what. But how many of those will there be? How many of those have there been?"

"Counting you and Father Antonio," said Columbus, "two."

"So—you will not win your victory by the force of your arguments, because they are feeble indeed. And the Spirit of God will not overwhelm everyone in your path, because God does not work that way. What do you have in your favor, Cristóbal?"

"Your friendship," he said at once.

"And your utter, absolute faith," said Father Perez. "Am I right, Father Antonio?"

Father Antonio nodded. "I see his point. Those who are weak in faith will adopt the faith of those who are strong. Your confidence must be absolute, and then others will be able to hold on to *your* faith and let it carry them."

"So," said Father Perez. "You never show doubt. You never show even the possibility of doubt."

"All right," said Columbus. "I can do that."

"And you always leave the impression that you know much more than you're telling," said Father Perez.

Columbus said nothing, for he could not tell Father Perez that his statement was the truth.

"This means that you never, never say to anyone, 'These are all my arguments, I've now told you everything I know.' If they ask you direct questions, you answer as if you were only letting a little bit of your knowledge escape. You act as if they should al-

ready know as much as you do, and you're disappointed that they do not. You act as if *everyone* should know the things you know, and you despair of teaching the uninitiated.''

''What you're describing sounds like arrogance,'' said Columbus.

''It's more than arrogance,'' said Father Antonio, laughing. ''It's *scholarly* arrogance. Believe me, Cristóbal, that's exactly how they'll be treating *you.*''

''True enough,'' said Columbus, remembering the attitude of King João's advisers back in Lisbon.

''And one more thing, Cristóbal,'' said Father Perez. ''You are good with women.''

Columbus raised an eyebrow. This was not the sort of thing he expected to hear from a Franciscan prior.

''I speak not of seduction, though I'm sure you could master those arts if you haven't already. I speak of the way they look at you. The way they pay attention to you. This is also a tool, for it happens that we live in a time when Castile is governed by a woman. A queen regnant, not just a queen consort. Do you think God leaves such things to chance? She will look at you as women look at men, and she will judge you as women judge men—not on the strength of their arguments, and not on their cleverness or prowess in battle, but rather on the force of their character, the intensity of their passion, their strength of soul, their compassion, and—ah, this above all—their conversation.''

''I don't understand how I'll use this supposed gift,'' said Columbus. He was thinking of his wife, and how badly he had treated her—and yet how much she had obviously loved him in spite of it all. ''You can't be suggesting that I seek some sort of private audience with Queen Isabella.''

''Not at all!'' cried Father Perez, horrified. ''Do you think I would suggest treason? No, you will meet with her publicly—that is why she has sent for you. My position as the queen's confessor has allowed me to send letters telling about you, and perhaps that helped pique her interest. Don Louis wrote to her, offering to contribute 4,000 ducats to your enterprise. Don Enrique wanted to mount the whole enterprise himself. All of these together have made you an intriguing figure in her eyes.''

"But what you'll receive," said Father Antonio, "is a royal audience. In the presence of the Queen of Castile and her husband the King of Aragon."

"Yet still I tell you that you must think of it as an audience with the Queen alone," said Father Perez, "and you must speak to her as a woman, after the way of women, and not after the way of men. It will be tempting for you to do as most courtiers and ambassadors do, and address yourself to the King. She hates that, Cristóbal. I betray no confidence of the confessional when I tell you *that*. They treat her as if she weren't there, and yet her kingdom is more than twice as large as the King's. Furthermore it is *her* kingdom that is a seafaring nation, looking westward into the Atlantic. So when you speak, you address them both, of course, for you dare not *offend* the King. But in all you say, you look first to the Queen. You speak to her. You explain to her. You *persuade* her. Remember that the amount you are asking for is not large. A few ships? This will not break the treasury. It is within her power to give you those ships even if her husband disdains you. And because she is a woman, it is within her power to believe in you and trust you and grant you your prayer even though all the wise men of Spain are arrayed against you. Do you understand me?"

"I have only one person to persuade," said Columbus, "and that is the Queen."

"All you have to do with the scholars is outlast them. All you have to do is never, never say to them, 'This is all I have, this is all my evidence.' If you ever admit that, they will rip those arguments to shreds and even Queen Isabella cannot stand against their certainty. But if you never do this, their report will sound much more tentative. It will leave room for interpretation. They will be furious at you, of course, and they will try to destroy you, but these are honest men, and they will have to leave open a few tiny doors of doubt, a few nuances of phrase that admit the possibility that while they *believe* you are wrong, they can't be absolutely, finally certain."

"And that will be enough?"

"Who knows?" said Father Perez. "It may have to be."

When God gave me this task, thought Columbus, I thought he

would open the way for me. Instead I find that such a slender chance as this is all that I can hope for.

"Persuade the Queen," said Father Perez.

"If I can," said Columbus.

"It's a good thing you're a widower," said Father Perez. "That's cruel to say, I know, but if the Queen knew you were married, it would dim her interest in you."

"*She* is married," said Columbus. "What can you possibly mean?"

"I mean that when a man is married, he is no longer half so fascinating to a woman. Even a married woman. Especially a married woman, since she thinks she knows what husbands are like!"

Father Antonio added, "Men, on the other hand, are not troubled by this aberration. Judging from my confessional, at least, I would say that men are *more* fascinated by married women than by single ones."

"Then the Queen and I are bound to fascinate each other," said Columbus dryly.

"I think so," said Father Perez, smiling. "But your friendship will be a pure one, and the children of your union will be caravels with the east wind behind them."

"Faith for women, evidence for men," said Father Antonio. "Does that mean that Christianity is for women?"

"Let us say rather that Christianity is for the faithful, and so there are more true Christians among women than among men," said Father Perez.

"But without understanding," said Father Antonio, "there can be no faith, and so it remains the province of men."

"There is the understanding of reason, at which men excel," said Father Perez, "and there is the understanding of compassion, at which women are far superior. Which do you think gives rise to faith?"

Columbus left them still disputing the point and finished his preparations for the journey to Córdoba, where the King and Queen were holding court as they prosecuted their more-or-less permanent war against the Moors. All the talk of what women want and need and admire and believe was ridiculous, he knew—what could celibate priests know of women? But then, Columbus had been married and certainly knew nothing about women all the same, and Father Perez and Father Antonio had both heard the confessions of many women. So perhaps they did know.

Felipa did believe in me, thought Columbus. I took that for granted, but now I realize that I needed her, I depended on her for that. She believed in me even when she did not understand my arguments. Perhaps Father Perez is right, and women can see past the superficial and comprehend the deepest heart of the truth. Perhaps Felipa saw the mission that the Holy Trinity put in my heart, and it led her to support me despite all. Perhaps Queen Isabella will also see this, and because she is a woman in a place normally reserved for men, she can turn the course of fate to allow me to fulfill the mission of God.

As it grew dark, Columbus grew lonely, and for the first time that he could remember, he missed Felipa and wanted her with him in the night. I never understood what you gave to me, he said to her, though he doubted she could hear him. But why couldn't she? If saints can hear prayers, why can't wives? And if she doesn't listen to me anymore—why should she?—I know she will be listening for the prayers of Diego.

With this thought he wandered through the torchlit monastery until he came to the small cell where Diego slept. His son was asleep. Columbus lifted him out of his bed and carried him through the gathering darkness to his own room, to his larger bed, and there he lay with his son curled into his arm. I'm here with Diego, he said silently. Do you see me, Felipa? Do you hear me? Now I understand you a little, he said to his dead wife. Now I know the greatness of the gift you gave me. Thank you. And if you have any influence in heaven, touch the heart of Queen Isabella. Let her see in me what you saw in me. Let her love me one-tenth as much as you did, and I will have my ships, and God will bring the cross to the kingdoms of the east.

Diego stirred, and Columbus whispered to him. "Go back to sleep, my son. Go back to sleep." Diego nestled tighter against him, and did not wake.

* * *

Hunahpu walked with Diko through the streets of Juba as if he thought the naked children and the grass huts were the most natural way to live; she had never had a visitor from out of town who didn't comment on it, who didn't ask questions. Some pretended to be quite blasé, asking questions about whether the grass used to make the huts was local or imported, or other nonsense that was really a circuitous way of saying, Do you people actually *live* like this? But Hunahpu seemed to think nothing of it, though she could sense that his eyes took in everything.

Inside Pastwatch, of course, everything *would* be familiar, and when they reached her station he immediately sat down at her terminal and began calling up files. He had not asked permission, but then, why should he? If he was to show her anything, he would have to be in charge; this was where she had led him, so why should he ask to use what she obviously intended him to use? He wasn't being discourteous. Indeed, he had said that he was terrified. Could this very calmness, this stillness, be the way he dealt with fear? Perhaps if he ever became truly relaxed, he would seem more tense! Laughing, joking, showing emotion, *engaged.* Perhaps it was only when he was fearful that he seemed utterly at peace.

"How much do you already know?" he asked. "I don't want to waste your time covering material you're familiar with."

"I know that the Mexica reached their imperial peak with the conquests of Ahuitzotl. He essentially proved the practical limits of Mesoamerican empire. The lands he conquered were so far away that Moctezuma II had to reconquer them, and they still didn't stay conquered."

"And you know why those were the limits?"

"Transportation," she said. "It was just too far, and too hard to supply an army. The greatest feat of Aztec arms was making the connection with Soconusco, far down the Pacific coast. And that only worked because they didn't take sacrificial victims from Soconusco, they traded with them. It was more of an alliance than a conquest."

"Those were the limits in space," said Hunahpu. "What about the social and economic limits?"

She felt as if she were being given an examination. But he was right—if he tested her knowledge first, he would know how deeply he could delve into the material that mattered, the new findings that he thought would answer the great question of why the Interveners had given Columbus the mission of sailing west. "Economically, the Mexica cult of sacrifice was counterproductive. As long as they kept conquering new lands, they took enough captives from warfare that the nearby territory could maintain enough of a workforce to provide food. But as soon as they began coming back from war with twenty or thirty captives instead of two or three thousand, they were left with a dilemma. If they took their sacrifices from the surrounding lands they already controlled, food production would go down. But if they left those men on the land, then they would have to cut down on their sacrifices, which would mean even *less* power in battle, even less favor from the state god—what was his name?"

"Huitzilopochtli," said Hunahpu.

"Well, they chose to increase the sacrifices. As a sort of proof of their faith. So production fell and there was hunger. And the people they ruled over were more and more upset at the taking of sacrifices, even though they were all believers in the sacrificial religion, because in the old days, before the Mexica with their cult of Witsil . . . Huitzil—"

"Huitzilopochtli."

"There'd be only a few sacrifices at a time, comparatively speaking. After ceremonial war, or even after star war. And after the ball games. The Mexica were new, with their profligate sacrificing. The people hated it. Their families were being torn apart, and because so many people were sacrificed it didn't seem to be such a sacred honor anymore."

"And within the Mexica culture?"

"The state thrived because it provided social mobility. If you distinguished yourself in war, you rose. The merchant classes could buy their way into the nobility. You could rise. But that ended immediately after Ahuitzotl, when Moctezuma virtually ended all possibility of buying your way from class to class, and when failure in war after war meant that there was little chance of rising through valor in battle. Moctezuma was in a holding pattern, and that was disastrous, since the entire Mexica social and economic structure depended on expansion and social mobility."

Hunahpu nodded.

"So," said Diko, "where do you disagree with any of this?"

"I don't disagree with it at all," he said.

"But the conclusion that is drawn from this is that even without Cortés, the Aztec empire would have collapsed within years."

"Within months, actually," said Hunahpu. "Cortés's most valuable Indie allies were the people of Tlaxcala. They were the ones who had already broken the back of the Mexica military machine. Ahuitzotl and Moctezuma threw army after army against them, and they always held on to their territory. It was a humiliation to the Mexica, because Tlaxcala was just to the east of Tenochtitlán, completely surrounded by the Mexica empire. And all the other people, both those who were still resisting the Mexica and those who were being ground to dust under their government, began to look to Tlaxcala as their hope of deliverance."

"Yes, I read your paper on this."

"It's like the Persian Empire after the Chaldean," said Hunahpu. "When the Mexica fell, it wouldn't have meant a collapse of the entire imperial structure. The Tlaxcalans would have moved in and taken over."

"That's one possible outcome," said Diko.

"No," said Hunahpu. "It's the only possible outcome. It was already under way."

"Now we come to the question of evidence, I'm afraid," said Diko.

He nodded. "Watch."

He turned to the TruSite II and began calling up short scenes. He had obviously prepared carefully, for he took her from scene to scene almost as smoothly as in a movie. "Here is Chocla," he said, and then showed her brief clips of the man meeting with the Tlaxcalan king and then meeting with other men in other contexts; then he named another Tlaxcalan ambassador and showed what he was doing.

The picture quickly emerged. The Tlaxcalans were well aware of the restiveness both of the subject peoples and of the merchant and warrior classes within the Mexica homeland. The Mexica were ripe for both a coup and a revolution, and whichever one happened first would certainly trigger the other. The Tlaxcalans were meeting with leaders of every group, forging alliances, preparing. "The Tlaxcalans were ready. If Cortés had not come along and thrown a monkey wrench into their plans, they would have slipped in and taken over the entire Mexica empire, whole. They were setting it up to have every subject nation that mattered revolt all at once and throw their might behind Tlaxcala, trusting in the Tlaxcalans because of their enormous prestige. At the same time, they were going to have a coup topple Moctezuma, which would break up the triple alliance as Texcozo and Tacuba abandoned Tenochtitlán and joined in a new ruling alliance with Tlaxcala."

"Yes," said Diko. "I think that's clear. I think you're right. That's what they planned."

"And it would have worked," said Hunahpu. "So all this talk about the Aztec Empire being ready to fall is meaningless. It would have been replaced by a newer, stronger, more vigorous empire. And, I might point out, one that was just as viciously committed to wholesale human sacrifice as the Mexica. The only difference between them was the name of the god—instead of Huitzilopochtli, the Tlaxcalans committed their butchery in the name of Camaxtli."

"This is all very convincing," said Diko. "But what difference does it make? The same limits that applied to the Mexica would apply to the Tlaxcala people as well. The limits on transportation. The impossibility of maintaining a program of wholesale slaughter and intensive agriculture at the same time."

"The Tlaxcala were not the Mexica," said Hunahpu.

"Meaning?"

"In their desperate struggle for survival against a relentless, powerful enemy—a struggle which the Mexica had never faced, I might add—the Tlaxcala abandoned the fatalistic view of history that had crippled the Mexica and the Toltecs and the Mayas before them. They were looking for change, and it was there to be had."

By now, it was getting late in the workday, and others were gathering around to watch Hunahpu's presentation. Diko saw now that the fear had left Hunahpu, and so he was becoming passionate and animated. She wondered if this was how the myth of the stoic Indie had begun—the cultural response to fear among the Indie looked like impassiveness to Europeans.

Hunahpu began to take her through another round of brief

scenes showing messengers from the king of Tlaxcala, but now they were not going to Mexica dissidents or subject nations. "It is well known that the Tarascan people to the west and north of Tenochtitlán had recently developed true bronze and were experimenting heavily with other metals and alloys," said Hunahpu. "What no one seems to have noticed is that the Mexica were completely unaware of this, but Tlaxcala was right on top of it. And they aren't just trying to *buy* the bronze. They're trying to co-opt it. They're negotiating for an alliance and they're trying to bring Tarascan smiths to Tlaxcala. They will certainly succeed, and that means that they'll have devastating and terrifying weapons unavailable to any other nations in the area."

"Would bronze make that big a difference?" asked one of the onlookers. "I mean, the flint hatchets of the Mexica could behead a horse with one blow, it's not as if they didn't have devastating weapons already."

"A bronze-tipped arrow is lighter and can fly farther and truer than a stone-tipped one. A bronze sword can pierce the padded armor that snagged and turned away flint points and flint blades. It makes a huge difference. And it wouldn't have stopped with bronze. The Tarascans were serious in their work with many different metals. They were starting to work with iron."

"No," said several at once.

"I know what everybody says, but it's true." He brought up a scene with a Tarascan metallurgist working with more-or-less pure iron.

"That won't work," said one onlooker. "It's not hot enough."

"Do you doubt that he'll find a way to make his fire hotter?" asked Hunahpu. "This clip is from a time when Cortés was already marching to Tenochtitlán. That's why the work with iron came to nothing. Because it hadn't succeeded by the time of the Spanish conquest it was not remembered. I found it because I'm the only one who believed that it mattered to try to look for it. But the Tarascans were on the verge of working with iron."

"So the Mesoamerican bronze age would have lasted for ten years?" someone asked.

"There's no law that says bronze has to come before iron, or that iron has to wait centuries after the discovery of bronze," said Hunahpu.

"Iron isn't gunpowder," said Diko. "Or are you going to show us Tarascans working with saltpeter?"

"My point isn't that they caught up with European technology all in a few years—I think that would be impossible. What I'm saying is that by allying themselves with the Tarascans and controlling them, the Tlaxcalans would have had weapons that would give them a devastating advantage over all the surrounding nations. They would cause so much fear that nations, once conquered, might stay conquered longer, might freely send the Tarascans tribute that the Mexica would have had to send an army to bring back. The boundaries would have increased and so would the stability of the empire."

"Possibly," said Diko.

"Probably," said Hunahpu. "And there's this, too. The Tlaxcala already dominated Huexotzingo and Cholula—small nearby cities, but it gives us an idea of *their* idea of empire. And what did they do? They interfered in the internal politics of their client states to a degree that the Mexica never dreamed of. They weren't just extracting tribute and sacrificial victims, they were establishing a centralized government with rigid control over the governments of conquered nations. A true politically unified empire, rather than a loose tribute network. This is the innovation that made the Assyrians so powerful, and which was copied by every successful empire after them. The Tlaxcalans have finally made the same discovery two thousand years later. But think what it did for the Assyrians, and now imagine what it will do for Tlaxcala."

"All right," said Diko. "Let me call in Mother and Father."

"But I'm not through," said Hunahpu.

"I was looking at your presentation to see if you were worth spending time on. You are. There was obviously a lot more going on in Mesoamerica than anybody thought, because everybody was studying the Mexica and nobody was looking for successor states. Your approach is clearly productive, and people with a lot more authority than I have need to see this."

Suddenly Hunahpu's animation and enthusiasm disappeared,

and he became calm and stoic-looking again. Diko thought: This means that he's now afraid again.

"Don't worry," she said. "They'll be as excited as I am."

He nodded. "When will we do this, then?"

"Tomorrow, I expect. Go to your room, sleep. The hotel restaurant will feed you, though I doubt they have much in the way of Mexican food so I hope standard international cuisine will do. I'll call you in the morning with our schedule for tomorrow."

"What about Kemal?"

"I don't think he'll want to miss this," said Diko.

"Because I never even got to the transportation issue."

"Tomorrow," said Diko.

The others were already drifting away, though some lingered, obviously hoping to speak to Hunahpu directly. Diko turned to them. "Let this man sleep," she said to them. "You'll all be invited to his presentation tomorrow, so why make him tell things tonight that he'll tell everybody tomorrow?"

She was surprised to hear Hunahpu laugh. She hadn't heard him laugh before, and she turned to him. "What's funny?"

"I thought when you stopped me it was because you didn't believe in me and you were being polite, with promises of meetings with Tagiri and Hassan and Kemal."

"Why would you think that, when I was saying that I thought this was important?" Diko was offended that he thought she was lying.

"Because I never before met someone who would do what you did. Stop a presentation that you thought was important."

She didn't understand.

"Diko," he said. "Most people want nothing more than to know something that people higher up don't know. To know things *first*. Here you had a chance to hear all of this *first,* and you stop it? You wait? And not only that, you promise others who are below you in the hierarchy that they can be there too?"

"That's the way it is in Pastwatch," said Diko. "The truth will still be true tomorrow, and everybody who needs to know it has an equal claim on learning it."

"That's the way it is in *Juba*," Hunahpu corrected her. "Or maybe that's the way it is in Tagiri's house. But everywhere else in the world, information is a coin, and people are greedy to acquire it and careful how and where they spend it.''

"Well, I guess we surprised each other,'' said Diko.

"Did I surprise you?''

"You're actually quite talkative,'' she said.

"To my friends,'' he said.

She accepted the compliment with a smile. His smile in return was warm and all the more valuable because it was so rare.

Santangel knew from the moment that Columbus began to speak that this was not going to be the normal courtier begging for advancement. For one thing, there was no hint of boastfulness, no swagger in the man. His face looked younger than his flowing white hair would imply, giving him an ageless, gnomic look. What captivated, though, was his manner. He spoke quietly, so that all the court had to fall silent to allow the King and Queen to hear him. And even though he looked equally at Ferdinand and Isabella, Santangel could see at once that this man knew who it was that he had to please, and it was not Ferdinand.

Ferdinand had no dreams of crusade; he worked to conquer Granada because it was Spanish soil, and his dream was of a single, united Spain. He knew it could not be achieved in a moment. He laid his plans with patience. He did not have to overwhelm Castile; it was enough to be married to Isabella, knowing that in their children the crowns would be united forever, and in the meantime he gave her great freedom of action in her kingdom as long as their military movements were under his direction alone. He showed the same patience in his war with Granada, never risking his armies in all-or-nothing pitched battles, but rather besieging, feinting, maneuvering, subverting, confusing the enemy, who knew that he meant to destroy them but could never quite find where to commit their forces to stop him. He would drive the Moors from Spain but he would do it without destroying Spain in the process.

Isabella, however, was more Christian than Spanish. She joined in the war against Granada because she wanted the land under Christian rule. She had long pressed for the purification of Spain by removing all non-Christians; it made her impatient that Ferdinand refused to let her expel the Jews until after the Moors were broken. "One infidel at a time," he said, and she consented, but she chafed under the delay, feeling the presence of any non-Christian in Spain like a stone in her shoe.

So when this Columbus began to speak of great kingdoms and empires in the east, where the name of Christ had never been spoken aloud, but lived only as a dream in the hearts of those who hungered for righteousness, Santangel knew that these words would burn like flame in Isabella's heart even as they put Ferdinand to sleep. When Columbus began to tell that these heathen nations were the special responsibility of Spain, "for we are nearer to them than any other Christian nation except Portugal, and *they* have set out on the longest possible voyage instead of the shortest, around Africa instead of due west into the narrow ocean that divides us from millions of souls who will flock to the banners of Christian Spain," her gaze on him became rapt, unblinking.

Santangel was not surprised when Ferdinand excused himself and left his wife to continue the interview alone. He knew that Ferdinand would immediately assign advisers to examine Columbus for him, and the process would not be an easy one. But this Columbus—hearing him, Santangel could not help but believe that if anyone could succeed at such a mad enterprise, it was this man. It was an insane time to try to put together an exploratory expedition. Spain was at war; every resource of the kingdom was committed to driving the Moors from Andalusia. How could the Queen possibly finance such a voyage? Santangel remembered well the fury in the King's eyes when he heard the letters from Don Enrique, the Duke of Sidonia, and from Don Luis de la Cerda, the Duke of Medina. "If they have such money they can afford to sink it in the Atlantic on pointless voyages, then why haven't they already given it to us to drive the Moor from their own doorstep?" he asked.

Isabella was also a practical sovereign, who never let her personal wishes interfere with the needs of her kingdom or overtax its resources. Nevertheless, she saw this matter differently. She saw that these two lords had become believers in this Genovese who had already failed at the court of the King of Portugal. She had the letter from Father Juan Perez, her confessor, attesting that Columbus was an honest man who asked for nothing more than the opportunity to prove his beliefs, with his own life if necessary. So she had invited him to Córdoba, a decision that Ferdinand patiently indulged, and she listened to him now.

Santangel now watched, staying as the agent of the King, to report to him all that Columbus said. Santangel already knew half of his report: We can spare no funds for such an expedition at this time. As King Ferdinand's treasurer and chief tax collector, Santangel knew that his duty required him to be absolutely honest and accurate, letting the king know exactly what Spain could afford and what it could not. Santangel was the one who had explained to the king why he should not be angry at the dukes of Medina and Sidonia. "They *are* paying all the tax they can afford to pay year in and year out. This expedition would happen but the once, and it would be a great sacrifice for them. We should see this, not as proof that they are cheating the Crown, but as proof that they truly believe in this Columbus. As it is, they pay as much toward the war out of their estates as any other lords, and to use this as a pretext to try to extract more from them would only make enemies out of them and make many other lords uneasy as well." King Ferdinand dropped the idea, of course, because he trusted Santangel's judgment on matters fiscal.

Now Santangel watched and listened as Columbus poured out his dreams and hopes to the Queen. What are you actually asking for? he asked silently. It wasn't until three hours into the interview that Columbus finally touched on *that* point. "No more than three or four ships—they could be mere caravels, for that matter," he said. "This is not a military expedition. We go only to mark the path. When we return with the gold and jewels and spices of the east, then the priests can go in great fleets, with soldiers to protect them from the jealous infidels. They can spread forth through Cipangu and Cathay, the Spice Islands and India, where millions will hear the sweet name of Jesus Christ and beg for baptism. They will become your subjects, and will look to you forever as the one who brought them the glad news of the resurrection, who taught them of their sins so they can repent. And with the gold and silver, with the wealth of the East at your command, there'll be no more struggling to finance a small war against the Moors of Spain. You can assemble great armies and liberate Constantinople. You can make the Mediterranean a

Christian sea again. You can stand in the tomb where the Savior's body lay, you can kneel and pray in the Garden of Gethsemane, you can raise the cross once more above the holy city of Jerusalem, over Bethlehem, the city of David, over Nazareth, where Jesus grew under the care of the carpenter and the Holy Virgin.''

It was like music, listening to him. And whenever Santangel began to think that this was nothing more than flattery, that this man, like most men, was out only for his own benefit, he remembered: Columbus intended to put his own life on the line, sailing with the fleet. Columbus asked for no titles, no preferment, no wealth until and unless he returned successfully from his voyage. It gave his impassioned arguments a ring of sincerity that was largely unfamiliar at court. He may be mad, thought Santangel, but he is honest. Honest and clever. He never raises his voice, noted Santangel. He never lectures, never harangues. Instead he speaks as if this were a conversation between a brother and sister. He is always respectful, but also intimate. He speaks with manly strength, yet never sounds as if he thinks her his inferior in matters of thought or understanding—a fatal mistake which many men had made over the years when speaking to Isabella.

At long last the interview ended. Isabella, always careful, promised nothing, but Santangel could see how her eyes shone. ''We will speak again,'' she said.

I think not, thought Santangel. I think Ferdinand will want to keep direct contact between his wife and this Genovese to a minimum. But she will not forget him, and even though at this moment the treasury can afford nothing beyond the war, if Columbus is patient enough and does nothing stupid, I think Isabella will find a way to give him a chance.

A chance for what? To die at sea, lost with three caravels and all their crews, starving or dying of thirst or broken up in some storm or swallowed up in a maelstrom?

Columbus was dismissed. Isabella, weary but happy, sank back in her throne, then beckoned to Quintanilla and Cardinal Mendoza, both of whom had also waited through the interview. To Santangel's surprise, she also beckoned to him.

''What do you think of this man?'' she asked.

Quintanilla, always the first to speak and the last to have anything valuable to say, merely shrugged. "Who can tell whether his plan has merit?"

Cardinal Mendoza, the man that some called "the third king," smiled. "He speaks well, Your Majesty, and he has sailed with the Portuguese and met with their king," he said. "But it will take much examination before we know whether his ideas have merit. I think his idea of the distance between Spain and Cathay, sailing west, is grossly wrong."

Then she looked at Santangel. This terrified him. He had not won his position of trust because he spoke up in the presence of others. He was not a speaker. Rather he acted. The King trusted him because when he promised he could raise a sum of money, he produced it; when he promised they could afford to carry out a campaign, the funds were there.

"What do I know of such matters, Your Majesty?" he asked. "Sailing west—what do I know of that?"

"What will you tell my husband?" she asked—teasingly, for of course he was an open observer, not a spy.

"That Columbus's plan is not as expensive as a siege, but more expensive than anything we can afford at present."

She turned to Quintanilla. "And can Castile not afford it, either?"

"At present, Your Majesty," said Quintanilla, "it would be difficult. Not impossible, but if it failed it would make Castile look foolish in the eyes of others."

No need to say that the "others" he referred to were Ferdinand and his advisers. Santangel knew that Isabella was always careful to retain the respect of her husband and the men he listened to, for if she gained a reputation for foolishness, it would be an easy matter for him to step in and take over more and more of her power in Castile with little resistance from the Castilian lords. Only her reputation for "manlike" wisdom allowed her to remain a strong rallying point for the Castilians, which in turn gave her a measure of independence from her husband.

"And yet," she said, "why did God make us queen, if not to bring his children to the Cross?"

Cardinal Mendoza nodded. "If his ideas have merit, then pursuing them would be worth any sacrifice, Your Majesty," he said.

"So let us keep him here with the court, so he can be examined, so his ideas can be discussed and compared to the knowledge we have from the ancients. There's no hurry, I think. Cathay will still be there in a month or two, or a year."

Isabella thought for a few moments. "The man has no estate," she said. "If we keep him here, then we must attach him to the court." She looked at Quintanilla. "He must be allowed to live as a gentleman."

He nodded. "I already gave him a small sum to keep him while he waited for this audience."

"Fifteen thousand maravedis out of my own purse," said the Queen.

"That is for the year, Your Majesty?"

"If it takes more than a year," she said, "we'll speak of this again." She waved her hand and looked away. Quintanilla left. Cardinal Mendoza also excused himself and took his leave. Santangel turned to go, but she called him back. "Luis," she said.

"Your Majesty."

She waited until Cardinal Mendoza had gone. "How extraordinary, that Cardinal Mendoza chose to listen to all that Columbus had to say."

"He's a remarkable man," said Santangel.

"Which? Columbus or Mendoza?"

Since Santangel wasn't sure himself, he had no ready answer.

"You heard him, Luis Santangel, and you are a hardheaded man. What do you think of him?"

"I believe him to be an honest man," said Santangel. "Beyond that, who can know? Oceans and sailing vessels and kingdoms of the east—I know nothing of that."

"But you do know how to judge whether a man is honest."

"He's not here to steal from the royal coffers," said Santangel. "And he meant every word that he said to you today. Of that I'm certain, Your Majesty."

"I am, too," said the Queen. "I hope he is able to make his case to the scholars."

Santangel nodded. And then, against his better judgment, he added a rather daring comment. "Scholars don't know everything, Your Majesty."

She raised her eyebrows. Then she smiled. "He won you over, too, did he?"

Santangel blushed. "As I said—I think him an honest man."

"Honest men don't know everything either," she said.

"In my line of work, Your Majesty, I have come to think of honest men as a precious rarity, while scholars are rather thick on the ground."

"And is that what you will tell my husband?"

"Your husband," he said carefully, "will not ask me the same questions that you asked."

"Then he will end up knowing less than he should know, don't you think?"

It was as close as Queen Isabella could come to openly admitting the rivalry between the two crowns of Spain, despite the careful harmony of their marriage. It would not do for Santangel to commit himself on such a dangerous question. "I cannot begin to guess what sovereigns should know."

"Neither can I," said the Queen softly. She looked away, a sort of melancholy drifting across her face. "It won't do for me to see him too often," she murmured. Then, as if remembering Santangel was there, she waved him off.

He left at once, but her words lingered. It won't do for me to see him too often. So, Columbus had struck deeper than he knew. Well, *that* was something the King didn't need to hear about. No reason to tell the King something that would lead to the poor Genovese dying on some dark night with a dirk between his ribs. Santangel would tell King Ferdinand only that what King Ferdinand would ask: Did Columbus's idea seem worth the cost? And to that, Santangel would answer honestly that at present it was more than the Crown could afford, but at some later date, with the war successfully concluded, it might be both feasible and desirable, if it were judged to have any chance at all of success.

And in the meantime, there was no need to worry about the Queen's last remark. She was a Christian woman and a clever queen. She would not jeopardize her place in eternity or on the throne for the sake of some brief yearning for this white-haired Genovese; nor did Columbus seem such a fool as to seek that dangerous avenue of preferment. Yet Santangel wondered if, in the back of Columbus's mind, there might not be some small hope of winning more than the mere approval of the Queen.

Well, what would it matter? It would come to nothing. If Santangel was any judge of men, he was certain that Cardinal Mendoza had left the court tonight determined to see to it that Columbus's examination would be hellish. The poor man's arguments would end up in shreds; after the scholars were through with him he would no doubt slink away from Córdoba in shame.

Too bad, thought Santangel. He made such an excellent start.

And then he thought: I want him to succeed. I want him to have his ships and make his voyage. What has he done to me? Why should I care? Columbus has seduced me as surely as he seduced the Queen.

He shuddered at his own fragility. He had thought he was a stronger man than that.

It was obvious to Hunahpu from the beginning that Kemal was annoyed at having to waste time listening to this unknown child from Mexico. He was cold and impatient. But Tagiri and Hassan were pleasant enough, and when Hunahpu looked to Diko he could see that she was perfectly at ease, and her smile was warm and encouraging. Perhaps Kemal was always like this. Well, no matter, thought Hunahpu. What mattered was the truth, and Hunahpu had that, or at least more of it than anyone else had put together yet about these matters.

It took an hour to get through all that he had shown to Diko in half that time, mostly because Kemal kept interrupting at first, challenging Hunahpu's statements. But as time went on, as it became clear that all of Kemal's challenges were easily dealt with using evidence that Hunahpu had already intended to include a bit later in his presentation, the hostility began to slacken, and he was allowed to proceed with fewer questions.

Now he had reached the end of the things that Diko had seen, and as if to signal that fact, she pulled her chair closer to the TruSite viewing area. The others who had watched yesterday also grew more attentive. "I have shown you that the Tarascans had the technology to establish a more dominant empire than the Mexica, and the Tlaxcalans were reaching for that technology. Their struggle for survival had made them more willing to embrace novelty—which we saw a bit later, of course, when they made alliance with Cortés. But this wasn't all. The Zapotecs of the northern coast of the Isthmus of Tehuantepec were also developing a new technology.''

The TruSite II at once began displaying shipbuilders at work. Hunahpu showed them the standard ocean-going kanoa of the Tainos and Caribs of the islands to the east, then the differences in the new ships that the Zapotecs were building. ''Rudders,'' he said, and they could see that the tiller was indeed being transformed into the more efficient steering device. ''And now,'' he said, ''look how they're making the ships larger.''

Sure enough, the Zapotecs were reaching for a greater carrying capacity than would ever be possible in a dugout canoe made from a single tree. At first it consisted of wide decks straddling the sides of the canoe and reaching beyond, but this became unwieldy, making the boat too likely to tip. A better solution was to shape a second tree into a vertical extension of the sides of the canoe, lashed to the hull by the use of holes bored into the sides. To make it watertight they smeared the surfaces with sap before they put them together, making a glue-like bond when it was lashed tight.

''Clever,'' said Kemal.

''It doubles the carrying capacity of the ships. But it slows them down, too—they tend to wallow in the water. What matters, though, is that they've learned to join wood and make it watertight. Single-tree construction is over. It's just a matter of time before the original one-tree canoe becomes the keel, and planks are used to make a much wider, shallower hull.''

''A matter of time,'' said Kemal. ''But you don't actually see any being made.''

''What they lack is adequate tools,'' said Hunahpu. ''When Tlaxcala takes over the Aztec empire, the bronze of the Tarascans will come to the Zapotecs, and they'll be able to make boards more efficiently and with more reliably smooth surfaces. The point is that when they make any innovation, it spreads quickly. And the Zapotecs are also under pressure from the Aztecs. They have to find sources of supply because the Mexican armies have forced them from their fields. In this swampy land, farming is always precarious. So look where they're sailing.''

He showed them the clumsy, wallowing Zapotec ships carrying large cargos from Veracruz and the Yucatán. "Slow as these ships are, they carry enough cargo on each trip to make the voyages profitable. They're far enough up the coast of Veracruz now to be in contact with the Tlaxcalans and the Tarascans. And here.'' Again the view changed. "This is the island of Hispaniola. And look who's coming to visit.''

Three Zapotecan ships slipped up to the shore.

"Unfortunately,'' said Hunahpu, "Columbus was already there.''

"But if he hadn't been there,'' said Diko, "it could have extended the reach of a Tlaxcalan empire out to the islands.''

"Exactly,'' said Hunahpu.

"There was already extensive contact between Mesoamerica and the Caribbean islands,'' said Kemal.

"Of course,'' said Hunahpu. "The Taino culture was actually an overlay by earlier raiders from the Yucatán. They brought the ball court with them, for instance, and established themselves as the ruling class. But they adopted the Arawak language and soon forgot their origins, and they certainly did *not* establish regular trade routes. Why should they? The boats didn't carry enough to make trade profitable. Only raiding was worth the effort, and the Caribs were the raiders, not the Taino, and since they came out of the southeastern Caribbean, Mesoamerica was even further out of reach. The Taino knew about Mesoamerica as a fabled land of gold and wealth and mighty gods—that's what they meant when they kept telling Columbus that the land of gold was to the west—but they had no regular contact. These Zapotecan ships would have changed all that. Especially as the ships got bigger and better. It would have been the beginning of a sailing tradition that would have led to ships that could cross the Atlantic.''

"Very speculative,'' said Kemal.

"Forgive me,'' said Diko, "but isn't that what your entire project is? Speculation?''

Kemal glowered at her.

"What matters," said Hunahpu, anxious not to antagonize Kemal, "is not the details. What matters is that the Zapotecs were innovating, they reached the islands with ships that could carry larger cargos, and they were also a familiar sight to the Tlaxcalans along the coast of Veracruz. It's unthinkable that the Tlaxcalans would not have seized upon this new technology just as they reached for the bronze-working of the Tarascans. It was an age of invention and innovation in Mesoamerica, and the only barrier was the ultraconservative Mexica leadership. That was doomed—everyone knows it—and it seems obvious to me from this evidence that the Tlaxcalans would have become the successor empire, and as the Persians far outstripped the empire of the Chaldeans, so also the innovative, politically sophisticated Tlaxcalan empire would have outreached the empire of the Mexica."

"You've made that case very well," said Kemal.

Hunahpu almost allowed himself a sigh of relief.

"But you have claimed much more than that, haven't you? And for those claims you have no evidence."

"Columbus's discovery erased all the other evidence," said Hunahpu. "But then, the Intervention also erased Columbus's crusade to the east. I think we're on equal ground here."

"Equally shaky," said Kemal.

"Kemal is heading the speculative aspects of our research," said Tagiri, "precisely because he is profoundly skeptical about it. He doesn't believe an accurate reconstruction is possible."

That thought had never occurred to Hunahpu—that Kemal was predisposed to reject *all* speculations. He had assumed that his only task was to bring Kemal to consider another possible scenario, not that he had to persuade him that it was possible to construct a scenario at all.

Diko seemed to sense his consternation. "Hunahpu," she said, "let's leave aside the issue of what can and can't be proved. You must have developed the rest of the story in your mind. Let's regard it as likely that Tlaxcala has conquered and unified the whole of the old Mexica empire, and that now it's running smoothly with Zapotecan ships trading far and wide and Tarascan bronzeworkers making weapons and tools for them. What then?"

Her guidance helped him recover his confidence. Trying to convince the great Kemal against his will was too much to contemplate; talking about ideas he could do. "First, you have to remember," said Hunahpu, "that there was one problem of the Mexica that the Tlaxcalans had *not* overcome. As with the Mexica, the Tlaxcalan practice of wholesale sacrifice to their bloodthirsty god would have drained away the manpower they needed to feed their population."

"So? How do you resolve it?" asked Kemal. "You wouldn't have come here if you didn't have an answer."

"I have a possibility, anyway. There's nothing in the evidence, because Tlaxcala hadn't had to govern a real empire yet. But they couldn't have succeeded if they made the same mistake the Mexica made, slaughtering the able-bodied men of their subject populations. So here's how I think they would have solved it. There is a hint of a doctrine among the priestly class that their warrior god Camaxtli becomes especially thirsty for blood *after* he has exerted himself to give Tlaxcala a victory. The existence of this idea makes it possible for the Tlaxcalans to evolve the practice of *only* offering huge mass sacrifices after a military victory, because that's the only time that Camaxtli is especially in need of blood. So if a city or nation or tribe willingly allies itself with Tlaxcala, submits to their overlordship, and allows the Tlaxcalan bureaucracy to administer their affairs, then instead of being sacrificed, their men are left to work the fields. Perhaps, if they prove to be trustworthy, they can even join the Tlaxcalan army, or fight alongside it. The mass sacrifices are *only* performed using captives from armies that resist. Aside from that, peacetime sacrifices in the Tlaxcalan empire would stay at a tolerable level—the way they were before the Mexica arose to form the Aztec empire in the first place."

"It gives the surrounding nations a reward for surrendering," said Hassan. "And a reason not to rebel."

"Just the way so much of the Roman Empire didn't have to be conquered," said Hunahpu. "The Romans seemed so irresistible that kings of neighboring countries would make the Roman senate the heir to their thrones, so that they could live as sovereigns until they died, and then their kingdoms would pass peacefully into the Roman system. It's the cheapest way to build an empire, and the best, since there's no war damage to the newly acquired lands."

"So," said Kemal. "If their god isn't bloodthirsty except *after* victory, they become peaceful and their god goes to sleep."

"Well, that would be nice," said Hunahpu, "but part of their theology was that besides *needing* sacrifices after victory, Camaxtli *liked* the blood. Camaxtli *liked* war. So they could put off the huge sacrifices until they won a victory, but they would still keep looking for more fights that might lead to such a victory. Besides, the Tlaxcalans had the same social-mobility system as the Mexica in their pre-Moctezuma days. The only way to rise within their society was either to make a lot of money or to prevail in battle. And making money was only possible for those who controlled trade. So there would have been constant pressure to start new wars with ever-more-remote neighbors. I think it wouldn't have taken the bronze-wielding Tlaxcalans long to reach the natural boundaries of their new seafaring empire: The Caribbean islands to the east, the mountains of Colombia to the south, and the deserts to the north. Conquests beyond those boundaries would not have been cost-effective, either because there were no large concentrated populations to exploit economically or to offer as sacrifices, or because the resistance would have been too strong as they came in contact with the Incas."

"So they turned to the empty Atlantic? Unlikely," said Kemal.

"I agree," said Hunahpu. "Left to themselves, I think they would never have turned eastward, or not for centuries. But they *weren't* left to themselves. The Europeans came to them."

"Then we're right back where we started," said Kemal. "The superior European civilization discovers the backward Indies and . . ."

"Not so backward now," said Diko.

"Bronze blades against muskets?" scoffed Kemal.

"Muskets weren't decisive," said Hunahpu. "Everyone knows that. The Europeans simply couldn't come in large enough numbers for their superior weapons to overcome the numerical advantage of the Indies. Besides, there's something else to consider. The Europeans wouldn't have come straight to the heart of the Caribbean this time. The later discovery would almost certainly have come from the Portuguese. Several Portuguese ships landed on or sighted the coast of Brazil quite independently of Columbus as early as the late 1490s. But the land they saw was dry and barren, and it didn't lead to India the way the coast of Africa would. So their exploration, instead of having the urgency that Columbus brought to it, would have been occasional and desultory. It would have taken years before Portuguese ships would have entered the Caribbean. By then, the Tlaxcalan empire would already be well established there. Now, instead of Europeans finding the sweet-natured Taino, they would meet the fierce and hungry Tlaxcalans, who would be getting frustrated by the fact that they weren't able to expand easily beyond their current borders around the Caribbean basin. What do the Tlaxcalans see? To them, the Europeans aren't gods from the east. To them, the Europeans are new victims that Camaxtli has brought to them, showing them how to get back on the path to productive warfare. And those big European boats and muskets aren't just strange miracles. The Tlaxcalans—or their Tarascan or Zapotecan allies—would immediately start taking them apart. Probably they'd sacrifice enough of the sailors to persuade the ship's carpenter and the ship's smith to make a deal, and unlike the Mexica, the Tlaxcalans would keep *them* alive and learn from them. How long would it take them to have muskets of their own? Big-bottomed ships? And in the meantime, the Europeans are hearing nothing at all about the Tlaxcalan empire, because any ships that reach Caribbean waters are being captured and their crews never get home."

"So the Tlaxcalans aren't independently developing technology anymore," said Tagiri.

"That's right. All they needed was to be advanced enough to understand the European technology when they encountered it, and to have an attitude that would allow them to exploit it. And that's what the Interveners understood. They had to get Europeans to discover the new world *before* the Tlaxcalans came to power, back with the relatively incompetent, decadent Mexica."

"That does work," said Kemal thoughtfully. "It does allow for a believable scenario. The Tlaxcalans build European-style ships and make European-style muskets, and then come to the shores of Europe fully prepared for a war whose purpose is to enlarge the empire and at the same time bring sacrifices to the temples of Camaxtli. I suppose the same pattern would apply in Europe, too. Any nation that resisted them would be slaughtered, while those that allied themselves to the Tlaxcalans would only have to endure a tolerable level of human sacrifice. I don't think it would be difficult to imagine Europe fragmenting over this. I don't think the Tlaxcalans would lack for allies. Particularly if Europe had been weakened by a long and bloody crusade.''

To Hunahpu, this sounded like victory. Kemal himself had completed the scenario for him.

"But it doesn't work anyway," said Kemal.

"Why not?" asked Diko.

"Smallpox," said Kemal. "Bubonic plague. The common cold. That was the great killer of the Indies. For every Indie who died of overwork in slavery or from Spanish muskets and swords, a hundred died of disease. Those plagues would still have come."

"Oh, yes," said Hunahpu. "That was one of the biggest problems, and there's no way to find evidence for what I'm about to say. But we do know the way diseases work in human populations. The Europeans carried these diseases because they were such a large population with lots of travel and trade and warfare—lots of contact between nations—so that as far as disease organisms were concerned, Europe was one vast caldron in which they could cook, just like China and India, which also had indigenous diseases. In a large population like that, successful diseases are the ones that evolve so they kill slowly and are *not* always fatal. That gives them time to spread, and leaves enough of the human population behind that it can recover and bring up a new, non-immune generation within a few years. These diseases eventually evolve into childhood epidemics, cycling around the large overall population pool, striking here and then there and then over there and finally here again. When Columbus came, there was no region of the Americas that had such a large population pool. Travel was too slow and the barriers were too great. There were a few indigenous diseases—syphilis comes to mind—but that one was exceptionally slow to kill in the American context. Fast-moving plagues were impossible because they would spend themselves in one locality and run out of human hosts before they could get carried to a new locality. But that changes with the Tlaxcalan empire."

"Zapotecan boats," said Diko.

"That's right. This empire is linked by ships carrying cargos and passengers all around the Caribbean basin. Now plagues can travel swiftly enough to spread and become indigenous.''

"That still doesn't mean that a new plague won't be devastating,'' said Kemal. ''It just means that smallpox would travel faster and strike the whole empire almost at the same time.''

"Yes,'' said Hunahpu. ''Just as bubonic plague devastated Europe in the fourteenth century. But there's a difference now. The plague will reach the Tlaxcala empire from those earlier accidental Portuguese visitors, *before* the Europeans come in force. It sweeps through the empire with exactly as much devastation as it had in Europe. Smallpox, measles—they have their terrible effect. But not one nation in Europe fell because of these plagues. No empire collapsed, any more than Rome collapsed because of the plagues in their time. In fact the plague has the effect of giving them more favorable population densities. With fewer mouths to feed, the Tlaxcalans can now produce a food surplus. And what if they interpret these plagues as a sign that Camaxtli wants them to go and win more captives for sacrifice? That might be the final spur to make them sail east. And now when they come, smallpox and measles and the common cold are *already* indigenous to the Tlaxcalans. They touch on European shores already immune to European diseases. But the Europeans have not been exposed to syphilis at all. And when syphilis first reached Europe in *our* history it struck viciously, killing quickly. It only gradually settled down to be the slow killer it had been among the Indies. And who knows what other diseases might have developed among the Tlaxcalans as their empire grew? This time I think the plagues would have worked the other way, against the Europeans and in favor of the Indies.''

"Possible,'' said Kemal. ''But it depends on so many suppositions.''

"Any scenario we think of will depend on suppositions,'' said Tagiri. ''But this one has one unique virtue.''

"And what is that?'' asked Kemal.

"This one would have created a future terrible enough for the Interveners to think it worthwhile to go back and erase their own time in order to eliminate the source of the disaster. Think of what it would have meant to human history, if the powerful, technology-wielding civilization that swept to dominance over the whole world was one that believed in human sacrifice. If Mesoamerican cults of torture and slaughter had come to India and China and Africa and Persia armed with rifles and linked by railroads.''

''And tied together with a single, unified, powerful, and efficient bureacracy, the way the Romans were,'' added Diko. ''The internal dissensions of Europe went a long way toward making their overlordship weaker and more tolerable.''

Tagiri went on. ''It's not hard to imagine that the Interveners, looking back, saw the Tlaxcalan conquest of Europe as the worst, most terrible disaster in the history of humanity. And then they saw Columbus's drive and ambition and personal charisma as the tool they could use to put a stop to it.''

''What does this mean, then?'' said Hassan. ''Do we abandon our entire project, because stopping Columbus would be worse than what he and those who came after him actually caused in our history?''

''Worse?'' asked Tagiri. ''Who is to say which is worse? What do you say, Kemal?''

Kemal looked triumphant. ''I say that if Hunahpu is right, which we can't prove, though he makes a good case, we learn only one thing: Meddling with the past is useless because, as the Interveners proved, the mess you make is little better than the mess you avoid.''

''Not so,'' said Hunahpu.

Everyone turned to look at him, and he realized that, caught up in the discussion, he had forgotten whom he was dealing with— that he was contradicting Kemal, and in front of Tagiri and Hassan, no less. He glanced over at Diko, and saw that, far from looking worried, she simply gazed at him with interest, waiting to hear what he would say. And he realized that this was how *all* of them were looking at him, except Kemal, and his scowl was probably not personal—it seemed to be his permanent expression. For the first time Hunahpu realized that he was being treated as an equal here, and they were not offended or contemptuous at his daring to speak. His voice was as good as anyone else's. The sheer marvel of it was almost enough to silence him.

''Well?'' asked Kemal.

''I think what we learn from this,'' said Hunahpu, ''is not that you can't intervene effectively in the past. After all, the Interveners *did* prevent exactly what they set out to prevent. I've seen a lot more of Mesoamerican culture than any of you, and even though it's my own culture, my own people, anyway, I can promise you that a world ruled by the Tlaxcalans or the Mexica—or even the Maya, for that matter—would never have given rise to the democratic and tolerant and scientific values that eventually emerged from European culture, despite all its bloody-handed arrogance toward other people.''

"You can't say that," said Kemal. "The Europeans sponsored slave trade, and then gradually repudiated it—who's to say that the Tlaxcalans wouldn't have repudiated human sacrifice? The Europeans conquered in the name of kings and queens, and by five centuries later they had stripped those monarchs, where they survived at all, of every shred of power they once had wielded. The Tlaxcalans would have evolved as well.''

"But outside the Americas, wherever the Europeans conquered, native culture survived," said Hunahpu. "Altered, yes, but still recognizably itself. I think the Tlaxcalan conquest would have been more like the Roman conquest, leaving behind little trace of the ancient Gallic or Iberian cultures.''

"This is all irrelevant," said Tagiri. "We aren't choosing between the Interveners' history and our own. Whatever else we do, we can't restore their history and we wouldn't want to. Whichever one was worse, ours or theirs, both were certainly terrible.''

"And both," said Hassan, "led to some version of Pastwatch, some future in which they were aware of their past and able to judge it.''

"Yes," agreed Kemal, rather nastily, "they both led to a time when meddlers with too much leisure on their hands decided to go back and reform the past to coincide with the values of the present. The dead are dead; let's study them and learn from them.''

"And help them if we can," said Tagiri, her voice thick with passion. "Kemal, all we learn from the Interveners is that what they did was not enough, not that it shouldn't have been attempted at all.''

"Not enough!''

"They were thinking only of the history they wanted to avoid, not of the history they would create. We must do better."

"How can we?" asked Diko. "As soon as we act, as soon as we change something, we run the risk of removing ourselves from history. So we can make only one change, as they did."

"They could make only one change," said Tagiri, "because they sent a message. But what if we send a messenger?"

"Send a person?"

"We have found, by careful examination, what the technology of the Interveners was. They didn't just send a message from their own time, because as soon as they started sending it, they would have destroyed themselves and the very instrument that was sending the message. Instead they sent an *object* back in time. A holographic projector, with their entire message contained within it. They knew exactly where to place it and when to trigger it. We've found the machine. It worked perfectly, and then it released powerful acids that destroyed the circuitry and, after about an hour, when no one was nearby, it released a burst of heat that melted itself into a lump of slag and then it exploded, scattering tiny molten fragments across several acres."

"You didn't tell us this," said Kemal.

"The team that is working on building a time machine has been aware of this for some time," said Tagiri. "They'll be publishing soon. What matters is this: They didn't just send a message, they sent an *object*. That was enough to change history, but not enough to shape it intelligently. We need to send back a messenger who can respond to circumstances, who can not only make one change but keep on introducing more changes. That way we can do more than simply avoid one dreadful path—we can deliberately, carefully create a new path that will make the rest of history infinitely better. Think of us as physicians to the past. It isn't enough just to give the patient one injection, one pill. We must keep the patient under our care for an extended period, adapting our treatment to the course of the disease."

"You mean send someone into the past," said Kemal.

"One person, or several people," said Tagiri. "One person might get sick or have an accident or be killed. Sending several people would build some redundancy into our effort."

"Then I must be one of the ones you send," said Kemal.

"What!" cried Hassan. "You! The one who believes we should make no intervention at all!"

"I never said that," said Kemal. "I only said that it was stupid to intervene when you had no way of controlling the consequences. If you *are* sending a team back into the past, I want to be one of them. So I can make sure it goes properly. So I can make sure it's worth doing."

"I think you have an inflated idea of your own powers of judgment," said Hassan crossly.

"Absolutely," said Kemal. "But I'll do it, all the same."

"If anyone goes at all," said Tagiri. "We need to go over Hunahpu's scenario and gather far more evidence. Then, whatever picture we emerge with, we must also plan what our changes will be. In the meantime we have scientists working on our machine—but working with confidence, because we've seen that a physical object can be pushed backward through time. When all these projects are complete—when we have the power to travel back in time, when we know exactly what it is we're trying to accomplish, and when we know exactly how we intend to accomplish it—then we'll make our report public and the decision whether to do it will be up to them. To everyone."

Columbus came home after dark in the chilly night, weary to the bone—not from the walk home, for it wasn't that far, but rather from the endless questions and answers and arguments. There were times when he longed to simply say, "Father Talavera, I've told you everything I can think of. I have no more answers. Make your report." But as the Franciscans of La Rábida had warned him, that would mean the end of his chances. Talavera's report would be devastating and thorough, and there would be no crack left through which he could escape with ships and crew and supplies for a voyage.

There were even times when Columbus wanted to seize the patient, methodical, brilliant priest and say, "Don't you know that I see exactly how impossible it looks to you? But God himself told me that I must sail west to reach the great kingdoms of the east!

So my reasoning must be true, not because I have evidence, but because I have the word of God!''

Of course he never succumbed to *that* temptation. While Columbus hoped that if he were ever charged with heresy, God might intervene and stop the priests from having him burned, he did not want to put God to the test on this. After all, God had told him to tell no one, and so he could hardly expect miraculous intervention if his own impatience put him in danger of the fire.

So it was that the days and the weeks and the months stretched on behind him, and it seemed that the path ahead would have at least as many days and weeks and months—why not years?—before at last Talavera. said, ''Columbus seems to know more than he's telling, but we must make our report and have done with it.'' How many years? It made Columbus tired just to think of it. Will I be like Moses? Will I win consent to launch the fleet when I'm already so old that I will only be able to stand on the coast and watch them sail away? Will I never enter the promised land myself?

No sooner had he laid his hand upon the door than it was flung open and Beatrice greeted him with an embrace only slightly encumbered by her thick belly. ''Are you mad?'' asked Columbus. ''It could have been anybody, and you opened the door without so much as asking who it was.''

''But it was you, wasn't it?'' she said, kissing him.

He reached behind him, shut the door, and then managed to extricate himself from her embrace long enough to bar it. ''You're doing no good for your own reputation, letting the whole street see that you wait for me in my rooms and greet me with kisses.''

''You think the whole street doesn't already know? You think even the two-year-olds don't already know that Beatrice has Cristóbal's baby in her womb?''

''Then let me marry you, Beatrice,'' he said.

''You say that, Cristóbal, only because you know that I'll say no.''

He protested, but in his heart he knew that she was right. He had promised Felipa that Diego would be his only heir, and so he could hardly marry Beatrice and make her child legitimate. Beyond that, though, was the reasoning that *she* always used, and it was correct.

She recited it even now. "You can't be burdened with a wife and child when the court moves to Salamanca in the spring. Besides which, right now you come before the court as a gentleman who consorted with nobility and royalty in Portugal. You are the widower of a woman of high birth. But marry me, and what are you? The husband of the cousin of Genovese merchants. That does *not* make you a gentleman. I think the Marquise de Moya wouldn't be as taken with you then, either."

Ah, yes, his other "affair of the heart," Isabella's good friend the Marquise. In vain had he explained to Beatrice that Isabella was so pious that she would not tolerate any hint that Columbus had dallied with her friend. Beatrice was convinced that Columbus slept with her regularly; she pretended elaborately that she didn't mind. "The Marquise de Moya is a friend and a help to me, because she has the ear of the Queen and because she believes in my cause," said Columbus. "But the only thing that I find beautiful about her is her name."

"De Moya?" teased Beatrice.

"Her Christian name," said Columbus. "Beatrice, just like you. When I hear that name spoken, it fills me with love, but only for you." He rested his hand on her belly. "I'm sorry to have burdened you like this."

"Your child is no burden to me, Cristóbal."

"I can never make him legitimate. If I win titles and fortune, they'll belong to Felipa's son Diego."

"He will have the blood of Columbus in him, and he will have my love and the love you gave me as his heritage."

"Beatrice," said Columbus, "what if I fail? What if there is no voyage, and therefore no fortune and no titles? What is your baby then? The bastard son of a Genovese adventurer who tried to involve the crowned heads of Europe in a mad scheme to sail into the unknown quarters of the sea."

"But you won't fail," she said, comfortably nestling closer to him. "God is with you."

Is he? thought Columbus. Or when I succumbed to your passion and joined you on your bed, did that sin—which I haven't the strength even now to forsake—deprive me of God's favor? Should I repudiate you now and repent of loving you, in order to win his favor back? Or should I forsake my oath to Felipa and follow the dangerous course of marrying you?

"God is with you," she said again. "God gave me to you. Marriage you must forsake for the sake of your great mission, but surely God does not mean you to be a priest, celibate and unloved."

She had always talked this way, even at the start, so that at first he had wondered if God had given him at last someone to whom he could talk about his vision on the beach near Lagos. But no, she knew nothing of that. And yet her faith in the divine origin of his mission was strong, and sustained him when he was at his most discouraged.

"You must eat," she said. "You have to keep up your strength for your jousting with the priests."

She was right, and he was hungry. But first he kissed her, because he knew that she needed to believe that she mattered more to him than anything, more than food, more than his cause. And as they kissed he thought, If only I had been this careful of Felipa. If only I had spent the little time it would have taken to reassure her, she might not have despaired and died so young, or if she died anyway, her life would have been happier until that day. It would have been so easy, but I didn't know.

Is that what Beatrice is? My chance to amend my mistakes with Felipa? Or simply a way to make new ones?

Never mind. If God wanted to punish Columbus for his illegitimate coupling with Beatrice, then so be it. But if God still wanted him to pursue his mission to the west, despite his sins and his weaknesses, then Columbus would keep trying with all his strength to accomplish it. His sins were no worse than King Solomon's, and a far sight gentler than King David's, and God gave greatness to both of them.

Dinner was delicious, and then they played together on the bed, and then he slept. It was the only happiness in these dark cold days, and whether God approved or not, he was glad of it.

Tagiri brought Hunahpu into the Columbus project, putting him and Diko jointly in charge of developing a plan of action for intervention in the past. For an hour or two, Hunahpu felt vindicated; he longed to go back to his old position just long enough to say good-bye, seeing the envy on the faces of those who had despised his private project—a project that now would form the basis of the great Kemal's own work. But the glow of triumph soon passed, and then came dread: He would have to work among people who were used to a very high level of thought, of analysis. He would have to supervise people—he who had always been impossible to supervise. How could he possibly measure up? They would all find him lacking, those above him and those below.

Diko was the one who brought him through these first days, being careful not to take over, but instead making sure that all decisions were jointly reached; that anytime he needed her advice even to know what the choices were, she prompted him only privately, where no one could see, so that the others wouldn't come to think of her as the "real" head of the intervention team. And soon enough Hunahpu began to feel more confident, and then the two of them really did lead together, often arguing over various points but never making a decision until both agreed. No one but Hunahpu and Diko themselves could have been surprised when, after several months together, each came to realize that their professional interdependence had turned to something much more intense and much more personal.

It was maddening to Hunahpu, that he worked with Diko every day, that every day he grew more sure that she loved him as much as he loved her, and yet she refused any hint, any proposal, any outright plea that they extend their friendship beyond the corridors of Pastwatch and into one of the grass huts of Juba.

"Why not?" he said. "Why not?"

"I'm tired," she said. "We have too much to do."

Normally he let this sort of answer stop him, but not today, not this time. "Everything is running smoothly in our project," he said. "We work together perfectly, and the team we've assembled is reliable and efficient. We go home every night at a reasonable hour. There is *time,* if only you took it, for us to—to eat a meal together. To sit and talk as a man and a woman."

"There is *no* time for that," she said.

"Why?" he demanded. "We're close to ready, our project is.

Kemal is still puttering along with his report on probable futures, and the machine is nowhere near done. We have plenty of time.''

The distress on her face usually would be enough to silence him, but not now. "This doesn't have to make you unhappy," he said. "Your mother and father work together just as we do, and yet they married and had a child."

"Yes," she said. "But we will not."

"Why not! What is it, that I'm so much smaller than you? I can't help the fact that Maya people are shorter than a Turko-Dongotona."

"You are so stupid, Hunahpu," she said. "Father is shorter than Mother, too. What kind of idiot do you think I am?"

"Such an idiot that you're in love with me just as I'm in love with you, only for some insane reason you refuse to admit it, you refuse even to take a chance on us being happy together."

To his surprise, tears came to her eyes. "I don't want to talk about this," she said.

"But I do," he said.

"You think you love me," she said.

"I know I love you."

"And you think I love you," she said.

"I hope for that."

"And maybe you're right," she said. "But there's something that both of us love more."

"What?"

"This," she said, indicating the room around them, filled with TruSite IIs and Tempoviews and computers and desks and chairs.

"People in Pastwatch love and live as human beings," he answered.

"Not Pastwatch, Hunahpu, our project. The Columbus project. We're going to succeed. We're going to assemble our team of three who will go back in time. And when they succeed, all of this will cease to be. Why should we marry and bring a child into the world in order to cause it to disappear in only a few more years?"

"We don't know that," said Hunahpu. "The mathematicians are still divided. Maybe all we create by intervening in the past is a fork in time, so that both futures continue to exist."

"You know that that is the least likely alternative. You know that the machine is being built according to the theory of metatime. Anything sent back in time is lifted out of the causal flow. It can no longer be affected by anything that happens to the timestream that originally brought it into existence, and when it enters the time-stream at a different point, it becomes an uncaused causer. When we change the past, this present will disappear.''

''Both theories can explain the way the machine works,'' said Hunahpu, ''so don't try to use your superior education in mathematics and time theory against me.''

''It doesn't matter anyway,'' said Diko. ''Because even if our time continues to exist, I won't be in it.''

There it was—the unspoken assumption that she would be one of the three who went back in time.

''That's ludicrous,'' he said. ''A tall black woman, going to live among the Taino?''

''A tall black woman with a detailed knowledge of events that still lie in the future for the people of the surrounding tribes,'' she said. ''I think I'll do well enough.''

''Your parents will never let you go.''

''My parents will do whatever it takes for this mission to succeed,'' she answered. ''I'm already far more qualified than anyone else. I'm in perfect health. I've been studying the languages I'll need for that aspect of the project—Spanish, Genovese, Latin, two Arawak dialects, one Carib dialect, and the Ciboney language that is still used in Putukam's village because they think it's so holy. Who else can match that? And I know the plan, inside and out, and all the thinking that went into it. Who can do better than I to adapt the plan if things don't go as expected? So I *will* go, Hunahpu. Mother and Father will fight it for a while, and then they'll realize that I am the best hope of success, and they'll send me.''

He said nothing. He knew that it was true.

She laughed at him. ''You hypocrite,'' she said. ''You've been doing just what I've been doing—you've designed the Mesoamerican part of the plan so that only you can possibly do it.''

That too was true. ''I'm as natural a choice as you are—more natural, because I'm a Maya.''

''A Maya who's more than a foot taller than the Mayas and Zapotecs of the period,'' she retorted.

"I speak two Mayan dialects, plus Nahuatl, Zapotec, Spanish, Portuguese, and both of the Tarascan dialects that matter. And all your arguments apply to me as well. Plus I know all the technologies we're going to try to introduce and the detailed personal histories of all the people we have to deal with. There *is* no choice but me."

"I know it," said Diko. "I knew it before you did. You don't have to persuade me."

"Oh," he said.

"You *are* a hypocrite," she said, and there was some emotion behind it. "You were all set to go yourself, and yet you expected *me* to stay behind. You had some foolish notion that we would marry and have a baby, and then I would stay behind on the off chance that there would *be* a future here while you went back and fulfilled your destiny."

"No," he said. "I never really thought of marriage."

"Then what, Hunahpu? Sneaking off to some sordid little rendezvous? I'm not your Beatrice, Hunahpu. I have work of my own to do. And unlike the Europeans and, apparently, the Indies, *I* know that to mate with someone without marriage is a repudiation of the community, a refusal to take one's proper role within the society. I won't mate like an animal, Hunahpu. When I marry it will be as a human being. And it will not be in this timestream. If I marry at all, it will be in the past, because that's the only place where I have a future."

He listened, leaden at heart. "The chance of our both living long enough to meet there is small, Diko."

"And that, my friend, is why I refuse all your invitations to extend our friendship beyond these walls. There's no future for us."

"Is the future, is the *past,* all that matters to you? Don't you have just a little bit of room for the present?"

Again the tears flowed down her cheeks. "No," she said.

He reached up and cleared her cheeks with his thumbs, then streaked his own cheeks with her tears. "I will love no one but you," he said.

"So you say now," she said. "But I release you from that promise and I forgive you already for the fact that you *will* love someone, and you *will* marry, and if we ever meet there, we will be friends and be glad to see each other and we will not regret for one moment that we did not act foolishly now.''

''We *will* regret it, Diko. At least *I* will. I regret it now, and I will regret it then, and always. Because no one that we meet in the past will understand what and who we really are, not the way we understand each other now. No one in the past will have shared our goals or worked as hard to help us achieve them as we've done for each other. No one will know you and love you as I do. And even if you're right, and there's no future for us, I for one would rather face whatever future I do have with the memory of knowing that we had each other for a while.''

''Then you *are* a romantic fool, just as Mother always said!''

''She said that?''

''Mother is never wrong,'' said Diko. ''She also said that I would never have a better friend than you.''

''She was right, then.''

''Be my true friend, Hunahpu,'' said Diko. ''Never speak of this to me again. Work with me, and when the time comes to go into the past, go with me. Let our marriage be the work we do together, and let our children be the future that we build. Let me come to whatever husband I *do* have without the memories of another husband or another lover to encumber me. Let me face my future with confidence in your friendship instead of guilt, whether it comes from denying you or accepting you. Will you do that for me?''

No, shouted Hunahpu silently. Because that isn't necessary, we don't have to do that, we can be happy now and *still* be happy in the future and you're wrong, completely wrong about this.

Except that if she believed that marriage or an affair would make her unhappy then it would make her unhappy, and so she was right—for herself—and loving him would be a bad thing—for her. So . . . did he love her or merely want to own her? Was it her happiness he cared about or satisfaction of his own needs?

''Yes,'' said Hunahpu. ''I'll do that for you.''

It was then, and only then, that she kissed him, leaned down to him and kissed him on the lips, not briefly but not with passion either. With love, simple love, a single kiss, and then she left, and left him desolate.

8

Dark Futures

Father Talavera had listened to all the eloquent, methodical, sometimes impassioned arguments, but he had known from the start that he had to make the final decision about Colón by himself. How many years had they listened to Colón—and harangued him, too—so that all were weary of the same conversations endlessly repeated? For so many years, since the Queen first asked him to lead the examination of Colón's claims, nothing had changed. Maldonado still seemed to regard Colón's very existence as an affront, while Deza seemed almost infatuated with the Genovese. The others still lined up behind one or the other, or, like Talavera himself, remained neutral. Or rather, they *seemed* neutral. They merely wavered like grass, dancing in whatever wind was blowing. How many times had each one come to him privately and spent long minutes—sometimes hours—explaining their views, which always amounted to the same thing: They agreed with everybody.

I alone am truly neutral, thought Talavera. I alone am swayed by no argument whatsoever. I alone can listen to Maldonado bring forth sentences from ancient, long-forgotten writings in languages so obscure that quite possibly no one ever spoke them except the original writer himself—I alone can listen to him and hear only the voice of a man who is determined not to allow the slightest new idea to disrupt his own perfect understanding of the world. I alone can listen to Deza eloquizing about Colón's brilliance in finding truths so long overlooked by scholars and hear only the voice of a man who yearned to be a knight-errant from the romances, championing a cause which is noble only because he champions it.

I alone am neutral, thought Talavera, because I alone understand the utter stupidity of the entire conversation. Which of these ancients they all quote with such certainty was lifted by the hand of God to see the Earth from an appropriate vantage point? Which of them was given calipers by the hand of God to make an accurate measurement of the diameter of the Earth? No one knew anything. The only serious attempt at measurement, more than a thousand years before, could have been disastrously flawed by the tiniest inconsistency in the original observations. All the argument in the world could not change the fact that if you build the foundation of your logic upon guesswork, then your conclusions will be guesswork also.

Of course Talavera could never say this to anyone else. He had not risen to his position of trust by freely expressing his skepticism about the wisdom of the ancients. On the contrary: All who knew him were sure that he was utterly orthodox. He had labored hard to make sure they had that opinion of him. And in a sense they were right. He simply defined orthodoxy quite differently from them.

Talavera did not put his faith in Aristotle or Ptolemy. He already knew what the examination of Colón was demonstrating in such agonizing detail: that for every ancient authority there was a contradictory authority just as ancient and (he suspected) just as ignorant. Let the other scholars claim that God had whispered to Plato as he wrote the Symposium; Talavera knew better. Aristotle was clever but his wise sayings were no likelier to be true than the opinions of other clever men.

Talavera put his faith in only one person: Jesus Christ. His were the only words that Talavera cared about, Christ's cause the only cause that stirred his soul. Every other cause, every other idea, every other plan or party or faction or individual, was to be judged in light of how it would either help or hinder the cause of Christ. Talavera had realized early in his rise within the Church that the monarchs of Castile and Aragon were good for the cause of Christ, and so he enlisted himself in their camp. They found him to be a valuable servant because he was deft at marshaling the resources of the Church in their support.

His technique was simple: See what the monarchs want and need in order to further their effort to make of Spain a Christian kingdom, driving the unbeliever from any power or influence, and then interpret all the pertinent texts to show how scripture, Church tradition, and all the ancient writers were united in supporting the course that the monarchs had already determined to pursue. The funny thing—or, when he was in another mood, the sad thing— was that no one ever caught on to his method. When he invariably brought in scholarship that would support the cause of Christ and the monarchs of Spain, everyone assumed that this meant that the course the monarchs were pursuing was the right one, not that Talavera had been clever about manipulating the texts. It was as if they did not realize the texts *could* be manipulated.

And yet they *all* manipulated and interpreted and transformed the ancient writings. Certainly Maldonado did it to defend his own elaborate preconceptions, and Deza just as much to attack them. But none of them seemed to know that this was what they were doing. They thought they were discovering truth.

How many times Talavera had wished to speak to them with utter scorn. Here is the only truth that matters, he wanted to say: Spain is at war, purifying Iberia as a Christian land. The King has conducted this war deftly and patiently, and he will win, driving the last Moors from Iberia. The Queen is now setting into motion what England wisely did years ago: the expulsion of the Jews from her kingdom. (Not that the Jews were dangerous by intent—Talavera had no sympathy with Torquemada's fanatical belief in the evil plots of the Jews. No, the Jews had to be expelled because as long as the weaker Christians could look around them and see unbelievers prospering, see them marrying and having children and living normal and decent lives, they would not be firm in their faith that only in Christ is there happiness. The Jews had to go, just as the Moors had to go.)

And what had Colón to do with this? Sailing west. So what?
Even if he was right, what would it accomplish? Convert the heathen in a far-off land when Spain itself was not yet unified in its
Christianity? That would be marvelous and well worth the effort—
as long as it didn't interfere in any way with the war against the
Moors. So, while the others argued about the size of the Earth and
the passability of the Ocean Sea, Talavera was always weighing far
more important matters. What would the news of this expedition
do to the prestige of the Crown? What would it cost and how would
the diversion of such funds affect the war? Would supporting Colón
cause Aragon and Castile to draw closer together or farther apart?
What do the King and Queen actually want to do? If Colón were
sent away, where would he go next and what would he do?

Until today, the answers had all been clear enough. The King
did not intend to spend one peso on anything but the war against
the Moors, while the Queen very much wanted to support Colón's
expedition. That meant that any decision at all would be divisive.
In the delicate balance between King and Queen, between Aragon
and Castile, any decision on Colón's expedition would cause one of
them to think that power had drifted dangerously in the other direction, and suspicion and envy would increase.

Therefore, regardless of all the arguments, Talavera was determined that no verdict would be reached until the situation changed.
It was easy enough at first, but as the years passed and it became
clear that Colón had nothing new to offer, it became harder and
harder to keep the issue alive. Fortunately, Colón was the only
other person involved in the process who seemed to understand it.
Or if he didn't understand it, at least he cooperated with Talavera
to this degree: He kept hinting that he knew more than he was
telling. Veiled references to information he learned while in Lisbon
or Madeira, mentions of proofs that had not yet been brought forward, this was what allowed Talavera to keep the examination
open.

When Maldonado (and Deza, for opposite reasons) wanted him
to force Colón to lay these great secrets on the table, to settle things
once and for all, Talavera always agreed that it would be a great
help if Colón would do so, but one must understand that anything
Colón learned in Portugal must have been learned under sacred

oath. If it was just a matter of fear of Portuguese reprisals, then no doubt Colón would tell, for he was a brave man and not afraid of anything King John might do. But if it was a matter of honor, then how could they insist that he break his oath and tell? That would be the same as asking Colón to damn himself to hell for all eternity, just to satisfy their curiosity. Therefore they must listen carefully to all that Colón said, hoping that, clever scholars that they were, they could determine just what it was he could not tell them openly.

And, by the grace of God, Colón himself played along. Surely the others had all taken him aside, at one time or another, trying to pry from him the secrets that he would not tell. And in all these long years, Colón had never given a hint of what his secret information was. Just as important, he had also never given a hint that there *was* no secret information.

For a long time Talavera had not studied the arguments—he had grasped those at the start and nothing important had been added in years. No, what Talavera studied was Colón himself. At first he had assumed that Colón was just another courtier on the make, but that impression was quickly dispelled. Colón was absolutely, fanatically determined to sail west, and could not be distracted by any other sort of preferment. Gradually, though, Talavera had come to see that this voyage west was not an end in itself. Colón had dreams. Not of personal wealth or fame, but rather dreams of power. Colón wanted to *accomplish* something, and this westward voyage was the foundation of it. And what was it that Colón wanted to do? Talavera had puzzled about this for months, for years.

Today, at last, the answer had come. Departing from his usual scholarly bludgeoning, Maldonado had remarked, rather testily, that it was selfish of Colón to try to distract the monarchs from their war with the Moors, and Colón had suddenly erupted in anger. "A war with the Moors? For what, to drive them from Granada, from a small corner of this dry peninsula? With the wealth of the East we could drive the Turk from Constantinople, and from there it is only a short step to Armageddon and the liberation of the Holy Land! And you tell me that I must not do *this*, because it might interfere with the war against Granada? You might as well tell a matador that he cannot kill the bull because it might interfere with the effort to stomp on a mouse!"

At once Colón had regretted his remarks, and was quick to reassure everyone that he had nothing but the greatest enthusiasm for the great war against Granada. "Forgive me for letting my passion rule my mouth," said Colón. "Never for a moment have I wished for anything but the victory of the Christian armies over the infidel in Granada."

Talavera had immediately forgiven him and forbidden anyone to repeat Colón's remarks. "We know that what you said was in zeal for the cause of Christ, wishing that we could accomplish even *more* than victory against Granada, not *less.*"

Colón himself seemed relieved indeed to hear Talavera's words. It could have been the death of his petition right on the spot, if his remarks had been taken as disloyalty—and the personal consequences could have been severe as well. The others had also nodded wisely. They had no wish to denounce Colón. For one thing, it would hardly redound to their credit if it had taken them this many years to discover that Colón was a traitor!

What Colón did not know, what none of them knew, was how deeply his words had touched Talavera's soul. A Crusade to liberate Constantinople! To break the power of the Turk! To plunge a knife into the heart of Islam! In a few sentences Colón had forced Talavera to view his life's work in a new light. All these years that Talavera had devoted himself to the cause of Spain for Christ's sake, and now he realized that next to Colón his own faith was childish. Colón is right: If we serve Christ, why are we chasing mice when the great bull of Satan struts through the greatest Christian city?

For the first time in years, Talavera realized that serving the King and Queen might not be identical to serving the cause of Christ. He realized that for the first time in his life he was in the presence of someone whose devotion to Christ might well be the match of his own. Such was my pride, thought Talavera, that it took me this many years to see it.

And in those years, what have I done? I have kept Colón trapped here, leading him on, keeping the question open year after year, all because making any kind of decision might weaken the relationship between Aragon and Castile. Yet what if it is Colón, and not Ferdinand and Isabella, who understands what will best serve the cause of Christ? How does the purification of Spain compare to the liberation of all the ancient Christian lands? And with the power of Islam broken, what then would stop Christianity from spreading forth to fill the world?

If only Colón had come to us with a plan for Crusade instead of this strange voyage to the west. The man was eloquent, forceful, and there was something about him that made you want to be on his side. Talavera imagined him going from king to king, from court to court. He might well have been able to convince the monarchs of Europe to unite in common cause against the Turk.

Instead, Colón seemed sure that the only way to bring about such a Crusade was to establish a direct, quick connection with the great kingdoms of the East. Well, what if he was right? What if God had put this vision in his mind? Certainly it was nothing an intelligent man would have thought of on his own—the most rational plan was to sail around Africa as the Portuguese were doing. But wasn't that, too, a species of madness? Weren't there ancient writers who had assumed that Africa extended all the way to the south pole, so there was no way to sail around it? Yet the Portuguese had persisted, finding again and again that no matter how far south they sailed, Africa was always there, extending even farther than they had imagined. Yet last year Dias at last returned with the good news—they had rounded a cape and found that the coast ran to the east, not to the south; and then, after hundreds of miles, it definitely ran to the northeast and then the north. They had rounded Africa. And now the irrational persistence of the Portuguese was widely known to be rational after all.

Couldn't Colón's irrational plans turn out the same way? Only instead of a years-long voyage, *his* route to the Orient would bring wealth much faster. And *his* plan, instead of enriching a tiny useless country like Portugal, would lead eventually to the Church of Christ filling the entire world!

So now, instead of thinking how to drag out the examination of Colón, waiting for the desires of the monarchs to resolve themselves, Talavera sat in his austere chamber trying to think how to force the issue. One thing he certainly could *not* do was suddenly, after all these years and with no significant new arguments, announce that the committee was deciding in favor of Colón. Maldonado and his supporters would protest directly to the King's men, and a power struggle would ensue. The Queen would almost certainly lose such an open struggle, since her support from the lords of her realm depended in large part on the fact that she was known to "think like a man." Disagreeing openly with the King would give the lie to *that* idea. Thus open support for Colón would lead to division and probably would not lead to a voyage.

No, Talavera thought, the one thing I cannot do is support Colón. So what *can* I do?

I can set him free. I can end the process and let him go on to another king, to another court. Talavera well knew that Colón's friends had made discreet inquiries in the courts of France and England. Now that the Portuguese had achieved their quest for an African route to the East, they might be able to afford a small exploratory expedition toward the west. Certainly the Portuguese advantage in trading with the Orient will be envied by other kings. Colón might well succeed somewhere. So whatever else happens, I must end his examination immediately.

But could there not also be a way to end the examination and yet turn things to the advantage of Colón's supporters?

With a half-formed plan in mind, Talavera sent to the Queen a note bearing his request for a secret audience with her on the matter of Colón.

Tagiri did not understand her own reaction to the news of success from the scientists working on time travel. She should be happy. She should be rejoicing to know that her great work could, physically, be accomplished. Yet ever since the meeting with the team of physicists, mathematicians, and engineers working on the time travel project, she had been upset, angry, frightened. The opposite of how she had expected she would feel.

Yes, they said, we can send a living person into the past. But if we do so there is no chance, no chance whatsoever, that our present world will survive in any form. To send someone into the past to change it is the end of ourselves.

They were so patient, trying to explain temporal physics to historians. "If our time is destroyed," Hassan asked, "then won't that also destroy the very people that we send back? If none of us are ever born, then the people we send won't have been born either, and therefore they could never have been sent."

No, explained the physicists, you're confusing causality with time. Time itself, as a phenomenon, is utterly linear and unidirectional. Each moment happens only once, and passes into the next moment. Our memories grasp this one-way flow of time, and in our minds we link it with causality. We know that if A causes B, then A must come *before* B. But there is nothing in the physics of time that requires this. Think of what your predecessors did. The machine they sent back in time was the product of a long causal network. Those causes were all real, and the machine actually existed. Sending it back in time did not undo any of the events that led to the creation of that machine. But in the moment that the machine caused Columbus to see his vision on that beach in Portugal, it began to transform the causal network so that it no longer led to the same place. All of those causes and effects really happened— the ones leading to the creation of the machine, and the ones following *from* the machine's introduction into the fifteenth century.

"But then you're saying that their future still exists," Hunahpu protested.

That depends on how you define existence, they explained. As a part of the causal network leading to the present moment, yes, they continue to exist in the sense that any part of their causal network that led to the existence of their machine in our time is still having effects in the present world. But anything peripheral or irrelevant to that is now utterly without effect in our timestream. And anything in *their* history that the introduction of that machine in *our* history caused *not* to happen is utterly and irrevocably lost. We can't go back into our past and view it because it didn't happen.

"But it *did* happen, because their machine exists."

No, they said again. Causality can be recursive, but time cannot. Anything that the introduction of their machine caused *not* to happen, did not in fact happen in time. There is no moment of time in which those events exist. Therefore they cannot be seen or visited because the temporal loci which they occupied are now occupied by different moments. Two contradictory sets of events cannot occupy the same moment: You are only confused because you cannot separate causality from time. And that's perfectly natural, because time is rational. Causality is irrational. We've been playing speculative games with the mathematics of time for centuries, but we would never have seen this distinction between time and causality ourselves if we hadn't had to account for the machine from the future.

"So what you're saying," Diko offered, "is that the other history still exists, but we just can't see it with our machines."

That's *not* what we're saying, they replied with infinite patience. Anything that was not causally connected to the creation of that machine cannot be said to have ever existed at all. And anything that *did* lead to the creation of that machine and its introduction into our time exists only in the sense that unreal numbers exist.

"But they *did* exist," Tagiri said, more passionately than she had expected. "They *did*."

"They did not," said old Manjam, who had let his younger colleagues speak for him till now. "We mathematicians are quite comfortable with this—we have never dwelt in the realm of reality. But of course your mind rebels against it because your mind exists in time. What you must understand is that causality is not real. It does not exist in time. Moment A does not really cause Moment B in reality. Moment A exists, and then Moment B exists, and between them are Moments A.a through A.z, and between A.a and A.b there are A.aa through A.az. None of these moments actually touches any other moment. That is what reality is—an infinite array of discreet moments unconnected with any other moment because each moment in time has no linear dimension. When the machine was introduced into our history, from that point forward a new infinite set of moments completely replaced the old infinite set of moments. There were no spare leftover moment-locations for the old moments to hang around in. And because there was no time for them, they didn't happen. But causality is unaffected by this. It isn't geometric. It has a completely different mathematics, one which does not fit well with concepts like space and time and *certainly* doesn't fit within anything that you could call 'real.' There is no space or time in which those events happened."

"What does that mean?" said Hassan. "That if we send somebody back in time, they will suddenly cease to remember anything about the time they came from, because that time no longer exists?''

"The person that you send back," said Manjam, "is a discrete event. He will have a brain, and that brain will contain memories that, when he accesses them, will give him certain information. This information will cause him to think he remembers a whole reality, a world and a history. But all that exists in reality is him and his brain. The causal network will only include those causal connections which led to the creation of his physical body, including his brain state, but any part of that causal network which is not part of the new reality cannot be said to exist in any way."

Tagiri was shaken. "I don't care that I don't understand the science of it," she said. "I only know that I hate it."

"It's always frightening to deal with something that is counter-intuitive," said Manjam.

"Not at all," said Tagiri, trembling. "I didn't say I was frightened. I'm not. I'm *angry* and . . . frustrated. Horrified."

"Horrified about the mathematics of time?"

"Horrified at what we are doing, at what the Interveners actually did. I suppose that I always felt that in some sense they went on. That they sent their machine and then went on with their lives, comforted in their miserable situation by knowing that they had done something to help their ancestors."

"But that was never possible," said Manjam.

"I know it," said Tagiri. "And so when I really thought about it, I imagined them sending the machine and in that moment they sort of—disappeared. A clean painless death for everyone. But at least they *had* lived, up to that moment."

"Well," said Manjam, "how is clean, painless nonexistence any worse than a clean, painless death?"

"You see," said Tagiri, "it's not. Not any worse. And not any better, either, for the people themselves."

"*What* people?" said Manjam, shrugging.

"*Us*, Manjam. We are talking about doing this to ourselves."

"If you do this, then there will have been no such people as ourselves. The only aspect of our causal network that will have any future *or* past are those that are connected to the creation of the physical bodies and mental states of the persons you send into the past.''

"This is all so silly," said Diko. "Who cares about what's real and what isn't real? Isn't this what we wanted all along? To make it so that the terrible events of our history never happened in the first place? And as for our own history, the parts that will be lost, who cares if a mathematician calls us dirty names like 'unreal'? They say such slanders about the square root of minus two, as well.''

Everyone laughed, but not Tagiri. They did not see the past as she saw it. Or rather, they didn't *feel* the past. They didn't understand that to her, looking through the Tempoview and the TruSite II, the past was alive and real. Just because the people were dead did not mean that they were not still part of the present, because she could go back and recover them. See them, hear them. Know them, at least as well as any human being ever knows any other. Even before the TruSite and the Tempoview, though, the dead still lived in memory, *some* kind of memory. But not if they changed the past. It was one thing to ask humankind of today to choose to give up their future in the hope of creating a new reality. That would be hard enough. But to also reach back and kill the dead, to uncreate them as well—and they had no vote. They could not be asked.

We must not do this, she thought. This is wrong. This will be a worse crime than the ones we are trying to prevent.

She got up and left the meeting. Diko and Hassan tried to leave with her, but she brushed them off. "I need to be alone," she said, and so they stayed behind, returning to a meeting that she knew would be in shambles. For a moment she felt remorse at having greeted the physicists' triumphant moment with such a negative response, but as she walked the streets of Juba that remorse faded, replaced by one far deeper.

The children playing naked in the dirt and weeds. The men and women going about their business. She spoke to them all in her heart, saying, How would you like to die? And not only you, but your children and their children? And not only them, but your parents, too? Let's go back into the graves, open them up, and kill them all. Every good and evil thing they did, all their joy, all their suffering, all their *choices*—let's kill them all, erase them, undo them. Reaching back and back and back, until we finally come to the golden moment that we have chosen, declaring it worthy to continue to exist, but with a new future tied to the end of it. And why must all of you and yours be killed? Because in our judgment they didn't make a good enough world. Their mistakes along the way were so unforgivable that they erase the value of any good that also happened. All must be obliterated.

How dare I? How dare we? Even if we got the unanimous consent of all the people of our own time, how will we poll the dead?

She picked her way down the bluffs to the riverside. In the waning afternoon, the heat of the day was finally beginning to break. In the distance, hippos were bathing or feeding or sleeping. Birds were calling, getting ready for their frenzied feeding on the insects of the dusk. What goes through your minds, Birds, Hippopotamuses, Insects of the late afternoon? Do you like being alive? Do you fear death? You kill to live; you die so others can live; it's the path ordained for you by evolution, by life itself. But if you had the power, wouldn't you save yourselves?

She was still there by the river when the darkness came, when the stars came out. For a moment, gazing at the ancient light of the stars, she thought: Why should I worry about uncreating so much of human history? Why should I care that it will be worse than forgotten, that it will be *unknown*? Why should that seem to be a crime, when all of human history is an eyeblink compared to the billions of years the stars have shone? We will all be forgotten in the last exhalation of our history; what does it matter, then, if some are forgotten sooner than others, or if some are caused to have never existed at all?

Oh, this is such a wise perspective, to compare human lives to the lives of stars. The only problem is that it cuts both ways. If in the long run it doesn't matter that we wipe out billions of lives in order to save our ancestors, then in the long run saving our ancestors doesn't matter, either, so why bother changing the past at all?

The only perspective that matters is the human one, Tagiri knew. We are the only ones who care; we are the actors and the audience as well, all of us. And the critics. We are also the critics.

The light of an electric torch bobbed into view as she heard someone approaching through the grass.

"That torch will only attract animals that we don't want," she said.

"Come home," said Diko. "It isn't safe out here, and Father's worried."

"Why should he be worried? My life doesn't exist. I never lived."

"You're alive now, and so am I, and so are the crocodiles."

"If individual lives don't matter," said Tagiri, "then why bother going back to make them better? And if they *do* matter, then how dare we snuff some out in favor of others?"

"Individual lives matter," said Diko. "But life also matters. Life as a whole. That's what you've forgotten today. That's what Manjam and the other scientists also forgot. They talk of all these moments, separate, never touching, and say that they are the only reality. Just as the only reality of human life is individuals, isolated individuals who never really know each other, never really touch at any point. No matter how close you are, you're always separate."

Tagiri shook her head. "This has nothing to do with what is bothering me."

"It has everything to do with it," said Diko. "Because you know that this is a lie. You know that the mathematicians are wrong about the moments, too. They *do* touch. Even if we can't really touch causality, the connections between moments, that doesn't mean they aren't real. And just because whenever you look closely at the human race, at a community, at a family, all you can ever find are separate individuals, that doesn't mean that the family is not also real. After all, when you look closely enough at a molecule, all you can see are atoms. There is no physical connection between them. And yet the molecule is still real because of the way the atoms affect each other."

"You're as bad as they are," said Tagiri, "answering anguish with analogies."

"Analogies are all I have," said Diko. "Truth is all I have, and truth is never a comfort. But *understanding* truth, that is what you taught me to do. So here is the truth. What human life *is,* what it's *for,* what we *do,* is create communities. Some of them are good, some of them are evil, or somewhere between. You taught me this, didn't you? And there are communities of communities, groups of group's, and—''

"And what *makes* them good or bad?'' demanded Tagiri. "The quality of the individual lives. The ones we're going to snuff out.''

"No,'' said Diko. "What we're going to do is go back and revise the ultimate community of communities, the human race as a whole, *history* as a whole here on this planet. We're going to create a new version of it, one that will give the new individuals who live within it a far, far better chance of happiness, of having a good life, than the old version. That's real, and that's good, Mother. It's worth doing. It is.''

"I've never known any groups,'' said Tagiri. "Just people. Just individual people. Why should I make those people pay so this imaginary thing called 'human history' can be better? Better for whom?''

"But Mother, individual people *always* sacrifice for the sake of the community. When it matters enough, people sometimes even die, willingly, for the good of the community that they feel themselves to be a part of. As well as a thousand sacrifices short of death. And why? Why do we give up our individual desires, leave them unfulfilled, or work hard at tasks we hate or fear because others need us to do them? Why did you go through such pain to bear me and Acho? Why did you give up all the time it took to take care of us?''

Tagiri looked at her daughter. "I don't know, but as I listen to you, I begin to think that perhaps it was worth it. Because *you* know things that I don't know. I wanted to create someone different from myself, better than myself, and willingly gave up part of my life to do it. And here you are. And you're saying that that's what the people of our time will be to the people of the new history we create. That we will sacrifice to create their history, as parents sacrifice to create healthy, happy children.''

"Yes, Mother,'' said Diko. "Manjam is wrong. The people who sent that vision to Columbus *did* exist. They were the parents of our age; we are their children. And now we will be the parents to another age.''

"Which just goes to show," said Tagiri, "that one can always find language to make the most terrible things sound noble and beautiful, so you can live with doing them."

Diko looked at Tagiri in silence for a long moment. Then she threw the electric torch to the ground at her mother's feet and walked away into the night.

Isabella found herself dreading the meeting with Talavera. It would be about Cristóbal Colón, of course. It must mean that he had reached a conclusion. "It's foolish of me, don't you think?" Isabella said to Lady Felicia. "Yet I am as worried about his verdict as if I myself were on trial."

Lady Felicia murmured something noncommittal.

"Perhaps I *am* on trial."

"What court on Earth can try a queen, Your Majesty?" asked Lady Felicia.

"That is my point," said Isabella. "I felt, when Cristóbal spoke that first day in court, so many years ago, that the Holy Mother was offering me something very sweet and fine, a fruit from her own garden, a berry from her own vine."

"He *is* a fascinating man, Your Majesty."

"Not *him,* though I do think him a sweet and fervent fellow." One thing Isabella would never do was leave the impression with anyone that she looked on any man but her husband with anything approaching desire. "No, I mean that the Queen of Heaven was giving me the chance to open a vast door that had long been closed." She sighed. "But the power even of queens is not infinite. I had no ships to spare, and the cost of saying yes on the spot would have been too great. Now Talavera has decided, and I fear that he is about to close a door whose key will only be given me that one time. Now it will pass into another hand, and I will regret it forever."

"Heaven cannot condemn Your Majesty for failing to do what was not within your power to do," said Lady Felicia.

"I'm not worried at this moment about the condemnation of heaven. That's between me and my confessors."

"Oh, Your Majesty, I was not saying that you face any kind of condemnation from—"

"No no, Lady Felicia, don't worry, I didn't take your remark as anything but the kindest reassurance."

Felicia, still flustered, got up to answer the soft knock on the door. It was Father Talavera.

"Would you wait by the door, Lady Felicia?" asked Isabella.

Talavera bowed over her hand. "Your Majesty, I am about to ask Father Maldonado to write the verdict."

The worst possible outcome. She heard the door of heaven clang shut against her. "Why today of all days?" she asked him. "You've taken all these years over this Colón fellow, and today it's suddenly an emergency that must be decided at once?"

"I think it is," he said.

"And why is that?"

"Because victory in Granada is near."

"Oh, has God spoken to you about this?"

"You feel it too. Not God, of course, but His Majesty the King. There is new energy in him. He is making the final push, and he knows that it will succeed. This next summer. By the end of 1491, all of Spain will be free of the Moor."

"And this means that you must press the issue of Colón's voyage now?"

"It means," said Talavera, "that one who wishes to do something so audacious must sometimes proceed very warily. Imagine, if you will, what would happen if our verdict were positive. Go ahead, Your Majesty, we say. This voyage is worthy of success. What then? At once Maldonado and his friends will seek His Majesty's ear, criticizing this voyage. And they will speak to many others, so that the voyage will soon be known as a folly. In particular, Isabella's folly."

She raised an eyebrow.

"I say only what will surely be said by those with malicious hearts. Now imagine if this verdict is reached when the war is over, and His Majesty can devote his full attention to the matter. The issue of this voyage could easily become quite a stumbling block in the relations between the two kingdoms."

"I see that in your view, supporting Colón will be disastrous," she said.

"Now imagine, Your Majesty, that the verdict is negative. In fact, that Maldonado himself writes it. From that point on, Maldonado has nothing to gossip about. There will be no whispers."

"There will also be no voyage."

"Won't there?" asked Talavera. "I imagine a day when a queen might say to her husband, 'Father Talavera came to me, and we agreed that Father Maldonado should write the verdict.' "

"But I don't agree."

"I imagine this queen saying to her husband, 'We agreed that Maldonado should write the verdict because we know that the war with Granada is the most vital concern of our kingdom. We want nothing to distract you or anyone else from this holy Crusade against the Moor. Most certainly we don't want to give King John of Portugal reason to think we are planning any kind of voyage through waters he thinks of as his own. We need his unflagging friendship during this final struggle with Granada. So even though in my heart I want nothing more than to take the chance and send this Colón west, to carry the cross to the great kingdoms of the East, I have set aside this dream.' "

"What an eloquent queen you have imagined," said Isabella.

"All controversy dies. The king sees the queen as a statesman of great wisdom. He also sees the sacrifice she has made for their kingdoms and the cause of Christ. Now imagine that time passes. The war is won. In the glow of victory, the queen comes to the king and says, 'Now let's see if this Colón still wants to sail west.' "

"And *he* will say, 'I thought that business was finished. I thought Talavera's examiners put a stop to all that nonsense.' "

"Oh, does he say that?" asked Talavera. "Fortunately, the queen is quite deft, and she says, 'Oh, but you know that Talavera and I agreed to have Maldonado write that verdict. For the good of the war effort. The matter was never really settled. Many of the examiners thought Colón's project was a worthy one with a decent chance of success. Who can know, anyway? We'll find out by sending this Colón. If he comes back successful, we'll know he was right and we'll send great expeditions at once to follow through. If he comes back empty-handed, then we'll put him in prison for defrauding the Crown. And if he never comes back, we'll waste no more effort on such projects.'''

"The queen *you* imagine is so *dry,*" said Isabella. "She talks like a cleric."

"It's a shortcoming of mine," said Talavera. "I haven't heard enough great ladies in private conversation with their husbands."

"I think this queen should say to her husband, 'If he sails and never returns, then we have lost a handful of caravels. Pirates take more than that every year. But if he sails and succeeds, then with three caravels we will have accomplished more than Portugal has achieved in a century of expensive, dangerous voyages along the African coast.'''

"Oh, you're right, that's much better. This king that you're imagining, he has a keen sense of competition."

"Portugal is a thorn in his side," said Isabella.

"So you agree with me that Maldonado should write the verdict?"

"You're forgetting one thing," said Isabella.

"And that is?"

"Colón. When the verdict comes, he will leave us and head for France or England. Or Portugal."

"There are two reasons why he will not, Your Majesty."

"And those are?"

"First, Portugal has Dias and the African route to the Indies, while I happen to know that Colón's first approaches to Paris and London, through intermediaries, did not meet with any encouragement."

"He has already turned to other kings?"

"After the first four years," said Talavera dryly, "his patience began to flag a little."

"And the second reason that Colón will not leave Spain between the verdict and the end of the war with Granada?"

"He will be informed of the verdict of the examiners in a letter. And that letter, while it will contain no promises, will nevertheless give him leave to understand that when the war ends, the matter can be reopened."

"The verdict closes the door, but the letter opens the window?"

"Just a little. But if I know Colón at all, that slight crack in the

window will be enough. He is a man of great hopes and great te-
nacity.''

"Do I take it, Father Talavera, that your own personal verdict
is in favor of the voyage?''

"Not at all," said Talavera. "If I had to guess which view of
the world is the more correct, I think I would favor Ptolemy and
Maldonado. But I would be guessing, because no one knows and
no one *can* know with the information we now have.''

"Then why did you come here today with all these—suggestions?''

"I think of them as imaginings, Your Majesty. I would not pre-
sume to suggest anything." He smiled. "While the others have
been trying to determine what is correct, I have been thinking more
along the lines of what is good and right. I have been thinking of
St. Peter stepping from the boat and walking on the water.''

"Until he doubted.''

"And then he was lifted up by the hand of the Savior.''

Tears came to Isabella's eyes. "Do you think Colón may be
filled with the Spirit of God?''

"The Maid of Orleans was either a saint or a madwoman.''

"Or a witch. They burned her as a witch.''

"My point exactly. Who could know, for certain, whether God
was in her? And yet by putting their trust in her as God's servant,
the soldiers of France drove the English from field after field. What
if she had been mad? What then? They would have lost one more
battle. What difference would that have made? They had already
lost so many.''

"So if Colón is a madman, we will only lose a few caravels, a
little money, a wasted voyage.''

"Besides, if I know His Majesty at all, I suspect he'll find a
way to get the boats for very little money.''

"They say that if you pinch the coins with his face on them,
they screech.''

Talavera's eyes went wide. "Someone told Your Majesty *that*
little jest?''

She lowered her voice. They were already talking so low that
Lady Felicia could not possibly hear them; still, he leaned toward
the Queen so he could hear her faint whisper. "Father Talavera,

just between you and me, when that little jest was first told, I was present. In fact, when that little jest was first told, I was speaking.''

"I will treat that," said Father Talavera, "with all the secrecy of a confession.''

"You are such a good priest, Father Talavera. Bring me Father Maldonado's verdict. Tell him not to make it too cruel.''

"Your Majesty, I will tell him to be *kind*. But Father Maldonado's kindness can leave scars.''

Diko came home to find Father and Mother both still awake, dressed, sitting up in the front room, as if they were waiting to go somewhere. Which turned out to be the case. "Manjam has asked to see us.''

"At this hour?" asked Diko. "Go then.''

"Us," said Father, "including you.''

They met in one of the smaller rooms at Pastwatch, but one designed for the optimum viewing of the holographic display of the TruSite II. It did not occur to Diko, however, that Manjam chose the room for anything but privacy. What would he need with the TruSite II? He was not of Pastwatch. He was a noted mathematician, but that was supposed to mean he had no use for the real world. His tool was a computer for number manipulation. And, of course, his own mind. After Hassan, Tagiri, and Diko arrived, Manjam had them wait just a moment more for Hunahpu and Kemal. Then they all sat.

"I must begin with an apology," said Manjam. "I realize in retrospect that my explanation of temporal effects was inept in the extreme.''

"On the contrary," said Tagiri, "it couldn't have been clearer.''

"I don't apologize for a lack of clarity. I apologize for a lack of empathy. It isn't one of the things mathematicians get much practice at. I actually thought that telling you that our own time would cease to be real would be a *comfort* to you. It would be to *me*, you see. But then, I don't spend my life looking at history. I didn't understand the great . . . compassion that fills your lives here. Tagiri, you especially. I know now what I should have said.

That the end will be painless. There will be no cataclysm. There will be no sense of loss. There will be no regret. Instead, there will be a new Earth. A new future. And in this new future, because of the wise plans that Diko and Hunahpu have devised, there will be far more chance of happiness and fulfilment than in our own time. There will still be unhappiness, but it will not be so pervasive. That's what I should have said. That you will indeed succeed in erasing much misery, while you will create no new sources of misery.''

''Yes,'' said Tagiri, ''you should have said that.''

''I'm not used to speaking in terms of misery and happiness. There is no mathematics of misery, you see. It doesn't come up in my professional life. And yet I do care about it.'' Manjam sighed. ''More than you know.''

Something that he said struck a wrong note in Diko's mind. She blurted out the question as soon as she realized what it was. ''Hunahpu and I have not finalized any plans.''

''Haven't you?'' said Manjam. He reached out his hands to the TruSite II, and to Diko's astonishment he manipulated the controls like an expert. In fact, he almost immediately called up a control screen that Diko had never seen before, and entered a double password. Moments later the holographic display came alive.

In the display, to Diko's astonishment, she saw herself and Hunahpu.

''It isn't enough to stop Cristforo,'' Diko was saying in the display. ''We have to help him and his crew on Hispaniola to develop a new culture in combination with the Taino. A new Christianity that adapts to the Indies the way that it adapted to the Greeks in the second century. But that also isn't enough.''

''I hoped you would see it that way,'' said Hunahpu in the display. ''Because I intend to go to Mexico.''

''What do you mean, Mexico?''

''That wasn't your plan?''

''I was *going* to say that we need to develop technology rapidly, to the point where the new hybrid culture can be a match for Europe.''

''Yes, that's what I thought you were going to say. But of course that can't be done on the island of Haiti. Oh, the Spaniards will try, but the Tainos are simply not ready to receive that level of technology. It will remain Spanish, and that means a permanent class division between the white keepers of the machines and the brown laboring class. Not healthy.''

Manjam paused the display. The images of Diko and Hunahpu froze.

Diko looked around at the others and saw that the fear and anger in their eyes was a match for what she felt.

''Those machines,'' said Hassan, ''they aren't supposed to be able to see anything more recent than a hundred years ago.''

''Normally they can't,'' said Manjam.

''Why does a mathematician know how to use the TruSite?'' asked Hunahpu. ''Pastwatch already duplicated all the lost private notes of the great mathematicians of history.''

''This is an unspeakable violation of privacy,'' said Kemal icily.

Diko agreed, but she had already leaped to the most important question. ''Who are you really, Manjam?''

''Oh, I'm really Manjam,'' he said.''But no, don't protest, I understand your real question.'' He regarded them all calmly for a moment. ''We don't talk about what we do, because people would misunderstand. They would think we are some kind of secret cabal that rules the world behind closed doors, and nothing could be farther from the truth.''

''That reassures me completely,'' said Diko.

''We do nothing political. Do you understand? We don't interfere with government. We care a great deal about what governments do, but when we want to achieve some goal, we act openly. I would write to a government official as myself, as Manjam. Or appear on a broadcast. Stating my opinions. Do you see? We are not a secret shadow government. We have no authority over human lives.''

''And yet you spy on us.''

''We monitor all that is interesting and important in the world. And because we have the TruSite II, we can do it without sending spies or openly talking to anybody. We just watch, and then, when something is important or valuable, we encourage.''

''Yes yes,'' said Hassan. ''I'm sure you're noble and very kind in your godlike role. Who are the others?''

''I'm the one who came to you,'' said Manjam.

"And why are you showing us this? Why are you telling us?" asked Tagiri.

"Because you have to understand that I know what I'm talking about. And I have to show you some things before you will understand why your project has been so encouraged, why you've had no interference, why you've been allowed to bring together so many people from the moment you discovered, Tagiri and Hassan, that we can reach back and affect the past. And most especially since you, Diko, discovered that someone had already done so, canceling their own time in order to create a new future."

"So show us," said Hunahpu.

Manjam typed in new coordinates. The display changed. It was a long-distance aerial view of a vast stony plain with only a few desert plants every square meter, except for thick trees and grass along the banks of a wide river.

"What is this, the Sahara project?" asked Hassan.

"This is the Amazon," said Manjam.

"No," murmured Tagiri. "That's how bad it was before the restoration began?"

"You don't understand," said Manjam. "That is the Amazon right now. Or, technically speaking, about fifteen minutes ago." The display moved quickly, mile after mile down the river, and nothing changed until at last, after what must have been a thousand miles, they came to scenes familiar from the broadcasts: the thick growth of the rain-forest restoration project. But in just a few moments they had passed through the entire rain forest and were back to stony ground growing almost nothing. And so it remained, all the way to the marshy mouth of the river where it flowed into the sea.

"That was all? That was the Amazon rain forest?" asked Hunahpu.

"But that project has been going for forty years," said Hassan.

"It wasn't *that* bad when they started," said Diko.

"Have they been lying to us?" asked Tagiri.

"Come now," said Manjam. "You've all heard about the terrible loss of topsoil. You all know that with the forests gone, erosion was uncontrolled."

"But they were planting grass."

"And it died," said Manjam. "They're working on new species that can live in the scarcity of important nutrients. Don't look so glum. Nature is on our side. In ten thousand years the Amazon should be right back to normal."

"That's longer than—that's older than civilization."

"A mere hiccup in the ecological history of Earth. It simply takes time for new soil to be brought down from the Andes and built up on the banks of the river, where grasses and trees will thrive and gradually push their way outward from the river. At the rate of about six to ten meters a year for the grass, in the good spots. Also, it would help if there were some really massive flooding now and then, to spread new soil. A new volcano in the Andes would be nice—the ash would be quite helpful. And the odds of one erupting in the next ten thousand years are pretty good. Plus there's always the topsoil blown across the Atlantic from Africa. You see? Our prospects are good."

Manjam's words were cheerful, but Diko was sure he was being ironic. "Good? That land is dead."

"Oh, well, yes, for now."

"What about Sahara restoration?" asked Tagiri.

"Going very well. Good progress. I give us five hundred years on that."

"Five hundred!" cried Tagiri.

"That's presupposing great increases in rainfall, of course. But our weather prediction is getting very good at the climatic level. *You* worked on part of that project for a while in school, Kemal."

"We were talking about restoring the Sahara in a hundred years."

"Well, yes, and that *would* happen, if we could continue to keep so many teams working on it. But that won't be possible for even ten more years."

"Why not?"

Again the display changed. The ocean in a storm, beating against a levee. It broke through. A wall of seawater broke across—fields of grain?

"Where is *that?*" demanded Diko.

"Surely you heard about the breaching of the Carolina dike. In America."

"That was five years ago," said Hunahpu.

"Right. Very unfortunate. We lost the coastal barrier islands fifty years ago, with the rising of the ocean. This section of the North American east coast had been converted from tobacco and lumber production to grain, in order to replace the farmland killed by the drying of the North American prairie. Now vast acreages are under water."

"But we're making progress on finding ways to reduce the greenhouse gases," said Hassan.

"So we are. We think that, with safety, we can reduce the greenhouse effect significantly within perhaps thirty years. But by then, you see, we won't *want* to reduce it."

"Why not?" asked Diko. "The oceans are rising as the ice cap melts. We *have* to stop global warming."

"Our climate studies show that this is a self-correcting problem. The greater heat and the increased surface area of the ocean lead to significantly greater evaporation and temperature differentials worldwide. The cloud cover is increasing, which raises the Earth's albedo. We will soon be reflecting more sunlight than ever before since the last ice age."

"But the weather satellites," said Kemal.

"They keep the extremes from getting unbearable in any one location. How long do you think those satellites can last?"

"They can be replaced when they wear out," said Kemal.

"Can they?" asked Manjam. "Already we're taking people out of the factories and putting them into the fields. But this won't really help, because we're already farming very close to one hundred percent of the land where there's any topsoil left at all. And since we've been farming at maximum yields for some time, we're already noticing the effects of the increasing cloud cover—fewer crops per hectare."

"What are you saying?" said Diko. "That we're already too late to restore the Earth?"

Manjam didn't answer. Instead, he brought onto the display a large region filled with grain silos. He zoomed in and they viewed the inside of silo after silo.

"Empty," murmured Tagiri.

"We're eating up our reserves," said Manjam.

"But why aren't we rationing?"

"Because politicians can't do that until the people as a whole see that there's an emergency. Right now they don't see it."

"Then warn them!" said Hunahpu.

"Oh, the warnings are there. And in a while people will start talking about it. But they'll do nothing, for the simple reason that there's nothing to be done. Crop yields will continue to go down."

"What about the ocean?" asked Hassan.

"The ocean has its own problems. What do you want us to do, scrape away all the plankton so that the ocean dies, too? We harvest as much fish as we dare. We are at maximum right now. Any more, and in ten years our yields will be a tiny fraction of what they are now. Don't you see? The damage our ancestors did was too great. It is not within our power to stop the forces that have already been in motion for centuries. If we started rationing right now, it would mean that the devastating famines would begin in twenty years instead of six. But of course we won't start rationing until the first famine. And even then, the areas that are producing enough food will become quite surly about having to go hungry in order to feed people in faraway lands. Right now we feel that all human beings are one tribe, so that no one anywhere is hungry. But how long do you think that will last, when the food-producing people hear their children pleading for bread and the ships are carrying so much grain away to other lands? How well do you think the politicians will do at containing the forces that will move through the world then?"

"So what is your little non-cabal doing about it?" asked Hassan.

"Nothing," said Manjam. "As I said, the processes have gone too far. Our most favorable projections show collapse of the present system within thirty years. That's if there *are* no wars. There simply won't be food enough to maintain the present population or even a major fraction of it. You can't keep up the industrial economy without an agricultural base that produces far more food than is needed just to sustain the food producers. So industry starts collapsing. Now there are fewer tractors. Now the fertilizer factories produce less, and less of what they do produce can get distributed because transportation can't be maintained. Food production falls

even further. Weather satellites wear out and can't be replaced.
Drought. Flood. Less land in production. More deaths. Therefore
less industry. Therefore lower food production. We have run a million different scenarios and there's not one of them that doesn't
lead us to the same place. A worldwide population of about five
million before we stabilize. Just in time for the ice age to begin in
earnest. At that point the population could start a slower decline
until it's down to about two million. That's if there's no warfare,
of course. All these projections are based on an assumption of a
completely docile response. We all know how likely *that* is. All it
will take is one full-fledged war in one of the major food-producing
countries and the drop will be *much* steeper, with the population
stabilizing at a much lower level."

No one could say anything to that. They knew what it meant.

"It's not all glum news," said Manjam. "The human race *will*
survive. As the ice age ends, our distant children will again start to
build civilizations. By then the rain forests will have been restored.
Herd animals will once more graze the rich grassland of the Sahara
and the Rub' al Khali and the Gobi. Unfortunately, all the easy iron
was taken out of the ground years ago. Also the easy tin and copper. In fact, one can't help but wonder what they'll do for metals
in order to rise out of the stone age. One can't help but wonder
what their transitional energy source is going to be, with all the oil
gone. There's still a little peat in Ireland. And of course the forests
will have come back, so there'll be charcoal until they burn all the
forests back down to nothing and the cycle starts over."

"You're saying that the human race *can't* rise again?"

"I'm saying that we've used up all the easy-to-find resources,"
said Manjam. "Human beings are very resourceful. Maybe they'll
find other paths into a better future. Maybe they'll figure out how
to make solar collectors out of the rusted debris of our skyscrap-
ers."

"I ask again," said Hassan. "What are you doing to prevent
this?"

"And I say again, nothing," said Manjam. "It can't be prevented. Warnings are useless because there's nothing that people
can do to change their behavior to make this problem go away. The
civilization we have right now cannot be maintained even for an-

other generation. And people do sense it, you know. The birthrates are falling all over the world. They all have their own individual reasons, but the cumulative effect is the same. People are choosing not to have children who will compete with them for scarce resources.''

''Why did you show us this, then, if there's nothing we can do?'' said Tagiri.

''Why did you search the past, when you believed there was nothing *you* could do?'' asked Manjam, smiling grimly. ''Besides, I never said that there was nothing *you* could do. Only that *we* could do nothing.''

''That's why we've been allowed to pursue time travel,'' said Hunahpu. ''So we can go back and prevent all this.''

''We had no hope, until you discovered the mutability of the past,'' said Manjam. ''Until then, our work was turned toward preservation. Collecting all of human knowledge and experience and storing it in some permanent form that might last in hiding for at least ten thousand years. We've come up with some very good, compact storage devices. And some simple nonmechanical readers that we think might last two or three thousand years. We could never do better than that. And of course we never managed to come up with the sum of all knowledge. Ideally what we *do* have we would have rewritten as a series of easy-to-learn lessons. Step by step through the acquired wisdom of the human race. That project lasted up through algebra and the basic principles of genetics and then we had to give it up. For the last decade we've just been dumping information into the banks and duplicating it. We'll just have to let our grandchildren figure out how to codify and make sense of it all, when and if they find the caches where we hide the stuff. That's what our little cabal exists for. Preserving the memory of the human race. Until we spotted *you*.''

Tagiri was weeping.

''Mother,'' said Diko. ''What is it?''

Hassan put his arm around his wife and drew her close. Tagiri raised her tear-streaked face and looked at her daughter. ''Oh, Diko,'' she said. ''For all these years I thought we lived in paradise.''

''Tagiri is a woman of astonishing compassion,'' said Manjam.

"When we found her, we watched her out of love and admiration. How could she endure the pain of so many other people? We never dreamed that it would be her compassion, and not the cleverness of our clever ones, that would finally lead us to the one road away from the disaster lying ahead of us." He rose and walked to Tagiri, and knelt before her. "Tagiri, I had to show you this, because we feared that you would decide to stop the Columbus project."

"I already did. Decide it, I mean," she said.

"I asked the others. They said we had to show you. Though we knew that you would not see this as parched earth or statistics or anything safe and distant and containable. You would see it as each life that was lost, each hope that was destroyed. You would hear the voices of the children born today, as they grew up cursing their parents for their cruelty in not having killed them in the womb. I'm sorry for the pain of it. But you had to understand that if in fact Columbus is a fulcrum of history, and stopping him opens a way to creating a new future for the human race, then we must do it."

Tagiri slowly nodded. But then she wiped the tears off her cheeks and faced Manjam, speaking fiercely. "Not in secret," she said.

Manjam smiled wanly. "Yes, some of us warned that you would feel that way."

"The people must consent to our sending someone back to undo our world. They must *agree*."

"Then we will have to wait to tell them," said Manjam. "Because if we asked today, they would say no."

"When?" asked Diko.

"You'll know when," said Manjam. "When the famines start."

"What if I'm too old to go?" asked Kemal.

"Then we'll send someone else," said Hassan.

"What if *I'm* too old to go?" asked Diko.

"You won't be," said Manjam. "So get ready. And when the emergency is upon us, and the people can see that their children are hungry, that people are dying, *then* they will consent to what you're going to do. Because then they'll finally have the perspective."

"What perspective?" asked Kemal.

"First we try to preserve ourselves," said Manjam, "until we see that we can't. Then we try to preserve our children, until we see that we can't. Then we act to preserve our kin, and then our village or tribe, and when we see that we can't preserve even them, then we act in order to preserve our memory. And if we can't do that, what is left? We finally have the perspective of trying to act for the good of humanity as a whole."

"Or despairing," said Tagiri.

"Yes, well, that's the other choice," said Manjam. "But I don't see that as an option for anyone in this room. And when we offer this chance to people who see their world collapsing around them, I think they'll choose to let you make the attempt."

"If they don't agree, then we won't do it," said Tagiri fiercely.

Diko said nothing, but she also knew that the decision was no longer Mother's to make. Why should the people of one generation have the right to veto the only chance to save the future of the human race? But it didn't matter. As Manjam said, the people would agree once they saw death and horror staring them in the face. After all, what had the old man and the woman in that village on Haiti Island prayed for, when they prayed? Not for deliverance, no. In their despair they asked for swift and merciful death. If nothing else, the Columbus project could certainly provide *that*.

Cristoforo sat back and let Father Perez and Father Antonio continue their analysis of the message from court. All he had really cared about was when Father Perez said to him, "Of course this is from the Queen. Do you think, after all these years, she would let you be sent a message without making sure she approved of the wording? The message speaks of the possibility of a reexamination at a 'more convenient time.' That sort of thing is not lightly said. Monarchs do not have time to be pestered by people about matters that are already closed. She invites you to pester her. Therefore the matter is *not* closed."

The matter is not closed. Almost he wished it were. Almost he wished that God had chosen someone else.

Then he shrugged off the thought and let his mind wander as the Franciscans discussed the possibilities. It didn't matter anymore what the arguments were. The only argument that really mattered to Cristoforo was that God and Christ and the dove of the Holy Ghost appeared to him on the beach and called him to sail west. All the rest—it must be true, of course, or God wouldn't have told him to sail west. But it had nothing to do with Cristoforo. He was bent on sailing west for . . . for God, yes. And why for God? Why had Christ become so important in his life? Other men—even churchmen—didn't deform their whole lives as he had. They pursued their private ambitions. They had careers, they planned their futures. And, oddly enough, it seemed that God was much kinder to those who cared little for him, or at least cared less than Cristoforo did.

Why do I care so much?

His eyes were looking across the table, toward the wall, but he was not seeing the crucifix there. Instead a memory washed through his mind. Of his mother huddling behind a table. Murmuring to him, as someone shouted in the distance. What was this memory? Why did it come to him now?

I had a mother; poor Diego has none. And no father either, in truth. He writes to me that he's tired of La Rábida. But what can I do? If I succeed in my mission, then his fortune is made, he will be son of a great man and therefore he will also be a great man. And if I fail, he had better be well educated, which no one can do better than Franciscans like these good priests. Nothing he would see or hear with me in Salamanca—or wherever I go next in pursuit of kings or queens—would prepare him for any life he is likely to lead.

Gradually, as Cristoforo's thoughts drifted toward sleep, he became aware that under the crucifix was a blackamoor girl, simply but brightly dressed, watching him intently. She was not really there, he knew, because he could still see the crucifix on the wall behind her. She must be very tall, for the crucifix was placed quite high. What should I be dreaming of blackamoor women, thought Cristoforo. Only I'm not dreaming, because I'm not asleep. I can still hear Father Perez and Father Antonio arguing about something. About Perez going to the Queen himself. Well, that's an idea. Why is that girl watching me?

Is this a vision? he wondered idly. Not as clear as it was on the beach. And this is certainly not God. Could a vision of a black woman come from Satan? Is that what I'm seeing? Satan's dam?

Not with a crucifix visible behind her head. This woman is like glass, black glass. I can see inside her. There's a crucifix inside her head. Does this mean that she dreams of crucifying Christ again? Or that the Son of Mary dwells always in her mind? I'm not good at visions and dreams. I need more clarity than this. So if you sent this, God, and if you mean something by it, I'm not understanding it well enough and you'll have to make things much clearer for me.

As if in answer, the blackamoor girl faded and Cristoforo became aware of someone else moving in the corner of the room. Someone who could not be seen through; someone solid and real. A young man, tall and handsome, but with questioning, uncertain eyes. He looked like Felipa. So much like Felipa. As if she dwelt in him, a continuous reproach to Cristoforo, a continuous plea. I did love you, Felipa. But I loved Christ more. That can't be a sin, can it?

Speak to me, Diego. Say my name. Demand what is yours by right: my attention, my respect for you. Don't stand there weakly waiting. Hoping for a crumb from my table. Don't you know that sons must be stronger than their fathers, or the world will die?

He said nothing. He said nothing.

Not all men have to be strong, thought Cristoforo. It is enough that some are simply good. That is enough for me to love my son, that he be good. I will be strong enough for us both. I have enough strength to hold you up as well.

"Diego, my good son," said Cristoforo.

Now the boy could speak. "I heard voices."

"I didn't want to wake you," said Cristoforo.

"I thought it was another dream."

Father Perez whispered, "He dreams of you, often."

"I dream of you, my son," said Cristoforo. "Do you also dream of me?"

Diego nodded, his eyes never leaving his father's face.

"Do you think the Holy Spirit gives these dreams to us, so we don't forget the great love we have for each other?"

He nodded again. Then he walked to his father, uncertainly at first; but then, as Cristoforo rose to his feet and held out his arms, the boy's strides became more certain. And when they embraced, Cristoforo was startled at how tall the boy had become, how long his arms, how strong he was. He held him, held him long.

"They tell me you're good at drawing, Diego."

"Yes, I am," said Diego.

"Show me."

As they walked toward Diego's room, Cristoforo talked to him. "I'm drawing again myself. Quintanilla cut off my funds a couple of years ago, but I fooled him. I didn't go away. I draw maps for people. Have you ever drawn a map?"

"Uncle Bartolomeu came and taught me how. I've mapped the monastery. Right down to the mouseholes!"

They laughed together all the way up the stairs.

"We wait and wait," said Diko. "We're not getting any younger."

"Kemal is," said Hunahpu. "He works out constantly. To the neglect of his other studies."

"He has to be strong enough to swim under the ships and set the charges," said Diko.

"I think we should have a younger man."

Diko shook her head.

"What if he has a heart attack, did you think of that? We send him back in time to stop Columbus, and he dies in the water. What good is that? I'll be among the Zapotecs. Will *you* set the charges and keep Columbus there? Or will he sail back to Europe and make the whole effort a waste?"

"Just by *going* we'll accomplish something. We'll be infected with the carrier viruses, you remember."

"So the New World will be immune to smallpox and measles. All that means is that more of them will survive to enjoy many years of slavery."

"The Spanish weren't *that* far ahead, technologically speaking. And without the plagues to make them think the gods are against them, the people won't lose heart. Hunahpu, we can't help but make things better, at least to some degree. But Kemal won't fail."

"No," said Hunahpu. "He's like your mother. Never say die."

Diko laughed bitterly. "He never says it, but he plans it all the same."

"Plans what?"

"He hasn't mentioned it in years. I think I only heard him say it as a half-formed thought, and then he simply decided to do it."

"What?"

"Die," said Diko.

"What do you mean?"

"He was talking, back in—oh, forever ago. About how the sinking of one ship is a misfortune. Two ships is a tragedy. Three ships is a punishment from God. What good will it do if Columbus thinks God is against him?"

"Well, that's a problem. But the ships have got to go."

"Listen, Hunahpu. He went on. He said, 'If only they knew that it was a Turk who blew up the boats. The infidel. The enemy of Christ.' Then he laughed. And then he stopped laughing."

"Why didn't you mention this before?"

"Because *he* chose not to mention it. But I thought you should understand why he isn't taking all the other learning assignments seriously. He doesn't expect to live to need them. All he needs is athletic ability, knowledge of explosives, and enough Spanish or Latin or whatever to tell Columbus's men that he is the one who blew up their ships, and that he did it in the name of Allah."

"And then he kills himself?"

"Are you joking? Of course not. He lets the Christians kill him."

"It won't be gentle."

"But he'll be taken up to heaven. He died for Islam."

"Is he really a believer?" asked Hunahpu.

"Father thinks so. He says that the older you get, the more you believe in God, whatever face he wears."

The doctor came back into the room, smiling. "All very excellent, just like I tell you. Your heads are very full of interesting things. No one in all of history has ever had so much knowledge in their heads as you and Kemal!"

"Knowledge and electromagnetic time bombs," said Hunahpu.

"Yes, well," said the doctor, "it is true that when the signaling device is set off, it could cause cancer after several decades of exposure. But it does not signal until a hundred years, so I think you are nothing but bones in the ground and cancer is not a big problem for you." He laughed.

"I think he's a ghoul," said Hunahpu.

"They all are," said Diko. "It's one of the classes in med school."

"Save the world, young man, young woman. Make a very good new world for my children."

For a horrible moment Diko thought that the doctor didn't understand that when they went, his children would all be snuffed out, like everyone else in this dead-end time. If only the Chinese made more of an effort to teach their people English so they could understand what the rest of the world was saying.

Seeing the consternation on their faces, the doctor laughed. "Do you think I'm so smart I can put phony bones in your skull, but so dumb I don't know? Don't you know Chinese were smart when all other people were stupid? When you go back, young man, young woman, then all the people of the new future, they are my children. And when they hear your phony bones talking to them, then they find the records, they find out about me and all the other people. So they remember us. They know we are their ancestors. This is very important. They know we are their ancestors, and they remember us." He bowed and left the room.

"My head hurts," said Diko. "Don't you think we could get more drugs?"

Santangel looked from the Queen to his books, trying to figure out what the monarchs wanted from him. "Can the kingdom afford this voyage? Three caravels, supplies, a crew? The war with Granada is over. Yes, the treasury can afford it."

"Easily?" asked King Ferdinand. So he really hoped to have it stopped for financial reasons. All Santangel had to do was say, Not easily, no, it will be a sacrifice right now, and then the King would say, Let's wait then, for a better time, and then the issue would never come up again.

Santangel did not so much as glance at the Queen, for a wise courtier never allowed it to seem that, before he could answer one of the monarchs, he had to look to the other one for some kind of signal. Yet he saw out of the corner of his eye that she gripped the arms of her throne. She cares about this, he thought. This matters to her. It does not matter to the King. It annoys him, but he has no passion about it either way.

"Your Majesty," said Santangel, "if you have any doubts about the ability of the treasury to pay for the voyage, I will be glad to underwrite it myself."

A hush fell over the court, and then a low murmur arose. At a stroke, Santangel had changed the whole mood. If there was one thing people were sure of, it was that Luis de Santangel knew how to make money. It was one of the reasons why King Ferdinand absolutely trusted him in financial matters. He did not have to cheat the treasury to be rich—he was extravagantly wealthy when he came into office and had the knack for easily making more without having to become a parasite on the royal court. So if he was enthusiastic enough about the voyage to offer to underwrite it himself . . .

The King smiled slightly. "And if I take you up on that generous offer?"

"It would be a great honor if your majesty allowed me to link my name to the voyage of Señor Colón."

The King's smile faded. Santangel knew why. The King was very sensitive to how people perceived him. Bad enough that he had to spend his life in this delicate balance with a reigning and ruling queen, in order to assure a peaceful unification of Castile and Aragon when one of them died. He did not like imagining the gossip. King Ferdinand wouldn't pay for this great voyage himself. Only Luis de Santangel had the foresight to fund it.

"Your offer was generous, my friend," said the King. "But Aragon does not shirk its responsibility."

"Nor does Castile," said the Queen. Her hands had relaxed.

Did she know that I would see how she tensed before? Was it a deliberate signal?

"Assemble this new council of examiners," said the King. "If their verdict is positive, we will give this voyager his caravels."

And so it began again, or so it seemed. Santangel, watching from a distance, soon realized that this time the fix was in. Instead of years it took weeks. The new council included most of the pro-

Colón faction from the previous group, and few of the conservative theologians who had so vehemently opposed him. It was no surprise when they made a perfunctory examination of Colón's proposals and returned with a favorable verdict. It remained only for the Queen to call Colón to court and tell him.

After all those years of waiting, after it had seemed a few months ago that it was all wasted, Santangel expected Colón to be joyful when he heard the news. He stood in the court and instead of gratefully accepting the Queen's commission, he began to list demands. It was unbelievable. First, this commoner wanted a noble title befitting the commission that was being given him. And that was only the beginning.

"When I return from the Orient," he said, "I will have done what no other captain has ever done or dared to do. I must sail with the authority and rank of Admiral of the Ocean-Sea, exactly equal in station to the Grand Admiral of Castile. Along with this rank, it will be appropriate that I be granted the powers of viceroy and governor-general of all lands that I might discover in the name of Spain. Furthermore these titles and powers must be hereditary, to be passed down to my son and his sons after him forever. It will also be appropriate that I be granted a commission of ten percent of all commerce that passes between Spain and the new lands, and the same commission on all mineral wealth found there."

After all these years in which Colón had shown not a sign of personal greed, did he now stand revealed before them as just another parasitic courtier?

The Queen was speechless for a moment. Then she curtly told Colón that she would take his requests under counsel, and dismissed him.

When Santangel took word of Colón's requests to the King, he was livid. "He dares to make *demands?* I thought he came to us as a supplicant. Does he expect kings to make contracts with commoners?"

"Actually, no, Your Majesty," said Santangel. "He expects you to make him a nobleman first, and *then* make a contract with him."

"And he doesn't budge on these points?"

"He is very courteous, but no, he simply does not bend, not a jot."

"Then send him away," said the King. "Isabella and I are preparing to enter Granada in a great procession, arriving there as liberators of Spain and champions of Christ. A Genovese mapmaker dares to demand the titles of viceroy and admiral? He does not even merit a *señor*."

Santangel was sure Colón would back down when he heard the King's reply. Instead, he coolly announced his departure and began packing to leave.

It was chaos all evening around the King and Queen. Santangel began to see that Colón was not such a fool to make these demands. For all these years he had to wait, because if he left Spain and went to England or France with his proposal, he would already have two failures behind him. Why would France or England be interested in him, when the two great seafaring nations of Europe had already rejected him? Now, though, it was widely known and witnessed by many that the monarchs of Spain had *accepted* his proposal and agreed to fund his voyage. The dispute was not over *whether* to give him ships, but rather what his reward would be. He could walk away today and be assured an eager welcome in Paris or London. Oh, were Ferdinand and Isabella unwilling to reward you for your great achievement? See how France rewards her great sailors, see how England honors those who carry the banners of the king to the Orient! At long last Colón was negotiating from strength. He could walk away from the Spanish offer, because Spain had already given him the first and most important thing he needed— and it had been given him for free.

What a negotiator, thought Santangel. If only he were in trade. What I could accomplish with a man like that in my service! I would soon hold the mortgage on St. Peter's in Rome! On the Hagia Sophia! On the Church of the Holy Sepulchre!

And then he thought: If Colón were in business, he would not be my agent, he would be my competitor. He shuddered.

The Queen vacillated. She truly wanted this voyage, and that made it very difficult for her. The King, however, was adamant. Why should he even have to *discuss* this foreigner's absurd demands?

Santangel watched how uselessly Father Diego de Deza tried to argue against the King's inclinations. Has this man no sense of how to deal with monarchs? Santangel was grateful when Father Talavera soon drew Deza out of the conversation. Santangel himself remained silent until at last the King asked for his opinion. "Of course these demands are just as absurd and impossible as they seem. The monarch who grants such titles to an untried foreigner is *not* the monarch who drove the Moors from Spain."

Almost everyone nodded wisely. They all assumed Santangel was playing the game of flattery, and like any careful courtier they were quick to agree with any praise of the King. Thus he was able to win the general approval for his most important stipulation: "untried foreigner."

"Of course, *after* the voyage, which Your Majesties have already agreed to authorize and fund, if he returns successful, then he will have brought such honor and wealth to the crowns of Spain that he would deserve all the rewards he has asked for, and more. He is so confident of success that he feels he already deserves them. But if he is that confident, surely he will accept without hesitation a stipulation on *your* part—that he receive these rewards only upon his successful return."

The King smiled. "Santangel, you fox. I know you want this Colón to sail. But you didn't get your wealth by paying people until *after* they delivered. Let *them* take the risk, is that it?"

Santangel bowed modestly.

The King turned to a clerk. "Write up a set of capitulations to Colón's demands. Only make them all contingent upon his *successful* return from the Orient." He grinned wickedly at Santangel. "Too bad I'm a Christian king and refuse to gamble. I would make a bet with you—that I will never have to grant these titles to Colón."

"Your Majesty, only a fool would bet against the conqueror of Granada," said Santangel. Silently he added: Only an even bigger fool would bet against Colón.

The capitulations were written in the small hours of the morning, after much last-minute consultation between the counselors of the King and the Queen. When at dawn a beadle was sent to deliver the message to Colón, he returned flustered and upset. "He's gone!" he cried.

"Of course he's gone," said Father Perez. "He was told that

his conditions were rejected. But he will only have left at dawn. And I suspect he will not be riding quickly.''

"Then fetch him back," said the Queen. "Tell him to present himself at once before me, for I am ready to conclude this affair at last. No, don't say 'at last.' Now hurry."

The beadle rushed from the court.

While they waited for Colón to be brought back, Santangel took Father Perez aside. "I didn't figure Colón for a greedy man."

"He's not," said Father Perez. "A modest man, in fact. Ambitious, but not the way you think."

"In what way is he ambitious, then, if not the way I think?"

"He wanted the titles to be hereditary because he has spent his life pursuing this voyage," said Perez. "He has no other inheritance for his son—no fortune, nothing. But with this voyage he will now be able to make his son, not just a gentleman, but a great lord. His wife died years ago, and he has many regrets. This is also his gift to her, and to her family, who are among the lesser nobility in Portugal."

"I know the family," said Santangel.

"You know the mother?"

"Is she still alive?"

"I think so," said Perez.

"Then I understand. I'm sure the old lady made him keenly aware that any claim to gentility he had came through her family. It will be sweet indeed for Colón if he can turn it backward, so that any claim of true nobility for *her* family comes through their connection to *him*."

"So you see," said Perez.

"No, Father Juan Perez, I see nothing yet. Why did Colón put this voyage at risk, solely to gain such lofty titles and absurd commissions?"

"Perhaps," said Father Perez, "because this voyage is not the end of his mission, but the beginning."

"The beginning! What can a man do, having discovered vast new lands for Christ and Queen? Having been made viceroy and admiral? Having been given wealth beyond imagining?"

"You, a Christian, you have to ask me *that?*" said Perez. Then he walked away.

Santangel thought himself a Christian, but he never *was* sure
what Perez meant. He thought of all sorts of possibilities, but they
all sounded ludicrous because no man could possibly dream of accomplishing such lofty purposes.

Then again, no man could possibly dream of getting monarchs
to agree to a mad voyage into unknown western seas with no high
probability of success. And yet Colón had achieved it. So if he had
dreams of reconquering the Roman Empire, or liberating the Holy
Land, or driving the heathen Turk from Byzantium, or making a
mechanical bird to fly to the moon, Santangel would not bet against
him.

There was famine now, only in North America, but there was no
surplus food anywhere else to relieve it. To send help required
rationing in many other places. The tales of bloodshed and chaos
in America persuaded the people of Europe and South America to
accept rationing so that some relief could be sent. But it would not
be enough to save everyone.

This hopeless inadequacy came to humanity as a terrible shock,
not least because they had believed for two generations that at last
the world was a good place to live. They had believed theirs was a
time of rebirth, rebuilding, restoration. Now they learned that it
was merely a rear guard action in a war whose conclusion was
already decided before they were even born. Their work was in
vain, because nothing could last. The Earth was too far gone.

It was in the midst of the agony of this realization that the
first news came out about the Columbus project. The discussion
was grim. When the choice came, it was not unanimous, but it
was overwhelming. What else was there, really? To watch their
children die of hunger? To take up arms again, and fight for the
last scraps of food-producing land? Could anyone happily choose
a future of caves and ice and ignorance, when there might be another way, if not for them and their children, then for the human
race as a whole?

Manjam sat with Kemal, who had come to wait out the voting
with him. When the decision came, and Kemal knew that he would
indeed be taking the voyage backward in time, he was at once

relieved and frightened. It was one thing to plan one's own death when the prospect was still remote. Now, though, it would be a matter of days before he went back in time, and then no more than weeks before he would stand scornfully before Columbus and say, "Did you think Allah would let a Christian discover these new lands? I spit on your Christ? He had not the power to sustain you against the power of Allah! There is no God but Allah, and Muhammad is his Prophet!"

And then someday perhaps, a future searcher in Pastwatch would see him standing there, and would nod his head and say, That was the man who stopped Columbus. That was the man who gave his life to create this good and peaceful world we live in. That was the man who gave the human race a future. As much as Yewesweder before him, this man chose the course of humanity.

That would be a life worth living, thought Kemal. To earn a place in history that could be spoken of in the same breath with Yewesweder himself.

"You seem melancholy, my friend," said Manjam.

"Do I?" said Kemal. "Yes. Sad and happy, both at once."

"How do you think Tagiri will take this?"

Kemal shrugged with some impatience. "Who can figure out this woman? She works all her life for this, and then we have to practically tie her down to keep her from going out urging people to vote *against* the very thing she worked for!"

"I don't think it's hard to understand her, Kemal," said Manjam. "It's as you said—it was the force of her will that caused the Columbus project to reach this point. She was responsible for it. That was too much of a burden for her to bear alone. Now, though, she can be satisfied inside herself that she opposed the destruction of our time, that the final decision was taken away from her, was forced on her by the will of the vast majority of humankind. Now her responsibility for the end of our time is not hers alone. It will be shared by many, borne on many shoulders. She can live with it now."

Kemal chuckled grimly. "She can live with it—for how many days? And then she will wink out of existence along with all the rest of humanity in this world. What does it matter now?"

"It matters," said Manjam, "because she *has* those few days, and because those few days are all the future she has. She will spend it with clean hands and a peaceful heart.''

''And is this not hypocrisy?'' asked Kemal. ''For she *did* cause it, just as much as ever.''

''Hypocrisy? No. The hypocrite knows what he really is, and labors to conceal it from others in order to gain from their misplaced faith in him. Tagiri fears the moral ambiguity in something that she knows she must do. She cannot live with *not* doing it, and yet fears she cannot live with doing it, either. So conceals it from herself in order to proceed with what she must do.''

''If there's a difference there, it's damned hard to see,'' said Kemal.

''That's right,'' said Manjam. ''There's a difference. And it's damned hard to see.''

From time to time, as he rode toward Palos, Cristoforo pressed his hand to his chest, to feel the stiff parchment tucked into his coat. For you, my Lord, my Savior. You gave this to me, and now I will use it for you. Thank you, thank you, for granting my prayer, for letting this also be a gift to my son, to my dead wife.

As he rode long into the day, Father Perez fell silent beside him, a memory came into his mind. His father, stepping forward eagerly toward a table where richly dressed men were seated. His father poured wine. When would that have happened? Father is a weaver. When did he pour wine? What am I remembering? And why does it come to me now of all times?

No answer came to his mind, and the horse plodded on, pounding dust up into the air with every step. Cristoforo thought of what lay ahead. Much work, outfitting a voyage. Would he even remember how, all these years since the last voyage he was really a part of? No matter. He would remember what he needed to remember, he would accomplish all he needed to accomplish. The worst obstacle was past. He had been lifted up by the arms of Christ, and Christ would carry him across the water and bring him home again. Nothing would stop him now.

9

Departures

Cristoforo stood near the helm, watching as the sailors readied the caravel for departure. A part of him longed to skim down from his lofty station and join in, to handle the sheets and sails aloft, to carry the last and freshest of the stores aboard, to be doing something with his hands, his feet, his body to make him a part of the crew, part of the living organism of the ship.

But that was not his role here. God had chosen him to lead, and it was in the nature of things that the captain of a ship, let alone the commander of an expedition, had to remain as aloof and unapproachable to the crew as Christ himself was to the Church he headed.

The people gathered at the shore and on the hills overlooking the sea were not there to cheer on his mission, Cristoforo knew. They were there because Martín Pinzón, their favorite among sailors, their hero, their darling, was taking a crew of their sons and brothers and uncles and cousins and friends out into the open ocean on a voyage of such bravery as to seem madness. Or was it of such madness as to seem bravery? It was Pinzón in whom their trust resided, Pinzón who would bring their menfolk home if anyone did

at all. What was this Cristóbal Colón to them, except a courtier who
had wangled his way into the favor of the Crown and won control
by fiat of what he could never have earned through seamanship?
They knew nothing of the boy Cristoforo's years haunting the docks
of Genova. They knew nothing of his voyages, nothing of his studies, nothing of his plans and dreams. Above all, they had no idea
that God had spoken to him on a beach in Portugal, not that many
miles to the west of them. They had no idea that this voyage was
already a miracle which could never have taken place were it not
that it had God's favor and therefore could not fail.

All was ready. The frenetic activity had settled to languor, the
languor to waiting, as eyes that had before watched the work now
turned to look at Colón.

Watch me, thought Cristoforo. When I raise my hand, I change
the world. With all their labors, not one of these other men can do
that.

He closed his fist. He lifted it high above his head. The people
cheered as the men cast off and and the caravels slipped away from
land.

Three hollow grey hemispheres formed a triangle, like three serving
bowls laid out for a feast. Each was filled with equipment for the
different missions that Diko, Hunahpu, and Kemal would carry
out. Each had a portion of the library that Manjam and his secret
committee had collected and preserved. If any one of them reached
the past and changed it so that the future was obliterated, then that
one portion of the library would contain enough information that
someday the people of the new future would be able to learn of the
future that had died for them. Would be able to build on their
science, wonder at their stories, profit from their technologies, learn
from their sorrows. It is a sad sort of feast these bowls contained,
thought Tagiri. But it is the way of the world. Always something
must die so that another organism can live. And now a community,
a world of communities must turn their dying into a banquet of
possibilities for another.

Diko and Hunahpu stood beside each other as they listened to
the final explanation from Sá Ferreira; Kemal was by himself, lis-

tening attentively enough but obviously not a part of what was going on. He was already gone, like a dik-dik in the jaws of a cheetah, past fear, past caring. The Christian martyrs must have looked like this, thought Tagiri, as they walked into the lion's den. It was not the look of sullen despair that Tagiri had seen on the faces of slaves being chained belowdecks in the ships of the Portuguese. Death is death, someone had said once to Tagiri, but she had not believed it then and did not believe it now. Kemal knows he is walking toward death, but it will mean something, it will achieve something, it is his apotheosis, it gives his life meaning. Such a death is to be not shunned but embraced. There is an element of pride in it, yes, but it is an honorable pride, not a vain one, that glories in sacrifice that will achieve a good end.

It is how we all should feel, for we all are being killed this day, by these machines. Kemal feels in his heart that he will die first, but it is not so. Of all the people in the world on this day, in this hour, he will be one of only three who do not die when the switch is thrown and the cargo and passengers of these hollow hemispheres hurtle back in time. Only two people alive today have a future longer than Kemal's.

And yet it was not wrong of him to relish his death. He would die surrounded by hate and rage, killed by those who did not understand what he was doing, but their hate would be a kind of honor, their rage a fitting response to his achievement.

Sá was nearly finished. "From the serious to the banal," he said. "Keep all your body parts inside the sphere. Don't stand up, don't raise your hands until you can see that you have arrived."

He pointed at the wires and cables dangling from the ceiling directly over the center of each hemisphere. "Those cables that hold up the field generators will be severed by the successful generation of the field. Thus your separation from the flow of time will have almost no duration. The field will exist, and in the moment it comes to exist, the generator will lose all power and the field will cease to exist. You'll be aware of none of that, of course. The only thing *you* will know is that the generator will suddenly drop. Since no part of your body will be under the generator—I'm hoping you will not risk breaking an ankle by testing whether I'm right or not . . ."

Diko laughed nervously. Hunahpu and Kemal were impassive.

"You will be in no danger from the fall of the generator. However, it will whip the cables down with it. They are heavy, but fortunately the fall is short and there won't be *that* much force in them. Still, you must be aware of the possibility of being struck with some violence by the cable. So even though you may wish to strike some gallant pose, I must beg you to assume a covered, protected position so that you do not jeopardize the success of your mission by exposing yourself to the risk of personal injury."

"Yes yes," said Kemal. "We will curl up like infants in the uterus."

"Then we're done here. Time to go."

There was only a moment's hesitation. And then the last good-byes began. Almost in silence, Hunahpu was embraced by his brothers, and Hassan and Tagiri, and their son Acho, held and kissed Diko for the last time. Kemal stood alone until Tagiri came also to him and kissed him lightly on the cheek, and Hassan gripped his shoulders and murmured something to him, words from the Quran, and then kissed him on the lips.

Kemal climbed alone into his hemisphere. Hunahpu walked with Diko to hers, and just before she climbed the ladder he embraced her and kissed her gently. Tagiri did not hear the words that passed between them, but she knew—they all knew, but did not speak of it—that Hunahpu and Diko had also made a personal sacrifice, perhaps not as complete as that of Kemal, but one with its own kind of pain, its own sweet bitterness. It was possible that Kemal and Diko might see each other again, for they were both going to the island of Hispaniola—no, the island of Haiti, for it was the native name for it that would survive now. But Hunahpu was going to the swamps of Chiapas in Mexico, and it was quite likely that either he or Diko would die during the long years before their paths could cross.

And that was assuming that all three hemispheres would arrive. The problem of simultaneity had never been overcome. Even though the wiring had been carefully measured so that it should take exactly as long for the signal to go from the switch to the three computers and from the computers to the three field generators, they knew that no amount of careful measurement could possibly make the signals arrive with true simultaneity. There would be some tiny but real difference in time. One of the signals would arrive first. One of the fields would exist, even if it was for just one nanosecond, before the others came into existence. And it was possible that because of the changes caused by the first field, the other fields would never come into being at all. The future in which they existed would have been obliterated.

Thus it was determined that each of the three must act as if the other two had already failed. Each must carry out the mission with as much care as if everything depended on him or her alone, for it very well might be true.

But they hoped that all three time machines would work, that all three travelers would reach their separate destinations. Diko would arrive in Haiti in 1488, Kemal in 1492; Hunahpu would reach Chiapas in 1475. "There is a certain sloppiness in nature," Manjam had told them. "True precision is never achieved, is never even possible, and so everything that happens depends on a certain amount of probability, has a little leeway, a bit of room to compensate for lapses and mistakes. Genetic molecules are filled with redundancy and can cope with a certain amount of loss or damage or extra insertions. Electrons moving through their quantum shells have a certain range of unpredictability about their exact location, for all that matters is that they remain at the same distance from the nucleus. Planets wobble in their orbits and yet persist for billions of years without falling into their motherstars. So there should be room for microseconds or milliseconds or centiseconds or even deciseconds of difference between the beginnings of the three fields. But we have no way of experimenting to see just what the tolerances are. We may have far exceeded them. We may have missed by a fraction of a nanosecond. We may have been so far from success as to have made this whole venture wasted time. Who can know these things?"

Why is it, thought Tagiri, that even though I know that within a few minutes I and my dear husband and my precious son Acho will almost certainly wink out of existence, it is Diko that I am grieving for? She is the one who will live. She is the one with the future. Yet the animal part of me, the part that feels emotion, does not comprehend my own death. It is *not* death, when the whole world dies with you. No, the animal part of me only knows that my child is leaving me, and that is what I grieve for.

She watched as Hunahpu helped Diko up the ladder, then walked to his own hemisphere and climbed.

And now it was Tagiri's own turn. She kissed and embraced Hassan and Acho, and then climbed her own ladder, up to the locked cage. She pressed the button to open it as Manjam and Hassan also pressed their widely separated buttons, as Diko and Hunahpu and Kemal pressed the buttons on their field generators. The lock clicked and she pushed open the door of the cage and stepped inside.

"I'm in," she said. "Release your buttons, travelers."

"Get in position," called Sá.

Tagiri was now above the hemispheres and could see as Kemal and Diko and Hunahpu curled up on top of their equipment and supplies, making sure that no part of their bodies was under the field generator or extending beyond the boundaries of the sphere that the field generator would create.

"Are you ready?" called Sá.

"Yes," answered Kemal at once.

"Ready," said Hunahpu.

"I'm ready," said Diko.

"Can you see them?" called Sá, now talking to Tagiri and to the other three watchers who were in position to see. All of them confirmed that the travelers seemed to be in a good position.

"When you are ready, Tagiri," said Sá.

Tagiri hesitated only a moment. *I am killing everyone so that everyone can live,* she reminded herself. *They chose this, as much as anyone with imperfect understanding can ever choose. From birth we all were fated to die, and so it is good that at least we can be sure our deaths today might bring about a good end, might make the world a better place.* This litany of justification passed quickly, and again she was left with the pain that had gnawed at her for the weeks, the years of this project.

For a fleeting moment she wished that she had never joined Pastwatch, rather than to face this moment, to have it be her hand that pulled the switch.

Who else's hand? she asked herself. *Who else should bear this* responsibility, if I cannot bear it? All the slaves waited for her to bring them freedom. All the unborn children of countless generations of humanity waited for her to save them from the withering death of the world. Diko waited for her to send her out into the great work of her life.

She grasped the handle of the switch.

"I love you," she said. "I love you all."

She pulled it down.

10

Arrivals

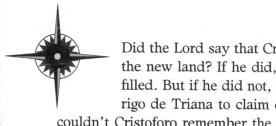

Did the Lord say that Cristoforo would be the first to see the new land? If he did, then the prophecy must be fulfilled. But if he did not, then Cristoforo could allow Rodrigo de Triana to claim credit for seeing land first. Why couldn't Cristoforo remember the exact words the Lord said? The most important moment in his life until now, and the wording escaped him completely.

No mistaking it, though. In the moonlight seeping through the clouds everyone could see the land; sharp-eyed Rodrigo de Triana had first seen it an hour ago, at two in the morning, when it was nothing but a different-colored shadow on the western horizon. The other sailors were gathered around him now, offering their congratulations and cheerfully reminding him of his debts, both real and imaginary. As well they should, for the first to see land had been promised a reward of ten thousand maravedis a year for life. It was enough to keep a fine household with servants; it would make de Triana a gentleman.

But what was it, then, that Cristoforo had seen earlier tonight, at ten o'clock? Land must have been close then, too, scarcely four hours before de Triana saw it. Cristoforo had seen a light, moving up and down, as if signaling him, as if beckoning him onward. God had shown land to him, and if he was to fulfill the words of the Lord, he must lay the claim.

"I'm sorry, Rodrigo," called Cristoforo from his place near the helm. "But the land you see now is surely the same land I saw at ten o'clock."

A hush fell over the company.

"Don Pedro Gutiérrez came to my side when I called him," said Cristoforo. "Don Pedro, what did we both see?"

"A light," said Don Pedro. "In the west, where the land now lies." He was the King's majordomo—or, to put it bluntly, the King's spy. Everyone knew he was no particular friend to Colón. Yet to the common sailors, all gentlemen were conspirators against them, as it certainly seemed to them now.

"I was the one cried 'land' before anyone," said de Triana. "You gave no sign of it, Don Cristóbal."

"I admit that I doubted it," said Cristoforo. "The sea was rough, and I doubted that land could be so near. I convinced myself that it could not be land, and so I said nothing because I didn't want to raise false hopes. But Don Pedro is my witness that I did see it, and what we all see now bears out the truth of it."

De Triana was outraged at what seemed to him to be plain theft. "All those hours I strained my eyes looking west. A light in the sky isn't land. No one saw land before I did, no one!"

Sánchez, the royal inspector—the King's official representative and bookkeeper on the voyage—immediately spoke up, his voice whipping sharply across the deck. "Enough of this. On the King's voyage, does anyone dare to question the word of the King's admiral?"

It was a daring thing for him to say, for only if Cristoforo reached Cipangu and returned to Spain would the title Admiral of the Ocean-Sea belong to him. And Cristoforo well knew that last night, when Don Pedro had affirmed that he saw the same light, Sánchez had insisted that there was no light, that there was nothing in the west. If anyone was going to cast doubt on Cristoforo's claim to first sighting, it would be Sánchez. Yet he had supported, if not Cristoforo's testimony, then his authority.

That would do well enough.

"Rodrigo, your eyes are indeed sharp," said Cristoforo. "If someone on shore had not been casting a light—a torch, or a bonfire—I would have seen nothing. But God led my eyes to the shore by that light, and you merely confirmed what God had already shown me."

The men were silent, but Cristoforo knew that they were not content. A moment ago they had been rejoicing in the sudden enrichment of one of their own; as usual, they had seen the reward snatched out of the hands of the common man. They would assume, of course, that Cristoforo and Don Pedro lied, that they acted from greed. They could not understand that he was on God's mission, and that he knew God would give him plenty of wealth without his having to take it from a common sailor. But Cristoforo dared not fail but to fulfill the Lord's instructions in every particular. If God had ordained that he be first to lay eyes upon the far-off kingdoms of the Orient, then Cristoforo could not thwart God's will in this, not even out of sympathy for de Triana. Nor could he even share some portion of the reward with Triana, for word would get out and people would assume that it was, not Cristoforo's mercy and compassion, but rather his guilty conscience that made him give the money. His claim to have seen land must stand unassailed forever, lest the will of God be undone. As for Rodrigo de Triana, God would surely provide him with decent compensation for his loss.

It *would* have been nice if, now that all the struggle was near fruition, God had let something be simple.

No measurements are exact. The temporal field was supposed to form a perfect sphere that exactly scoured the inside of the hemisphere, sending the passenger and his supplies back in time while leaving the metal bowl behind in the future. Instead, Hunahpu found himself rocking gently in a portion of the bowl, a fragment of metal so thin that he could see leaves through the edges of it. For a moment he wondered how he would get out, for metal so thin would surely have an edge that would slice right through his skin. But then the metal shattered under the strain and fell in thin crumbling sheets on the ground. His supplies tumbled down among the fragile shards.

Hunahpu got up and walked gingerly, gathering up the thin sheets carefully and making a pile of them near the base of a tree. Their biggest fear, in delivering him on land, was that the sphere of his temporal field would bisect a tree, causing the top half of it to drop like a battering ram onto Hunahpu and his supplies. So they had put him as near the beach as they dared without running a serious risk of dropping him in the ocean. But the measurements were not exact. One large tree was not three meters from the edge of the field.

No matter. He had missed the tree. The slight miscalculation in the size of the field had at least been in the direction of including too much rather than slicing off a portion of his equipment. And with luck they would have come close enough to the right timeframe that he would be in good time to accomplish his work before the Europeans came.

It was early morning, and Hunahpu's greatest danger would come from being sighted too soon. This stretch of beach had been chosen because it was rarely visited; only if they had missed their target date by several weeks would someone be within sight of him. But he had to act as if the worst had happened. He had to be careful.

Soon he had everything out of sight among the bushes. He sprayed himself again with insect repellent, just to be sure, and began the labor of carrying everything from the shore to the hiding place he had selected among the rocks a kilometer inland.

It took him most of the day. He rested then, and allowed himself the luxury of pondering his future. I am here in the land of my ancestors, or at least a place near to it. There is no retreat. If I don't bring it off, I'll end up as a sacrifice to Huitzilopochtli or perhaps some Zapotecan god. Even if Diko and Kemal made it, their target dates were years in the future from this place where I am now. I am alone in this world, and everything depends on me. Even if the others fail, I have it in my power to undo Columbus. All I have to do is turn the Zapotecs into a great nation, link up with the Tarascans, accelerate the development of ironworking and shipbuilding, block the Tlaxcalans and overthrow the Mexica, and prepare these people for a new ideology that does not include human sac-rifice. Who couldn't do *that?*

It had looked so easy on paper. So logical, such a simple pro-gression from one step to the next. But now, knowing no one in this place, all alone with the most pathetic of equipment, really, which could not be replaced or repaired if it failed. . . .

Enough of that, he told himself. I still have a few hours before dark. I must find out when I have arrived. I have rendezvous to keep.

Before dark he had located the nearest Zapotec village, Ate-tulka, and, because he had watched this village over and over again on the TruSite II, he recognized what day it was from what he saw the people doing. There had been no important error in the tem-poral field, so far as date was concerned. He had arrived when he was supposed to, and he had the option of making himself known to this village in the morning.

He winced at the thought of what he would have to do to make ready, and then walked back to his cache in the dusk. He waited for the jaguar that he had watched so many times, dropped it with a tranquilizer dart, then killed it and skinned it, so he could arrive at Atetulka wearing the skin. They would not lay hands readily upon a Jaguar Man, especially when he identified himself as a Maya king from the inscrutable underworld land of Xibalba. The days of Mayan greatness were long in the past, but they were well remembered all the same. The Zapotecs lived perpetually in the great shadow of the Maya civilization of centuries past. The Inter-veners had come to Columbus dressed up in the image of the God he believed in; Hunahpu would do the same. The difference was that he would have to live on with the people he was deceiving and continue to manipulate them successfully for the rest of his life.

This all had seemed like such a good idea at the time.

Cristoforo wouldn't let any of the ships sail for land until full light. It was an unknown coast, and, impatient as they all were to set foot on solid earth again, there was no use in risking even one ship when there might be reefs or rocks.

The daylight passage proved him right. The approaches were

treacherous, and it was only by deft sailing that Cristoforo was able to guide them in to shore. Let them say he was no sailor *now,* thought Cristoforo. Could Pinzón himself have done better than I just did?

Yet none of the sailors seemed disposed to give him credit for his navigation. They were still sullen over the matter of de Triana's reward. Well, let them pout. There would be wealth enough for all before this voyage was done. Hadn't the Lord promised so much gold that a great fleet could not carry it all? Or was that what Cristoforo's memory had made up for the Lord to have said?

Why couldn't I have been permitted to write it down when it was fresh in mind! But Cristoforo had been forbidden, and so he had to trust his memory. There was gold here, and he would bring it home.

"At this latitude, we must surely be at the coast of Cipangu," said Cristoforo to Sánchez.

"Do you think so?" asked Sánchez. "I can't think of a stretch of the Spanish coast where there would be no sign of human habitation."

"You forget the light that we saw last night," said Don Pedro.

Sánchez said nothing.

"Have you ever seen such a lush and verdant land," said Don Pedro.

"God smiles on this place," said Cristoforo, "and he has delivered it into the hands of our Christian King and Queen."

The caravels were moving slowly, for fear of running aground in uncharted shallows. As they moved closer to the luminous white beach, figures emerged from the forest shadows.

"Men!" cried one of the sailors.

And so they obviously were, since they wore no clothing except for a string around their waists. They were dark, but not, Cristoforo thought, as dark as the Africans he had seen. And their hair was straight, not tight-curled.

"Such men as these," said Sánchez, "I have never seen before."

"That is because you have never been to the Indies before," said Cristoforo.

"Nor have I been to the moon," murmured Sánchez.

"Haven't you read Marco Polo? These are not Chinese because their eyes are not pinched-off and slanted. There is no yellowness to their skin, nor blackness either, but rather a ruddiness that tells us they are of India."

"So it's not Cipangu after all?" said Don Pedro.

"An outlying island. We have come perhaps too far north. Cipangu is to the south of here, or the southwest. We can't be sure how accurate Polo's observations were. He was no navigator."

"And you *are?*" asked Sánchez dryly.

Cristoforo did not even bother to look at him with the disdain that he deserved. "I said that we would reach the Orient by sailing west, Señor, and here we are."

"We're somewhere," said Sánchez. "But where this place may be on God's green Earth, no man can say."

"By God's own sacred wounds, man, I tell you that we are in the Orient."

"I admire the admiral's certainty."

There it was again, that title—admiral. Sánchez's words seemed to express doubt, and yet he gave the title that could only be given to Cristoforo if his expedition succeeded. Or did he use the title ironically? Was Cristoforo being mocked?

The helmsman called to him. "Do we head for land now, sir?"

"The sea is still too rough," said Cristoforo. "And you can see the waves breaking over rocks. We have to circle the island and find an opening. Sail two points west of south until we round the southern end of the reef, and then west."

The same command was signaled to the other two caravels. The Indians on the shore waved at them, shouting something incomprehensible. Ignorant and naked—it was not appropriate for the emissary of Christian kings to make his first overtures to the poorest people of this new land. Jesuit missionaries had traveled to the far corners of the East. Someone who knew Latin would surely be sent to greet them, now that they had been sighted.

About midday, now sailing northward up the western coast of the island, they found a bay that made a good entrance. By now it was clear that this was an island so small as to be insignificant. Even the Jesuits couldn't be bothered with a place so small, so Cristoforo was reconciled to waiting another day or two before reaching someone worthy of receiving the emissaries of the King and Queen.

The sky had cleared and the sun shone hot and bright as Cristoforo descended into the launch. Behind him down the ladder came Sánchez and Don Pedro and, shaky as ever, poor Rodrigo de Escobedo, the notary who had to make an official record of all deeds done in the name of Their Majesties. He had cut a fine figure at court, a promising young functionary, but on board ship he had quickly been reduced to a puking shadow rushing from his cabin to the gunwale and staggering back—when he had strength to rise from his bed at all. By now, of course, he had got something like sea legs, and he even ate food that didn't end up staining the sides of the caravel. But yesterday's storms had felled him again, and so it was an act of sheer courage that he could come to shore and perform the duty for which he had been sent. Cristoforo admired him enough for his silent strength that he determined that no log of his would record the fact of Escobedo's seasickness. Let him keep his dignity in history.

Cristoforo noted that the launch put away from Pinzón's caravel before all the royal officials had made it down into his launch. Let Pinzón beware, if he thinks he can be the first to set foot on this island. Whatever he thinks of me as a sailor, I am still the emissary of the King of Aragon and the Queen of Castile, and it would be treason for him to try to preempt me on such a mission as this.

Pinzón must have realized this halfway to the beach, for his launch lay still in the water as Cristoforo's passed him and ran up onto the beach. Before the boat staggered to a stop, Cristoforo swung over the side and tramped through the water, the low breakers soaking him up to the waist and dragging at the sword at his hip. He held the royal standard high over his head as he broke from the water and strode forward on the smooth wet sand of the beach. He walked on until he was above the tide line, and there in the dry sand he knelt down and kissed the earth. Then he rose to his feet and turned to see the others behind him, also kneeling, also kissing the ground as he had done.

"This small island will now bear the name of the holy Savior who led us here."

Escobedo wrote on the paper he held on the small box he had carried from the caravel: "San Salvador."

"This land is now the property of Their Majesties King Ferdinand and Queen Isabella, our sovereigns and the servants of Christ."

They waited as Escobedo finished writing what Cristoforo had said. Then Cristoforo signed the deed, and so also did every other man there. None had the temerity to dare to sign above him, or to sign more than half as large as his bold signature.

Only then did the natives begin to emerge from the forest. There was a large number of them, all naked, none armed, brown as treebark. Against the vivid greens of the trees and underbrush, their skin looked almost red. They walked timidly, deferently, awe obvious on their faces.

"Are they all children?" asked Escobedo.

"Children?" asked Don Pedro.

"No beards," said Escobedo.

"Our captain shaves his face, too," said Don Pedro.

"They have no whiskers at all," said Escobedo.

Sánchez, hearing them, laughed loudly. "They're stark naked, and you look at their *chins* to see if they're men?"

Pinzón overheard the joke and laughed even louder, passing the story on.

The natives, hearing the laughter, joined in. But they could not keep from reaching up and touching the beards of those Spaniards nearest them. It was so obvious that they had no harmful intent that the Spaniards permitted their touch, laughing and joking.

Still, even though Cristoforo had no beard to attract them, they obviously recognized that he was the leader, and it was to him that the oldest of them came. Cristoforo tried several languages on him, including Latin, Spanish, Portuguese, and Genovese, to no avail. Escobedo tried Greek and Pinzón's brother, Vicente Yáñez, tried the smattering of Moorish he had learned during his years of smuggling along the coast.

"They have no language at all," said Cristoforo. Then he reached out to the gold ornament the chief wore in his ear.

Without a word the man smiled, took it out of his ear, and laid it in Cristoforo's hand.

The Spaniards sighed in relief. So these natives understood things well enough, language or not. Whatever gold they had belonged to Spain.

"More of this," said Cristoforo. "Where do you dig it out of the ground?"

Met by incomprehension, Cristoforo acted it out, digging in the sand and "finding" the gold ornament there. Then he pointed inland.

The old man shook his head vigorously and pointed out to sea. To the southwest.

"The gold apparently doesn't come from this island," said Cristoforo. "But we could hardly expect a place as small and poor as this to have a gold mine, or there would have been royal officials from Cipangu here to oversee the labor of digging it."

He laid the gold ornament back into the old man's hand. To the other Spaniards he said, "We'll soon see gold in such quantities as to make this a trifle."

But the old man refused to keep the gold. He pressed it upon Cristoforo again. It was the clear sign he was looking for. The gold of this place was being given to him by God. No man would freely give away something so precious if God had not impelled him. Cristoforo's dream of a crusade to liberate Constantinople and then the Holy Land would be financed by the ornaments of savages. "I take this, then, in the name of my sovereign lords the King and Queen of Spain," he said. "Now we will go in search of the place where the gold is born."

It was not the safest group of Zapotecs to run into in the forest—they were a war party, bent on finding a captive for sacrifice at the start of the rainy season. Their first thought would be that Hunahpu would make a splendid victim. He was taller and stronger than any man they had ever seen before, quite suitable for an offering of exceptional value.

So he had to preempt them—to appear to them as one who already belonged to the gods. In the end, he virtually had to capture them. He had been blithely confident back in Juba that his plan would work. Here, when he was surrounded by the birdcalls and whining insects of the marshy land of Chiapas, the plan seemed ludicrous, embarrassing, and painful.

He *would* have to imitate the most savage royal sacrifice ritual anywhere that didn't actually leave the king dead. Why had the Mayas been so inventively self-abusive?

Everything else was ready. He had hidden the library of the lost future in its permanent resting place and sealed the opening. He had cached the items he would need later in their weatherproof containers, and memorized all the permanent landmarks that would allow him to find them again. And the items he would need now, for the first year, were bundled in packaging that would not look too bizarre to the eyes of the Zapotecs. He himself was naked, his body painted, his hair feathered and beaded and jeweled to look like a Maya king's after a great victory. And, most important, on his head and draped down his back were the head and skin of the jaguar he had killed.

He had thirty minutes before the war party from the village of Atetulka would reach this clearing. If his blood was to be fresh he had to wait until the last minute, and now the last minute had arrived. He sighed, knelt in the soft leafmeal of the shadowed clearing, and reached for the topical anesthetic. The Mayas did this without anesthetic, he reminded himself as he applied it liberally to his penis and then waited a few minutes for it to become numb. Then, with a hypodermic gun, he deadened the entire genital area, hoping that he would have some opportunity to reapply the anesthetic in about four hours, when it began to wear off.

One genuine stingray needle and five imitation ones made of different metals. He took them one at a time in his hand and pushed each one crosswise into the loose skin along the top of his penis. The blood flow was copious, dripping all over his legs. Stingray needle, then silver, gold, copper, bronze, and iron. Even though there was no pain, he was dizzy by the end of it. From loss of blood? He doubted it. It was almost certainly the psychological effect of perforating his own penis that made him feel faint. Being a king among the Mayas was a serious business. Could he have done this without anesthetic? Hunahpu doubted it, saluting his ancestors even as he shuddered at their barbarism.

When the hunting party trotted silently into the clearing, Hu-

nahpu stood in a shaft of light. The high-intensity lamp pointing
upward between his legs caused the metal spines to glint and shim-
mer with the trembling of his body. As he had hoped, their eyes
went right to where the blood still trickled down his thighs and
dripped from the tip of his penis. They also took in his body paint
and, just as he had expected, they seemed to recognize at once the
significance of his appearance. They prostrated themselves.

"I am One-Hunahpu," he said in Maya. Then he repeated himself in Zapotecan. "I am One-Hunahpu. I come from Xibalba to
you, dogs of Atetulka. I have decided that you will no longer be
dogs, but men. If you obey me, you and all who speak the language
of the Zapotec will be masters of this land. No longer will your sons
go up to the altar of Huitzilopochtli, for I will break the back of the
Mexica, I will tear out the heart of the Tlaxcala, and your ships will
touch the shores of all the islands of the world."

The men lying on the ground began to tremble and moan.

"I command you to tell me why you are afraid, foolish dogs!"

"Huitzilopochtli is a terrible god!" cried one of them—Yax, his
name was. Hunahpu knew them all, of course, had studied their
village and key people in the other Zapotec villages for years.

"Huitzilopochtli is almost as terrible as Fat Jaguar Girl," said
Hunahpu.

Yax raised his head at this mention of his wife, and several of
the other men laughed.

"Fat Jaguar Girl beats you with a stick when she thinks you
have been planting corn in the wrong field," said Hunahpu, "but
still you plant corn where you want."

"One-Hunahpu!" cried Yax. "Who told you about Fat Jaguar
Girl?"

"In Xibalba I watched you all. I laughed at you when you cried
under Fat Jaguar Girl's stick. And you, Flower-eating-Monkey, do
you think I didn't see you pee on old Great-Skull-Zero's cornmeal
and make them into frycakes for him? I laughed when he ate
them."

The other men also laughed, and Flower-eating-Monkey raised
his head with a smile. "You liked my revenge joke?"

"I told of your monkey tricks to the lords of Xibalba, and they
laughed until they cried. And when Huitzilopochtli's eyes were

filled with tears, I jabbed him with my thumbs and popped out his eyeballs.'' With this, Hunahpu reached into the pouch hanging from the string around his waist and brought out the two acrylic eyeballs he had brought with him. ''Now Huitzilopochtli has to have a boy lead him around Xibalba, telling him what he sees. The other lords of Xibalba set obstacles in his path and laugh when he falls down. And now I have come here to the surface of Earth to make you into people.''

''We will build a temple and sacrifice every man of the Mexica to you, O One-Hunahpu!'' cried Yax.

Exactly the reaction he had expected. At once he threw one of the eyeballs of Huitzilopochtli at Yax, who yelped and rubbed his shoulder where it had hit him. Hunahpu had been a pretty good Little League pitcher with a decent fastball.

''Pick up the eyeball of Huitzilopochtli and hear my words, dogs of Atetulka!''

Yax scrabbled around in the leafmeal until he found the acrylic eye.

''Why do you think the lords of Xibalba were glad and didn't punish me when I took the eyes of Huitzilopochtli? Because he was fat from the blood of so many men. He was greedy and the Mexica fed him on blood that should have been out planting corn. Now all the lords of Xibalba are sick of blood, and they will make Huitzilopochtli go hungry until he is thin as a young tree.''

They moaned again. The fear of Huitzilopochtli ran deep—the success of the Mexica in war after war had seen to that—and to hear such terrible threats against a powerful god was a heavy burden to place upon them. Well, they're tough little bastards, thought Hunahpu. And I'll give them plenty of courage when the time comes.

''The lords of Xibalba have called upon their king to come from a far country. He will forbid them to drink the blood of men or women ever again. For the King of Xibalba will shed his own blood, and when they drink of his blood and eat of his flesh they will never thirst or hunger anymore.''

Hunahpu thought of his brother the priest and wondered what he would think of what was happening to the Christian gospel right now. In the long run, he would surely approve. But there would be some uncomfortable moments along the way.

"Rise up and look at me. Pretend to be men." They arose carefully from the forest floor and stood looking at him. "As you see me shed my blood here, so the King of Xibalba has already shed his blood for the lords of Xibalba. They will drink, and never thirst again. In that day will men cease to die to feed their god. Instead they will die in the water and rise up reborn, and then eat the flesh and drink the blood of the King of Xibalba just as the lords of Xibalba do. The King of Xibalba died in a faraway kingdom, and yet he lives again. The King of Xibalba is returning and he will make Huitzilopochtli bow down before him and will not let him drink of his blood or eat of his flesh until he is thin again, and that will take a thousand years, that old pig has eaten and drunk so much!"

He looked around at them, at the awe on their faces. Of course they were hardly taking this in, but Hunahpu had worked out with Diko and Kemal the doctrine he would teach to the Zapotecs and would repeat these ideas often until thousands, millions of people in the Caribbean basin could repeat them at will. It would prepare them for the coming of Columbus, if the others succeeded, but even if they did not, even if Hunahpu was the only one of the time travelers to reach his destination, it would prepare the Zapotecs to receive Christianity as something they had long expected. They could accept it without giving up one iota of their own native religion. Christ would simply be the King of Xibalba, and if the Zapotecs believed that he bore some small but bloody wounds in a place not often depicted in Christian art, it would be a heresy that the Catholics could learn to live with—as long as the Zapotecs had the technology and the military power to stand against Europe. If the Christians could accommodate the Greek philosophers and a plethora of barbarian holidays and rituals and pretend that they had been Christian all along, they could deal with the slightly perverse spin that Hunahpu was putting on the doctrine of Jesus' sacrifice.

"You are wondering if *I* am the King of Xibalba," said Hunahpu, "but I am not. I am only the one who comes before, to announce his coming. I am not worthy to braid a feather into his hair."

Take that, Juan Batista.

"Here is the sign that he is coming to you. Every man of you will be taken sick, and every person in your village. This sickness will spread throughout the land, but you will not die of it unless your heart belonged to Huitzilopochtli. You will see that even among the Mexica, there were few who truly loved that gluttonous fat god!''

Let that be the story that would travel with and explain the virulent therapeutic plague that these men were already catching from him. The carrier virus would kill no more than one in ten thousand, making it an exceptionally safe vaccine as it left its "victims" with antibodies capable of fighting off smallpox, bubonic plague, cholera, measles, chicken pox, yellow fever, malaria, sleeping sickness, and as many other diseases as the medical researchers had been able to pile on back in the lost future. The carrier virus would remain as a childhood disease, reinfecting each new generation—infecting the Europeans, too, when they came, and eventually all of Africa and Asia and every island of the sea. Not that disease would become unknown—no one was foolish enough to think that bacteria and viruses would not evolve to fill the niches left by the defeat of these old killers. But disease would not give an advantage to one side over the other in the cultural rivalries to come. There would be no smallpox-infected blankets to kill off annoyingly persistent Indie tribes.

Hunahpu squatted down and picked up the high-intensity light from between his feet. It was enclosed in a basket. "The lords of Xibalba gave me this basket of light. It holds within it a small piece of the sun, but it only works for me.'' He shone the light in their eyes, temporarily blinding them, then reached one finger into a gap in the basket, pressing it on the identification plate. The light turned off. No reason to waste batteries—this "basket of light" would have only a limited life, even with the solar collectors around the rim, and Hunahpu didn't want to waste it.

"Which of you will carry the gifts that the lords of Xibalba gave to One-Hunahpu when he came to this world to tell you of the coming of the King?''

Soon they were all reverently carrying bundles of equipment that Hunahpu would need during the coming months. Medical supplies for pertinent healings. Weapons for self-defense and for taking the courage out of enemy armies. Tools. Reference books stored in digital form. Appropriate costumes. Underwater breathing equipment. All sorts of useful little magic tricks.

The journey wasn't easy. Every step caused the weight of the metal spines to tug at his skin, opening the wounds wider and causing more bleeding. Hunahpu toyed with having the removal ceremony now, but decided against it. It was Yax's father, Na-Yaxhal, who was headman of the village, and to cement his authority and place him in the proper relationship with Hunahpu, he had to be the one to remove the spines. So Hunahpu walked on, slowly, step by step, hoping that the blood loss would remain minor, wishing that he had chosen a location just a little closer to the village.

When they were near, Hunahpu sent Yax on ahead, carrying the eyeball of Huitzilopochtli. Whatever jumble he might make of the things that Hunahpu had said to him, the gist of it would be clear enough, and the village would be turned out and waiting.

Waiting they were. All the other men of the village, armed with spears, ready to throw them, the women and children hidden in the woods. Hunahpu cursed. He had chosen this village specifically because Na-Yaxhal was smart and inventive. Why would Hunahpu imagine that he would believe at face value his son's story of a Maya king from Xibalba.

"Stop there, liar and spy!" cried Na-Yaxhal.

Hunahpu leaned back his head and laughed, as he inserted his finger into the basket of light and activated it. "Na-Yaxhal, does a man who woke up with painfully loose bowels twice in the night dare to stand before One-Hunahpu, who brings a basket of light from Xibalba?" With that he shone the light directly in Na-Yaxhal's eyes.

Six-Kauil's-Daughter, Na-Yaxhal's wife, cried out, "Spare my foolish husband!"

"Silence, woman!" answered Na-Yaxhal.

"He *was* up twice in the night with loose bowels, and he groaned with the pain of it!" she shouted. All the other women moaned with this confirmation of the stranger's secret knowledge, and the spears wavered and dipped.

"Na-Yaxhal, I will make you sick indeed. For two days your bowels will run like a fountain, but I will heal you and make you a man who serves the King of Xibalba. You will rule many villages and build ships to sail to every shore, but only if you kneel now before me. If you do not, I will cause you to fall over dead with a hole in your body that will not stop bleeding until you are dead!''

I won't have to shoot him, Hunahpu told himself. He'll obey and we'll become friends. But if he makes me, I can do it, I can kill him.

''Why does the man of Xibalba choose me for this greatness, when I am a dog?'' called out Na-Yaxhal. It was a very promising rhetorical position for him to take.

''I choose you because you are the closest to human of all the dogs who bark in Zapotec, and because your wife is already a woman for two hours every day.'' There, that would reward the old bat for speaking out in Hunahpu's support.

Na-Yaxhal made up his mind and, as rapidly as his aging body—he was nearly thirty-five—would allow, he prostrated himself. The others in the village followed suit.

''Where are the women of Atetulka? Come out of hiding, you and all your children. Come out and see me! Among men I would be a king, but I am only the humblest servant of the King of Xibalba. Come out and see me!'' Let's lay the groundwork of somewhat more egalitarian treatment of women now, at the beginning. ''Stand with your families, all of you!''

They milled around, but it took only a few moments—they already oriented themselves by clan and family, even when confronting an enemy, so it took little rearrangement to obey his command.

''Now, Na-Yaxhal, come forward. Take the first spine from my penis and paint the blood from it on your forehead, for you are the man who will be first king in the Kingdom of Xibalba-on-Earth, as long as you serve me, for I am the servant of the King of Xibalba!''

Na-Yaxhal came forward and pulled out the stingray spine. Hunahpu did not wince because there was no pain, but he could tell how the stingray spine tugged at his skin and imagined how nasty the pain would be tonight. If I ever see Diko again I don't want to hear her complain about anything she had to go through for the sake of our mission. Then he thought of the price Kemal intended to pay, and was ashamed.

Na-Yaxhal painted his forehead and nose, his lips and chin with the blood on the stingray spine.

"Six-Kauil's-Daughter!" The woman emerged from the midst of the leading clan of the village. "Draw out the next spine. What is it made of?"

"Silver," she said.

"Paint your neck with my blood."

She drew the long silver spine across her neck.

"You will be the mother of kings and your strength will be in the ships of the Zapotec people, if you serve the King of Xibalba-on-Earth, and me, the servant of the King of Xibalba!"

"I will," she murmured.

"Speak loudly!" Hunahpu commanded. "You did not whisper when you spoke wisely of the loose bowels of your husband! The voice of a woman can be heard as loud as the voice of a man, in the Kingdom of Xibalba-on-Earth!"

That's about all we can do for egalitarianism right now, Hunahpu said silently, but it should be revolutionary enough as the story spreads.

"Where is Yax!" cried Hunahpu.

The young man came forward timidly.

"Will you obey your father, and when he is carried to Xibalba will you lead this people in mercy and wisdom?"

Yax prostrated himself before Hunahpu.

"Take out the next spine. What is it made of?"

"Gold," said Yax, when he had it out.

"Paint your chest with my blood. All the gold of the world will be yours to command, when you are worthy to become king, as long as you remember that it belongs to the King of Xibalba, and not to you or any man. You will share it freely and fairly with all who drink the blood and eat the flesh of the King of Xibalba." That should help get the Catholic Church on the side of conciliation with the strange heretical proto-Christians when the two cultures met. If gold flowed freely to the Church, but only on condition that they confessed that they were eating the flesh and drinking the blood of the King of Xibalba, the heresy should find itself well on the way to become an acceptable variant of Catholic dogma. I wonder, thought Hunahpu, if I will be declared a saint. There will certainly be no lack of miracles, for a while, at least.

"Bacab, toolmaker, metalworker!" A thin young man came forward, and Hunahpu had him withdraw the next spine.

"It is copper, Lord One-Hunahpu," said Bacab.

"Do you know copper? Can you work it better than any man?"

"I work it better than any man in this village, but there are surely other men in other places who work it better than I do."

"You will learn to mix it with many metals. You will make tools that no one in the world has seen. Paint my blood upon your belly!"

The coppersmith did as he was told. After a king, a king's wife, and a king's son, the metalworkers would now have the most prestige in the new kingdom.

"Where is Xocol-Ha-Man? Where is the master shipbuilder?"

A strong man with massive shoulders emerged from another clan, smiling in pride and slapping his shoulders in piety.

"Take out the next spine, Xocol-Ha-Man. You who are named for a great river in flood, you must tell me, have you ever seen this metal before?"

Xocol-Ha-Man fingered the bronze, getting blood all over his fingers. "It looks like copper, only brighter," he said. "I've never seen it."

Bacab looked at it too, and also shook his head.

"Pee on this metal, Xocol-Ha-Man. Make the current of the ocean within you flow upon it! For you will not paint my blood on your body until you have found this metal in another land. You will build ships and you will sail them until you find the land in the north where they know the name of this metal. When you bring back the name of this metal to me, then you will paint my blood upon your groin."

Only the iron spine remained. "Where is Xoc? Yes, I mean the slavegirl, the ugly girl you captured and no one would marry her!"

She was thrust forward, a filthy thirteen-year-old with a harelip.

"Take out the last spine, Xoc. Paint my blood upon your feet. For by the power of this last metal will the King of Xibalba make all slaves free. Today you are a free citizen of the Kingdom of Xi-

balba-on-Earth, Xoc. You belong to no man or woman, for no man
or woman belongs to any other. The King of Xibalba commands it!
There are no captives, no slaves, no servants-for-life in the Kingdom
of Xibalba-on-Earth!''

For you, Tagiri.

But what he had given in pity was used in power. Xoc drew
the iron spine from his penis and then, just as a Maya queen would
have done, she stuck out her tongue, gripped the tip of it with her
left hand, and with her right hand drove the spine through it. Blood
flooded down her chin as the spine and her lips made a strange
cross.

The people gasped. What Xoc was demanding was not the kindness of a lord toward a slave he plans to free, but the honor of a
king for the queen who will bear his children.

What do I do with *this?* Who could have guessed, watching
Xoc's abject servility during her months of slavery, that she had
this kind of ambition? What did she mean to accomplish? Hunahpu
studied her face and saw in it—what, defiance? It was as if she saw
through his whole charade and dared him to refuse her.

But no, it was not defiance. It was bravery in the face of fear.
Of course she acted boldly. This kingly man who claimed to come
from the land of the gods was the first chance she had to rise above
her miserable condition. Who could blame her for acting as desperate people so often do, seizing on the first opportunity to reach
far beyond all reasonable hope? What did she have to lose? In her
despair, all salvation had seemed equally impossible. So why not
try to be queen, as long as this One-Hunahpu seemed disposed to
help her?

She is so ugly.

But smart and brave. Why close a door?

He reached down and drew the iron spine from her tongue.
''Let truth flow from your mouth forever as blood does now. I am
no king, and so I have no queen. But because you mixed your blood
with mine upon this last spine, I promise that for the rest of your
life, I will listen every day to one thing that you choose to tell me.''

Gravely she nodded, her face showing relief and pride. He had
turned away her bid to be a consort, but had accepted her as a
counselor. And as he knelt and painted her feet with the bloody

spine, she could not help but know that her life had been changed completely and forever. He had made her great in the eyes of those who had mistreated her.

As he rose to his feet, he put both hands on her shoulders and leaned close so he could whisper in her ear. "Do not seek vengeance now that you have power," he said in pure Maya, knowing that her native dialect was close enough that she would understand him well enough. "Earn my respect by your generosity and truthfulness."

"Thank you," she answered.

Now back to the original script. I hope, thought Hunahpu, that there aren't too many more surprises like this.

But of course there would be. All he could ever do was improvise. His plans would all have to be adapted; only his purposes were unchangeable.

He flung out his voice over the crowd. "Let Bacab touch this metal. Let Xocol-Ha-Man see it!"

The men came forward, studied it in awe. Alone of all the spines, it would not bend, not even slightly. "I have never seen a metal so strong," said Bacab.

"Black," said Xocol-Ha-Man.

"There are many kingdoms, far across the sea, where this metal is as common as copper is here. They will know how to smelt it until it shines white as silver. These kingdoms already know the King of Xibalba, but he has hidden many secrets from them. It is the will of the King of Xibalba that the Kingdom of Xibalba-on-Earth find this metal and master it, if you are worthy of it! But for now, this black metal spine will stay with Xoc, who once was a slave, and you will come to her or to her children in order to see if you have found the hard black metal. The faraway people call it *ferro* and *herro* and *iron* and *fer,* but you will call it *xibex,* for it comes from Xibalba and must only be used in the service of the King."

The last of the spines was out of his body now. It made him feel pleasantly light, as if the weight of them had dragged him down.

"Let this now be a sign to all of you, that the King of Xibalba touches all men and women of the world. This village will be struck with a plague, but not one of you will die of it." That promise had a chance of failure—the immunologists said that one in 100,000 would die of it. If one of those bad reactions came in Atetulka, Hunahpu would deal with it well enough. And compared to the millions who died of smallpox and other diseases in the old history, it was a small price to pay. "The plague will go forth from this village to every land, until all people have been touched by the finger of the King. And they will all say, From Atetulka came the sickness of the lords of Xibalba. It came first to you, because I came first to you, because the King of Xibalba chose you to lead the world. Not as the Mexica lead, in blood and cruelty, but as the King of Xibalba leads, in wisdom and strength." Might as well make the immunity virus part of the divinity show.

He looked around at their faces. Awe, and surprise, and, here and there, resentment. Well, that was to be expected. The power structure in this village was going to be transformed many times over before this was finished. Somehow these people would become leaders of a great empire. Only a few of them would be up to the challenge; many would be left behind, because they were suited only to the life of a village. There was no dishonor in that, but some would feel left out and hurt. Hunahpu would try to teach them to be content with what was possible to them, teach them to take pride in the achievements of others. But he could not change human nature. Some of them would go to their graves hating him for the changes that he brought. And he could never tell them how their lives might have ended, had he not interfered.

"Where will One-Hunahpu live?" he asked.

"In my house!" cried Na-Yaxhal at once.

"Will I take the house of the king of Atetulka, when he is only now becoming a man? It has been the house of dog-men and women! No, you must build me a new house, here, on this very spot." Hunahpu sat down cross-legged in the grass. "I will not move from this place until I have a new house around me. And over me, I will have a roof thatched from the roofs of all the houses of Atetulka. Na-Yaxhal, prove to me that you are a king. Organize your people to build me my house before darkness comes, and teach them their duties well enough that those who build it can do it without speaking a word."

It was already midday, but impossible as the task might look to the people, Hunahpu knew that it was well within their capacity to do it. The story of the building of One-Hunahpu's house would spread, and it would make others believe that they were indeed worthy to be the greatest city among the cities of the new Kingdom of Xibalba-on-Earth. Such stories were needed in forging a new nation with a will to empire. The people had to have an unshakable belief in their own worthiness.

And if they didn't make it before nightfall, Hunahpu would simply fire up the basket of light and declare that the lords of Xibalba were lengthening the day with this piece of sunlight so they could finish building the house before nightfall. Either way, the story would be a good one.

The people quickly left him alone as Na-Yaxhal organized them to build him a house. Able to relax at last, Hunahpu got the disinfectant out of one of his bags and applied it to his wounded penis. It contained agents to promote clotting and healing, and soon the flow of blood would become mere seepage and then stop. Hunahpu's hands trembled as he applied the salve. Not from pain, for that had not yet begun, nor even from loss of blood, but rather from relief after the tension of the ceremonies just past.

In retrospect it had been as easy to overawe these people as he had imagined it would be back when he had proposed his plan to the others in the lost future. Easy, but Hunahpu had never been so frightened in his life. How did Columbus manage it, boldly creating a future? Only because he knew so little of how futures could go wrong, Hunahpu decided, only because of ignorance could he shape the world so fearlessly.

"It's hard to imagine that these are the great kingdoms of the east that we read about in Marco Polo's account," said Sánchez.

Cristoforo could hardly argue with him. Colba seemed vast enough to be the mainland of Asia, but the Indians insisted that it was an island and that another island to the southeast, called Haiti, was much richer and had far more gold. Could that be Cipangu? Possibly. But it was discouraging to have to keep assuring the sailors and, above all, the royal functionaries that untold wealth was just a few more days' sailing away.

When would God allow him the moment of triumph? When would all the promises of gold and great kingdoms be obviously, clearly fulfilled so that he could return to Spain as Viceroy and Admiral of the Ocean-Sea?

"What does that matter?" said Don Pedro. "The greatest wealth of this place is before you in plain sight."

"What do you mean?" asked Sánchez. "The only thing this land is wealthy in is trees and insects."

"And people," said Don Pedro. "The gentlest, most peaceful people I've ever seen. It will be no trouble at all to get them to work, and they'll obey their masters perfectly. There's no fight in them at all, can't you see that? Can't you imagine what price they would fetch as the most docile of servants?"

Cristoforo frowned. That same thought had occurred to him, but it troubled him all the same. Was it what the Lord had had in mind, to convert them and enslave them at the same time? Yet there was no other source of wealth in sight, here in the land God had led him to. And it was obvious that these savages were completely unfit to be made into soldiers in a Crusade.

If God had meant these savages to be free Christians, he would have taught them to wear clothing instead of going about naked.

"Of course," said Cristoforo. "We will bring a sample of these people back to Their Majesties when we return. But I imagine that it will be more profitable to keep them here in the land they're acclimated to, and use them to mine gold and other precious metals while we teach them of Christ and see to their salvation."

The others heard him without disagreement—how could they argue with something so obviously true? Besides, they were still weak and weary from the illness that had swept through the crews of all three ships, obliging them to drop anchor and rest for several days. No one died from it—it was nowhere near as virulent as the terrible plagues that the Portuguese had run into in Africa, forcing them to build their forts on offshore islands. But it had left Cristoforo with quite a headache, and he was sure the others suffered from it, too. If it didn't hurt so much, he might wish for it to continue forever, since it kept them from raising their voices. The royal functionaries were much more tolerable when pain kept them from becoming strident.

They had been livid back when they reached the city called Cubanacán. Cristoforo had thought that the last syllable of the name referred to the Great Khan of Marco Polo's writing, but when they reached the "city" the natives had babbled about, it turned out to be a miserable collection of huts, perhaps a bit more populated than the other squalid villages that they had seen on this island. City of the Khan indeed. Sánchez had dared to raise his voice then, in front of the men. Maybe this minor plague was God's remonstrance against his insubordinate complaining. Maybe God wanted to give him something to whine about.

Tomorrow or the next day they would sail for Haiti. Perhaps there they would see some sign of the great civilizations of Cipangu or Cathay. And in the meantime, these miserable islands would at least be a source of slaves, and as long as the royal functionaries were willing to back him up, that might be enough to justify the cost of a second voyage, should they fail to find the Khan himself on this first trip.

Kemal sat glumly on the crest of the promontory, looking out to the northwest for a sail. Columbus was late.

And if he was late, all bets were off. It meant that some change had already been introduced, something that would delay him in Colba. Kemal might have been encouraged to think of this as proof that one of the others had successfully made the trip into the past, except that he was quite aware that the change might have been caused by him. The only influence that could reach from the island of Haiti to the island of Colba was the carrier virus—and even though he had only been here for two months, that was plenty of time for the virus to have been spread to Colba by a raiding party in a seagoing canoe. The Spaniards must have contracted the virus.

Or worse. The gentle plague might have caused a change in behavior by the Indies. There might have been bloodshed, bad enough to make the Europeans head for home. Or Columbus might have been told something that led him to take a different route—

circling Haiti counterclockwise, for instance, instead of charting the north shore.

They had known that the virus could upset their plans, because it would move faster and farther than the time travelers could. Yet it was also the surest, most basic aspect of their plan. What if only one traveler got through, and then was killed immediately? Even so, the virus would be communicated to those who touched the body during the first few hours. If no other change could be introduced, this one might be enough—to keep the Indies from being swept away in a tide of European diseases.

So it's a good thing, Kemal told himself. A good thing that Columbus is late, because it means that the virus is doing its work. We've already changed the world. We've already succeeded.

Only it didn't feel like success to him. Living on stored rations, hiding out here on this isolated promontory, watching for the sails, Kemal wanted to accomplish something more personal than being the carrier of a healing virus. Allah wills whatever happens, he knew, but he was not so pious that he could keep himself from wishing he could whisper a word or two in Allah's ear. A few pointed suggestions.

It wasn't until the third day that he saw a sail. Too early in the day. In the old version of history, Columbus had arrived later, which was why the *Santa Maria* wrecked, running against a submerged reef in the darkness. Now it wouldn't be dark. And even if it were, the currents and winds would not be the same. Kemal would have to destroy all three ships. Worse, without the the the accident with the *Santa Maria,* there would be no reason for the *Niña* to drop anchor. Kemal would have to follow along the shore and watch for his opportunity. If it came.

If I fail, thought Kemal, the others may still succeed. If Hunahpu manages to preempt the Tlaxcalans and create a Zapotec-Tarascan empire that has abandoned or downplayed human sacrifice, then the Spanish won't have such an easy time of it. If Diko is somewhere in the highlands, she may be able to create a new proto-Christian religion and, conceivably, a unified Caribbean empire that the Spaniards will not easily crack. After all, Spanish success depended almost entirely upon the inability of the Indies to organize serious resistance. So even if Columbus gets back to Europe, history will still be different.

He could whisper all these reassuring things, but they tasted like ashes in his mouth. If I fail, America loses its fifty years of preparation before the Europeans come.

Two ships. Not three. That was a relief. Or was it? As long as history was changing, it might have been better for Columbus's fleet to stay together. Pinzón had taken the *Pinta* away from the rest of the fleet, just as in the former history. But now who could guess whether Pinzón would have his change of heart and sail back to Haiti to rejoin Columbus? This time he might simply go on eastward, arriving in Spain first and claiming all the credit for Columbus's discovery.

That's out of my hands, Kemal told himself. The *Pinta* will either come back or it will not. I have the *Niña* and the *Santa Maria*, and I must make sure that they, at least, never return to Spain.

Kemal watched until he could see that the ships were turning south, to round the Cape of San Nicolas. Would they take the same course they had followed in the prior history, sailing south a bit more, then turning back to chart the north coast of the island of Haiti? Nothing was predictable anymore, even if logic proclaimed that whatever reasons Columbus had for his actions in the other history, the same reasons would hold sway this time, too.

Kemal picked his way carefully down to the stand of trees near the water where he had concealed his inflatable boat. Unlike lifeboats, this one was not bright orange. Rather it was a greenish blue, designed to be invisible on the water. Kemal pulled on his wet suit, also greenish blue, and pulled the boat into the water. Then he loaded it with enough underwater charges to deal with both the *Santa Maria* and the *Niña*, should the opportunity present itself. Then he started up the engine and put out to sea.

It took him a half hour to be far enough from shore to be reasonably confident of being invisible to the keen-eyed watchers on the Spanish caravels. Only then did he sail westward far enough to see the Spanish sails. To his relief, they had dropped anchor off Cape San Nicolas and small boats were putting to shore. It might be December ninth rather than the sixth, but Columbus was making the same decisions he had made before. The weather was getting cold, for this part of the world, and Columbus would have the same problems getting through the channel between Tortuga and Haiti until the fourteenth of December. Perhaps Kemal would be better off if he put back to shore and waited for history to repeat itself.

Or perhaps not. Columbus would be anxious to sail east in order to beat Pinzón back to Spain, and this time he might go out around Tortuga, tacking into the trade winds and completely avoiding the treacherous shore winds that would drive him onto the reefs. This might be Kemal's last chance.

But then, Cape San Nicolas was far from where Diko's tribe lived—if in fact she had succeeded in becoming part of the village that had first called to the people of the future to save them. Why make things harder for her?

He would wait and watch.

At first when the *Pinta* started slipping farther and farther away, Cristoforo supposed that Pinzón was avoiding some hazard in the water. Then, as the caravel drifted nearer the horizon, Cristoforo tried to believe what the men were telling him—that the *Pinta* must be unable to read the signals that Cristoforo was sending. This was nonsense, of course. The *Niña* also lay to portside, and was having no trouble at all staying on course. By the time the *Pinta* dropped over the horizon, Cristoforo knew that Pinzón had betrayed him, that the onetime pirate was now determined to sail direct for Spain and report to Their Majesties before Cristoforo could get there. Never mind that it would be Cristoforo who was recognized officially as the head of the expedition, or that the royal officials traveling with the expedition would report Pinzón's perfidy—it would be Pinzón who would reap the first fame, Pinzón whose name would live through history as the man who returned first to Europe from the westward route to the Orient.

Pinzón had never sailed far enough south to know that this steady east wind gave way, in lower latitudes, to the steady west wind that Cristoforo had felt when he sailed in Portuguese vessels. So there was a good chance that if Cristoforo could just get far enough south, he could reach Spain long before Pinzón, who would no doubt be tacking his way across the Atlantic, a slow proposition at best. There was a good chance that Pinzón's progress would be so slow that he would have to give up and return to these islands to resupply his caravel.

A good chance, but no certainty, and Cristoforo could not shake the sense of urgency—and barely suppressed fury—that Pinzón's disloyalty had provoked. Worst of all, there was no one in whom he could confide, for the men were doubtless all rooting for Pinzón to win, while in front of the officers and the royal officials Cristoforo could show no weakness or worry.

So it was that Cristoforo took little pleasure in charting the unknown coast of the great island the natives called Haiti, and which Cristoforo had named Hispañola. Perhaps he might have enjoyed the charting more if it had proceeded steadily, but the east wind was against him all along the coast. They had to harbor for days at the place that the men called Mosquito Bay, and again for several days at Paradise Valley. The men had made much of these stops, for the people here were taller and healthier, and two of the women light enough of skin that they were nicknamed "the Spaniards" by the men. As a Christian commander, Cristoforo had to pretend not to know what else was going on between the sailors and the women who came out to the caravels. Some of the tension of the voyage eased at Paradise Valley. But not for Cristoforo, who counted every day's delay as that much better a chance for Pinzón to arrive first in Spain.

When Cristoforo finally got them moving, it was by sailing in the evening and hugging the coastline, where the breeze from shore counteracted the prevailing easterlies and carried them smoothly eastward. Even though the nights were clear, it was a dangerous business, sailing at night on an unfamiliar coastline, for no one knew what hazards there might be beneath the water. But Cristoforo could see no choice. It was either sail west and south around the island, which could be so huge that it would take months to circumnavigate it, or sail at night on the shore breezes. God would protect the ships, because if he didn't, the voyage would fail, or at least Cristoforo's part of it. What mattered now was getting back to Spain with glorious reports that concealed the disappointing amount of gold and the generally low level of civilization, so that

Their Majesties would outfit a real fleet and he could do some serious exploring until he found the lands Marco Polo had written of.

What bothered Cristoforo most, however, was something that he could not explain even to himself. During the days, as they lay at anchor and Cristoforo worked on charting the coast, he would sometimes turn away from the coast and look out over the open sea. It was then that he sometimes saw something out on the water. It would be visible only for a few moments at a time, and no one else reported seeing it at all. But Cristoforo knew that he had seen it, whatever it was—a patch of water that was slightly different in color from the water around it, and several times a shape like a man standing half in and half out of the water. The first time he saw the manshape, he immediately remembered all the Genovese sailors' tales of mermen and other monsters of the deep. But whatever it was, it was always far out to seaward, and came no closer. Was it some spiritual apparition, some sign from the Lord? Or was it a sign of the enmity of Satan, watching, waiting for some chance to disrupt this Christian expedition?

Once, just once, Cristoforo caught a glimpse of light as if whatever it was had a glass of its own and was watching him as steadily as he was watching it.

Of this Cristoforo wrote nothing in his log. Indeed, he tended to dismiss it as a sign of some slight madness brought about by tropical latitudes and the worries about Pinzón. Until disaster struck in the early hours of Christmas morning.

Cristoforo was awake in his cabin. It was hard for him to sleep when the ship was sailing so dangerously close to land, and so he stayed awake most nights, studying his charts or writing in his log or his private diary. Tonight, though, he had done nothing more than lie on his bed, thinking about all that had happened in his life so far, marveling at how things had worked out despite all adversity, and finally praying, giving thanks to God for what had looked at the time like divine neglect, but now looked like miraculous shepherding. Forgive me for misunderstanding you, for expecting you to measure time by the short moments of a man's life. Forgive me for my fears and doubts along the way, for I see now that you were always at my side, watching over me and protecting me and helping me to accomplish your will.

A shudder ran through the boat, and from the deck came a scream.

Kemal watched through his nightsights, hardly believing his good fortune. Why had he ever worried? Weather had been the cause of Columbus's delays in the prior history, and the same weather determined his progress now. Waiting for favorable winds had brought him to this spot just past Cape Haitien on Christmas Eve, within fifteen minutes of when he had arrived in Kemal's former past. The same currents and similar winds had caused the *Santa Maria* to drift onto a reef, just as before. It was still possible for everything to work just right.

Of course, it had always been the human factor, not the weather, that was expected to change. For all the talk of how a butterfly's wing in Beijing could cause a hurricane in the Caribbean, Manjam had explained to Kemal that pseudochaotic systems like weather were actually quite stable in their underlying patterns, and swallowed up random tiny fluctuations.

The real problem was the decision making of the men on the voyage. Would *they* do what they had done before? Kemal had watched the sinking of the *Santa Maria* a hundred times or more, since so much depended on it. The ship sank because of several factors, any one of which might be changed on a whim. First, Columbus had to be sailing at night—and to Kemal's relief, he was consistently doing just that in order to fight the trade winds. Then, both Columbus and Juan de la Cosa, the owner and master of the ship, had to be belowdecks, leaving the piloting of the ship in the hands of Peralonso Niño—which was proper enough, since he was the pilot. But Niño then had to take a nap, leaving the helm in the hands of one of the ship's boys, giving him a star to steer by, which would be fine for an ocean voyage but was hardly helpful when sailing along a treacherous and unfamiliar coast.

In the event, the only difference was that it wasn't the same ship's boy—from his height and manner, Kemal could tell even at a distance that this time it was Andrés Yévenes, a bit older. But whatever experience Andrés had would hardly help him now—no one had charted this coast, so even the most experienced pilot wouldn't have known that shelves of coral would be so close to the surface without making any visible change in the sea.

Even this had still been recoverable even in the prior history, for Columbus immediately gave orders which, if they had been obeyed, would have saved the ship. What really sank the *Santa Maria* was its owner, Juan de la Cosa, who panicked and not only disobeyed Columbus's orders but made it impossible for anyone else to obey him. From that point the caravel had been doomed.

Kemal, studying de la Cosa from the beginning of his life to the end, was unable to discover why he did such an inexplicable thing. De la Cosa never told the same story twice, and obviously lied every time. Kemal's only conclusion was that de la Cosa had panicked at the prospect of the ship sinking and had simply got away as quickly and effectively as possible. By the time it became obvious that there was plenty of time to take all the men off without serious danger, it was far too late to save the ship. At that point, de la Cosa could hardly admit to cowardice—or whatever his motive was.

The ship shuddered from the impact, then listed over to one side. Kemal watched anxiously. He was in full scuba gear, ready to come in close and put an explosive charge under the caravel in case it looked as though Columbus was about to save it. But it would be better if this ship could sink without inexplicable fires or explosions.

Juan de la Cosa stumbled out of his cabin and clambered up to the quarterdeck, not quite awake, but definitely inside a nightmare. His caravel had run aground! How could such a thing have happened? There was Colón, already on deck and angry. As always, Juan was filled with anger at the very sight of the Genovese courtier. If Pinzón had been in charge, there would have been no such nonsense as sailing at night. It was all Juan could do to get to sleep at night, knowing that his caravel was coasting a strange shore in darkness. And, just as he had feared, they had run aground. They would all drown, if they couldn't get off the ship before it sank.

One of the ship's boys—Andrés, the one that Niño fancied this week—was offering his pathetic excuses. "I kept my eye fixed on the star he pointed at, and kept the mast lined up with it.'' He looked and sounded terrified.

The ship lurched heavily to one side.

We will sink, thought Juan. I will lose everything. ''My caravel,'' he cried out. ''My little ship, what have you done to it!''

Colón turned to him with icy coldness. ''Were you sleeping well?'' he asked acidly. ''Niño certainly was.''

And shouldn't the ship's master be asleep? Juan wasn't the pilot and he wasn't the navigator. He was just the *owner*. Hadn't it been made clear to him that he had almost no authority, except as bestowed on him by Colón? As a Basque, Juan was as much a foreigner among these Spaniards as Colón himself, so that he got condescension from the Italian, contempt from the Spanish royal officers, and mockery from the Spanish sailors. But now, after having all control and respect stripped away, it was suddenly *his* fault that the ship ran aground?

The ship listed further to port.

Colón was speaking, but Juan had trouble concentrating on what he said. ''The stern is heavy, and we've dragged onto an underwater reef or shelf. We'll make no headway forward. There's no choice for it but to warp the ship off.''

This was the stupidest thing Juan had ever heard of. It was dark, the ship was sinking, and Colón wanted to try some stupid maneuver instead of *saving lives?* That's what you'd expect of an Italian—what were Spanish lives to him? And when it came to that, what was a Basque life to the Spaniards? Colón and the officers would get first call on the boats, but they wouldn't care what happened to Juan de la Cosa. While the men would never let him into a boat if they had a choice. He could see it, had always seen it in their eyes.

''Warp the ship off,'' said Cristoforo again. ''Take the launch out, carry the anchor to sternward, drop it, and then use the windlass to draw us off the rock.''

''I know what warping is,'' Juan answered. This fool, did he think he could teach seamanship to *him?*

''Then see to it, man!'' Cristoforo commanded. ''Or do you want to lose your caravel here in these waters?''

Well, let Colón give his orders—he knew nothing. Juan de la

Cosa was a better Christian than any of these men. The only way to get all the crew off was to bring the Niña's boats over to help. Forget drawing the anchor out—that would be slow and time-consuming and men would die. Juan would save every life on this ship, and the men would know who cared for them. Not that braggart Pinzón, who selfishly took off on his own. Certainly not Colón, who thought only of the success of his expedition, never mind if men died in the doing of it. I'm the one, Juan de la Cosa, the Basque, the northerner, the outsider. *I* am the one who will help you live to return to your families in Spain.

Juan immediately set several men to lowering the launch. In the meantime, he heard Colón barking orders to furl the sails and free the anchor. Oh, what an excellent idea, thought Juan. The ship will sink *with sails furled*. That will make a huge difference to the sharks.

The launch dropped into the water with a splash. At once the launch's crew of three oarsmen scrambled down the lines and began untying the knots to free the launch from the caravel. In the meantime, Juan tried to climb down the rope ladder, which, with the ship tilting, dangled in midair and swayed dangerously. Let me live to reach the launch, Holy Mother, he prayed, and then I will be a hero to save the others.

His feet found the boat but he could not pry his fingers away from the rope ladder.

"Let go!" demanded Peña, one of the seamen.

I'm trying, thought Juan. Why aren't my hands working?

"He's such a coward," muttered Bartolomé. They pretend to speak softly, thought Juan, but they always make sure I can hear them.

His fingers opened. It had only been a moment. No one could be expected to act with perfect control when death by drowning lurked only moments away.

He clambered over Peña to get to his place at the stern, controlling the tiller. "Row," he said.

As they began pulling, Bartolomé, sitting in the bow, called the rhythm. He had once been a soldier in the Spanish army, but was arrested for stealing—he was one of those who joined the voyage as a criminal hoping for pardon. Most of the criminals were treated badly by the others, but Bartolomé's military experience had earned him some grudging respect from the others—and the slavish devotion of the other criminals. "Pull," he said. "Pull."

As they rowed, Juan turned the tiller hard to port.

"What are you doing?" demanded Bartolomé, when he saw that the launch was pulling away from the *Santa Maria* instead of heading for the bow, where the anchor was already beginning to descend.

"Do your job and I'll do mine!" shouted Juan.

"We're supposed to lie under the anchor!" answered Bartolomé.

"Do *you* trust your life to the Genovese? We're going to the *Niña* for help!"

The seamen's eyes widened. This was a direct contravention of orders. It bordered on mutiny against Colón. They still didn't resume pulling on the oars. "De la Cosa," said Peña, "aren't you going to try to save the caravel?"

"It's *my* ship!" cried Juan. "And it's *your* lives! Pull on your oars and we can save everyone! Pull! Pull!"

Bartolomé took up the chant, and they pulled.

Only now did Colón trouble to notice what they were doing. Juan could hear him crying out from the quarterdeck. "Come back! What are you doing? Come and lie under the anchor!"

But Juan looked fiercely at the seamen. "If you want to live to see Spain again, then all we can hear is the splashing of the oars."

Wordlessly they rowed, hard and fast. The *Niña* grew larger in the distance, the *Santa Maria* smaller behind them.

It's amazing which events turn out to have been inevitable, thought Kemal, and which can be changed. The sailors all slept with different native women in Paradise Valley this time, so that apparently the choice of bedmates was entirely by random whim. But when it came to disobeying the only order that could have saved the *Santa Maria*, Juan de la Cosa apparently made the same choice no matter what. Love is random; fear is inevitable. Too bad I'll never get a chance to publish this finding.

I'm done with telling stories. I can only act out the end of my

life. Who then will decide the meaning of *my* death? I will, as best
I can. But then it will be out of my hands. They will make of me
whatever they want, if they remember me at all. The world in
which I discovered a great secret of the past and became famous
no longer exists. Now I'm in a world where I was never born and
have no past. A lone Muslim saboteur, who somehow made his
way to the New World? Who in the future will believe such a fan-
tastic tale? Kemal imagined what the learned articles would sound
like, explaining the psychosocial origin of the Lone Muslim Bomber
legends from the voyage of Columbus. It brought a smile to his face,
as the crew of the *Santa Maria* rowed for the *Niña.*

Diko came back to Ankuash with two full baskets of water hanging
from the yoke over her shoulder. She had made the yoke herself,
when it became clear to them all that no one in the village was as
strong as Diko. It shamed the others, to see her carry her water so
easily when for them it was so hard. So she made the yoke so she
could carry twice as much, and then she insisted on hauling the
water alone, so that no one else could be compared to her. She
made three trips a day to the stream under the falls. It kept her
strong, and she appreciated the solitude.

The others were waiting for her, of course—the water from her
large baskets would be poured out into many smaller vessels, most
of them clay pots. But she could see even from a distance that there
was an eagerness to them. News, then.

"The white men's canoe was taken by the spirits in the water!"
cried Putukam, as soon as Diko was close enough to hear. "On the
very day you said!"

"So now maybe Guacanagarí will believe the warning and protect his young girls." Guacanagarí was the cacique over most of
northwestern Haiti. He fancied sometimes that his authority extended all the way up the mountains of Cibao to Ankuash, though
he had never attempted to test this theory in battle—there was nothing this high up in Cibao that he wanted. Guacanagarí's dreams of
being ruler of all of Haiti had led him in the prior history to make
a fatal alliance with the Spanish. If they had not had him and his

people to spy for them and even fight beside them, the Spanish might not have prevailed; other Taino leaders might have been able to unite Haiti in some kind of effective resistance. But that would not happen this time. Guacanagarí's ambition would still be his guiding principle, but it would not have the same devastating effect. For Guacanagarí would only be a friend to the Spanish when they seemed strong. As soon as they seemed weak, he would be their deadliest enemy. Diko knew enough not to trust his word even for a moment. But he was still useful, because he was predictable to one who understood his hunger for glory.

Diko squatted down to take the yoke from her shoulders. Others held up the water baskets and began to pour them off into other vessels.

"Guacanagarí, listen to a woman of Ankuash?" said Baiku skeptically. He was taking water into three pots. Little Inoxtla had cut himself badly in a fall, and Baiku was preparing a poultice, a tea, and a steam for him.

One of the younger women immediately rushed to Diko's defense. "He must believe Sees-in-the-Dark! All her words come true."

As always, Diko denied her supposed prophetic gifts, though it had been her intimate knowledge of the future that kept her from living as a slave or the cacique's fifth wife. "It is Putukam who sees true visions, and Baiku who heals. I haul water."

The others fell silent, for none of them had ever understood why Diko would say something which was so obviously false. Who ever heard of a person who refused to admit what she did *well?* Yet she was the strongest, tallest, wisest, and holiest person they had ever seen or heard of, and so if she said this, then there must be some meaning in it, though it could not be taken at face value, of course.

Think what you want, Diko said silently. But I know that the day has now come when I will have no more knowledge of the future than you have, because it will not be the future that I remembered.

"And what of the Silent Man?" she asked.

"Oh, they say he is still in his boat made of water and air, watching."

Another added, "They say these white people can't see him at all. Are they blind?"

"They don't know how to watch things," said Diko. "They don't know how to see anything but what they expect to see. The Tainos down on the coast know how to see his boat made of water and air, because they saw him make it and put it into the water. They *expect* to see it. But the white men have never seen it before, so their eyes don't know how to find it."

"Still they're very stupid not to see," said Goala, a teenage boy freshly into his manhood.

"You are very bold," said Diko. "I'd be afraid to be your enemy."

Goala preened.

"But I'd be even more afraid to be your friend in battle. You are sure your enemy is stupid because he doesn't do things as you would do them. It will make you careless, and your enemy will surprise you, and your friend will die."

Goala went silent, while the others laughed.

"You haven't seen the boat made of water and air," said Diko. "So you don't know how hard or easy it is to see it."

"I want to see it," said Goala quietly.

"It will do you no good to see it," said Diko, "because no one in the world has the power to make one like it, and no one *will* have such power for more than four hundred years." Unless technology moved even faster in this new history. With luck, this time technology would not outstrip the ability of human beings to understand it, to control it, to clean up after it.

"You make no sense at all," said Goala.

The others gasped—only a man so young would speak so disrespectfully to Sees-in-the-Dark.

"Goala is thinking," said Diko, "that it is the thing that will only be seen once in five hundred years that a man should go and see. But I tell you that it is only the thing that a man can learn from and use to help his tribe and his family that is worth going to see. The man who sees the boat made of water and air has a story that his children will not believe. But the man who learns how to make a great wooden canoe like the ones the Spaniards sail in can cross oceans with heavy cargo and many passengers. It is the Spaniard's canoes you want to see, not the boat made of water and air.''

''I don't want to see the white men at all,'' said Putukam with a shudder.

''They are only men,'' said Diko. ''Some of them are very bad, and some of them are very good. All of them know how to do things that no one in Haiti knows how to do, and yet there are many things that every child in Haiti knows that these men do not understand at all.''

''Tell us!'' several of them cried.

''I've told you all these stories about the coming of the white men,'' said Diko. ''And today there's work to do.''

They voiced their disappointment like children. And why shouldn't they? Such was the trust within the village, within the tribe, that no one was afraid to tell what he desired. The only feelings they had to hide from their fellow villagers were the truly shameful feelings, like fear and malice.

Diko carried her yoke and her empty water baskets back to her house—a hut, really. Thankfully no one was waiting for her there. She and Putukam were the only women to have houses of their own, and ever since the first time Diko had taken in a woman whose husband was angry at her and threatened to beat her, Putukam had joined her in making her house available as a refuge for women. There had been a great deal of tension at the beginning, since Nugkui, the cacique, correctly saw Diko as a rival for power in the village. It only came to violence once, when three men came in the shadow of night, armed with spears. It had taken her about twenty seconds to disarm all three of them, break the spear shafts, and send them staggering away with many cuts and bruises and sore muscles. They were simply no match for her size and strength—and her martial-arts training.

It wouldn't have kept them from trying something later—an arrow, a dart, a fire—except that Diko had taken action at first light. She gathered up her belongings and began giving them away as gifts to other women. This immediately aroused the whole village. ''Where are you going?'' they demanded. ''Why are you leaving?'' She had answered disingenuously: ''I came to this village because I thought I heard a voice calling me here. But last night I had a vision of three men attacking me in the darkness, and I knew that the voice must have been wrong, it was not this village, because this village doesn't want me. I must go now and find the right village, the one that has a need for a tall black woman to carry their water.'' After much remonstrance, she agreed to stay for three days. ''By the end of that time, I will go unless everybody in Ankuash has asked me, one at a time, to stay, and promised to make me their aunt or their sister or their niece. If even one person does not want me here, I will go.''

Nugkui was no fool. Much as he might resent her authority, he knew that having her in the village gave Ankuash enormous prestige among the Taino who lived farther down the mountain. Didn't they send their sick to Ankuash now to be healed? Didn't they send messengers to ask the meanings of events or to learn what Sees-in-the-Dark predicted for the future? Until Diko came, the people of Ankuash were despised as the people who lived in the cold place on the mountain. It was Diko who had explained that their tribe was the first to live on Haiti, that their ancestors were the first to be brave enough to sail from island to island. ''For a long time, the Taino have had their way here, and the Caribs want to do the same to them,'' she explained. ''But the time is soon coming when Ankuash will once again lead all the people of Haiti. For this is the village that will tame the white men.''

Nugkui was not about to let this exalted future slip away. ''I want you to stay,'' he had said, gruffly.

''I'm glad to hear that. Have you seen Baiku about that nasty bruise on your forehead? You must have bumped into a tree when you went out to pee in the dark.''

He glared at her. ''Some say you do things a woman shouldn't do.''

''But if I do them, then they must be things that I believe a woman *should* do.''

''Some say that you are teaching their wives to be rebellious and lazy.''

''I never teach anyone to be lazy. I work harder than anybody, and the best women of Ankuash follow my example.''

''They work hard, but they don't always do what their husbands tell them.''

"But they do almost everything that their husband *ask* them to do," said Diko. "Especially when their husbands do everything the women ask *them* to do."

Nugkui had sat there for a long while, sucking on his anger.

"That cut on your arm looks ugly," said Diko. "Was somebody careless with his spearpoint on yesterday's hunt?"

"You change everything," said Nugkui.

Here was the crux of the negotiation. "Nugkui, you are a brave and wise leader. I watched you for a long time before I came here. Wherever I went, I knew that I would make changes, because the village that teaches the white men how to be human has to be different from all other villages. There will be a dangerous time when the white men are not yet tamed, when you may need to lead our men in war. And even in peace, you are the cacique. When people come to me for judgment, don't I always send them to you? Don't I always show you respect?"

Grudgingly he admitted that she did.

"I have seen a terrible future, in which the white men come, thousands upon thousands of them, and make our people into slaves—the ones they don't kill outright. I have seen a future in which on the whole island of Haiti there is not one Taino, not one Carib, not one man or woman or child of Ankuash. I came here to prevent that terrible future. But I can't do it alone. It depends on you as much as on me. I don't want you to obey me. I don't want to rule over you. What village would respect Ankuash, if the cacique took orders from a woman? But what cacique deserves respect, if he can't learn wisdom just because a woman teaches it to him?"

He watched her impassively, and then said, "Sees-in-the-Dark is a woman who tames men."

"The men of Ankuash are not animals. Sees-in-the-Dark came here because the men of Ankuash have already tamed themselves. When women took refuge in my tent, or Putukam's, the men of this village could have torn apart the walls and beaten their wives, or killed them—or Putukam, or even me, because I may be clever and strong but I am not immortal and I can be killed."

Nugkui blinked at that statement.

"But the men of Ankuash are truly human. They were angry

with their wives, but they respected the door of my house and the door of Putukam's house. They stayed outside, and waited until their anger had cooled. Then their wives came out, and no one was beaten, and things were better. They say that Putukam and I were making trouble, but you are the cacique. You know that we were helping make peace. But it only worked because the men and women of this village *wanted* peace. It only worked because you, as cacique, allowed it to work. If you saw another cacique act as you have acted, wouldn't you call him wise?''

"Yes," said Nugkui.

"I also call you wise," said Diko. "But I won't stay unless I can also call you my uncle."

He shook his head. "That wouldn't be right. I'm no uncle to you, Sees-in-the-Dark. No one would believe it. They would know that you were only pretending to be my niece."

"Then I can't stay," she said, rising to her feet.

"Sit down," he said. "I can't be your uncle, and I won't be your nephew, but I can be your brother."

Diko had fallen to her knees before him then, and embraced him where he sat on the ground. "Oh, Nugkui, you *are* the man I hoped for."

"You are my sister," he said again, "but I thank every pasuk that lives in these woods that you are not my wife." With that he got up and left her house. From then on they were allies—once Nugkui's word was given, he didn't break it or allow any of the angry men to break it either. The result was inevitable. The men learned that rather than have the public humiliation of their wives taking refuge in the house of Diko or Putukam, they would control their anger, and no woman had been beaten in Ankuash for more than a year. Now women were more likely to come to Diko's house to complain about a husband who had lost his desire for her, or to ask her for magic or prophecy. She gave them neither, but instead offered sympathy and commonsense advice.

Alone in her house, she took up the calendar she was keeping, and reviewed in her mind the events that would come in the next few days. Down on the coast, the Spanish would be turning to Guacanagarí for help. In the meantime, Kemal—the one the Indies called Silent Man—would be destroying the other Spanish ships. If he failed, or if the Spanish succeeded in building new ships and sailed for home, then her work would be to unify the Indies to prepare them to beat off the Spanish. But if the Spanish were stranded here, then her work would be to spread stories that would lead Columbus to her. As social order broke down in the expedition—a near certainty, once they were stranded—Columbus would come to need a refuge. That would be Ankuash, and it would be her job to get him and any who came with him under control. If she had had to do a number on the Indies to get them to accept her, wait till they saw what she did to the white men.

Ah, Kemal. She had prepared the ground for him by saying that a person of power might come, a silent man, who would do marvelous things but would keep to himself. Leave him alone, she said in all her telling of this tale. All this time, she had no idea whether he would come or not—for all she knew, she had been the only one to succeed in reaching her destination. It was such a relief when word reached her that the Silent Man was living in the forest near the seashore. For several days she toyed with the idea of going to see him. He had to be even lonelier than she was, disconnected from her own time, from all the people she had loved. But it wouldn't do. When he succeeded in his work, he would be perceived by the Spanish as their enemy; she could not be linked with him, even in Indie legend, for soon enough all those stories would reach Spanish ears. So she let it be known that she wanted to know all about his movements—and that she thought it would be wise to leave him alone. Her authority wasn't all-pervasive, but Sees-in-the-Dark was regarded with enough awe, even by far-off villagers who had never spoken with her, that her advice concerning this strange bearded man was taken seriously.

Someone clapped outside her house.

"Be welcome," she said.

The woven reed flap was lifted aside, and Chipa came in. She was a young girl, perhaps ten years old, but smart, and Diko had chosen her to be her messenger to Cristoforo.

"*Estás pronta?*" Diko asked her.

"*Pronta mas estoy con miedo.*" I'm ready but I'm afraid.

Chipa's Spanish was solid. Diko had taught her for two years now—the two of them never spoke any other language between each other anymore. And of course Chipa was already fluent in the Taino language that was the lingua franca on Haiti, even though the villagers of Ankuash often spoke a different and much older language among each other, especially on solemn or sacred occasions. Language came easily to Chipa. She would do well as an interpreter.

Interpretation was the one thing that Cristoforo had never had on his first voyage. What could be communicated by hand signs and pointing and facial expressions wasn't much. The lack of a common language had forced both the Indies and the Europeans to depend on guesswork about what the other side really meant. It made for ludicrous misunderstandings. Any syllable that sounded like *khan* sent Cristoforo chasing after Cathay. And at this moment, in Guacanagarí's main village, Cristoforo was no doubt asking where more gold could be found; when Guacanagarí pointed up the mountain and said *Cibao*, Cristoforo would hear it as a version of *Cipangu*. If it really *had* been Cipangu, the samurai would have made short work of him and his men. But the most disturbing thing was that in the prior history it never crossed Cristoforo's mind that he didn't have the right to go straight to any gold mine he might find on Haiti and take possession of it.

She remembered what Cristoforo wrote in his log when Guacanagarí's people worked long and hard to help him load all his equipment and supplies off the wrecked *Santa Maria*: "They love their neighbor as themselves." He was capable of thinking of them as having exemplary Christian virtues—and then turn right around and assume that he had the right to take from them anything they owned. Gold mines, food, even their freedom and their lives—he was incapable of thinking of them as having rights. After all, they were strangers. Dark of skin. Unable to speak any recognizable language. And therefore not people.

It was one of the hardest things for novices in Pastwatch to get used to, in studying the past—the way that most people in most times were able to speak to people of other nations, treat with them, make promises to them, and then go off and act as if those very people were beasts. What were promises made to beasts? What respect did you owe to property claimed by animals? But Diko had learned, as most did in Pastwatch, that for most of human history, the virtue of empathy was confined to one's kinship group or tribe.

People who were not members of the tribe were not people. Instead they were animals—either dangerous predators, useful prey, or beasts of burden. It was only now and then that a few great prophets declared people of other tribes, even of other languages or races, to be human. Guest- and host-rights gradually evolved. Even in modern times, when such attractive notions as the fundamental equality and fraternity of humankind were preached in every corner of the world, the idea that the stranger is not a person still remained just under the surface.

What am I expecting of Cristoforo, really? Diko wondered. I am asking him to learn a degree of empathy for other races that would not become a serious force in human life until nearly five hundred years after his great voyage, and did not prevail worldwide until many bloody wars and famines and plagues after that. I am asking him to rise out of his own time and become something new.

And this girl, Chipa, will be his first lesson and his first test. How will he treat her? Will he even listen to her?

"You are right to be afraid," said Diko in Spanish. "The white men are dangerous and treacherous. Their promises mean nothing. If you don't want to go, I won't compel you."

"But why else did I learn Spanish?" she asked.

"So you and I could tell secrets." Diko grinned at her.

"I'll go," said Chipa. "I want to see them."

Diko nodded, accepting her decision. Chipa was too young and ignorant to understand the real danger that the Spanish would mistreat her; but then, most adults made most of their decisions without a clear understanding of the possible consequences. And Chipa was both clever and good-hearted—the combination would probably serve her well enough.

An hour later, Chipa was out in the center of the village, plucking at the woven-grass shift that Diko had made for her. "It feels awful," said Chipa in Taino. "Why should I wear such a thing?"

"Because in the white men's country, it is a shameful thing for people to be naked."

Everybody laughed. "Why? Are they so ugly?"

"It's very cold there sometimes," said Diko, "but even in the summer they keep their bodies covered. Their God commanded them to wear things like this."

"It's better to sacrifice blood to the gods a few times a year, as the Taino do," said Baiku, "than for everybody to have to wear such ugly small houses on their bodies all the time."

"They say," said the boy Goala, "that the white men wear shells like a turtle."

"Those shells are strong, and spears don't go through them very easily," said Diko.

The villagers fell silent then, thinking about what this might mean if it ever came to battle.

"Why are you sending Chipa to these turtle men?" asked Nugkui.

"These turtle men are dangerous, but they're also powerful, and some of them have good hearts if we can only teach them how to be human. Chipa will bring the white men here, and when they're ready to learn from me, I'll teach them. And the rest of you will teach them, too."

"What can we teach to men who can build canoes as big as a hundred of ours?" asked Nugkui.

"They'll teach us, too. But not until they're ready."

Nugkui still looked skeptical.

"Nugkui," said Diko, "I know what you're thinking."

He waited to hear what she would say.

"You don't want me to send Chipa as a gift to Guacanagarí, because then he'll think that this means he rules over Ankuash."

Nugkui shrugged. "He already thinks that. But why should I make him sure?"

"Because he'll have to give Chipa to the white men. And once she's with them, she'll serve Ankuash."

"She'll serve Sees-in-the-Dark, you mean." It was a man's voice, from behind her.

"Your name may be Yacha," she said without turning around, "but you are not always wise, my cousin. But if I'm not a part of Ankuash, tell me now, and I'll go to another village and let them become the teachers of the white men."

The uproar among the villagers was immediate. A few moments later, Baiku and Putukam were leading Chipa down the mountain, out of Ankuash, out of Ciboa, to begin her moment of peril and greatness.

* * *

Kemal swam under the hull of the *Niña*. He had more than two hours' breathing mixture left in the tanks, which was five times longer than he would need, if everything went as he had practiced it. It took a little longer than he had expected to chip away the barnacles from a strip of hull near the waterline—you couldn't build up much momentum wielding a chisel under water. But the job was done soon enough, and then from his belly pouch he drew out the array of shaped incendiaries. He put the heating surface of each one against the hull, and then tripped the automatic self-driving staples that would hold them tight to the wood. When they were all in place, he pulled the cord at the end. At once he could feel the water growing warmer. Despite being shaped to put most of their energy into the wood, they still gave off enough heat into the water that before long it would be boiling. Kemal swam quickly away, back toward his boat.

In five minutes, the wood inside the hull burst into fierce flames. And still the heat from the incendiaries continued, helping the fire to spread rapidly.

The Spanish would have no idea how a fire could have started in the bilge. Long before they could get near the *Niña* again, the wood that the incendiaries were attached to would be ash, and the metal shells of the charges would drop to the bottom of the sea. They would give off a faint sonar pulse for several days, allowing Kemal to swim back and retrieve them later. The Spanish would have no idea that the burning of the *Niña* was anything but a terrible accident. Nor would anyone else who searched the site of the wreck in future centuries.

Now everything depended on whether Pinzón remained true to character and brought the *Pinta* back to Haiti. If he did, Kemal would blow the last caravel to bits. There would be no way to believe it an accident. Everyone would look at the ship and say, An enemy has done this.

11

Encounters

Chipa was frightened when Guacanagarí's women brought her forward. Hearing about the bearded white men was different from coming into their presence. They were large men, and they wore the most fearsome clothing. Truly it was as if each of them wore a house on his shoulders— and a roof on his head! The metal of the helmets shone so brightly in the sunlight. And the colors of their banners were like captured parrots. If I could weave a cloth like that, thought Chipa, I would wear their banners and live under a roof made of the metal they put on their heads.

Guacanagarí was busy plying her with last-minute instructions and warnings, and she had to pretend to listen, but she already had her instructions from Sees-in-the-Dark, and once she was speaking Spanish with the white men, it would hardly matter what Guacanagarí's plans might be.

"Tell me *exactly* what they *really* say," said Guacanagarí. "And don't add a single word to what I say to them beyond what I tell you. Do you understand me, you little snail from the mountains?"

"Great Cacique, I will do all that you say."

"Are you sure you can really speak their awful language?"

"If I can't, you'll soon see it by their faces," Chipa answered.

"Then say this to them: The great Guacanagarí, cacique of all of Haiti from Cibao to the sea, is proud to have found an interpreter."

Found an interpreter? Chipa was not surprised by his attempt to cut Sees-in-the-Dark out of things, but she was disgusted by it. Nevertheless, she turned to the white man in the most flamboyant costume and started to speak. But she had hardly got a sound from her mouth when Guacanagarí pushed her from behind with his foot, throwing her facedown on the ground.

"Show respect, mountain slug!" shouted Guacanagarí. "And that's not the chief, anyway, stupid girl. It's *that* man, the white-haired one."

She should have known—it wasn't by the volume of his clothing, it was by his age, by the respect his years had earned, that she could recognize the one that Sees-in-the-Dark had called Colón.

Lying on the ground, she began again, stammering a bit at first, but still making the Spanish words very clearly. "My Lord Cristobal Colón, I have come here to interpret for you."

She was answered by silence. She raised her head to see the white men, in wide-eyed astonishment, conferring among themselves. She strained to hear, but they spoke too rapidly.

"What are they saying?" asked Guacanagarí.

"How can I hear when you're talking?" answered Chipa. She knew she was being impudent, but if Diko was right, Guacanagarí would soon have no power over her.

Colón finally stepped forward and spoke to her.

"How did you learn Spanish, my child?" he asked.

He spoke rapidly, and his accent was different from Sees-in-the-Dark, but this was exactly the question that she had been told to expect.

"I learned this language so that I might learn about Christ."

If they had been flustered before by her command of Spanish, these words brought consternation upon the white men. Again there was a flurry of whispered conversation.

"What did you say to him?" demanded Guacanagarí.

"He asked me how I came to speak his language, and I told him."

"I told you not to speak of Sees-in-the-Dark!" Guacanagarí said angrily.

"I didn't," she said. "I spoke of the God they worship."

"I think you're betraying me," said Guacanagarí.

"I'm not," said Chipa.

Now when Colón stepped forward, the man in the voluminous clothing was beside him.

"This man is Rodrigo Sánchez de Segovia, the royal inspector of the fleet," said Colón. "He would like to ask you a question."

The titles meant nothing to Chipa. She had been told to talk to Colón.

"How do you know of Christ?" asked Segovia.

"Sees-in-the-Dark told us to look for the coming of a man who would teach us about Christ."

Segovia smiled. "I am that man."

"No sir," said Chipa. "Colón is the man."

It was easy to read the expressions on the white men's faces—they showed everything they were feeling. Segovia was very angry. But he stepped back, leaving Colón alone in front of the other white men.

"Who is this Sees-in-the-Dark?" asked Colón.

"My teacher," Chipa answered. "She sent me as a gift to Guacanagarí, so he would bring me to you. But he is not my master."

"Sees-in-the-Dark is your mistress?"

"No one is my master but Christ," she said—exactly the statement that Sees-in-the-Dark had told her was the most important she could make. And now, with Colón looking at her, speechless, she said the one sentence that she did not understand, for it was in another language. The language was Genovese, and therefore only Cristoforo understood her as she said words that he had heard before, on a beach near Lagos: "I saved you alive so you could carry the cross."

He sank to his knees. He said something that sounded like the same strange language.

"I don't speak that language, sir," she said.

"What's happening?" demanded Guacanagarí.

"The cacique is angry at me," said Chipa. "He will beat me for not saying what he told me to say."

"Never," said Colón. "If you give yourself to Christ, then you are under our protection."

"Sir, don't provoke Guacanagarí for my sake. With both your ships destroyed, you need to keep his friendship."

"The girl is right," said Segovia. "It won't be the first time she's been beaten."

But it *would* be the first time, thought Chipa. In the white men's land, were they accustomed to beating children?

"You could ask for me as a gift," said Chipa.

"Are you a slave, then?"

"Guacanagarí thinks so," said Chipa, "but I never was. *You* won't make me a slave, will you?" Sees-in-the-Dark had told her that it was very important that she say this to Colón.

"You will never be a slave," said Colón. "Tell him that we are very pleased, and we thank him for his gift to us."

Chipa had expected him to ask for her. But she saw at once that his way was much better—if he assumed that the gift was already given, Guacanagarí could hardly take it back. So she turned to Guacanagarí and prostrated herself before him as she had done only yesterday, when she first met the cacique of the coastlands. "The great white cacique, Colón, is very pleased with me. He thanks you for giving him such a useful gift."

Guacanagarí showed nothing on his face, but she knew that he was furious. That was all right with her—she didn't like him.

"Tell him," said Colón behind her, "that I give him my own hat, which I would never give to any man but a great king."

She translated his words into Taino. Guacanagarí's eyes widened. He reached out a hand.

Colón took the hat from his head and, instead of putting it in the cacique's hand, placed it on Guacanagarí's head himself. Guacanagarí smiled. Chipa thought he looked even stupider than the white men did, wearing such a roof on his head. But she could see that the other Tainos around Guacanagarí were impressed. It was a good exchange. A powerfully talismanic hat for a troublesome disobedient mountain girl.

"Rise to your feet, girl," said Colón. He gave her his hand to help her up. His fingers were long and smooth. She had never touched such smooth skin, except on a baby. Did Colón never do any work? "What is your name?"

"Chipa," she said. "But Sees-in-the-Dark said you would give me a new name when I was baptized."

"A new name," said Colón. "And a new life." And then, quietly, so only she could hear: "This woman you call Sees-in-the-Dark—can you lead me to her?"

"Yes," said Chipa. Then she added something that perhaps Sees-in-the-Dark didn't mean for her to say. "She told me once that she gave up her family and the man she loved so that she could meet you."

"Many people have given up many things," said Colón. "But now would you be willing to interpret for us? I need to have Guacanagarí's help in building shelters for my men, now that our ships have been burnt. And I need him to send a messenger with a letter for the captain of my third ship, asking him to come here to find us and carry us home. Will you go back to Spain with us?"

Sees-in-the-Dark had said nothing about going to Spain. In fact, she had said that the white men would never leave Haiti. But she decided this was not a good time to mention this particular prophecy. "If you go there," she said, "I'll go with you."

Pedro de Salcedo was seventeen years old. He might be page to the Captain-General of the fleet, but this never made him feel superior to the common seamen or the ship's boys. No, what made him feel superior was the way that these men and boys lusted after these ugly Indian women. He could hear them talking sometimes—though they had learned not to try to engage him in these conversations. Apparently they couldn't get over the fact that the Indian women went about naked.

Not the new one, though. Chipa. *She* wore clothing, and spoke Spanish. Everyone else was amazed by this, but not Pedro de Salcedo. Clothing and Spanish were to be expected from civilized people. And she was certainly civilized, even if she wasn't yet a Christian.

Indeed, she wasn't a Christian at all, as far as Pedro could tell.

He had heard all her words to the Captain-General, of course, but when he was assigned to provide her with safe quarters, he took the opportunity to converse with her. He quickly found that she hadn't the faintest idea who Christ was, and her idea of Christian doctrine was pathetic at best. But then, she did say that this mystical Sees-in-the-Dark had promised that Colón would teach her about Christ.

Sees-in-the-Dark. What kind of name was that? And how did it happen that an Indian woman had received a prophecy telling of Colón and Christ? Such a vision must have come from God—but to a woman? And not a Christian woman, either.

Though, come to think of it, God spoke to Moses, too, and he was a Jew. That was back when Jews were still the chosen people instead of being the filthy vile thieving Christ-killing scum of the earth, but still, it made you think.

Pedro was thinking about a lot of things. Anything to keep him from thinking about Chipa. Because *those* thoughts were the ones that disturbed him. Sometimes he wondered if he wasn't just as low and vulgar as the seamen and the ship's boys, so hungry for venery that even these Indian women could become attractive to him. But it wasn't that, not really. He didn't particularly lust after Chipa. He could still see that she was ugly, and for heaven's sake, she didn't even have a woman's shape, she was a *child*, what kind of pervert would he have to be to lust after her? Yet he also saw something in her voice, her face, that made her beautiful to him.

What was it? Her shyness? The obvious pride she felt when she said difficult sentences in Spanish? Her eager questions about his clothing, his weapons, the other members of the expedition? Those sweet little gestures she made when she was embarrassed at making a mistake? The sheer translucence of her face, as if a light shone through from beneath the skin? No, that was impossible, she didn't really glow. It was an illusion. I've been lonely too long.

Yet he found that the only part of his duties that he looked forward to these days was tending to Chipa, watching over her, conversing with her. He lingered with her as long as possible, and sometimes neglected his other tasks. Not that he meant to; he simply forgot anything but her when he was with her. And it was useful for him to spend time with her, wasn't it? She was teaching him the Taino language, too. If he learned it well, then there would be two interpreters, not just one. That would be good, wouldn't it?

He was also teaching her the alphabet. She seemed to like that most of all, and she was very clever about it. Pedro couldn't think of why she wanted it so much, since there was nothing in a woman's life that made reading necessary. But if it amused her and helped her understand Spanish better, why not?

So Pedro was making letters in the dirt, and Chipa was naming them, when Diego Bermúdez came looking for him. "The boss wants you," he said. At twelve, the boy had no sense of propriety. "And the girl. He's going on an expedition."

"Where?" asked Pedro.

"To the moon," said Diego. "We've *been* everywhere else."

"He's going to the mountain," said Chipa. "To meet Sees-in-the-Dark."

Pedro looked at her in consternation. "How would you know that?"

"Because Sees-in-the-Dark said he would come to her."

More of that mystical claptrap. What was Sees-in-the-Dark, anyway, a witch? Pedro could hardly wait to meet her. But he'd have his rosary triple-wrapped around his wrist and hold the cross in his hand the whole time. No sense taking chances.

Chipa must have done well, Diko decided, for runners had been coming up the mountain all morning, telling of the coming of the white men. The most annoying messages were from Guacanagarí, full of half-veiled threats about any attempt by an obscure mountain village like Ankuash daring to interfere with the great cacique's plans. Poor Guacanagarí—in the prior version of history, he had also had the illusion that he was in control of relations with the Spanish. The result was that he ended up being a quisling, betraying other Indie leaders until he, too, was destroyed. Not that he was any stupider than others who have fooled themselves into thinking that they've got the tiger under control just because they're holding on to its tail.

It was midafternoon when Cristoforo himself came into the

clearing. But Diko was not outside to meet him. She listened to the noise from inside her house, waiting.

Nugkui made a great show of greeting the great white cacique, and Cristoforo for his part was gracious. Diko listened with pleasure at the confidence in Chipa's voice. She had taken to her role and did it well. Diko had clear memories of Chipa's death in the other history. By then she was in her twenties, and her children were murdered in front of her before she was raped to death. She would never know that horror now. It gave Diko confidence, as she waited in her house.

The preliminaries ended, Cristoforo was now asking for Sees-in-the-Dark. Nugkui of course warned him that it was a waste of time talking to the black giant, but this only intrigued Cristoforo all the more, as Diko had expected. Soon he was in front of her door, and Chipa ducked inside. "Can he come in?" she asked in Taino.

"You're doing well, my niece," said Diko. She and Chipa had spoken only in Spanish for so long that it felt odd to Diko to revert to the local language with her. But it was necessary, for the moment, at least, if Cristoforo was not to understand what they said to each other.

Chipa smiled at that, and ducked her head. "He brought his page with him. He's very tall and fine and he likes me."

"He'd better not like you too well," said Diko. "You're not a woman yet."

"But he's a man," said Chipa, with a laugh. "Should I let them in?"

"Who is with Cristoforo?"

"All the big-house people," said Chipa. "Segovia, Arana, Gutiérrez, Escobedo. Even Torres." She giggled again. "Did you know that they brought him along to be an interpreter? He doesn't speak a *word* of Taino."

He didn't speak Mandarin either, or Japanese or Cantonese or Hindi or Malay or any of the other languages he would have needed if Cristoforo had actually reached the Far East as he intended. The poor myopic Europeans had sent Torres because he could read Hebrew and Aramaic, which they considered to be the matrices of all language.

"Let the Captain-General come in," said Diko. "And you can bring in your page, too. Pedro de Salcedo?"

Chipa did not seem surprised that Diko knew the name of her page. "Thank you," she said, and then stepped outside to bring in the guests.

Diko could not help feeling nervous—no, why quibble? She was terrified. To finally meet him, the man who had consumed her life. And the scene they would play would be one that had never existed before in any history. She was so used to knowing what he would say before he said it. What would it be like, now that he had the capacity to surprise her?

No matter. *She* had a far greater ability to surprise *him,* and she used it immediately, speaking to him first in Genovese. "I've waited a long time to meet you, Cristoforo."

Even in the darkness inside her house, Diko could see how his face flushed at her lack of respect. Yet he had the good grace not to insist that she call him by his titles. Instead, he concentrated on the real question. "How is it that you speak the language of my family?"

She answered in Portuguese. "Would this be the language of your family? This is how your wife spoke, before she died, and your older son still thinks in Portuguese. Did you know that? Or have you spoken to him often enough to know what he thinks about anything?"

Cristoforo was angry and frightened. Just what she was hoping for. "You know things that no one knows." He was not speaking of family details, of course.

"Kingdoms will fall at your feet," she said, imitating as much as possible even the intonation of the voice in Cristoforo's vision from the interveners. "And millions whose lives are saved will call you blessed."

"We don't need an interpreter, do we," said Cristoforo.

"Shall we let the children go?" said Diko.

Cristoforo murmured to Chipa and Pedro. Pedro got up at once and went to the door, but Chipa didn't move.

"Chipa is not your servant," Diko pointed out. "But I will ask her to leave." In Taino she said, "I want the Captain-General to speak about things that he won't want anyone else to hear. Would you go outside?''

Chipa got up at once and headed for the door. Diko noticed with pleasure that Pedro held the flap open for her. The boy was already thinking of her, not just as a human, but as a lady. It was a breakthrough, even if no one was aware of it yet.

They were alone.

"How do you come to know these things?" asked Cristoforo at once. "These promises—that kingdoms would fall at my feet, that—"

"I know them," said Diko, "because I came here by the same power that first gave those words to you." Let him interpret that how he would—later, when he understood more, she would remind him that she hadn't lied to him.

She pulled a small solar-powered lantern from one of her bags and set it between them. When she switched it on, he shielded his eyes. His fingers also formed a cross. "It isn't witchcraft," she said. "It's a tool made by my people, of another place, where you could never voyage in all your traveling. But like any tool, it will someday wear out, and I won't know how to make another."

He was listening, but as his eyes adjusted, he was also looking at her. "You're as dark as a Moor."

"I *am* an African," she said. "Not a Moor, but from farther south."

"How did you come here, then?"

"Do you think you're the only voyager? Do you think you're the only one who can be sent to faraway lands to save the souls of the heathen?"

He rose to his feet. "I can see that after all my struggles, I have only now begun to face opposition. Did God send me to the Indies only to show me a Negress with a magic lamp?"

"This is not India," said Diko. "Or Cathay, or Cipangu. Those lie far, far to the west. This is another land entirely."

"You quote the words spoken to me by God himself, and then you tell me that God was wrong?"

"If you think back carefully, you will remember that he never said Cathay or Cipangu or India or any other such name," said Diko.

"How do you know this?"

"I saw you kneeling on the beach, and heard you take your oath in the name of the Father, the Son, and the Holy Ghost."

"Then why didn't I see you? If I could see the Holy Trinity, why were *you* invisible?"

"You dream of a great victory for Christianity," said Diko, ignoring his question because she couldn't think of an answer that would be comprehensible to him. "The liberation of Constantinople."

"Only as a step along the way to freeing Jerusalem," said Cristoforo.

"But I tell you that here, in this place, there are millions of souls who would accept Christianity if only you offer it to them peacefully, lovingly."

"How else would I offer it?"

"How else? Already you have written in your logbooks about how these people could be made to work. Already you talk about enslaving them."

He looked at her piercingly. "Who showed you my log?"

"You are not yet fit to teach these people Christianity, Cristoforo, because you are not yet a Christian."

He reached back his hand to strike at her. It surprised her, because he was not a violent man.

"Oh, will hitting me prove how Christian you are? Yes, I remember all the stories about how Jesus whipped Mary Magdelene. And the beatings he gave to Mary and Martha."

"I didn't hit you," he said.

"But it was your first desire, wasn't it?" she said. "Why? You are the most patient of men. You let those priests badger you and torment you for years, and you never lost your temper with them. Yet with me, you felt free to lash out. Why is that, Cristoforo?"

He looked at her, not answering.

"I'll tell you why. Because to you I'm not a human being, I'm a dog, less than a dog, because you would not beat a dog, would you? Just like the Portuguese, when you see a black woman you see a slave. And these brown people—you can teach them the gospel of Christ and baptize them, but that doesn't stop you from wanting to make slaves of them and steal their gold from them."

"You can teach a dog to walk on its hind legs, but that doesn't make it a man."

"Oh, that's a clever bit of wisdom. That's just the kind of argument that rich men make about men like your father. Oh, he can dress in fine clothing, but he's still a country bumpkin, not worth treating with respect."

Cristoforo cried out in rage. "How dare you speak of my father that way!"

"I tell you that as long as you treat these people even worse than the rich men of Genova treated your father, you will never be pleasing to God."

The flap of the door opened wide, and Pedro and Escobedo stuck their heads into the house. "You cried out, my lord!" said Escobedo.

"I'm leaving," said Cristoforo.

He ducked and walked through the door. She turned off her lamp and followed him out into the afternoon light. All of Ankuash was gathered around, and the Spaniards all had their hands on their sword hilts. When they saw her—so tall, so black—they gasped, and some of the swords began to rise out of their sheaths. But Cristoforo waved the weapons back into place. "We're going," he announced. "There's nothing for us here."

"I know where the gold is!" cried Diko in Spanish. As she expected, it brought her the complete attention of all the white men. "It doesn't come from this island. It comes from farther west. I know where it is. I can take you there. I can show you so much gold that stories of it will be told forever."

It wasn't Cristoforo, but Segovia, the Royal Inspector, who answered her. "Then show us, woman. Take us there."

"Take you there? Using what boat?"

The Spaniards remained silent.

"Even when Pinzón returns, he won't be able to take you back to Spain," she said.

They looked at each other in consternation. How did this woman know so much?

"Colón," she said. "Do you know when I will show you that gold?"

He was with the other white men now, as he turned to face her. "When is that?"

"When you love Christ more than gold," Diko answered.

"I already do," said Cristoforo.

"I will know when you love Christ more than gold," said Diko. She pointed to the villagers. "It will be when you look at *these* and see, not slaves, not servants, not strangers, not enemies, but brothers and sisters, your equals in the eyes of God. But until you learn that humility, Cristóbal Colón, you will find nothing but one calamity after another."

"Devil," said Segovia. Most of the Spaniards crossed themselves.

"I do not curse you," she said. "I bless you. Whatever evil comes upon you comes as a punishment from God, because you looked at his children and saw only slaves. Jesus warned you: Whoever harms one of these little ones, it would be better for him to tie a millstone around his neck and throw himself into the sea."

"Even the devil can quote scripture," said Segovia. But his voice didn't sound very confident.

"Remember this, Cristoforo," Diko said. "When all is lost, when your enemies have brought you down to the depths of despair, come to me in humility and I will help you do the work of God in this place."

"*God* will help me do the work of God," said Cristoforo. "I need no heathen witch when I have him on my side."

"He will not be on your side until you have asked these people to forgive you for thinking that *they* were savages." She turned her back on him and went back into her house.

Outside, she could hear the Spaniards shouting at each other for a few moments. Some of them wanted to seize her and put her to death on the spot. But Cristoforo knew better. Angry as he was, he knew that she had seen things that only God and he had known.

Besides, the Spanish were outnumbered. Cristoforo was nothing if not prudent. You don't commit to battle until you know that you'll win—that was his philosophy.

When they were gone, Diko emerged again from her house. Nugkui was livid. "How dare you make these white men so angry?

Now they'll be friends with Guacanagarí and never visit us again!''

"You don't want them as friends until they learn how to be human," said Diko. "Guacanagarí will beg for them to be friends with someone else before this story is played out. But I tell you this. No matter what happens, let it be known that no harm is to come to the one they call Colón, the white-haired one, the cacique. Tell it to every village and clan: If you harm Colón, the curse of Sees-in-the-Dark will come upon you."

Nugkui glowered.

"Don't worry, Nugkui," she said. "I think Colón will be back."

"Maybe I don't want him back," Nugkui retorted. "Maybe I just wish you and he *both* would go away!" But he knew the rest of the village wouldn't stand for it if she left. So she said nothing, until he turned and walked out into the forest. Only then did she return to her house, where she sat on her sleeping mat and trembled. Wasn't this exactly what she had planned? To make Cristoforo angry but plant the seeds of transformation in his mind? Yet in all her imagining of this encounter, she had never counted on how powerful Cristoforo was in person. She had watched him, had seen the power he had over people, but he had never looked her in the eye until this day. And it left her as disturbed as any of the Europeans who had confronted him. It gave her new respect for those who resisted him, and new understanding of those who bent completely to his will. Not even Tagiri had so much fire burning behind her eyes as this man had. No wonder the Interveners chose him as their tool. Come what may, Cristoforo would prevail, given time enough.

How had she ever imagined that she could tame this man and bend him to her own plan?

No, she said silently, no, I'm not trying to tame him. I'm only trying to show him a better, truer way to fulfill his own dream. When he understands that, those eyes will look at me with kindness, not with fury.

It was a long trip down the mountain, not least because some of the men seem disposed to take out their anger on the girl, Chipa. Cristoforo was caught up in his own thoughts when he became aware that Pedro was doing his best to shield the girl from the shoving and curses of Arana and Gutiérrez. "Leave her alone," Cristoforo said.

Pedro looked at him with gratitude, and the girl, too.

"She's not a slave," said Cristoforo. "Nor is she a soldier. She helps us of her own free will, so that we'll teach her about Christ."

"She's a heathen witch, just like that other one!" retorted Arana.

"You forget yourself," said Cristoforo.

Sullenly Arana bowed his head in acknowledgment of Cristoforo's superior rank.

"If Pinzón doesn't return, we'll need the help of the natives to build another ship. Without this girl, we'd be back to trying to talk to them with signs and grunts and gestures."

"Your page is learning their babble," said Arana.

"My page has learned a few dozen words," said Cristoforo.

"If anything happened to the girl," said Arana, "we could always come back up here and take that black whore and make *her* interpret for us."

Chipa spoke up in fury. "She would *never* obey you."

Arana laughed. "Oh, by the time we were through with her, she'd obey, all right!" His laugh got darker, uglier. "And it'd be good for her, too, to learn her place in the world."

Cristoforo heard Arana's words and they made him uncomfortable. A part of him agreed completely with Arana's sentiments. But another part of him couldn't help but remember what Sees-in-the-Dark had said. Until he saw the natives as equals . . .

The thought made him shudder. These savages, his equals? If God meant them to be his equals, he would have let them be born as Christians. Yet there was no denying that Chipa was as smart and good-hearted as any Christian girl. She wanted to be taught the word of Christ, and to be baptized.

Teach her, baptize her, put her in a fine gown, and she would still be brown-skinned and ugly. Might as well put a monkey in a dress. Sees-in-the-Dark was denying nature, to think it could be otherwise. Obviously she was the devil's last-ditch effort to stop him, to distract him from his mission. Just as the devil had led Pinzón to sail the *Pinta* away.

It was near dark when he returned to the half-completed stockade where the Spanish were encamped. He could hear the sound
of laughter and revelry in the camp, and was prepared to be angry
about the lack of discipline, until he realized why. There, standing
beside a large fire, regaling the gathered seamen with some tale or
other, was Martín Alonzo Pinzón. He had come back.

As Cristoforo strode across the open area between the gate of
the stockade and the fire, the men around Pinzón became aware of
him, and fell silent, watching. Pinzón, too, watched Cristoforo's
approach. When he was near enough for them to speak without
shouting, Pinzón began his excuses.

"Captain-General, you can't imagine my dismay when I lost
you in the fog coming away from Colba."

Such a lie, thought Cristoforo. The *Pinta* still was clearly visible
after the coastal fog dissipated.

"But I thought, why not explore while we're separated? We
stopped at the island of Babeque, where the Colbanos said we'd
find gold, but there wasn't a bit of it there. But east of here, along
the coast of this island, there were vast quantities of it. For a little
strip of ribbon they gave me gold pieces the size of two fingers, and
sometimes as large as my hand!"

He held up his large, strong, callused hand.

Cristoforo still did not answer, though now he stood not five
feet from the captain of the *Pinta*. It was Segovia who said, "Of
course you will give a full accounting of all this gold and add it to
the common treasury."

Pinzón turned red. "What do you accuse me of, Segovia?" he
demanded.

He might accuse you of treason, thought Cristoforo. Certainly
of mutiny. Why did you turn back? Because you couldn't make
any better headway against the east wind than I did? Or because
you realized that when you returned to Spain without me, there
would be questions that you couldn't answer? So not only are you
disloyal and untrustworthy, but you are also too cowardly even to
complete your betrayal.

All of this remained unsaid, however. Cristoforo's rage
against Pinzón, though it was every bit as justified as his anger
toward Sees-in-the-Dark, had nothing to do with the reason God

had sent him here. The royal officials might share Cristoforo's contempt for Pinzón, but the seamen all looked at him as if he were Charlemagne or El Cid. If Cristoforo made an enemy of him, he would lose his control over the crew. Segovia and Arana and Gutiérrez didn't understand this. They believed that authority came from the King. But Cristoforo knew that authority came from obedience. In this place, among these men, Pinzón commanded much more obedience than the King. So Cristoforo would swallow his anger so that he could make use of Pinzón in accomplishing God's work.

"He accuses you of nothing," said Cristoforo. "How can anyone think of accusing you? The one who was lost is now found. If we had a fatted calf, I'd have it slaughtered now in your honor. In the name of Their Majesties, I welcome you back, Captain Pinzón."

Pinzón was obviously relieved, but he also got a sly look in his eyes. He thinks he has the upper hand, thought Cristoforo. He thinks he can get away with anything. But once we're back in Spain, Segovia will support my view of events. We'll see who has the upper hand then.

Cristoforo smiled, held out his arms, and embraced the lying bastard.

Hunahpu watched as the three Tarascan metalsmiths handled the iron bar he had taught them how to smelt, using the charcoal he had taught them how to make. He watched them test it against bronze blades and arrowheads. He watched them test it against stone. And when they were done, the three of them prostrated themselves on the ground before him.

Hunahpu waited patiently until their obeisance was done—it was the respect due to a hero from Xibalba, whether they were impressed by iron or not. Then he told them to rise from the ground and stand like men.

"The lords of Xibalba have watched you for years. They saw how you worked with bronze. They saw the three of you working with iron. And they argued among themselves. Some of them wanted to destroy you. But some of them said, No, the Tarascans are not bloodthirsty like the Mexica or the Tlaxcalans. They will not use this black metal to slaughter thousands of men so that barren fields burn under the sun, without anyone to plant maize.''

No, no, agreed the Tarascans.

"So now I offer you the same covenant I offered to the Zapotecs. You've heard the story a dozen times by now.''

Yes, they had.

"If you vow that you will never again take a human life as sacrifice to any god, and that you will only go to war to defend yourselves or to protect other peaceloving people, then I will teach you even more secrets. I'll teach you how to make this black metal even harder, until it shines like silver.''

We would do anything to know these secrets. Yes, we take this vow. We will obey the great One-Hunahpu in all things.

"I'm not here to be your king. You have your own king. I ask only that you keep this covenant. And then let your own king be as a brother to Na-Yaxhal, the king of the Zapotecs, and let the Tarascans be brothers and sisters to the Zapotecs. They are masters of the great canoes that sail the open sea, and you are masters of the fire that turns stone into metal. You will teach them all your secrets of metalwork, and they will teach you all their secrets of shipbuilding and navigation. Or I will return to Xibalba and tell the lords that you are ungrateful for the gift of knowledge!''

They listened wide-eyed, promising everything. His words would be relayed to the king soon enough, but when they showed him what iron could do, and warned him that One-Hunahpu knew how to make an even harder metal, he would agree to the alliance. Hunahpu's plotting would be complete, then. The Mexica *and* the Tlaxcalans would be surrounded by an enemy with iron weapons and large fast ships. Huitzilopochtli, you old faker, your days of drinking human blood are numbered.

I've done it, thought Hunahpu, and ahead of schedule. Even if Kemal and Diko failed, I will have suppressed the practice of human sacrifice, unified the people of Mesoamerica, and given them a high enough technology to be able to resist the Europeans whenever they come.

Yet even as he congratulated himself, Hunahpu felt a wave of homesickness sweep over him. Let Diko be alive, he prayed silently. Let her do her work with Columbus and make of him a bridge between Europe and America, so that it never comes to bloody war.

It was suppertime in the Spanish camp. All the officers and men were gathered for the meal, except for the four men on watch around the stockade and the two men who watched the ship. Cristoforo and the other officers ate apart from the others, but all ate the same food—most of which was provided by the Indians.

It was not served by Indians, however. The men served themselves, and the ship's boys served the officers. There had been serious difficulties over that, beginning when Chipa refused to translate Pinzón's orders to the Indians. "They're not servants," said Chipa. "They're friends."

In reply, Pinzón had started beating the girl, and when Pedro tried to intervene, Pinzón knocked him down and gave him a solid beating, too. When the Captain-General demanded that he apologize, Pinzón gladly agreed to apologize to Pedro. "He shouldn't have tried to stop me, but he *is* your page and I apologize for punishing him when that should be left to you."

"The girl, too," Colón had said.

To which Pinzón had replied by spitting and saying, "The little whore refused to do what she was told. She was insolent. Servants have no business talking to gentlemen that way."

When did Pinzón become a gentleman? thought Pedro. But he held his tongue. This was a matter for the Captain-General, not for a page.

"She is not your servant," Colón said.

Pinzón laughed insolently. "All brown people are servants by nature," he said.

"If they were servants by nature," said Colón, "you wouldn't have to beat them to get them to obey. It's a brave man who beats a little child. They'll no doubt write songs about your courage."

That had been enough to silence Pinzón—at least in public. Ever since then, there had been no attempt to get the Indians to give personal service. But Pedro knew that Pinzón had not forgiven or forgotten the scorn in the Captain-General's voice, or the humiliation of having been forced to back down. Pedro had even urged Chipa to leave.

"Leave?" she had said. "You don't speak Taino well enough yet for me to leave."

"If something goes wrong," Pedro had told her, "Pinzón will kill you. I know he will."

"Sees-in-the-Dark will protect me," she said.

"Sees-in-the-Dark isn't *here*," said Pedro.

"Then *you'll* protect me."

"Oh, yes, that worked so well *this* time." Pedro couldn't protect her and she wouldn't leave. It meant that he lived with constant anxiety, watching how the men watched Chipa, how they whispered behind the Captain-General's back, how they gave many signs of their solidarity with Pinzón. There was a bloody mutiny coming, Pedro could see it. It awaited only an occasion. When Pedro tried to talk to the Captain-General about it, he refused to listen, saying only that he knew the men favored Pinzón, but they would not rebel against the authority of the crown. If Pedro could only believe that.

So this evening Pedro directed the ship's boys in serving the officers. The unfamiliar fruits had grown familiar, and every meal was a feast. All the men were healthier now than at any time before in the voyage. From outward appearances everything was perfectly pleasant between the Captain-General and Pinzón. But by Pedro's count, the only men that Colón could count on his side in a crisis were himself, Segovia, Arana, Gutiérrez, Escobedo, and Torres. In other words, the royal officers and the Captain-General's own page. The ship's boys and some of the craftsmen would be on Colón's side in their hearts, but they wouldn't dare to stand against the men. For that matter, the royal officers had no personal loyalty to Colón himself. Their loyalty was simply to the idea of proper order and authority. No, when the trouble came, Colón would find himself almost friendless.

As for Chipa, she would be destroyed. I will kill her myself, thought Pedro, before I let Pinzón get his hands on her. I will kill her, and then I will kill myself. Better still, why not kill Pinzón? As long as I'm thinking of murder, why not strike at the one I hate instead of the ones I love?

These were Pedro's dark thoughts as he handed another bowl of melon slices to Martín Pinzón. Pinzón winked at him and smiled. He knows what I'm thinking, and he laughs at me, thought Pedro. He knows that I know what he's planning. He also knows that I'm powerless.

Suddenly a terrible blast shattered the quiet evening. Almost at once the earth shook under him and a shock of wind from seaward knocked Pedro down. He fell right across Pinzón, and almost at once the man was hitting and cursing him. Pedro got off him as quickly as possible, and it soon became clear even to Pinzón that it wasn't Pedro's clumsiness that had caused their collision. Most of the men had been bowled over by the blast, and now smoke and ash filled the air. It was thickest toward the water.

"The *Pinta!*" cried Pinzón. At once everyone else took up the cry, and ran through the thickening smoke toward the shore.

The *Pinta* wasn't on fire. It simply wasn't there at all.

The evening breeze was gradually clearing the smoke when they finally found the two men who were supposed to be on watch. Pinzón was already laying on them with the flat of his sword before Colón could get a couple of men to pull him off.

"My ship!" cried Pinzón. "What have you done to my ship?"

"If you stop beating them and shouting at them," said Colón, "perhaps we can learn from them what happened."

"My ship is gone and they were supposed to watch it!" cried Pinzón, struggling to get free of the men who restrained him.

"It was *my* ship, given me by the King and Queen," said Colón. "Will you stand alone like a gentleman, sir?"

Pinzón furiously nodded, and the men let go of him.

One of the men who had been on watch was Rascón, who was part owner of the *Pinta*. "Martín, I'm sorry, what could we do? He made us get into the launch and row for shore. And then he made us get behind that rock. And then the ship—blew up."

"He?" asked Colón, ignoring the fact that Rascón had reported to Pinzón instead of to the Captain-General.

"The man who did it."

"Where is he now?" asked Colón.

"He can't be far," said Rascón.

"He went off that way," said Gil Pérez, the other watchman.

"Señor Pinzón, would you kindly organize a search?"

His fury properly focused now, Pinzón immediately divided the men into search parties, not forgetting to leave a good contingent behind to guard the stockade against theft or sabotage. Pedro could not help but see that Pinzón was a good leader, quick of mind and able to make himself understood and obeyed at once. That only made him more dangerous, as far as Pedro was concerned.

When the men had dispersed, Colón stood on the shore, looking out over the many bits of wood that were bobbing on the waves. "Not even if all the gunpowder on the *Pinta* exploded all at once," said the Captain-General, "not even then could it destroy the ship so completely."

"What could have done it, then?" said Pedro.

"God could do it," said the Captain-General. "Or perhaps the devil. The Indians know nothing about gunpowder. If they find this man who supposedly did it, do you think he'll be a Moor?"

So the Captain-General was remembering the curse of the mountain witch. One calamity after another. What could be worse than this, to lose the last ship?

But when they found him, the man wasn't a Moor. Nor was he an Indian. He was white and bearded, a large man, a strong one. His clothing had obviously been bizarre even before the men tore much of it from him. They held him, a garrotte around his neck, forcing him to his knees in front of the Captain-General.

"It was all I could do to keep him alive long enough for you to speak to him, sir," said Pinzón.

"Why did you do this?" asked Colón.

The man answered in Spanish—thickly accented, but understandable. "When I first heard about your expedition I vowed that if you succeeded, you would never return to Spain."

"Why?" demanded the Captain-General.

"My name is Kemal," said the man. "I'm a Turk. There is no God but Allah, and Mohammad is his Prophet."

The men muttered in rage. Infidel. Heathen. Devil.

"I will still return to Spain," said Colón. "You haven't stopped me."

"Fool," said Kemal. "How will you return to Spain when you're surrounded by enemies?"

Pinzón immediately roared out, "*You're* the only enemy, infidel!"

"How do you think I got here, if I hadn't had the help of some of *these.*" With his head, he indicated the men around him. Then he looked Pinzón in the eye and winked.

"Liar!" cried Pinzón. "Kill him! Kill him!"

The men who held the Turk obeyed at once, even though Colón raised his voice and cried out for them to stop. It was possible that in the roar of fury they didn't hear him. And it didn't take long for the Turk to die. Instead of strangling him, they pulled the garrotte so tight and twisted it so hard that it broke his neck and with only a twitch or two he was gone.

At last the tumult ended. In the silence, the Captain-General spoke. "Fools. You killed him too quickly. He told us nothing."

"What could he have told us, except lies?" said Pinzón.

Colón took a long, measured look at him. "We'll never know, will we? As far as I can tell, the only people glad of that would be the ones he might have named as his conspirators."

"What are you accusing me of?" demanded Pinzón.

"I haven't accused you at all."

Only then did Pinzón seem to realize that his own actions had pointed the finger of suspicion at him. He began to nod, and then smiled. "I see, Captain-General. You finally found a way to discredit me, even if it took blowing up my caravel to do it."

"Watch what you say to the Captain-General." Segovia's voice whipped out across the crowd.

"Let him watch what he says to *me*. I didn't have to bring the *Pinta* back here. I've proved my loyalty. Every man here knows *me*. I'm not the foreigner. How do we know that this Colón is even a Christian, let alone a Genovese? After all, that black witch and the little whore interpreter both knew his native language, when not one honest Spaniard could understand it."

Pinzón hadn't been present on either occasion, Pedro noted. Obviously there had been a lot of talk about who spoke what language to whom.

Colón looked at him steadily. "There would have been no expedition if I had not spent half my life arguing for it. Would I destroy it now, when success was so close?"

"You would never have gotten us home anyway, you posturing fool!" cried Pinzón. "*That's* why I came back, because I saw how difficult it was to sail east against the wind. I knew you weren't sailor enough to bring my brother and my friends back home."

Colón allowed himself a hint of a smile. "If you were such a fine sailor, you'd know that to the north of us the prevailing wind blows from the west."

"And how would *you* know that?" The scorn in Pinzón's voice was outrageous.

"You're speaking to the commander of Their Majesties' fleet," said Segovia.

Pinzón fell silent for the moment; perhaps he had spoken more openly than he intended, for now at least.

"When you were a pirate," said Colón quietly, "I sailed the coast of Africa with the Portuguese."

From the growling of the men, Pedro knew that the Captain-General had just committed a serious mistake. The rivalry between the men of Palos and the sailors of the Portuguese coast was intensely felt, all the more so because the Portuguese were so clearly the better, farther-reaching sailors. And to throw in Pinzón's face his days of piracy—well, that was a crime that all of Palos was guilty of, during the hardest days of the war against the Moors, when normal trade was impossible. Colón might have buttressed his credentials as a sailor, but he did it at the immediate cost of losing what vestiges of loyalty he might have commanded among the men.

"Dispose of the body," said the Captain-General. Then he turned his back on them and returned to the camp.

The runner from Guacanagarí couldn't stop laughing as he told the story of the death of the Silent Man. "The white men are so stupid that they killed him first and tortured him afterward!"

Diko heard this with relief. Kemal had died quickly. And the *Pinta* had been destroyed.

"We must watch the white men's village," said Diko. "The white men will turn against their cacique soon, and we must make sure he comes to Ankuash, and not to any other village."

12

Refuge

 The woman up in the mountain *had* cursed him, but Cristoforo knew that it was not by any sort of witchery. The curse was that he couldn't think of anything but her, anything but what she had said. Every subject kept leading back to the challenges she had issued.

Could God have possibly sent her? Was she, at last, the first reaffirmation he had received since that vision on the beach? She knew so much: The words that the Savior had spoken to him. The language of his youth in Genova. His sense of guilt about his son, left to be raised by the monks of La Rábida.

Yet she was nothing like what he looked for. Angels were dazzling white, weren't they? That's how all the artists showed them. So perhaps she wasn't an angel. But why would God send her a woman—an African woman? Weren't black people devils? Everyone said so, and in Spain it was well known that black Moors fought like demons. And among the Portuguese it was well known that the black savages of the Guinea coast engaged in devil worship and magic, and cursed with diseases that quickly killed any white man who dared set foot on African shores.

On the other hand, his purpose was to baptize the people he

found at the end of his voyage, wasn't it? If they could be baptized, it meant they could be saved. If they could be saved, then perhaps she was right, and once they were converted these people would be Christian and have the same rights as any European.

But they were *savages.* They went about naked. They couldn't read or write.

They could learn.

If only he could see the world through his page's eyes. Young Pedro was obviously smitten with Chipa. Dark as she was, squat and ugly, she did have a good smile, and no one could deny that she was as smart as any Spanish girl. She was learning about Christ. She insisted on being baptized at once. When that happened, shouldn't she have the same protection as any other Christian?

"Captain-General," said Segovia, "you must pay attention. Things are getting out of hand with the men. Pinzón is impossible—he obeys only those orders he happens to agree with, and the men obey only those orders that he consents to."

"And what would you have me do?" asked Cristoforo. "Clap him in irons?"

"That's what the King would have done."

"The King *had* irons. Ours are at the bottom of the sea. And the King also had thousands of soldiers to see to it his words were obeyed. Where are my soldiers, Segovia?"

"You have not acted with sufficient authority."

"I'm sure you would have done better in my place."

"That is not impossible, Captain-General."

"I see that the spirit of insubordination is contagious," said Cristoforo. "But rest easy. As the black woman in the mountain said, it will be one calamity after another. Perhaps after the next calamity, you'll find yourself in command of this expedition as the King's inspector."

"I could not do a worse job of it than you."

"Yes, I'm sure that's right," said Cristoforo. "That Turk would not have blown up the *Pinta*, and you would have peed on the *Niña* and put the fire out."

"I see that you forget in whose name I speak."

"Only because you have forgotten whose charter I bear. If you have authority from the King, kindly remember that I have a greater authority from the same source. If Pinzón chooses to blow over the last remnants of that authority, I am not the only one who will fall in that wind.''

Yet no sooner was Segovia gone than Cristoforo was once again trying to puzzle out what God expected of him. Was there anything he could do now to bring the men back under his command? Pinzón had them building a ship, but these weren't the shipbuilders of Palos here, these were common sailors. Domingo was a good cooper, but making a barrel wasn't the same as laying a keel. López was a caulker, not a carpenter. And most of the other men were clever enough with their hands, but what none of them had in his head was the knowledge, the *practice* of building a ship.

They had to try, though. Had to try, and if they failed the first time, try again. So there was no quarrel between Cristoforo and Pinzón over the effort to build a ship. The quarrel came over the way the men were treating the Indians that they needed to help them. The generous spirit of cooperation that Guacanagarí's people had shown in helping unload the *Santa Maria* had long since faded. The more the Spaniards ordered them around, the less the Indians did. Fewer and fewer of them showed up each day, which meant that those who did got treated even worse. They seemed to think that every Spaniard, no matter how low in rank or station, was entitled to give commands—and punishments—to any Indian, no matter how young or old, no matter . . .

These thoughts come from her, Cristoforo realized again. Until I spoke with *her*, I didn't question the right of white men to give commands to brown ones. Only since she poisoned my mind with her strange interpretation of Christianity did I start seeing the way the Indians quietly resist being treated like slaves. I would have thought of them the way Pinzón does, as worthless, lazy savages. But now I see that they are quiet, gentle, unwilling to provoke a quarrel. They endure a beating quietly—but then don't return to be beaten again. Except that even some who *have* been beaten still return to help, of their own free will, avoiding the cruelest of the Spaniards but still helping the others as much as they can. Isn't this what Christ meant when he said to turn the other cheek? If a man compels you to walk a mile with him, then walk the second mile by your own choice—wasn't that Christianity? So who were the Christians? The baptized Spaniards, or the unbaptized Indians?

She has turned the world upside down. These Indians know nothing of Jesus, and yet they live by the Savior's word, while the Spanish, who have fought for centuries in the name of Christ, have become a bloodthirsty, brutal people. And yet no worse than any other people in Europe. No worse than the bloody-handed Genovese, with their feuds and murders. Was it possible that God had brought him here, not to bring enlightenment to the heathen, but to learn it from them?

"The Taino way is not always better," said Chipa.

"We have better tools," said Cristoforo. "And better weapons."

"I meant, how do you say? The Taino kill people for the gods. Sees-in-the-Dark said that when you taught us about Christ, we would understand that one man already died as the only sacrifice ever needed. Then the Taino would stop killing people. And the Caribs would stop eating them."

"Holy Mother," said Pedro. "They do that?"

"The people from the lowlands say so. The Caribs are terrible monster people. The Taino are better than they are. And we of Ankuash are better than the Taino. But Sees-in-the-Dark says that when you are ready to teach us, we will see that you are the best of all."

"We Spanish?" asked Pedro.

"No, him. You, Colón."

It's nothing but flattery, Cristoforo told himself. That's why Sees-in-the-Dark has been teaching Chipa and the other people of Ankuash to say things like that. The only reason I'm so happy when I hear such things is because it makes such a contrast to the malicious rumors being spread among my own crew. Sees-in-the-Dark wants me to think of the people of Ankuash as if they were my true people, instead of the Spanish crew.

What if it was true? What if the whole purpose of this voyage was to bring him here, where he could meet the people God had prepared to receive the word of Christ?

No, it couldn't be that. The Lord spoke of gold, of great nations, of crusades. Not an obscure mountain village.

She said that when I was ready, she'd show me the gold.

We have to build a ship. I have to hold the men together long enough to build a ship, return to Spain, and come back with a larger force. One with more discipline. One without Martín Pinzón. But I'll also bring priests, many of them, to teach the Indians. That will satisfy Sees-in-the-Dark. I can still do all of it, if I can just hold things together here long enough to get the ship built.

Putukam clucked her tongue. "Things are very bad, Chipa says."

"How bad?" asked Diko.

"Chipa says that her young man, Pedro, is always begging Colón to leave. She says that some of the boys have tried to warn Pedro, so he can warn the cacique. They plan to kill him."

"Who?"

"I can't remember the names now, Sees-in-the-Dark," said Putukam, laughing. "Do you think I'm as smart as you?"

Diko sighed. "Why can't he see that he has to leave, he has to come here?"

"He may be white, but he's still a man," said Putukam. "Men always think they know the right thing, and so they don't listen."

"If I leave the village to go down the mountain and watch over Colón, who will carry the water here?" asked Diko.

"We carried water before you came," said Putukam. "The girls are all getting fat and lazy now."

"If I leave the village to watch over Colón and bring him safely here, who will watch over my house so Nugkui doesn't move someone else in here, and give away all my tools?"

"Baiku and I will take turns watching," said Putukam.

"Then I'll go," said Diko. "But I won't make him come. He has to come here under his own power, of his own free will."

Putukam looked at her, impassively.

"I don't make people do things against their will," said Diko.

Putukam smiled. "No, Sees-in-the-Dark. You just refuse to leave them alone until they change their minds. Of their own free will."

* * *

The mutiny finally came out in the open because of Rodrigo de Triana, perhaps because he had more reason to hate Colón than any other, having been cheated out of his prize for being first to see land. Yet it didn't happen according to anyone's plan, as far as Pedro could see. The first he knew about it was when the Taino named Dead Fish came running. He spoke so rapidly that Pedro couldn't understand him, even though he had been making progress with the language. Chipa understood, though, and she looked angry. "They're raping Parrot Feather," she said. "She's not even a woman. She's younger than me."

At once Pedro called out to Caro, the silversmith, to go fetch the officers. Then he ran with Chipa, following Dead Fish outside the stockade.

Parrot Feather looked like she was dead. Limp as a rag. It was Moger and Clavijo, two of the criminals who had signed on in order to get a pardon. They were the ones who had obviously been doing the rape—but Rodrigo de Triana and a couple of other sailors from the Pinta were looking on, laughing.

"Stop it!" Pedro screamed.

The men looked at him like a bug on their bed, to be flicked away.

"She's a child!" he shouted at them.

"She's a woman now," said Moger. Then he and the others burst out laughing again.

Chipa was already heading for the girl. Pedro tried to stop her. "No, Chipa."

But Chipa seemed oblivious to her own danger. She tried to get around one of the men to see to Parrot Feather. He shoved her out of the way—and into the hands of Rodrigo de Triana. "Let me see if she's alive," Chipa insisted.

"Leave her alone," said Pedro. But now he wasn't shouting.

"Looks like this one's a volunteer," said Clavijo, running his fingers along Chipa's cheek.

Pedro reached for his sword, knowing that there was no hope of him prevailing against any of these men, but knowing also that he had to try.

"Put the sword away," said Pinzón, behind him.

Pedro turned. Pinzón was at the head of a group of officers. The Captain-General was not far behind.

"Let go of the girl, Rodrigo," said Pinzón.

He complied. But instead of heading back toward safety, Chipa made for the girl, still lying motionless on the ground, putting her head to the girl's chest to listen for a heartbeat.

"Now let's get back to the stockade and get to work," said Pinzón.

"Who is responsible for this?" demanded Colón.

"I've taken care of it," said Pinzón.

"Have you?" asked Colón. "The girl is obviously just a child. This was a monstrous crime. And it was stupid, too. How much help do you think we'll get from the Indians now?"

"If they don't help us willingly," said Rodrigo de Triana, "then we'll go get them and *make* them help."

"And while you're at it, you'll take their women and rape them all, is that the plan, Rodrigo? Is that what you think it means to be a Christian?" asked Colón.

"Are you a Captain-General, or a bishop?" asked Rodrigo. The other men laughed.

"I said I've taken care of it, Captain-General," said Pinzón.

"By telling them to get back to work? What kind of work will we get done if we have to defend ourselves against the Taino?"

"These Indians aren't fighters," said Moger, laughing. "I could fight off every man in the village with one hand while I was taking a shit and whistling."

"She's dead," said Chipa. She arose from the body of the girl and started back toward Pedro. But Rodrigo de Triana caught her by the shoulder.

"What happened here shouldn't have happened," said Rodrigo to Colón. "But it's not that important, either. Like Pinzón said, let's get back to work."

For a few moments, Pedro thought that the Captain-General was going to let this pass, just as he had let so many other slights and contemptuous acts go by unremarked. Keeping the peace, Pedro understood that. But this was different. The men started to disperse, heading back toward the stockade.

"You killed a girl!" Pedro shouted.

Chipa was heading for Pedro, but once again Rodrigo reached out his hand to catch her. I should have waited a little longer, thought Pedro. I should have held my tongue.

"Enough," said Pinzón. "Let's have no more of this."

But Rodrigo couldn't let the accusation go unanswered. "Nobody meant her to die," said Rodrigo.

"If she was a girl of Palos," said Pedro, "you would kill the men who did this to her. The law would demand it!"

"Girls of Palos," said Rodrigo, "don't go around naked."

"You are not civilized!" shouted Pedro. "Even now, by holding Chipa that way, you are threatening to murder again!"

Pedro felt the Captain-General's hand on his shoulder. "Come here, Chipa," said Colón. "I will need you to help me explain this to Guacanagarí."

Chipa immediately tried to obey him. For a moment, Rodrigo restrained her. But he could see that no one was behind him on this, and he let her go. At once Chipa returned to Pedro and Colón.

But Rodrigo could not resist a parting shot. "So, Pedro, apparently *you're* the only one who gets to go rutting on Indian girls."

Pedro was livid. Pulling at his sword, he stepped forward. "I've never touched her!"

Rodrigo immediately began to laugh. "Look, he intends to defend her *honor!* He thinks this little brown bitch is a *lady!*" Other men began to laugh.

"Put the sword away, Pedro," said Colón.

Pedro obeyed, stepping back to rejoin Chipa and Colón.

Again the men began moving toward the stockade. But Rodrigo couldn't leave well enough alone. He was making comments, parts of them clearly audible. "Happy little family there," he said, and other men laughed. And then, a phrase, "Probably plowing his own furrow in her, too."

But the Captain-General seemed to be ignoring them. Pedro knew that this was the wisest course, but he couldn't stop thinking about the dead girl lying back there in the clearing. Was there no justice? Could white men do anything to Indians, and no one would punish them?

The officers were first through the stockade gate. Other men had gathered there, too. The men who had been involved in the rape—whether doing it or merely watching—were the last. And as they reached the gate and it closed behind them, Colón turned to Arana, the constable of the fleet, and said, "Arrest those men, sir. I charge Moger and Clavijo with rape and murder. I charge Triana, Vallejos, and Franco with disobedience to orders."

Perhaps if Arana had not hesitated, the sheer force of Colón's voice would have carried the day. But he did hesitate, and then spent a few moments looking to see which of the men would be likely to obey his orders.

That gave Rodrigo de Triana time enough to collect himself. "Don't do it!" he shouted. "Don't obey him! Pinzón already told us to go back to work. Are we going to let this Genovese flog us because of a little accident?"

"Arrest them," said Colón.

"You, you, and you," said Arana. "Put Moger and Clavijo under—"

"Don't do it!" shouted Rodrigo de Triana.

"If Rodrigo de Triana advocates mutiny again," said Colón, "I order you to shoot him dead."

"Wouldn't you like that, Colón! Then there'd be nobody to argue over who saw land that night!"

"Captain-General," said Pinzón quietly. "There's no need to talk of shooting people."

"I have given an order to arrest five seamen," said Colón. "I am waiting for obedience."

"Then you'll have a hell of a long wait!" cried Rodrigo.

Pinzón put out a hand and touched Arana's arm, urging him to delay. "Captain-General," said Pinzón. "Let's just wait until tempers cool down."

Pedro gasped. He could see that Segovia and Gutiérrez were just as shocked as he was. Pinzón had just mutinied, whether he meant it that way or not. He had come between the Captain-General and the Constable, and had restrained Arana from obeying Colón's order. Now he stood there, face to face with Colón, as if daring him to do anything about it.

Colón simply ignored him, and spoke to Arana. "I'm waiting."

Arana turned to the three men he had called upon before. "Do as I ordered you, men," he said.

But they did not move. They looked at Pinzón, waiting.

Pedro could see that Pinzón did not know what to do. Probably didn't know what he wanted. It was obvious now, if it had not been obvious before, that as far as the men were concerned, Pinzón was the commander of the expedition. Yet Pinzón was a good commander, and knew that discipline was vital to survival. He also knew that if he ever intended to return to Spain, he couldn't do it with a mutiny on his record.

At the same time, if he obeyed Colón now, he would lose the support of the men. They would feel betrayed. It would diminish him in their minds.

So . . . what was the most important to him? The devotion of the men of Palos, or the law of the sea?

There was no way of knowing what Pinzón would have chosen. For Colón did not wait until he finally made up his mind. Instead he spoke to Arana. "Apparently Pinzón thinks that it is for him to decide whether the orders of the Captain-General will be obeyed or not. Arana, you will arrest Martín Pinzón for insubordination and mutiny."

While Pinzón dithered about whether to cross the line, Colón had recognized the simple fact that he had already crossed it. Colón had law and justice on his side. Pinzón, however, had the sympathy of almost all the men. No sooner had Colón given the order than the men roared their rejection of his decision, and almost at once they became a mob, seizing Colón and the other officers and dragging them to the middle of the stockade.

For a moment, Pedro and Chipa were forgotten—the men had apparently been thinking of mutiny for long enough to have figured out who it was that they needed to subdue. Colón himself, of course, and the royal officers. Also Jácome el Rico, the financial agent; Juan de la Cosa, because he was a Basque, not a man of Palos, and therefore couldn't be trusted; and Alonso the physician, Lequeitio the gunner, and Domingo the cooper.

Pedro moved as unobtrusively as possible toward the gate of the stockade. He was about thirty yards from where the officers and loyal men were being restrained, but someone would be bound to notice when he opened the gate. He took Chipa by the hand, and said to her, in halting Taino, "We will run. When gate open."

She squeezed his hand to show that she understood.

Pinzón had apparently realized that it looked very bad for him, that he and his brothers had not been restrained with the other officers. Unless they killed all the royal officials, someone would testify against him in Spain. "I oppose this," he said loudly. "You must let them go at once."

"Come on, Martín," shouted Rodrigo. "He was charging you with mutiny."

"But Rodrigo, I am not guilty of mutiny," said Pinzón, speaking very clearly, so that everyone could hear. "I oppose this action. I won't allow you to continue. You will have to restrain me, too."

After a moment, Rodrigo finally got it. "You men," he said, giving orders as naturally as if he had been born to it. "You'd better seize Captain Pinzón and his brothers." From where he was standing, Pedro couldn't see whether Rodrigo winked as he said this. But he hardly needed to. Everyone knew that the Pinzóns were only being restrained because Martín had asked for it. To protect him from a charge of mutiny.

"Harm no one," said Pinzón. "If you have any hope of seeing Spain again, harm no one."

"He was going to flog me, the lying bastard!" cried Rodrigo. "So let's see how he likes the lash!"

If they dared to lay the lash to Colón, Pedro realized, then there was no hope for Chipa. She would end up like Parrot Feather, unless he got her out of the stockade and safely into the forest.

"Sees-in-the-Dark will know what to do," Chipa said quietly in Taino.

"Quiet," said Pedro. Then he gave up on Taino and continued in Spanish. "As soon as I get the gate open, run through it and head for the nearest trees."

He dashed for the gate, lifted the heavy crossbar, and let it drop out of the way. At once an outcry arose among the mutineers. "The gate! Pedro! Stop him! Get the girl! Don't let her get to the village!"

The gate was heavy and hard to move. It felt like it was taking a long time, though it was only moments. Pedro heard the discharge of a musket, but didn't hear any bullet striking nearby—at that range, muskets weren't very accurate. As soon as Chipa could squeeze through, she did, and a moment later Pedro was behind her. But there were men in pursuit of them, and Pedro was too frightened to dare to stop and look to see how close they were.

Chipa ran light as a deer across the clearing and dodged into the undergrowth at the forest's edge without so much as disturbing the leaves. By comparison, Pedro felt like an ox, clumping along, his boots pounding, sweat flowing under his heavy clothing. His sword smacked against his thigh and calf as he ran. He thought he could hear footsteps behind him, closer and closer. Finally, with a killing burst of speed he broke into the underbrush, vines tangling around his face, gripping his neck, trying to force him back out into the open.

"Quiet," said Chipa. "Hold still and they won't be able to see you."

Her voice calmed him. He stopped thrashing at the leaves, and then discovered that by moving slowly it was easy to duck through the vines and thin branches that had been holding him. Then he followed Chipa to a tree with a low-forking branch. She lifted herself easily up onto the branch. "They're going back into the stockade," she said.

"Nobody's following us?" Pedro was a little disappointed. "They must not think we matter."

"We have to get Sees-in-the-Dark," said Chipa.

"No need," said a woman's voice.

Pedro looked around frantically, but still couldn't see where the voice was coming from. It was Chipa who spotted her. "Sees-in-the-Dark!" she cried. "You're here already!"

Now Pedro could see her, dark in the shadows. "Come with me," she said. "This is a very dangerous time for Colón."

"Can you stop them?" asked Pedro.

"Be quiet and follow me," she answered.

But he could only follow Chipa, for he lost sight of Sees-in-the-Dark from the moment she moved away. Soon he found himself at the base of a tall tree. Looking up, he could see Chipa and Sees-in-the-Dark perched on high branches. Sees-in-the-Dark had some kind of complicated musket. But how could a weapon be of any use from this far away?

*   *   *

Diko watched through the scope of the tranquilizer gun. While
was busy intercepting Pedro and Chipa, the mutineers had stripp
Cristoforo to the waist and tied him to the cornerpost of one of the
cabins. Now Moger was preparing to lay on the lash.

Which were the ones whose anger was driving the mob? Rodrigo de Triana, of course, and Moger and Clavijo. Anyone else?

Behind her, clinging to another branch, Chipa spoke quietly.
"If you were here, Sees-in-the-Dark, why didn't you help Parrot
Feather?"

"I was watching the stockade," said Diko. "I didn't know anything was wrong until I saw Dead Fish run in and get you. You
were wrong, you know. Parrot Feather isn't dead."

"I couldn't hear her heart."

"It was very faint. But after all the white men left, I gave her
something that will help. And I sent Dead Fish to get the women
of the village to help her."

"If I hadn't said that Parrot Feather was dead, then all the rest
of this—"

"It was going to happen, one way or another," said Diko.
"That's why I was here, waiting."

Even without the scope, Chipa could see that Colón was being
flogged. "They're whipping him," she said.

"Quiet," said Diko.

She took careful aim at Rodrigo and pulled the trigger. There
was a popping sound. Rodrigo shrugged. Diko aimed again, this
time at Clavijo. Another pop. Clavijo scratched his head. Aiming at
Moger was harder, because he was moving so much as he laid on
with the lash. But when she got the shot off, it also struck true.
Moger paused and scratched his neck.

It was the weapon of last resort for her, firing these tiny laser-
guided missiles that struck and dropped off immediately, leaving
behind a dart as tiny as a bee sting. It took only seconds for the
drug to reach their brains, quickly damping down their aggression,
making them passive and lackadaisical. It wouldn't kill anybody,
but with the leaders suddenly losing interest, the rest of the mob
would cool off.

* * *

stoforo had never been beaten like this before, not even as a
boy. It hurt far worse than any physical pain he had ever suffered
before. And yet the pain was also far less than he had feared, because he found that he could bear it. He grunted involuntarily with
each blow, but the pain wasn't enough to quell his pride. They
would not see the Captain-General beg for mercy or weep under
the lash. They would remember how he bore their treachery.

To his surprise, the flogging ended after only a half dozen
blows. "Oh, that's enough," said Moger.

It was almost unbelievable. His rage had been so hot only a few
moments before, screaming about how Colón had called him a murderer and he'd see what it felt like when Moger actually *tried* to
hurt somebody.

"Cut him down," said Rodrigo. He, too, sounded more calm.
Almost bored. It was as if the hate in them had suddenly spent
itself.

"I'm sorry, my lord," whispered Andrés Yévenes as he untied
the knots that held his hands. "They had the guns. What could we
boys have done?"

"I know who the loyal men are," whispered Cristoforo.

"What are you doing, Yévenes, telling him what a good boy
you are?" demanded Clavijo.

"Yes," said Yévenes defiantly. "I'm not with you."

"Not that anyone cares," said Rodrigo.

Cristoforo could not believe how Rodrigo had changed. He
looked uninterested. For that matter, so did Moger and Clavijo, the
same kind of dazed look on their faces. Clavijo kept scratching his
head.

"Moger, you keep guard on him," said Rodrigo. "You too,
Clavijo. You've got the most to lose if he gets away. And you men,
put the rest of them into Segovia's cabin."

They obeyed, but everyone was moving slower, and most of the
men looked sullen or thoughtful. Without the fire of Rodrigo's rage
to drive them, many of them were obviously having second
thoughts. What would happen to them when they got back to Palos?

Only now did Cristoforo realize how much the lash had hurt
him. When he tried to take a step, he discovered he was dizzy from
loss of blood. He staggered. He heard several men gasp, and some

murmured. I'm too old for this, thought Cristoforo. If I had to be
whipped, it should have happened when I was younger.

Inside his cabin, Cristoforo endured the pain as Master Juan
laid on some nasty salve, then laid a light cloth over his back. "Try
not to move much," said Juan—as if Cristoforo needed to be told.
"The cloth will keep the flies off, so leave it there."

Lying there, Cristoforo thought back over what had happened.
They meant to kill me. They were filled with rage. And then, suddenly, they were not even interested in hurting me anymore. What
could have caused that, but the Spirit of God softening their hearts?
The Lord *does* watch over me. He does not want me to die yet.

Moving slowly, gently, so as not to disturb the cloth or cause
too much pain, Cristoforo crossed himself and prayed. Can I still
fulfill the mission you gave me, Lord? Even after the rape of that
girl? Even after this mutiny?

The words came into his mind as clearly as if he were hearing
the woman's own voice: "One calamity after another. Until you
learn that humility."

What humility was that? What was it he was supposed to learn?

Late in the afternoon, several Tainos from Guacanagarí's village
made their way over the wall of the stockade—did the white men
really think a bunch of sticks were going to be a barrier to men
who had been climbing trees since boyhood?—and soon one of them
returned to make his report. Diko was waiting for him with Guacanagarí.

"The men who are guarding him are asleep."

"I gave them a little poison so they would," said Diko.

Guacanagarí glared at her. "I don't see why any of this should
be your concern."

None of the others shared their cacique's attitude toward the
black shaman-woman from the old mountain village of Ankuash.
They were in awe of her, and had no doubt that she could poison
anybody she wanted to, at any time.

"Guacanagarí, I share your anger," said Diko. "You and your
village have done nothing but good for these white men, and see
how they treat you. Worse than dogs. But not all the white men

are like this. The white cacique tried to punish the men who raped Parrot Feather. That's why the evil men among them have taken away his power and given him such a beating.''

''So he wasn't much of a cacique after all,'' said Guacanagarí.

''He is a great man,'' said Diko. ''Chipa and this young man, Pedro, both know him better than anyone but me.''

''Why should I believe this white boy and this tricky lying girl?'' demanded Guacanagarí.

To Diko's surprise, Pedro had learned enough Taino to be able to speak up and say, clearly, ''Because we have seen with our eyes, and you have not.''

All of the Taino war council, gathered in the forest within sight of the stockade, were surprised by the fact that Pedro could understand and speak their language. Diko could tell they were surprised, because they showed no expression on their faces and waited in silence until they could speak calmly. Their controlled, impassive-seeming response reminded her of Hunahpu, and for a moment she felt a terrible pang of grief at having lost him. Years ago, she told herself. It was years ago, and I've already done all my grieving. I am over all feelings of regret.

''The poison will wear off,'' said Diko. ''The evil men among them will remember their anger.''

''We will remember our anger, too,'' said one of Guacanagarí's young men.

''If you kill *all* the white men, even the ones who did no harm, then you are just as bad as they are,'' said Diko. ''I promise you that if you kill in haste, you will be sorry.''

She said it quietly, but the menace in her words was real—she could see that they were all considering very carefully. They knew that she had deep powers, and none of them would be reckless enough to oppose her openly.

''Do you dare to forbid us to be men? Will you forbid us to protect our village?'' asked Guacanagarí.

''I would never forbid you to do anything,'' said Diko. ''I only *ask* you to wait and watch a little longer. Soon white men will begin leaving the stockade. I think that first there will be loyal men trying to save their cacique. Then the other good men who don't want to harm your people. You must let them find their way up the mountain to me. I ask you not to hurt them. If they are coming to me, please let them come."

"Even if they're searching for you to kill you?" asked Guacan-agarí. It was a sly question, leaving him an opening to kill whoever he wanted, claiming he did it in order to protect Sees-in-the-Dark.

"I can protect myself," said Sees-in-the-Dark. "If they are heading up the mountain, I ask you not to hinder or hurt them in any way. You'll know when the only ones left are the evil ones. It will be plain to all of you, not just to one or two. When that day comes, you can act as men should act. But even then, if any of them escape and head for the mountain, I ask you to let them go."

"Not the ones who raped Parrot Feather," said Dead Fish at once. "Never them, no matter what way they run."

"I agree," said Diko. "There is no refuge for them."

Cristoforo awoke in the darkness. There were voices outside his tent. He couldn't hear the words, but he didn't care, either. He understood now. It had come clear to him in his dream. Instead of dreaming about his own suffering, he had dreamed about the girl they had raped and killed. In his dream he saw the faces of Moger and Clavijo as they must have seemed to her, filled with lust and mockery and hate. In his dream, he begged them not to hurt her. In his dream, he told them he was just a girl, just a child. But nothing stopped them. They had no mercy.

These are the men I brought to this place, thought Cristoforo. And yet I called them Christian. And the gentle Indians, I called them savages. Sees-in-the-Dark said nothing but the simple truth. These people are the children of God, waiting only to be taught and baptized in order to be Christian. Some of my men are worthy to be Christians along with them. Pedro has been my example in this all along. He learned to see Chipa's heart when all I or anyone else could see was her skin, the ugliness of her face, her strange manner. If I had been like Pedro in my heart, I would have believed Sees-in-the-Dark, and so I would not have had to suffer these last calamities—the loss of the *Pinta*, the mutiny, this beating. And the worst calamity of all: my shame at having refused the word of God because he didn't send the kind of messenger I expected.

The door opened, then closed again quickly. Quiet footsteps approached him.

"If you have come to kill me," said Cristoforo, "be man enough to let me see the face of my murderer."

"Quiet, please, my lord," said the voice. "Some of us have had a meeting. We'll free you and get you out of the stockade. And then we'll fight these damned mutineers and—"

"No," said Cristoforo. "No fighting, no bloodshed."

"What, then? Do we let these men rule over us?"

"The village of Ankuash, up the mountain," said Cristoforo. "I'll go there. The same with all loyal men. Get away quietly, without a fight. Follow the stream up the mountain—to Ankuash. That is the place that God prepared for us."

"But the mutineers will build the ship . . ."

"Do you think mutineers could ever build a ship?" asked Cristoforo scornfully. "They'll look each other in the eye, and then look away, because they'll know they can't trust each other."

"That's true, my lord," said the man. "Already some of them are muttering about how Pinzón was interested only in making sure you knew that he wasn't a mutineer. Some of them remembered how the Turk accused Pinzón of helping him."

"A stupid charge," said Cristoforo.

"Pinzón listens when Moger and Clavijo talk about killing you, and he says nothing," said the man. "And Rodrigo stamps about, cursing and swearing because he didn't kill you this afternoon. We have to get you out of here."

"Help me get to my feet."

The pain was sharp, and he could feel the fragile scabs on some of the wounds break open. Blood was trickling on his back. But it couldn't be helped.

"How many of you are there?" asked Cristoforo.

"Most of the ship's boys are with you," he said. "They were all ashamed of Pinzón today. Some of the officers talk about negotiating with the mutineers, and Segovia talked with Pinzón for a long time, so I think maybe he's trying to work out a compromise. Probably wants to put Pinzón in command—"

"Enough," said Cristoforo. "Everyone is frightened, everyone is doing what he thinks is best. Tell your friends this: I will know who the loyal men are, because they will make their way up the mountain to Ankuash. I will be there, with the woman Sees-in-the-Dark.''

"The black witch?''

"There is more of God in her than in half the so-called Christians in this place,'' said Cristoforo. "Tell them all—if any man wishes to return to Spain with me as a witness that he was loyal, then he will get away from here and join me in Ankuash.''

Cristoforo was standing now, and had his hose on, with a shirt loosely thrown over his back. More clothing than that he couldn't bear, and on this warm night he wouldn't suffer from being so lightly dressed. "My sword,'' he said.

"Can you carry it?''

"I'm Captain-General of this expedition,'' said Cristoforo. "I will have my sword. And let it be known—whoever brings me my logbooks and charts will be rewarded beyond his dreams when we return to Spain.''

The man opened the door, and both of them looked carefully to see if anyone was watching them. Finally they saw a man—Andrés Yévenes, from his lean boyish body—waving for them to come on. Only now did Cristoforo have a chance to see who it was who had come for him. It was the Basque, Juan de la Cosa. The man whose cowardly disobedience had led to the loss of the *Santa Maria*. "You have redeemed yourself tonight, Juan,'' said Cristoforo.

Cosa shrugged. "We Basques—you never know what we're going to do.''

Leaning on de la Cosa, Cristoforo moved as quickly as he could across the open area to the stockade wall. In the distance, he could hear the laughter and singing of drunken men. That was why he had been so badly guarded.

Andrés and Juan were joined by several others, all ship's boys except for Escobedo, the clerk, who was carrying a small chest. "My log,'' said Cristoforo.

"And your charts,'' said Escobedo.

De la Cosa grinned at him. "Should I tell him about the reward you promised, or will you, my lord?''

"Which of you are coming with me?'' asked Cristoforo.

They looked at each other in surprise. "We thought to help you over the wall," said de la Cosa. "Beyond that . . ."

"They'll know I couldn't have done it alone. Most of you should come with me now. That way they won't start searching through the stockade, accusing people of having helped me. They'll think all my friends left with me."

"I'll stay," said Juan de la Cosa, "so I can tell people the things you told me. All the rest of you, go."

They hoisted Cristoforo up onto the stockade. He braced himself against the pain, and swung down and landed on the other side. Almost at once he found himself face to face with one of the Taino. Dead Fish, if he could tell one Indian from another by moonlight. Dead Fish put his fingers against Cristoforo's lips. Be silent, he was saying.

The others came over the wall much more quickly than Cristoforo had. The only trouble was with the chest containing the logs and charts, but it was eventually handed over the top, followed by Escobedo.

"That's all of us," said Escobedo. "The Basque is already heading back to the drinking before he's missed."

"I fear for his life," said Cristoforo.

"He feared much more for yours."

The Tainos all carried weapons, but they did not brandish them or seem to be threatening in any way. And when Dead Fish took Cristoforo by the hand, the Captain-General followed him toward the woods.

Diko carefully removed the bandages. The healing was going well. She thought ruefully of the small quantity of antibiotics she had left. Oh, well. She had had enough for this, and with any luck she wouldn't need any more.

Cristoforo's eyes fluttered.

"So you aren't going to sleep forever after all," said Diko.

His eyes opened, and he tried to lift himself from the mat. He fell back at once.

"You're still weak," she said. "The flogging was bad enough,

but the journey up the mountain wasn't good for you. You ar
a young man anymore.''

He nodded weakly.

''Go back to sleep. Tomorrow you'll feel much better.''

He shook his head. ''Sees-in-the-Dark,'' he began.

''You can tell me tomorrow.''

''I'm sorry,'' he said.

''Tomorrow.''

''You are a daughter of God,'' he said. It was hard for him to
speak, to get the breath for it, to form the words. But he formed
them. ''You are my sister. You are a Christian.''

''Tomorrow,'' she said.

''I don't care about the gold,'' he said.

''I know,'' she answered.

''I think you come to me from God,'' he said.

''I have come to you to help you make true Christians of the
people here. Beginning with me. Tomorrow you'll start to teach me
about Christ, so I can be the first baptized in this land.''

''This is why I came here,'' he murmured.

She stroked his hair, his shoulders, his cheek. As he drifted
back to sleep, she answered him with the same words. ''This is
why I came here.''

Within a few days, the royal officers and several more loyal men
found their way up the mountain to Ankuash. Cristoforo, now able to
stand and walk for a while each day, set his men to work at once,
helping the villagers with their work, teaching them Spanish and
learning Taino as they did. The ship's boys took to this humble work
quite naturally. It was much harder for the royal officers to swallow
their pride and work alongside the villagers. But there was no com-
pulsion. As long as they refused to help, they were simply ignored,
until they finally realized that in Ankuash, the old hierarchical rules
no longer applied. If you weren't helping, you didn't matter. These
were men who were determined to matter. Escobedo was the first to
forget his rank, and Segovia the last, but that was to be expected. The
heavier the burden of office, the harder it was to set it down.

Runners from the valley brought news. With the royal officers ~ne, Pinzón had accepted command of the stockade, but work on .ne new ship soon stopped, and there were tales of fighting among the Spaniards. More men slipped away and came up the mountain. Finally it came to a pitched battle. The gunfire could be heard all the way to Ankuash.

That night a dozen men arrived in the village. Among them was Pinzón himself, wounded in the leg and weeping because his brother Vincente, who had been captain of the *Niña,* was dead. When his wound had been treated, he insisted on publicly begging the Captain-General's forgiveness, which Cristoforo freely gave.

With the last restraint removed, the two dozen men remaining in the stockade ventured out to try to capture some Tainos, to make them into slaves or whores. They failed, but two Tainos and a Spaniard died in the fighting. A runner came to Diko from Guacanagarí. "We will kill them now," said the messenger. "Only the evil ones are left."

"I told Guacanagarí it would be obvious when the time came. But because you waited, there will only be a few of them, and you'll beat them easily."

The remaining mutineers slept in foolish security within their stockade, then woke in the morning to find their watchmen dead and the stockade filled with angry and well-armed Tainos. They learned that the gentleness of the Tainos was only one aspect of their character.

By the summer solstice of 1493, all the people of Ankuash had been baptized, and those Spaniards who had learned enough Taino to get along were permitted to begin courting young women from Ankuash or other villages. As the Spanish learned Taino ways, so also the villagers began to learn from the Spanish.

"They're forgetting to be Spanish," Segovia complained to Cristoforo one day.

"But the Taino are also forgetting to be Taino," Cristoforo replied. "They're becoming something new, something that has hardly been seen in the world before."

"And what is that?" demanded Segovia.

"I'm not sure," said Cristoforo. "Christians, I think."

In the meantime, Cristoforo and Sees-in-the-Dark talked for

many hours each day, and gradually he began to realize that desp...
all the secrets that she knew and all the strange powers that sh...
seemed to have, she was not an angel or any other kind of supernatural being. She was a woman, still young, yet with a great deal
of pain and wisdom in her eyes. She was a woman, and she was
his friend. Why should that have surprised him? It was always from
the love of strong women that he had found whatever joy had been
granted him in his life.

13

Reconciliations

It was a meeting that would live in history.

Cristobal Colón was the European who had created the Carib League, a confederation of Christian tribes in all the lands surrounding the Carib Sea on the east, the north, and the south.

Yax was the Zapotec king who, building on his father's work in uniting all the Zapotec tribes and forming an alliance with the Tarascan Empire, conquered the Aztecs and brought his ironworking and shipbuilding kingdom to the highest cultural level achieved in the western hemisphere.

Their achievements were remarkably parallel. Both men had put a stop to the ubiquitous practice of human sacrifice in the lands they governed. Both men had adopted a form of Christianity, which was easily united when they met. Colón and his men had taught European navigation and some shipbuilding techniques to the Tainos and, when they were converted to Christianity, the Caribs as well; under Yax, Zapotec ships traded far and wide, along both coasts of the Zapotec Empire. While the Carib islands were too poor in iron for them to match the achievements of the Tarascan metalsmiths, when Colón and Yax united their empires into one nation, there were still enough of Colón's European crew who knew iron-working that they were able to help the Tarascans make the leap forward into gunsmithing.

Historians looked back on their meeting at Chichén Itzá as the greatest moment of reconciliation in history. Imagine what would have happened if Alexander, instead of conquering the Persians, had united with them. If the Romans and Parthians had become a single nation. If the Christians and Muslims, if the Mongols and the Han . . .

But it was unimaginable. The only reason they could believe it was possible with the Carib League and the Zapotec Empire was that it actually happened.

In the great central plaza of Chichén Itzá, where once human sacrifice and torture had been offered to Mayan gods, the Christian Colón embraced the heathen Yax, and then baptized him. Colón presented his daughter and heir, Beatrice Tagiri Colón, and Yax presented his son and heir, Ya-Hunahpu Ipoxtli. They were married on the spot, whereupon both Colón and Yax abdicated in favor of their children. Of course they would both remain the powers behind the throne until their deaths, but the alliance held, and the nation known as Caribia was born.

It was a well-governed empire. While all the different tribes and language-groups that were included within it were allowed to govern themselves, a series of uniform laws were imposed and impartially enforced, allowing trade and free movement through every part of Caribia. Christianity was not established as a state religion, but the principles of nonviolence and communal control of land were made uniform, and human sacrifice and slavery were strictly forbidden. It was because of this that historians dated the beginning of the humanist era from the date of that meeting between Yax and Colón: the summer solstice of the year 1519, by the Christian reckoning.

The European influence that came through Colón was powerful, considering that only he and the merest handful of his officers and men were available to promulgate their culture. But, having come to Haiti, a land without writing, it should not have been astonishing that the Spanish alphabet was adopted to write the Taino and Carib languages, or that Spanish should eventually be adopted as the language of trade, government, and record-keeping throughout the Carib League. After all, Spanish was the language that already had the vocabulary to deal with Christianity, trade, and law. Yet by no means was this a European conquest. It was the Spanish who gave up the idea of personal ownership of land, which had long been a cause of great inequities in the old world; it was the Spanish who learned to tolerate different religions and cultures and languages without trying to enforce uniformity. When the behavior of the Colón's Spanish expedition in the new world is compared to the record of intolerance marked by the Inquisition, the expulsion of the Jews, and the war against the Moors in Spain itself, it is obvious that while Spanish culture provided a few useful tools—a lingua franca, an alphabet, a calendar—it was the Tainos who taught the Spanish what it meant to be Christian.

There was another similarity between Yax and Colón. Each of them had an enigmatic adviser. It was said that Yax's mentor, One-Hunahpu, came direct from Xibalba itself, and commanded the Zapotecs to end human sacrifice and to look for a sacrificial god that they later believed was Jesus Christ. Colón's mentor was his wife, a woman so dark she was said to be African, though of course that could not have been true. The woman was called Sees-in-the-Dark by the Taino, but Colón—and history—came to know her as Diko, though the meaning of that name, if it had one, was lost. Her role was not as clear to historians as that of One-Hunahpu, but it was known that when Colón fled the mutineers, it was Diko who took him in, nursed him back to health, and by embracing Christianity helped him to begin his great work of conversion among the people of the Carib Sea. Some historians speculated that it was Diko who tamed the brutality of the Spanish Christians. But Colón himself was such a powerful figure that it was hard for historians to get a clear look at anyone in his shadow.

On that day in 1519, when the official ceremonies were over, as the feasting and dancing for the wedding of the two kingdoms ran far into the night, there was another meeting, one that was not witnessed by anyone but the participants. They met on the top of the great pyramid of Chichén Itzá, the last hour before dawn.

She was there first, waiting for him in the darkness. When he came to the top of the tower and saw her, at first he was wordless, nd so was she. They sat across from each other. She had brought mats so they wouldn't have to sit on the hard stone. He had brought a little food and drink, which he shared. They ate in silence, but the true feast was in the way they looked at each other.

Finally she broke the silence. "You succeeded better than we dreamed, Hunahpu."

"And you, Diko."

She shook her head. "No, it wasn't hard after all. He changed himself. The Interveners chose well, when they made him their tool."

"And is that what we made him? Our tool?"

"No, Hunahpu. I made him my husband. We have seven children. Our daughter is Queen of Caribia. It's been a good life. And your wife, Xoc. She seems a loving, gentle woman."

"She is. And strong." He smiled. "The third strongest woman I ever knew."

Suddenly tears flowed down Diko's face. "Oh, Hunahpu, I miss my mother so much."

"I miss her too. I still see her sometimes in my dreams, reaching up to pull down the switch."

She reached out her hand, laid it on his knee. "Hunahpu, did you forget that once we loved each other?"

"Not for a day. Not for an hour."

"I always thought: Hunahpu will be proud of me for doing this. Was that disloyal of me? To look forward to the day when I could show you my work?"

"Who else but you would understand what I achieved? Who else but me could know how far beyond our dreams you succeeded?"

"We changed the world," she said.

"For now, anyway," said Hunahpu. "They can still find their own ways to make all the old mistakes."

She shrugged.

"Did you tell him?" asked Hunahpu. "About who we are, and where we came from?"

"As much as he could understand. He knows that I'm not an angel, anyway. And he knows that there was another version of

history, in which Spain destroyed the Caribian people. He wept f
days, once he understood.''

Hunahpu nodded. "I tried to tell Xoc, but to her there was little
difference between Xibalba and Pastwatch. Call them gods or call
them researchers, she didn't see much practical difference. And
you know, I can't think of a significant difference, either.''

"It didn't seem as if we were gods, when we were among them.
It was just Mother and Father and their friends," said Diko.

"And to me, it was a job. Until I found you. Or you found me.
Or however that worked.''

"It worked," said Diko with finality.

He cocked his head and looked at her sideways, to let her know
that he knew he was asking a loaded question. "Is it true you aren't
going with Colón when he sails east?''

"I don't think Spain is likely to be ready for an ambassador
married to an African. Let's not make them swallow too much.''

"He's an old man, Diko. He might not live to come home.''

"I know," she said.

"Now that we're making Atetulka the capital of Caribia, will
you come there to live? To wait for his return?''

"Hunahpu, you aren't expecting that at our age we would start to
set a bad example, are you? Though I admit to being curious about the
twelve scars that legend says you carry on your . . . person.''

He laughed. "No, I'm not proposing an affair. I love Xoc, and
you love Colón. We both still have too much work to do for us to
put it at risk now. But I hoped for your company. For many conversations.''

She thought about it, but in the end, she shook her head. "It
would be too . . . hard for me. *This* is too hard for me. Seeing you
brings back another life. A time when I was another person. Maybe
now and then. Every few years. Sail to Haiti and visit us in Ankuash.
My Beatrice will want to come home to the mountain—Atetulka must
be sweltering, there on the coast.''

"Ya-Hunahpu is dying to go to Haiti—he hears that the women
wear no clothing.''

"In some places they still go naked. But bright colors are all
the fashion. I think he'll be disappointed.''

Hunahpu reached out and took her hand. "I'm not disappointed."

"Neither am I."

They held hands like that, for a long time.

"I was thinking," said Hunahpu, "of the third one who earned a place atop this tower."

"I was thinking of him, too."

"We remade the culture, so that Europe and America—Caribia—could meet without either being destroyed," said Hunahpu. "But he's the one who bought us the time to do it."

"He died quickly," said Diko. "But not without planting seeds of suspicion among the Spaniards. It must have been quite a death scene. But I'm glad I missed it."

The first light of dawn had appeared over the jungle to the east. Hunahpu noticed it, sighed, and stood. Then Diko stood, unfolding herself to her full height. Hunahpu laughed. "I forgot how tall you were."

"I'm stooping a little these days."

"It doesn't help," he said.

They went down the pyramid separately. No one saw them. No one guessed that they knew each other.

Cristóbal Colón returned to Spain in the spring of 1520. No one looked for him anymore, of course. There were legends about the disappearance of the three caravels that sailed west; the name Colón had become synonymous, in Spain, at least, with the idea of mad ventures.

It was the Portuguese who had made the link to the Indies, and Portuguese ships now dominated all the Atlantic sea routes. They were just starting to explore the coast of a large island they named for the legendary land of Hy-Brasil, and some were saying that it might be a continent, especially when a ship returned with reports that northwest of the desert lands first discovered was a vast jungle with a river so wide and powerful that it made the ocean fresh twenty miles from its mouth. The inhabitants of the land were poor and weak savages, easily conquered and enslaved—much easier to deal with than the fierce Africans, who were also guarded by plagues invariably fatal to white men. The sailors who landed Hy-Brasil got sick, but the disease was quick and never killed. Indeed, those who caught it reported that they were healthier afterward than they had ever been before. This "plague" was now spreading through Europe, doing no harm at all, and some said that where the Brasilian plague had passed, smallpox and black death could no longer return. It made Hy-Brasil seem magical, and the Portuguese were preparing an expedition to explore the coast and look for a site for supply stations. Perhaps the madman Colón was not so mad after all. If there was a suitable coast for resupply, it might be possible to reach China by sailing west.

That was when a fleet of a thousand ships appeared off the Portuguese coast near Lagos, sailing eastward toward Spain, toward the straits of Gibraltar. The Portuguese galleon that spotted the strange ships at first sailed boldly toward them. But then, when it became obvious that these strange vessels filled the sea from horizon to horizon, the captain wisely turned about and raced for Lisboa. The Portuguese who stood on the southern shores said that it took three days for the whole fleet to pass. Some ships came close enough to the shore that the watchers could say with confidence that the sailors were brown, of a race never seen before. They also said that the ships were heavily armed; any one of them would be a match for the fiercest war galleon of the Portuguese fleet.

Wisely, the Portuguese sailors put in to port and stayed there while the fleet passed. If it was an enemy, better not to provoke them, but instead hope they would find some better land to conquer farther east.

The first of the ships put in to port at Palos. If anyone noticed that it was the same port from which Colón had set sail, the coincidence went unremarked at the time. The brown men who disembarked from the ships shocked everyone by speaking fluent Spanish, though with many new words and odd pronunciations. They said they came from the kingdom of Caribia, which lay on a vast island between Europe and China. They insisted on speaking to the monks of La Rábida, and it was to these holy men that they gave three chests of pure gold. "One is a gift to the King and Queen of Spain, to thank them for sending three ships to us, twenty-eight years ago," said the leader of the Caribians. "One is a gift to the holy Church, to help pay for sending missionaries to teach the gospel of Jesus Christ in every corner of Caribia, to any who will freely listen. And the last is the price we will pay for a piece of land, well-watered with a good harbor, where we can build a palace fitting for the father of our Queen Beatrice Tagiri to receive the visit of the King and Queen of Spain.''

Few of the monks of La Rábida remembered the days when Colón had been a frequent visitor there. But one remembered very well. He had been left there as a boy to be educated while his father pressed his suit at court, and later when he sailed west in search of a mad goal. When his father never returned, he had taken holy orders, and was now distinguished for his holiness. He took the leader of the Caribian party aside and said, "The three ships you say that Spain sent to you. They were commanded by Cristóbal Colón, weren't they?"

"Yes, they were," said the brown man.

"Did he live? Is he still alive?"

"He is not only alive, but he is the father of our Queen Beatrice Tagiri. It is for him that we build a palace. And because you remember him, my friend, I can tell you, in his heart he is not building this palace for the King and Queen of Spain, though he will receive them there. He is building this palace so he can invite his son, Diego, to learn what has become of him, and to beg his forgiveness for not returning to him for all these years."

"I am Diego Colón," said the monk.

"I assumed you were," said the brown man. "You look like him. Only younger. And your mother must have been a beauty, because the differences are all improvements." The brown man didn't smile, but Diego saw at last the twinkle in his eyes.

"Tell my father," said Diego, "that many a man has been separated from his family by fortune or fate, and only an unworthy son would ask his father to apologize for coming home."

The land was purchased, and seven thousand Caribians began trading and purchasing throughout southern Spain. They caused much comment and not a little fear, but they all claimed to be Christians, they spent gold as freely as if they had dug it up like dirt, and their soldiers were heavily armed and highly disciplined.

It took a year to build the palace for the father of Queen Beatrice

Tagiri, and when it was finished it was clear that it was really more of a city than a palace. Spanish architects had been hired to design a cathedral, a monastery, an abbey, and a university; Spanish workers had been well paid to do much of the labor, working side by side with the strange brown men of Caribia. Gradually the women who had come with the fleet began to venture out in public, wearing their lightweight, bright-colored gowns all through the summer, and then learning to wear warmer Spanish clothing when winter came. By the time the city of the Caribians was finished, and the King and Queen of Spain were invited to come and visit, the city was populated by as many Spaniards as Caribians, working and worshiping together.

Spanish scholars were teaching Caribian and Spanish students in the university; Spanish priests taught Caribians to speak Latin and say the mass; Spanish merchants came to the city to sell food and other supplies, and came away with strange artworks made of gold and silver, copper and iron, cloth and stone. Only gradually did they learn that many of the Caribians were *not* Christians, after all, but that among the Caribians it did not matter whether a person was Christian or not. All were equal citizens, free to choose what they might believe. This idea was strange indeed, and it did not occur to anyone in authority in Spain to adopt it, but as long as the pagans among the Caribians did not try to proselytize in Christian Spain, their presence could be tolerated. After all, these Caribians had so much gold. And so many fast ships. And so many excellent guns.

When the King and Queen of Spain arrived—trying their pathetic best to look impressive amid the opulence of the Caribian city—they were brought into a great throne room in a magnificent building. They were led to a pair of thrones and invited to sit on them. Only then did the father of the Queen of the Caribians present himself, and when he came in, he knelt before them.

"Queen Juana," he said, "I'm sorry that your mother and father did not live to see my return from the expedition on which they sent me in 1492."

"So Cristóbal Colón was not a madman," she said. "And it was not a folly for Isabella to send him."

"Cristóbal Colón," he said, "was the true servant of the King and Queen. But I *was* wrong about how far it is to China. What I found was a land that no European had ever known before.'' On a table before their thrones he set a small chest, and took from it four books. ''The logs of my voyage and all my acts since then. My ships were destroyed and I could not return, but as Queen Isabella charged me, I did my best to bring as many people as I could to the service of Christ. My daughter has become Queen Beatrice Tagiri of Caribia, and her husband is King Ya-Hunahpu of Caribia. Just as your parents joined Aragon and Castile through their marriage, so my daughter and her husband have united two great kingdoms into one nation. May their children be as good and wise rulers of Caribia as you have been of Spain.''

He listened as Queen Juana and King Henrique made gracious speeches accepting his logs and journals. As they spoke, he thought of what Diko had said—that in another history, the one in which his ships had not been destroyed, and he had sailed home with the *Pinta* and the *Niña*, his discovery had made Spain so rich that Juana had been given in marriage to a different man, who had died young. It had driven her mad, and first her father and then her son had ruled in her place. What an odd thing, that among all the changes that God had made through him, one of them should be to save this gracious queen from madness. She would never know, for he and Diko would never tell.

Their speeches were done, and in return they had offered him many fine gifts—by Spanish standards—to take back to King Ya-Hunahpu and Queen Beatrice Tagiri. He accepted them all.

''Caribia is a large land,'' he said, ''and there are many places where the name of Christ has not yet been heard. Also, the land is rich in many things, and we welcome trade with Spain. We ask you to send priests to teach our people. We ask you to send merchants to trade with them. But since Caribia is a peaceful land, where an unarmed man can walk from one end of the kingdom to the other without harm, there will be no need for you to send any soldiers. Indeed, my daughter and her husband ask you to do them the great favor of telling all the other sovereigns of Europe that, while they are welcome to send priests and merchants, any ships that sail into Caribian waters bearing weapons of any kind will be sent to the bottom of the sea.''

The warning was clear enough—it had been clear from the moment that the thousand ships of the Caribian fleet were first seen off the coast of Portugal. Already word had come back from the King of Portugal that all plans to explore Hy-Brasil had been abandoned, and Cristoforo was confident that other monarchs would be as prudent.

Documents were prepared and signed, affirming the eternal peace and special friendship that existed between the monarchs of Spain and Caribia. When they were signed, it was time for the audience to end. "I have but one last favor to ask of Your Majesties," said Cristoforo. "This city is known to all as La Ciudad de los Caribianos. This is because I would not give the city a name until I could ask you, in person, for permission to name it for the gracious queen your mother, Isabella of Castile. It was because of her faith in Christ and her trust in me that this city was built, and such great friendship exists between Spain and Caribia. Will you give me your consent?"

Consent was freely given, and Juana and Henrique stayed another week in order to lead the ceremonies involved in naming the Ciudad Isabella.

When they left, the serious work began. Most of the fleet would return to Caribia soon, but only the crews would be Caribian. The passengers would be Spanish—priests and merchantmen. Cristoforo's son Diego had turned down the wealth that his father offered him, and asked instead to be allowed to be one of the Franciscan contingent among the missionaries to Caribia. Discreet inquiry located Cristoforo's other son, Fernando. He had been brought up to take part in the business of his grandfather, a merchant of Córdoba. Cristoforo invited him to Ciudad Isabella, where he recognized him as a son and gave him one of the Caribian ships to hold his trade goods. Together they decided to name the ship *Beatrice de Córdoba*, after Fernando's mother. Fernando was also pleased at the name that his father had given to the daughter who became queen of Caribia. It is doubtful that Cristoforo ever let him know that there might be some ambiguity about which Beatrice the queen was named for.

Cristoforo watched from his palace as eight hundred Caribian ships set sail for the new world, carrying his first two sons on their different missions there. He watched as another hundred and fifty ships set forth in groups of three or four or five to carry ambassadors and traders to every port of Europe and to every city of the Muslims. He watched as ambassadors and princes, great traders and scholars and churchmen came to Ciudad Isabella to teach the Caribians and learn from them.

Surely God had fulfilled the promises made on that beach near Lagos. Because of Cristoforo the word of God was being carried to millions. Kingdoms had fallen at his feet, and the wealth that had passed through his hands, under his control, was beyond anything he could have conceived of as a child in Genova. The weaver's son who had once cowered in fear at the cruel doings of great men had become one of the greatest of all, and had done it without cruelty. On his knees Cristoforo gave thanks many times for God's goodness to him.

But in the silence of the night, on his balcony overlooking the sea, he thought back to his neglected wife Felipa; to his patient lover Beatrice in Córdoba; to Lady Beatrice de Bobadilla, who had died before he could return to her in triumph in Gomera. He thought back to his brothers and sisters in Genova, who were all in the grave before his fame could ever reach them. He thought of the years he might have spent with Diego, with Fernando, if he had never left Spain. Is there no triumph without loss, without pain, without regret?

He thought then of Diko. She could never have been the woman of his dreams; there were times when he suspected that she had once loved another man, too, that was as lost to her as both his Beatrices were to him. Diko had been his teacher, his partner, his lover, his companion, the mother of many children, his true queen when they had shaped a great kingdom out of a thousand villages on fifty islands and two continents. He loved her. He was grateful to her. She had been a gift of God to him.

Was it so disloyal of him, then, to wish for one hour's conversation with Beatrice de Bobadilla? To wish that he could kiss Beatrice de Córdoba again, and hear her laugh loudly at his stories? To wish that he could show his charts and logbooks to Felipa, so she would know that his mad obsession had been worth the pain it caused to all of them?

There is no good thing that does not cost a dear price. That is what Cristoforo learned by looking back upon his life. Happiness is not a life without pain, but rather a life in which the pain is traded for a worthy price. That is what you gave me, Lord.

Pedro de Salcedo and his wife, Chipa, reached Ciudad Isabella in the fall of 1522, bringing letters to Colón from his daughter, his son-in-law, and, most important, from his Diko. They found the old man napping on his balcony, the smell of the sea strong in the rising breeze that promised rain from the west. Pedro was loath to wake him, but Chipa insisted that he wouldn't want to wait. When Pedro shook him gently, Colón recognized them at once. "Pedro," he murmured. "Chipa."

"Letters," Pedro said. "From Diko, most of all."

Colón smiled, took the letters, and laid them unopened in his lap. He closed his eyes again, and it seemed he meant to doze off again. Pedro and Chipa lingered, watching him, with affection, with nostalgia for early days and great achievements. Then, suddenly, he seemed to rouse from his slumber. His eyes flew open and he raised one hand, his finger pointing out to sea. "Constantinople!" he cried.

Then he fell back in his chair, and his hand dropped into his lap. What dream was this? they wondered.

A few moments later, Pedro realized that there was a different quality to the old man's posture now. Ah, yes, that's the difference: He isn't breathing now. He bent down and kissed his forehead. "Good-bye, my Captain-General," he said. Chipa also kissed his white hair. "Go to God, my friend," she murmured. Then they left to tell the palace staff that the great discoverer was dead.

Epilogue

In the year 1955, a Caribian archaeologist, heading a dig near the traditional location of the landing place of Cristóbal Colón, observed that the nearly perfect skull found that day was heavier than it should be. He noted the anomaly, and a few weeks later, when he had occasion to return to the University of Ankuash, he had it x-rayed. It showed a metal plate embedded inside the skull.

Inside the skull? Impossible. Only upon close examination did he find the hairline marks of surgery that had made the metal implant possible. But bones did not heal this neatly. What kind of surgery was this, to leave so little damage? It was not possible in 1955, let alone in the late fifteenth century, to do a job like this.

Photographing every step of the process, and with several assistants as witness, he sawed open the skull and removed the plate. It was of an alloy he had never seen before; later testing would reveal that it was an alloy that had never existed, to anyone's knowledge. But the metal was hardly the issue. For once it was detached from the skull, it was found that the metal separated into four thin leaves, on which there was a great deal of writing—all of it almost microscopically small. It was written in four languages—

Spanish, Russian, Chinese, and Arabic. It was full of circumlocutions, for it was speaking of concepts which could not be readily expressed in the vocabulary available in any of those languages in 1500. But the message, once deciphered, was clear enough. It told which radio frequency to broadcast on, and in what pattern, in order to trigger a response from a buried archive.

The broadcast was made. The archive was found. The story it told was incredible and yet could not be doubted, for the archive itself was clearly the product of a technology that had never existed on Earth. When the story became clear, a search was made for two other archives. Together, they told a detailed history, not only of the centuries and millennia of human life before 1492, but also of a strange and terrifying history that had not happened, of the years between 1492 and the making of the archives. If there had been any doubt before about the authenticity of the find, all was dispelled when digs at the locations specified in the archives led to spectacular archaeological finds confirming everything that could be confirmed.

Had there once been a different history? No, *two* different histories, both of them obliterated by interventions in the past?

Suddenly the legends and rumors about Colón's wife Diko and Yax's mentor One-Hunahpu began to make sense. The more-obscure stories of a Turk who supposedly sabotaged the *Pinta* and was killed by Colón's crew were revived and compared to the plans talked about in the archives. Obviously, the travelers had succeeded in journeying into their past, all three of them. Obviously they had succeeded.

Two of the travelers already had tombs and monuments. All that was left was to build a third tomb there on the Haitian shore, lay the skull within it, and inscribe on the outside the name Kemal, a date of birth that would not come for centuries, and as the date of death, 1492.

Sources

Michael F. Brown, *Tsewa's Gift: Magic and Meaning in an Amazonian Society* (Smithsonian Institution Press, 1985). Though the culture studied by Brown is not directly related to any known people of the Caribbean, I found his exploration of magic use very helpful; it was for the sake of using this magic culture that I made the village of Ankuash a remnant of a pre-Taino tribe, which could well have had common roots with the tribe Brown studied in the upper Amazon.

Geoffrey W. Conrad and Arthur A. Demarest, *Religion and Empire* (Cambridge University Press, 1984). A remarkably perceptive book that stresses the role of religion and ideology in the creation of the two great American empires that the Europeans discovered—and conquered—in the 16th century. Not only are their ideas perceptive and often quite convincing, but also they are exemplars of rational perspective: They don't think their ideas explain "everything," as far too many do. They merely think their ideas explain *something*, and that other explanations that don't include religion and ideology are inadequate, which seems obvious enough despite the fact that religion and ideology are often ignored or downplayed by historians, journalists, archaeologists, and even cultural anthropologists, who should know better.

Gianni Granzotto, *Christopher Columbus* (University of Oklahoma Press, 1985; trans. Stephen Sartarelli). The best-written and most balanced and helpful of the biographies of Columbus that I read. Granzotto neither judged Columbus by the ethics of our day nor idolized him; what emerged from his book was the best glimpse of the living man possible from documents and speculation alone.

Francine Jacobs, *The Tainos: The People Who Welcomed Columbus* (Putnam, 1992). It took a young-adult novel, published long after I should have turned in my own book for publication, to provide me with the details of the daily life and tribal politics of the people of Hispaniola. The writing is not scholarly, of course, but the information is valuable, and even though my project was undoing the events chronicled by Jacobs, I recommend this book highly for those who want to know what really happened in our version of history.

Alvin M. Josephy, Jr., *America in 1492: The World of the Indian Peoples Before the Arrival of Columbus* (Knopf, 1991). If I had turned this novel in on time, I would have had to do it without the help of this excellent overview of Native American cultures. Besides helping with specific details concerning the long-lost tribes of the Caribbean islands, it gave me a good grounding in the sorts of generalities that Pastwatch might be bandying about—though the conclusions reached by characters concerning the cultures of the Americas are either mine or the characters' own; if there are errors, Josephy and his contributors are responsible only for the fact that I was not even more mistaken.

Linda Schele and David Freidel, *A Forest of Kings: The Untold Story of the Ancient Maya* (Morrow, 1990). A friend of mine, Dave Dollahite, thrust this book upon me even though I insisted that I was working with the Mexica, not the Maya. He was wiser than I. The Mexica were keenly aware of their cultural dependence on the Toltecs and, before them, on the Maya, and this excellent book served me as a guide into the Mesoamerican mindset. The authors are rigorously scholarly without being needlessly obscure, and their loyalty to Maya culture makes their book in some ways a view from the inside. The authors' determination to be nonjudgmental sometimes goes too far, as they occasionally slip from their morally neutral view of the culture of sacrifice to one that seems apologetic and even, occasionally, admiring. When the suffering of the victims of torture and sacrifice is merely "unfortunate" one realizes that there is such a thing as getting too much moral distance from one's subject matter. Nevertheless, even this trait made *A Forest of Kings* all the more valuable to me: Watching how contemporary American scientists were able to become comfortable with a culture of sacrifice helped me see how the Mesoamericans themselves could accept it.

Dennis Tedlock, trans., *Popul Vuh* (Simon & Schuster, 1985). A fluid, clear translation of the Maya holy book, a truly alien mythology. I found this book invaluable in helping me get and give a feel for the culture and mindset of the Mesoamerican people at the time of the coming of the Spanish. The story of Hunahpu One and Seven and their sons is derived entirely from this text; I only regret that I could not include more of it.

Tzvetan Todorov, *The Conquest of America* (Harper & Row, 1984; French edition 1982; trans. Richard Howard). This was the book that made me want to write a novel about Columbus. Todorov's analysis of the conflicting cultures, the mindsets on both sides that led to the European conquest of America—and most particularly his view of Columbus, Cortés, and Moctezuma—rang true with me and illuminated much that had been mysterious to me in the American past. This is not only a profound essay on cultures in conflict, but also a textbook on how to think about the public mind.